ONE WORLD TWO

A SECOND GLOBAL ANTHOLOGY OF SHORT STORIES

ONE WORLD TWO

A SECOND GLOBAL ANTHOLOGY OF SHORT STORIES

New Internationalist

ONE WORLD TWO

A second global anthology of short stories

First published in 2016 by
New Internationalist Publications Ltd
Oxford OX4 1JE
newint.org

Compiled and edited by Ovo Adagha and Chris Brazier.
Designed by Juha Sorsa.

The front cover design incorporates a photograph from the Tomb of
Hafez in Shiraz, Iran by Catalin Marin, momentaryawe.com

'The War Years' by Viet Thanh Nguyen was first published in
TriQuarterly in 2009.
'Absence' by Daniel Alarcon was first published in *War by Candlelight*
(Harper Collins, 2005).
'Bitter Kola' by Aminatta Forna was first published in Ancestor Stones
(Bloomsbury, 2006).
'The David Thuo Show' by Samuel Munene was first published in the 2010
Caine Prize for African Writing anthology (New Internationalist).
'Dosas' by Edwidge Danticat was first published in *Sable* in 2007.

Printed by TJ International Ltd, Cornwall UK
Who hold environmental accreditation 14001.

British Library Cataloguing-in-Publication Data.
A catalogue record for this book is available from the British Library.

Library of Congress Cataloguing-in-Publication Data.
A catalogue for this book is available from the Library of Congress.

ISBN: 978-1-78026-330-4
(ebook ISBN: 978-1-78026-315-1)

CONTENTS

FOREWORD BY ELLEKE BOEHMER

Short stories open doors onto others' lives, perhaps even more memorably than longer fiction. Short stories lead us outdoors, invite us to step forward, as we read, into another space. The stories collected in this dynamic collection *One World Two* are no exception. Each one offers not only a link or a bridge, as its theme suggests, but also creates an opening onto something new. By throwing wide a door each story offers a shift in the light, a new perspective, a step up, a stirring in the air around us, all the things that happen when a space opens up, or when a window is unlatched. Stories are not only representations of lives, but technologies of imaginative travel, taking us through our reading into other imaginative worlds, as the stories collected here manifestly do.

Across the period of time during which this volume was produced, our television screens have been filled with images of people blocked at Europe's borders, crowded into small blow-up boats, queuing to get through checkpoints, or walking in ragged groups along railway lines and motorways. These have been poignant and often painful scenes, but in the media they have largely been silent, lacking distinct voices. The individuals we have seen walking have not generally spoken to camera and therefore, unless they were very young, like the drowned boy Aylan Kurdi, have not been granted a name or an identity. In this gated world that has replaced the borderless spaces beloved of the late 20th century, those pressing at the wire cannot be granted individuality. They must be treated *en masse*, as barbarians and faceless crowds.

The stories we encounter in *One World Two* are important because they give (back to) individuals from communities located beyond many different borderlines a viewpoint, a back-story, a face, a life. Often tracing pathways between different countries, and different consciousnesses, the characters moving along streets and across fields that we encounter here gain a singular and recognizable voice, something that 'pinches at the back of [our] ears like a lemon', to borrow a memorable image from Yewande Omotoso's story 'The Leftovers'. And indeed the eye-catching or ear-holding image, that centers us as readers in a completely different world and grounds us in its particularity, is something that anyone who opens these pages will carry away with them.

'An aerosol of grease clung to the air, along with the warm, wet socks of cooked rice,' writes Viet Thanh Nguyen in 'The War Years'. Aminatta Forna's Asana turns 'thoughts around and around in my head, the way I examine a pawpaw before I buy it in the market'. Elsie in Edwidge Dandicat's 'Dosas' presents 'her wide bottom spiked up in the air'.

In these times of globalization, when the World Wide Web and international flows of goods and money are meant to interconnect us all, short stories from around the world such as we find between these covers, confront readers with an appropriately global question. Apart from the fact that the stories are in English (both originally written in English, and translated), are there particular thematic or formal features that run like a connecting thread through them all? Is something of our own world citizenship reflected back at us through the very forms and styles used in the collection?

In the 1980s we might have expected to find in a collection of 'world' stories the imprint of magic realism, fostered by Latin American writers keen to capture something of a world deformed by late colonial power and corruption. Around the millennium we encountered a recognizable 'expressivist' turn, manifested in extreme bodily effects, eruptions, effusions, emissions – something resembling the Thing in Okwiri Oduor's haunting story 'That Balmy September Day'.

In this collection, it is interesting that realism has rallied and seems to be in good health, though always with local adaptations. Realism like the television in Samuel Munene's 'The David Thuo Show' gives the memory work so crucial to many of these writers shape and solidity. It reminds us of the monotony of life in a refugee camp, as in Vamba Sherif's 'Homecoming'. It resurrects dialogue, in so many of the stories, and recreates familiar but distant scenes, like Ana Menendez's ghostly Prague. It etches new possibilities – the horses in the New Zealand back paddock for Heidi North-Bailey. It is something like the identifying name that Olivia in Dandicat's 'Dosas' writes on her feet, so that when abducted and beheaded she will retain her identity. And, finally, realism immerses us as readers in new worlds that are interconnected through the power of the story itself. All of the stories in *One World Two* give testimony to that power. Readers, enjoy!

Elleke Boehmer is Professor of World Literature in English at Oxford University. Also an acclaimed novelist and short-story writer, her most recent novel is *The Shouting in the Dark* (Sandstone Press, 2015).

INTRODUCTION BY OVO ADAGHA

Beginning in January 2008, a group of 23 writers from 14 different countries came together to work on a book project. Working collaboratively online, in a dedicated Zoetrope office, the writers anthologized 23 stories to drive the concept of *One World*.

The *One World* project was designed with the aim of redefining national borders through the short story. It was a literary voyage that brought together stories from many corners of the earth: from the cane fields of Puerto Rico, from the schoolyards of Botswana and India, from living rooms in London and organic farmsteads in Zimbabwe, right through to the funeral homes of Nigeria and the waterfronts of Bangladesh. The success of the project itself lay in the unity of purpose – diverse writers, some already well known and others just starting out, transformed into ambassadors from different parts of the world, most of them not having met each other in the flesh.

Since 2009 when it was published, *One World* has continued to function as an agent of change. It has been used as a recommended textbook on world literature in many schools and colleges across the globe. More than just an anthology of short stories, the book conveys the reader on thought-provoking journeys across continents, cultures and landscapes. This purpose may be particularly significant in the context of global preoccupations with conflict in the shape of wars, racism, terrorism, religion and economics. The project recognized the potential of literature to contribute to peaceful bonding and mutual co-operation between people.

But some may ask, why? How did the materially challenged short-story genre become the vehicle of choice through which we can navigate to distant lands and cultures? What qualifies the short story as a visionary tool to enrich the mind of the reader? A collection like this provides the reader with privileged glimpses into the heart of other cultures and places they may never otherwise have the opportunity to know. The reason for this is simple enough: we can see ourselves in short stories because they give us a thousand eyes, a thousand points of view and a thousand revealing moments, because, in the words of Lorrie Moore, 'they represent life itself, organic to the occasion, and second to none in power and efficiency'.

The theme of this second volume, *One World Two*, which has been more than three years in the making, is building bridges. It is interested in the human condition as a dynamic central line linking individuals, cultures and experiences: east and west, north and south, and, perhaps most importantly, past, present and future. In a world where artificial borders between nations struggle to contain human populations, the bridges theme is well suited to filling in gaps, stirring empathy and emphasizing similarities rather than differences.

One World Two is even more geographically diverse than its predecessor. We – I and my co-editor at New Internationalist, Chris Brazier – have pulled together an entirely new cast of writers, a large number of whom hail from two, and sometimes three, countries – they may have been born in one, brought up in a second and be working now in a third, just as I myself grew up in Nigeria but have since lived in both Scotland and Canada. Altogether there are 21 writers representing 26 different countries. There was not the peer-review process of the previous volume but on the other hand there have been numerous instances where we have developed stories over a period of weeks or months and arrived at a result that satisfied us all. So there has been the same sense of creative adventure.

The stories in this collection are intended to gratify readers of different tastes. New and established voices merge – and emerge with greater strength in the collective environment. While each story in the anthology has a characteristic tone, a circumstance that is peculiar and self-contained, the thematic link between stories helps to draw the fragments of the collection into a whole.

As the anthology unfolds, we can move through the stories much as we navigate through rooms in a house. There, we can look for ourselves in the crafted descriptions and conversations of characters, and in those unique perceptions of places and scenes that are unfamiliar yet familiar. What we may find in this journey is the hope of what is lost, the resources to begin to strip our societies of incompatibility, injustice and inequality.

The *One World* project does not end here. We are optimistic that there will be further anthologies in the series and that this book will find its way into the hands of the rising generation, to engage with it rather as one having a compelling conversation with a neighbor or a friend who ends up seeing the world as they have not seen it before.

As an ongoing concern, we hope the *One World* series will continue to champion the cause of the less privileged. A portion of the royalties from *One World Two* will be donated to the International Committee of the Red Cross.

Share with us, dear reader, this unifying concept of One World.

Ovo Adagha is a Nigerian scholar and writer currently living in Calgary, Canada. His work has appeared in *One World: a global anthology of short stories* (New Internationalist, 2009), the 2010 Caine Prize anthology, *African Writing, Eclectica, Angle Journal, Santa Fe Writers Project* and *The Stockholm Review of Literature*. He is a contributing editor with *African Writing* journal.

YEWANDE OMOTOSO
Nigeria/Barbados/South Africa

THE LEFTOVERS

The conversations of those nights should be filed as those had while drunk, and those while sober, or perhaps those had in pairs and those in groups. Although, when I look, I notice that the sober conversations happened in pairs and drunkenness required an audience. When I think back we were always drunk and in the parlor. I was sober in the shower and the corridor; I was sober on the patio, in the hallway. A hallway, a place of exits and entrances, nothing more sobering than that.

I've often wondered how we got left behind, the accident of that. And the convenience of a house there and ready to have us. I'm older now. I haven't managed to fall in love again. It's possible that you only really love once and fully; everything else is a mucking about. But this house and the wine and the man who couldn't hear English. The loss was still new, I was still thinking how precious life is and fleeting. A thing had slipped by; the insult of time walking casually past, saying 'hey, bye now'.

The house took on a magical quality. On the day of the funeral it had seemed a village, with alleys and porticoes along almost every edge, people everywhere, gorging themselves and checking for the correct placement of their make-up in mirrors, on the backs of silver spoons, in the visors of other people's sunglasses. I myself didn't much care for my reflection. I saw it in the morning when I brushed my teeth, I saw it nightly when I brushed my teeth, and any other meetings during the day were accidents. I may not have cared for my reflection but didn't begrudge others theirs – even when we bury the dead we must look good.

Once everyone had left, though, and only we remained, the house squeezed in like a toothpaste tube, squeezed in on itself until, when I slept at night, I thought I could feel its sides brushing against my bare skin. It became a house with only one corridor, with a single patio at the back by the braai unit, and it had no functioning mirrors.

There were five of us in the house, although at dusk I sometimes felt that Kaiser was still around, somehow. I'd removed his wedding ring and it fit my thumb. I kept turning and troubling it, new and uncomfortable.

Apart from myself, there was a woman named Amanda, who was a colleague of Kaiser's – she had a streak of purple in her hair. There was Kaiser's best friend from Bishops days, although I knew they hadn't spoken since high school; his name was Thandabantu and he'd come with his girlfriend. There was also a man who went on in the rare dialect spoken in a Croatian village I will never visit.

There was wine. Amanda discovered the rack the first night. Well stocked, she said. As if unfamiliar to me, I took some moments to study the contents of the rack. There was Bilton, Shiraz, the year 2008. Meerkat, a 2014 Pinotage, a pair of them. Accredited to a Schalk Burger and Sons. The Pinot had a string of meerkats around the waist of the bottle, standing as if in a Disney shot, and a hefty proclamation on the label that this was South Africa's most gregarious wine. We drank those bottles first. The bottle with the most motes of dust on its neck was a Laibach Merlot. There was a white box of three which we left alone and only opened on the last night: Sauvignon Blanc, Elsenburg College of Agriculture.

Thandabantu's girlfriend, Juliet, told a story of sitting on the toilet and noticing a spider's web designed between the floor and the curves of a sink stand, and the spider, proud, splayed on top of a weave of strands.

'I tried to blow it,' she said. 'Right from the toilet seat, not interrupting my business. I took a big puff and went whooooosh.'

'And?' Thandabantu asked. He was sitting beside her, pressing her ear between his thumb and forefinger. They made a habit of this until it felt obscene, the rhythmic rubbing, the ardent way he worked, as if towards a goal.

'What happened to the spider?' he asked again.

'It wavered a bit. When I finished I stamped the thing out.'

That was the general nature of the drunken conversations; infused with a misguided sense of importance, propelled by urgent (if maladroit) forward movement towards underdeveloped and disappointing conclusions. Anything could be turned into a metaphor for our existence.

Juliet got drunk the fastest, the deepest. Alcohol animated her. I noticed soon into our first evening together, we five, that I was studying her. I couldn't look away from the flesh on the underside of her arms, and if she reached for something – usually a bottle – I would stare. Her voice pinched me at the back of my ears like a lemon. She giggled. She'd never been poor. Her skin blonde as her hair, her eyes green, she'd never had to wonder as to her beauty in the world – she and her sisters shone on magazine pages, she was coveted standard and she laughed like she knew it. It felt good to be jealous – it released me from just being devastated.

I should mention Juliet and I had an odd encounter. We'd both been elected to choose some wine for dinner. She'd just been telling more stories. She'd winked at Thandabantu as we left the room. I followed behind her. She turned to say, 'I love your skin'. She wasn't drunk yet but she still smelt of the drunkenness from previous nights and, when she reached for my wrist, her touch was clammy; the sensation made me feel sordid. Her teeth were yellow, which was a relief. We both studied the rack.

'Do you want?' she asked.

'Want what?'

'For the grief. To ease the grief.'

It took me a moment to realize she was being generous. Before understanding her, I wheeled through so many other equally insane but more likely possibilities. I thought she had dagga tucked artfully in her brassiere. Then I thought, it won't be dagga it will be something harder, a line of cocaine to really send me into Arcadia. Then I thought she looked hippie enough to do mushrooms and messed up enough to be offering me a blade to gently (not too deep) slice at the skin above my wrists – above the wrist to cope, at the wrists if you want to die.

'Want what?' I asked again when I felt tired of not guessing.

'You know.'

She changed her standing position, which immediately conveyed that we were talking about sex. But now I again was puzzled. I wasn't attracted to women and she knew this. Did she think herself so appealing as to be able to unravel my heterosexuality? Or was it the opposite, was she attracted to *me*? And then I saw her smile in a controlled way. In the adjoining room, Thandabantu laughed, and she jerked her head a bit, in the direction of the sound.

'Oh, Jesus.'

'Sorry. Not to offend.' She relaxed into normality, apologetic for being inappropriate and suddenly riddled with decorous intentions.

'Listen–'

'No no no, I'm sorry,' she said. 'And just… think of me as His Pimp and it's on the house… Oh God, that's vile, I'm sorry. I'm an idiot… but do think about it. Don't answer now. Don't say anything further. I won't.'

We selected four bottles. I remember the Laibach Merlot was amongst them. I carried it and set it down on the dinner table, brushing the dust off my fingers, brushing away the dust of His Pimp's offer. I excused myself early in the night. Thandabantu and the Croatian were playing charades, with Juliet and Amanda looking on amused. If not for the grace of Hollywood and the ubiquity of blockbuster movies, the two strangers, Ezra from God-knows-where and Thandabantu from the depths of Khayelitsha, son of a char, adopted by Jews and Bishops-schooled, would have had nothing to play about.

He wasn't unhandsome and I wasn't above certain needs. By the time of his death, despite my begging, Kaiser and I had not made love in almost a year.

In the corridor Thandabantu bumped into me, hard to do in a space wide enough for two to pass. 'Sorry,' he said and winked but maybe it was a nervous tick.

'Does he know?' I asked Juliet.

'What?'

We were at the entrance of the bathroom, she was trying to come out and I suppose, in a way, I was blocking her passage.

'What you said to me the other night. Does he know?'

'Oh, no, I haven't told him yet. It's totally my idea, I didn't want to tell him unless you were… you know… keen… are you?'

'No,' I said and let her pass.

Amanda of the purple hair and skin the color of honey made some moves on Ezra that seemed to work. I noticed they shared a room, took showers together, held hands, which requires no language at all.

I cooked the dinners. For the first few days there had been leftovers from the funeral, people had brought food. An aunt of mine had made four trays of lasagna. Someone, I don't know who, had brought two buckets of amagwinya, bronze on the outside, fluffy within. One moment I remember was someone wheeling in crates of Fanta and Coke. When a man with hair on his face and on the backs of his hands hugged me I thought I'd break. Neither of my parents were present: having never acknowledged my relationship with Kaiser, they'd struggled with taking part in any ceremonies that marked the end of it. Kaiser's parents came but deferred to me; they'd had an uneasy relationship with their son and, when we'd fallen in love and moved in together, they'd seemed relieved to relinquish him to me; their discomfort survived his death.

When the food started to run out, I put meals together.

'Can I help?' Thandabantu asked early one evening. The other three were playing Monopoly, Juliet strident in her attempts to translate for Ezra.

'Just knocking some stuff together.'

'Yes. Give me something to chop.' He grinned, came to stand next to me. I shoved over the bell peppers.

'You eat pasta?' I asked, as if he were a house guest, a proper one.

'I eat anything,' he replied, making our talk even more mundane.

He chopped the peppers in fine lines.

'You don't have to do that,' I said.

'I took a course. In fact, did… not sure if he ever mentioned it. We took a course together. The famous one across the way from our school.'

I appreciated his fear of saying Kaiser's name.

'Oh.' I searched for a deep pot for the spaghetti.

'I was rubbish actually. Except at this. This, I was good at.' He certainly did chop well.

'And Kaiser?' I asked and met his eyes when he looked up, met them straight so I was certain he could see right through me.

'Yeah, much better. And the wine-thing must have started back then. The pairing. A Sommelier came to some classes and after that… well, you can imagine. You know your husband. Knew.'

'A little. Why didn't you stay friends? After school and everything?'

He made a face.

'Life, I guess,' I said when he still hadn't answered.

'I guess so.'

We cooked without talking. I liked him in my kitchen, and I liked the sounds of laughter from Amanda. Even Juliet's belonging didn't grate. And Ezra in the back, with broken English swaddled in his mother tongue.

'You all should have left a few days ago – or perhaps I should kick you out,' I said. 'I'm avoiding something.'

'When you want us to leave, we'll go.'

'And why is she offering you to me? Haven't black bodies been traded enough?'

He looked confused, of course, and I hated myself for saying anything, but hating myself was preferable to feeling grief, right at that moment. Same as being a hostess. Being jealous. Being lonely. All preferable to being bereaved.

'Juliet. She offered you to me.'

He looked something I hadn't expected: hurt.

'How well do you know her?' I asked.

He shook his head. 'It's not that... she... she thinks I like you.'

'I'm not following.' Getting entangled in nonsense, getting drunk with strangers, mourners, strange mourners – all preferable.

I tested and felt the pasta was ready. I'd used the colander the day before, now where was it. I opened cupboards.

'She's done this before... it's... I... I'm embarrassed but I mentioned to her that I thought you looked beautiful and very sad. At the service.'

'So... what... she offers you to me before you help yourself, before I steal you? Did she forget the part that I'm a widow... that I won't be at my husband's funeral... scoping for... shit... the colander, where's the colander?'

He came to get my hands because I'd been raking them through the shelves, upsetting the dishes. He took my hands as if his were what I was looking for. He offered his hands to say, 'here it is.'

I steadied.

'She's sorry,' he said.

'Kaiser cheated.'

'I–'

'Just once. He said. Just... the one time.'

'Sorry.'

'Yes. I made him tell me.'

'Sorry.'

'Yes. I dug in and goaded him and made him tell me. I didn't want to know why, I wanted to know what.'

He looked at his Julienned peppers. I'd memorized all the details, tortured myself with them.

'When?'

'About, just over a year ago. I don't know her. Business trip. Just once.'

'And he told you now?'

I nodded. 'Said to forgive him.'

Right then Thandabantu and I both spotted the colander, sitting on top of the fridge, grinning. I snorted and he laughed too. The moment was finished.

'Look,' I said, embarrassed so soon, 'I don't care how blonde she is, you're in love with a maniac.' We laughed some more, harder this time.

'Who says it's love?' he said. And then, 'Was yours?'

'Yes. Yes, mine was.'

He helped me pile a stack of plates on the counter.

'I'm sorry I said all that. Kaiser was sick,' I said.

'It's okay.'

'No, I'm just saying that. I just wanted to say to you that… towards the end he was very sick. Inside,' I pointed to my forehead. 'And also I wanted to ask you something.'

'Anything.'

'Why did you come? Any of you?'

'Well, you have to ask the others.'

'No. I'm asking you. I'm too tired to ask the others.'

'I–'

'Let's start with Amanda. Why did she come? I saw you speaking to her at the service, do you know her?'

'No. We just got talking. She worked with Kaiser as you know. She said he was kind and she had to come. All the other Directors ignored her or paid keen attention to her breasts. Kaiser looked her in the eye, that's all she said.'

I nodded. 'And Ezra?'

'Him… I'm supposing it must have been from the merger. That's practically the only English word he knows.' Thandabantu laughed.

'Merger?'

'Yeah, merger. He keeps saying it. I'm guessing Ezra is from the other company.'

'Why does he care?'

'I don't know. I don't speak Croatian well enough to work that out.'

'And you?'

'I had to come.'

'Why?'

'Kaiser… you don't forget someone like that.'

'Like what?'

'You don't forget the first person you fall in love with who isn't family. Doesn't matter if you never speak to each other again – you never forget. Anyway, I heard about it from my mom–'

'Your Jewish mom?'

He frowned at me. 'No, my mother. She told me about it. I'd heard of the company and how well everything was going. Read about it... I don't know, somewhere, Business Day or something. I called and spoke to Kaiser's secretary for the details and... well, Juliet came with me because I asked her to.'

'And why are you all still here?'

'Because you haven't asked us to leave.'

He smiled and I smiled back.

We ate dinner. Amanda egged him on and Ezra made a speech, impassioned and pleasingly unintelligible to my ears or to any of the others present. It felt good to not understand something innocuous.

Much later I heard Ezra and Amanda got married; much much later that they had a baby. No one told me they had called him Kaiser until the boy was four and in full possession of his name; if he'd been younger and less capable I would have taken the name back. I'd wanted to set it in resin, embalm it. That is, after all, what we ought to do with the dead things we cannot let go of.

Would you imagine that I met her? She wrote to me. Seven or eight years had passed. The only other people who remained loyal to the postal service were my bank and insurance company. It was a white envelope, without the familiar mastheads. Is it too trite to claim that I knew who it was from? I'd just spent several weeks in the caves where I'd wondered what could have been so important that it deserved to be drawn on stone. Despite so many years since his death, I hadn't been able to shake seeing everything through Kaiser. Wondering what he would make of a remark or a scene in a film. I burnt the letter before reading it, which is why, when she rang the doorbell, I had no way of knowing she'd sent word of her visit. Unlike the envelope, I couldn't place her immediately. But she called herself 'Sandra'. And of course I'd put the name to memory. She didn't look as I'd imagined. No woman could possibly have lived up to what I had imagined.

It wasn't long. She made a point of saying that she had meant nothing to him. And that she felt she owed me that assurance; she offered her hatred of me, her jealousy, as proof of where his true love lay. She spoke the most and, throughout, I resisted the urge to slap her. She was being nervous. I wondered if I should tell her that he'd lied to me, that he'd approximated their lengthy affair to one ruffled night.

'Why now?' I asked.

Wet-eyed, she spoke of her new religion, redemption, forgiveness and ecstasy – words I had no reason to use. But when she said 'demon' my heart popped. When she said 'haunted', I nodded. When we hugged, she cried and thanked me and I wondered who I could visit, who I could beseech for absolution.

Little Kaiser. I visited the family more, grew a friend in Amanda, understood what Kaiser had liked about her. Ezra by then, of course, had learnt English. Sometimes I arrived at their home for dinner and thought – tonight. Other visits I knew I would never say anything.

All the while I wondered if Ezra could retrospectively decipher what I'd told him on the last night of that strange, protracted gathering. He never intimated as much. I'd got up around 2am and wanted to eat something. I noticed a draft. I followed it to the open patio doors and Ezra, propped on the arm of a chair, smoking. The darkness, the smoke, the lack of common tongue meant we made no sounds at each other. I sat with him a while, enjoying his company. He offered me a pull and I accepted.

'Ezra, he told me that he was going to do it.' I handed back the cigarette, shook my head when he offered it a second time. 'He told me that he was going to do it and that I should release him. That if I loved him... if I truly loved him, he said, I would let him be.'

Ezra looked apologetic. 'Don't know English,' he said.

'On and on. On and on, he said that.'

Ezra scrunched his face, helpless.

'He was sick. He was functioning but... he was very very... very sick. You don't know that sickness. No doctor could fix it. No drug. Nobody knows it.'

'Don't know.'

'You don't know.'

'I sorry.'

'You don't know.'

There was so much darkness that night. Beyond the house the world had jumped off a cliff. We were what was left.

Yewande Omotoso is a Barbadian-Nigerian who grew up in Cape Town and currently lives in Johannesburg. An architect, she completed a Masters in Creative Writing at the University of Cape Town. Her debut novel *Bomboy* (Modjaji Books), was shortlisted for the 2012 *Sunday Times* Fiction Prize, the MNet Film Award and the 2013 Etisalat Prize for Literature. It won the South African Literary Award First Time Author Prize. Her short stories include 'Two Old

People' in the anthology *Speaking for the Generation: Contemporary Stories from Africa*, 'How About The Children' published in *The Kalahari Review*, 'Things Are Hard' in the 2012 Caine Prize Anthology and 'Fish' published in *The Moth*. Yewande was a 2013 Norman Mailer Fellow and a 2014 Etisalat Fellow. She is a 2015 Miles Morland Scholar. Yewande's second novel *The Woman Next Door* (Chatto and Windus) will be published in May 2016.

VIET THANH NGUYEN
United States/Vietnam

THE WAR YEARS

Before Mrs Hoa broke into our lives in the summer of 1985, nothing my mother did surprised me. Her routine was as predictable as the rotation of the earth, beginning with how she rapped on my door every morning, at six, six-fifteen, and six-thirty, until at last I was awake. When I emerged from my bedroom, she was already dressed, inevitably wearing a short-sleeved blouse and skirt of matching pastels. She owned seven such outfits, and if she had on fuchsia, I knew it was Monday. Before we departed, she switched off the lights, checked the burners, tugged on the black iron bars guarding our windows, always in that order, and then, in the car, ordered me to lock my door.

As my father steered the Oldsmobile and I sat in the back reading a comic book, my mother worked on her makeup. By the time we arrived at St Patrick 10 minutes later, she was finished, the flags of blush on her cheeks blending in with her foundation. Perfume was the last touch, a pump of the spray on either side of her neck. Her dizzying scent of gardenias clung to me in Ms Korman's summer-school classroom, where, for seven hours every day, I spoke only English. I liked school, even summer school. It was like being on vacation from home and, at three o'clock, I was always a little disappointed to walk the four blocks to the grocery store my parents owned, the New Saigon Market, where English was hardly ever spoken and Vietnamese was loud.

My mother and father rarely left their posts, the cash registers flanking the entrance of the New Saigon. Customers always crowded the market, one of the few places in San José where the Vietnamese could buy the staples and spices of home: jasmine rice and star anise, fish sauce and fire-engine red chilies. People haggled endlessly with my mother over everything, beginning with the rock sugar, which I pretended was yellow Kryptonite, and ending with the varieties of meat in the freezer, from pork chops and catfish with a glint of light in their eyes to shoestrings of chewy tripe and packets of chicken hearts, small and tender as button mushrooms.

'Can't we just sell TV dinners?' I asked once. It was easy to say *TV dinners* in Vietnamese since the word for television was *ti-vi*, but there were no Vietnamese words for other things I wanted. 'And what about bologna?'

'*Cai gi vay?*' My mother's brow furrowed. 'If I can't pronounce it, my customers won't buy it. Now go stamp the prices on those cans.'

'They're just going to ask for a lower price.' I was 13, beginning to be brave enough to say what I had suspected for a while, that my mother wasn't always right. 'Why do they haggle over everything? Why can't they just pay the price that's there?'

'Are you going to be the kind of person who always pays the asking price?' my mother demanded. 'Or the kind who fights to find out what something's really worth?'

I wasn't sure. All I knew was that in the New Saigon, my chore every afternoon was to price the cans and packages. I was on my knees, rummaging for the stamp pad in the counter behind my mother, when Mrs Hoa introduced herself. Like my mother, she was in her late forties and dressed in monochrome, a white jacket, white pants and white shoes, with bug-eyed sunglasses obscuring her face. As my mother bagged her purchases, Mrs Hoa said, 'I'm collecting funds for the fight against the Communists, my dear.' I knew the basics of our history as well as I knew the story of Adam and Eve: the Communists had marched from North Vietnam in 1975 to invade South Vietnam, driving us out, all the way across the Pacific to California. I had no memories of the war, but Mrs Hoa said others had not forgotten. A guerrilla army of former South Vietnamese soldiers was training in the jungles of Thailand, preparing to counter-attack into unified Vietnam. The plan was to stir the unhappy people against their Communist rulers, incite a revolution, and resurrect the Republic of the South.

'Our men need our support,' Mrs Hoa said. 'And we need good citizens like yourself to contribute.'

My mother rubbed one ankle against the other, her nylons scratching. A seam had opened behind her knee, but my mother would keep wearing the same hose until the run nipped at her heels. 'I wish I could help, Mrs Hoa, but times are hard,' my mother said. 'Our customers are cutting back on everything, what with the recession and the gas prices. And our daughter's in college. Her tuition is like a down payment on a house every year.'

'I struggle making ends meet, too.' Mrs Hoa unclasped and reclasped the silver latch on her purse. A thin gold band encircled her ring finger, and the red enamel on her nails was as polished and glossy as a new car's paint. 'But people talk. Did you hear about Mrs Binh? People say she's a Communist sympathizer, and all because she's too cheap to give anything. There's even talk of boycotting her store.'

My mother knew Mrs Binh, owner of the Les Amis Beauty Salon a few blocks further west downtown, but my mother changed the topic to the steamy June weather and the price of gold. Mrs Hoa agreed about the temperature, smiling and displaying a formidable wall of teeth. I had just learned the word for their color in art class: ochre. Mrs Hoa glanced at me before leaving my mother with this: 'Think about it, dear. Taking back our homeland is a noble cause for which we should all be proud to fight.'

'Idiot,' my mother muttered after Mrs Hoa was gone. As we drove home that evening along Tenth Street, my mother recounted the episode to my father, who had been too busy at his own register to overhear the conversation. When she mentioned the guerrillas, I imagined them to be unshaven, mosquito-bitten men with matted hair wearing ragged tiger-stripe fatigues, living on rainwater, wild boar and aphids, practising hand-to-hand combat skills by bayoneting jackfruit. From the backseat, I said, 'How much are you giving Mrs Hoa?'

'Nothing,' she replied. 'It's extortion.'

'But they're fighting the Communists,' I said. Also known as Chinese and North Koreans, with Cubans and Sandinistas threatening infiltration and invasion from south of our border, as President Reagan explained on *World News Tonight*. 'Shouldn't we help them?'

'The war's over.' My mother sounded tired. 'There's no fighting it again.'

I was outraged, for Mrs Hoa's appearance proved the war was not over, having somehow followed us from the old Saigon to the new one. What was more, I had read *Newsweek* in the dentist's office and knew we were in the midst of an epic battle against the Evil Empire of the Soviet Union. But if I was unhappy with my mother's response, I was even more upset with my father's.

'The war may be over,' he said, wiggling his little finger in his ear, 'but paying a little hush money would make our lives a lot easier.'

My mother said nothing, merely drumming her fingers on the armrest. I knew she would have her way with my father, a bald man with the deliberate moves and patient eyes of a turtle. Late that night, hurrying from the kitchen to my room with a glass of water, I heard my mother working to persuade him behind their closed door. There was no time to eavesdrop. We had recently read *The Fall of the House of Usher* in Ms Korman's class, and the fear of seeing someone undead in the dark hallway made me rush past their door, just as my mother said, 'I've dealt with worse than her.'

Dread was stronger than curiosity. I shut my door and jumped into bed shivering, pushing aside my summer textbooks, wrapped in brown covers I had cut from a shopping bag and upon which I had scrawled *Math* and *American History*. Perhaps my mother was talking about the famine at the end of the Second World War, when she was nine. Last year, an evening television report on the Ethiopian famine had prompted my mother to mention this other famine while I plucked the grey hairs from her head.

'Do you know a dozen children in my village starved to death?' she said, even though I obviously did not know. 'Older people, too, sometimes right on the street. One day I found a girl I used to play with dead on her doorstep.'

My mother lapsed into silence as she stared at a point on the wall above the television, and I did not say anything. It was the kind of story she told all the time, and in any case, I was too distracted to ask questions. She was paying me for every strand I found and I was intent on my search, each grey hair bringing me one nickel closer to the next issue of *Captain America*.

In the days and nights that passed, my mother never brought up Mrs Hoa, but the woman had unsettled her. My mother began talking during our evening book-keeping, a time when she was usually and completely focused on calculating the daily receipts. We worked at the dining table, counting cash, rolling coins into paper packages the size of firecrackers, and stamping the New Saigon's address onto the back of the personal checks, the Monopoly money food stamps and the yellow coupons from Aid to Families with Dependent Children. When I added the sums with a humming mechanical calculator bigger than our rotary telephone, I never needed to look at the keypad. I knew every number's place by heart.

As we did the day's reckoning, my mother reported on the rumors of former South Vietnamese soldiers organizing not only a guerrilla army in Thailand but also a secret front here in the United States, its purpose to overthrow the Communists. Grimmer than rumors was how unknown assailants had firebombed a Vietnamese newspaper editor's office in Westminster (he lived), while another editor had been shot to death, along with his wife, in the doorway of their Oakland house (the murderers were never caught). 'They just said in public what a lot of people already say in private,' my mother said, wetting her fingers on a sponge. 'Making peace with the Communists might not be such a bad thing.'

I wrote down figures in a ledger, never looking up. My father and I worked in T-shirts and shorts, but my mother wore only a nightgown of sheer green fabric without a bra. She didn't notice how her breasts swayed like anemones under shallow water, embarrassing me whenever I saw those dark and doleful aureoles with their nipples as thick as my index finger. My mother's breasts were nothing like what I imagined belonged to the girls of my class, a fantasy confirmed the previous week when Emmy Tsuchida had leaned over to peek at my quiz on the causes of the Civil War and I had seen her nipple through the gap between two buttons of her shirt, pink and pert, exactly like the eraser on the pencil in my hand. Without raising my gaze from the ledger, I said, 'But you always tell me the Communists are bad people.'

'O-ho!' my father said with a chortle. 'So you do pay attention. Sometimes I can't tell what's going on behind those thick glasses of yours.'

'The Communists are evil.' My mother riffled through a stack of 20-dollar bills. She had never finished grade school, her father forcing her to stay at home to care for her siblings, and yet she could count money by hand and add figures in her head more quickly than I could on the calculator. 'There's no doubt about it. They don't believe in God and they don't believe in money.'

'But they believe in taking other people's money,' my father said. He spoke often of his auto parts store, which according to his brothers no longer had any parts to sell under Communist ownership. We had lived above the store, and sometimes I wondered if a Communist child was sleeping in my bed and, if so, what kinds of books a Red read, and what kind of movies he saw. *Captain America* was out of the question, but he must have seen Luke Skywalker crossing light sabers with Darth Vader. I had seen *Star Wars* a dozen times on videotape, and if anyone was so deprived as to have not watched it even once, then the country in which he lived surely needed a revolution. But my mother would not have agreed. She wrapped a paper band around the twenties and said: 'I hate the Communists as much as Mrs Hoa, but she's fighting a war that can't be won. I'm not throwing away my money on a lost cause.'

My father ended the conversation by standing and sweeping the cash, coins, checks and food stamps into the vinyl satchel he carried every morning to the Bank of America, where he would deposit them. My parents kept some of their profits in the bank, donated a portion to the church, and wired another percentage to the relatives in Vietnam, who periodically mailed us thin letters thick with trouble, summed up for me by my mother to the tune of no food and no money, no school and no hope. Their relatives' experiences and their own had taught my parents to believe that no country was immune to disaster, and so they secreted another percentage of the profits at home, just in case some horrendous calamity wiped out the American banking system. My mother wrapped blocks of hundred-dollar bills in plastic and taped them underneath the lid of the toilet tank, buried dog-tag sized ounces of gold in the rice, and stashed her jade bracelets, 24-karat gold necklaces and diamond rings in a portable fireproof safe, hidden in the crawlspace underneath the house. To distract thieves, she devised decoys, placing a large glass vase heavy with coins high on a bookshelf by the front door, and a pair of gold bracelets on top of her dresser.

Her fear of robbery was proven justified one evening last October, when, on an otherwise forgettable Tuesday evening, someone knocked on the door. My father was in the kitchen, having just switched on the stove, and I reached the door a few steps ahead of my mother, already in her nightgown. When I peered through the peephole, I saw a white man who said, 'I got mail for you, sir.' If he had spoken in Vietnamese or Spanish, I never would have unlocked the door, but because he spoke English, I did. He used his left hand to push his way into the house, a young man in his twenties with feathered hair the color of old straw, long enough to brush the collar of his frayed blue-jean jacket. Not much taller than my mother, he was slightly built; when he spoke, his voice squeaked like rubber soles on a gym floor.

'Get back,' he said. His forehead was slick with sweat, and the muzzle of the black-barreled .22 revolver in his right hand was shaking as he stepped past the threshold, kicking at the jumble of shoes we kept there and forgetting to close the door. My mother concluded later that he was an amateur, perhaps an addict desperate for money to buy drugs. He pointed the gun past me, at her, and said, 'You understand English? Get on the floor!'

I backed away, while my mother threw her hands in the air, saying, '*Khong, khong, khong.*' My father had appeared, halfway between the kitchen and the front door, and the man fixed his aim on my father, saying, 'Get down, mister.' My father got onto his knees, raising his hands high. 'No shoot,' my father said in English, his voice faint. 'No shoot, please.'

I had never seen my father on his knees outside of church, and I had never seen my mother tremble and shake with fear. Pity overwhelmed me, knowing this was neither the first nor the last time someone would humiliate them like this. As if aware of my thoughts, the man pointed the gun at me wordlessly, and I got down on my knees, too. Only my mother did not sink to her knees, her back against the wall and her face, freshly peeled of makeup, very white. Her breasts undulated behind her nightgown, like the heads of twin eels, as she kept saying *no*. The man was still aiming his gun at me as he said, 'What's her problem, kid?'

When my mother screamed, the sound froze everyone except her. She pushed past the man, nudging the gun aside with her hand and bumping him with her shoulder as she ran outside. He stumbled against the bookshelf by the door, knocking over the glass vase full of coins. Falling to the ground, it shattered, spraying pennies, nickels and dimes all over, along with some quarters and a few Susan B Anthonys, the coins mixed with shards of glass. 'Jesus Christ!' the man said. When he turned towards the door, my father leapt up off his knees and hurled himself against the man's back, shoving him across the threshold and then slamming the door shut. Outside, the gun went off with a short, sharp little *pop*, the bullet ricocheting off the sidewalk and lodging itself in the wall next to the mailbox, where a policeman would dig it out a few hours later.

On Sunday morning before we left for church, my mother used a dab of Brylcreem and a black Ace comb to slick my hair and part it down the middle. I was horrified at the way I looked, like Alfalfa from *Little Rascals*, but I didn't protest, just as I hadn't said anything to her after the police brought my mother back home from a neighbors' house. 'I saved our lives, you coward!' she yelled at my father, who smiled weakly at the police sergeant taking down our report while we sat at the dining table. To me, as she yanked my ear, she said, 'What did I say about opening the door to strangers? How come you never listen to me?' All this was in Vietnamese, and since I had been translating for my father, the police sergeant asked me what she had said. I rubbed my ear, focused on his nametag – Rodriguez – and said, 'She's just scared, officer.' The police never caught the man, and, after a while, there was no more reason to mention him. Even so, I thought about him every now and again, especially on Sunday mornings when salvation was on my mind, with my father singing *Ave Maria* and *Amazing Grace* in a slightly off-key way as he drove us to St Patrick. It was the only occasion when we had music in the car.

By the time the Vietnamese mass started, every seat of every pew was taken. The leader of the congregation, Father Dinh, had been born in the last century. According to my mother, he was already middle-aged when he led his flock, including my parents, from the north of Vietnam to the south in 1954, after the Communists had kicked out the French and seized

VIET THANH NGUYEN

the northern half of the country. Fantastically, Father Dinh still had more hair than my father, a tuft of white thread that shone under the light illuminating the stained-glass windows. His voice trembled when he said, 'In the name of the Father, the Son, and the Holy Spirit'. While he sermonized about the miracle of Jesus feeding a hungry crowd with only a basket of loaves and fishes, I dozed in the hard-backed pew, remembering Emmy Tsuchida's nipple and looking forward only to the end of mass, after the Eucharist was locked in the tabernacle, when the priest finally allowed us to rise from the thinly cushioned kneelers.

It was in the crowd jostling for the exit that Mrs Hoa touched my mother's elbow. 'Didn't you enjoy the Father's sermon?' Mrs Hoa said. Her eyes were curiously flat, as if painted onto her face. My mother's back stiffened, and she barely turned her head to say, 'I liked it very much.'

'I haven't heard from you yet about your donation, dear. Next week, perhaps? I'll come by.' Mrs Hoa was dressed formally, in an *ao dai* of midnight velvet embroidered with a golden lotus over the breast. It must have been unbearably hot in summer weather, but no perspiration showed on her temples. 'Meanwhile, here's something to read.'

She produced a sheet of paper from her purse, the same fake alligator-skin one with the silver clasp I'd seen last week, and offered it to me. The mimeograph was in Vietnamese, which I could not read, but the blurry photograph said it all, gaunt men standing at attention in rank and file under fronds of palm trees, wearing exactly the tiger-stripe fatigues I'd imagined.

'What a handsome boy.' Mrs Hoa's tone was unconvincing. She wore the same white high heels I'd seen before. 'And you said your daughter's in college?'

'On the East Coast.'

'Harvard? Yale?' Those were the only two East Coast schools the Vietnamese knew. My mother, who could not pronounce Bryn Mawr, said, 'Another one.'

'What's she studying? Law? Medicine?'

My mother looked down in shame when she said, 'Philosophy.' She had scolded my sister Loan during her Christmas vacation, telling her she was wasting her education. My father had agreed, saying: 'Everyone needs a doctor or a lawyer, but who needs a philosopher? We can get advice for free from the priest.'

Mrs Hoa smiled once more and said, 'Excellent!' After she was gone, I handed the mimeograph to my mother, who shoved it into her purse. In the parking lot, crammed with cars and people, my mother pinched my father and said, 'I'm following Mrs Hoa. You and Long run the market by yourselves for a few hours.'

My father grimaced and rubbed his hand over his head. 'And what, exactly, are you planning to do?'

'She knows where we work. I'll bet she knows where we live. It's only fair I know the same things, isn't it?'

'Okay.' My father sighed. 'Let's go, son.'

'I want to go with Ma.'

'You, too?' my father muttered.

I was curious about Mrs Hoa, and helping my mother was an excuse not to spend my morning at the New Saigon. My mother and I followed her in our Oldsmobile, heading south. Mrs Hoa drove a small Datsun sedan the color of an egg yolk, peppered with flakes of rust. Superimposed upon the Datsun was the Virgin Mary, her image reflected in the windshield from her picture on the dash, as dim as our handful of fading color photos from Vietnam. My favorite featured a smiling young couple sitting on a grassy slope in front of a pink country church, Ba in his sunglasses as he embraced Ma, who wore a peach *ao dai* over silk cream pants, her abundant hair whipped into a bouffant.

'*Nam xu*,' my mother said, turning left onto Story Road. Thinking she wanted a translation into English, I said, 'A nickel?'

'Five cents is my profit on a can of soup.' As my mother drove, she kept her foot on the brake, not the accelerator. My head bounced back and forth on the headrest like a ball tethered to a paddle. 'Ten cents for a pound of pork, 25 cents for 10 pounds of rice. That woman wants 500 dollars from me, but you see how we fight for each penny?'

'Uh-huh.' Beads of sweat trickled from my armpit. I rolled down the window, but when I flung out my hand to surf the breeze, my mother said, 'A bus might come along and rip your arm off.' I pulled my arm back in and sighed. I yearned for the woman she once was in that old photograph, when my sister and I were not yet born and the war was nowhere to be seen, when my mother and father owned the future. Sometimes I tried to imagine what she looked like when she was even younger, at nine, and I could not. Without a photo, my mother as a little girl no longer existed anywhere, perhaps not even in her own mind. More than all those people starved by famine, it was the thought of my mother not remembering what she looked like as a little girl that saddened me.

Mrs Hoa turned off King Road onto a side street, a neighborhood of one-story homes with windows too small for the walls. Well-worn Ford pickups and Chrysler lowriders with chrome rims parked on the lawns. The front yard of Mrs Hoa's house was paved over, and her yellow Datsun joined a white Toyota Corolla with a crushed bumper and a green Honda Civic missing a hubcap. After Mrs Hoa walked inside, my mother cruised forward to inspect the house, painted with a newish coat of cheap, bright turquoise, the garage transformed into a storefront with sliding glass doors and a red neon sign that said NHA MAY. The blinds on the tailor shop's windows and the curtains of the living room were drawn, showing their white backs. The man who had broken into our house must have followed us home in the same way, but my mother did not seem to recognize this. Instead, her voice was full of satisfaction when she spoke. 'Now,' she said, easing her foot off the brake, 'we know where she lives.'

When Mrs Hoa came to the New Saigon on Wednesday afternoon of the following week, I was in the wooden loft my father had hammered together above the kitchenware at the rear of the store. We stored enough long-grain rice in the loft to feed a village, stacked nearly to the ceiling in burlap sacks of 10, 25 and 50 pounds. The clean carpet scent of polished jasmine permeated the air as I sat astride a dike of rice sacks, reading about Reconstruction. I had reached the part about the scalawags and carpetbaggers who had come from the North to help rebuild, or perhaps swindle, the South, when I saw Mrs Hoa at the doorway, wearing the white outfit from her first visit.

By the way my mother gripped the sides of the cash register as if it were a canoe rocking in the waves while Mrs Hoa talked to her, I knew there would be trouble. I climbed down the ladder, made my way past aisles stocked with condensed milk and cellophane noodles, shrimp chips and dried cuttlefish, lychees and green mangoes, ducking my head to avoid the yellow strips of sticky flypaper dangling from the ceiling, and reached the front of the store as my mother was saying, 'I'm not giving you any money'. A crack showed in her foundation, a line creasing her cheek from nose to jawbone. 'I work hard for my money. What do you do? You're nothing but a thief and an extortionist, making people think they can still fight this war.'

I stood behind a row of customers, one of them reading the same mimeograph Mrs Hoa gave me in church. Mrs Hoa's face had turned as white as her outfit, and red lipstick smeared her ochre teeth, bared in fury. She glared at the customers and said: 'You heard her, didn't you? She doesn't support the cause. If she's not a Communist, she's just as good as a Communist. If you shop here, you're helping Communists.'

Mrs Hoa slammed a stack of mimeographs on the counter by the register and, with that, she left. My mother stared at my father at the register across from her, and neither said a word as the Datsun sputtered into life outside. The customers in front of me shifted uneasily. Within an hour, they would be on their telephones, each one telling their friends, who in turn would tell their friends, who then would tell more people, until everyone in the community knew. My mother turned to the customers with her face as carefully composed as the letters she sent to her relatives, showing no signs of worry, and said, 'Who's next?'

Throughout the rest of the day, my mother made no more mention of Mrs Hoa, and I thought that she would simply ignore her, hoping she would not return. But the moment we got in the car, my mother began talking about her counter-attack, and I realized that she had been simmering for hours, keeping quiet for the sake of the customers. My mother would go to Mrs Hoa's and demand an apology, for her accusation could cost my mother her reputation and her business, given the depth of anti-Communist fervor in our Vietnamese community. My mother would call Mrs Hoa a disgrace and slap her if she refused. My mother would point out the hopelessness and self-delusion of Mrs Hoa's cause, reducing her to tears with logic. As my mother rehearsed her plans, my father said nothing, and neither did I. We knew better than to oppose her, and when we reached our house, he went wordlessly inside to start dinner, as instructed. My mother drove on to Mrs Hoa's, taking me as her co-pilot because, she said, 'That woman won't do anything crazy with you there.'

It was eight-thirty when my mother parked the car in Mrs Hoa's driveway, behind the Datsun. Mrs Hoa answered the door wearing an orange tank top and a pair of shorts in a purple floral print. Her hair was pinned back in a bun and her face, bereft of mascara, lipstick or foundation, belonged to a woman years older, creviced, pitted, cracked. Her small breasts were no bigger than those of Emmy Tsuchida's, and a map of varicose veins on her skinny thighs and shins led south to gnarled toes, the yellowing nails spotted with red dabs of chipped polish.

'What are you doing here?' Mrs Hoa said.

'I want to speak to you,' my mother said. 'Aren't you going to invite us in?'

Mrs Hoa hesitated and then stepped back grudgingly. We took off our shoes and picked our way past the loafers, sneakers, pumps and flip-flops jammed around the door. Racks on wheels, crammed with hangers for girls' clothes, hid the window, while a pair of bunk beds ran along two walls of the living room. In the center was a long folding table, stacked with notebooks and textbooks.

'We're having dinner,' Mrs Hoa said. Other voices rang from the dining room. An aerosol of grease clung to the air, along with the warm, wet socks of cooked rice. 'Have you eaten yet?'

'Yes.' If my mother was surprised at Mrs Hoa's politeness, she didn't show it. 'I'd like to talk in private.'

Mrs Hoa shrugged and led us past the dining room. At the packed table sat eight or nine people with heads turned our way, little girls with bowl cuts, a quartet of grandparents, and a man and woman around my mother's age, the shadows under their eyes so pronounced they looked as if someone had punched them again and again. Just as crowded was Mrs Hoa's bedroom, the first one down the hall. An industrial steel-frame table, a sewing machine fastened to it, dominated the middle of the room, while the velvet *ao dai* and the white jacket and pants hung from the bunk bed blocking the window. Mrs Hoa sat on the only chair, behind the sewing machine, and said, 'What do you want?'

My mother glanced at the closet, doors removed to reveal hand-built pine shelves stacked with bolts of silk and cotton. One of the two clothing racks behind Mrs Hoa was hung with everyday clothing – women's slacks and blouses, men's suits and dress shirts – while the other was hung with uniforms, olive-green fatigues and camouflage outfits patterned with blotches of brown, black and green in varying shades, the same kind issued to the Marines who had liberated Grenada not long ago. My mother said, 'You tailor uniforms for the soldiers?'

'Yes, besides the usual tailoring we do. American sizes are too large for Vietnamese men and the proportions aren't right. Plus the men want their names sewn on, and their ranks and units.' Mrs Hoa reached under the sewing table and lifted a cardboard box, and when we leaned over the table to peek inside, we saw plastic sandwich bags filled with chevrons and the colorful badges of Vietnamese units. 'Some of these uniforms are for the guerrilla army in Thailand, but others are for our men here.'

I wondered if she meant the rumored secret front, or the men my father's age and younger that I saw at Tet festivals, veterans of the vanquished South Vietnamese army who welcomed the New Year by wearing military uniforms and checking tickets at the fairgrounds where the festivals happened.

'Your husband's a soldier?' my mother said.

'He's a commando. The CIA parachuted him into North Vietnam in 1963. I haven't heard from him since.' Mrs Hoa spoke without any change in inflection, clutching the box to her chest. 'The Americans sent my younger son's division to Laos in 1972. He never returned. As for my eldest son, he was in the army, too. The Communists killed him. I buried him in 1969. My daughter wrote to tell me the Communists bulldozed his grave at Bien Hoa.'

My mother was silent, fingering a tiger-stripe camouflage jacket hanging from the rack. At last, she said, 'I'm sorry to hear about your husband and your sons.'

'Sorry for what?' Mrs Hoa's voice was shrill. 'Who ever said my husband was dead? No one saw him die. No-one saw my youngest son die, either. They're alive, and no-one like you is going to tell me otherwise.'

I studied the patterns in the beige carpet, shapes of a frog and a tree, trapped there along with odors of garlic and sesame, sweat and moisturizer. My mother broke the silence by opening her purse and digging inside. From the crumpling of paper, I knew she was opening the envelope with the day's cash. She extracted two hundred-dollar bills and laid them on the sewing table in front of Mrs Hoa, smoothing the face of Benjamin Franklin on each bill, the same way she ran her palm over my hair before entering church.

'That's it,' my mother said. 'That's all I have.'

I calculated the cans of soup, the pounds of rice, and the hours of standing on her feet that made those 200 dollars possible, and I was astonished that my mother had surrendered the money. When Mrs Hoa looked at the cash, I thought she might demand the 500 dollars she'd asked for, but she swept up the bills, folded them, and dropped them into the box on her lap. As she and my mother stared at each other after that, I thought about how, years ago, my mother had bribed a general's wife with an ounce of gold, buying my father's freedom from the draft. My mother had mentioned the incident one night to my father as they inspected another ounce they had just purchased, and he, glancing at me, had said, 'Let's not talk about that'. They would file this incident with Mrs Hoa under the same category of things better left unspoken.

'We'll see ourselves out,' my mother said.

'You see how the Communists weren't satisfied with killing my son once?' Mrs Hoa aimed her gaze at me. 'They killed him twice when they desecrated his grave. They don't respect anybody, not even the dead.'

Her voice was urgent, and when she suddenly leaned forward, I was afraid she was going to reach across the sewing machine and grasp my hand. I willed myself not to back away from her fingers, two of them bandaged as if she had pricked herself with needles. I felt that I had to say something, and so I said, 'I'm sorry'. I meant that I was sorry for all that had happened, not only to her but also to my mother, the accumulation of everything I could do nothing about. My apology made utterly no difference, but Mrs Hoa nodded gravely, as if understanding my intentions. In a subdued tone, she said, 'I know you are'.

Those were her last words to me. She did not say goodbye when we left, and indeed, did not even look at us, for as my mother closed the bedroom door, Mrs Hoa was gazing down into the box, her bent head revealing a furrow of white roots running through her scalp, where the hair's natural color revealed itself past the receding tide of black dye. It was a trivial secret, but one I would remember as vividly as my feeling that while some people are haunted by the dead, others are haunted by the living.

When my mother exited the freeway, she surprised me for the second time. She pulled into the parking lot of the 7-11 off the freeway, two blocks from home, and said: 'You've been such a good boy. Let's get you a treat.' I didn't know what to say. My parents did not grant me so much as an allowance. When I had asked for one in the fourth grade, my father had frowned and said, 'Let me think it over'. The next night he had handed me an itemized list of expenses that included my birth, feeding, education and clothing, the sum total being $24,376. 'This doesn't include emotional aggravation, compound interest or future expenses,' my father said. 'Now when can you start paying *me* an allowance?'

My mother stopped under the bright lights at the door of the 7-11, pulled a crisp five-dollar bill out of her purse, and handed it to me. 'Go buy,' she said in English, motioning me inside. Whenever she spoke in English, her voice took on a higher pitch, as if, instead of coming from inside her, the language was outside, squeezing her by the throat. 'Anything you want.'

I left her on the sidewalk and went in, the five-dollar bill as slick as wax paper in my hand. The 7-11 was empty except for the two Sikh men at the registers, who gave me bored looks and returned to their conversation. Disinfectant tinted the air. I ignored the bank of arcade games and the racks of comic books, even though the covers of *Superman* and *Iron Man* caught my eye and the electronic whirring of *Pac-Man* called to me. Past the cleaning products and canned soups was an aisle stocked with chips, cookies and candy. I glanced down the aisle, saw the glint of gold foil on a chocolate bar, and froze. While the clerks chatted in a language I could not understand, I hesitated, yearning to take everything home and unable to choose.

Instinctively, I looked back at my mother for help. She was visible through the glass doors at the other end of the store, wearing lavender, head bent, shoulders stooped and purse clutched under her arm, worn and diminished under fluorescent light. Her lips moved as she used the fingers of one hand to count something on the fingers of her other hand, each beat taking me back in time to the moment I got up off my knees and saw her dashing by the living-room window, barefoot on the sidewalk before all the people in their cars, hands raised high in the air and wearing only her nightgown in the twilight, shouting something I could not hear, demanding to be heard.

Viet Thanh Nguyen was born in Vietnam and travelled to the United States in 1975 as a refugee with his family. His first novel, *The Sympathizer,* has been listed as one of the best or most notable books of 2015 nearly 20 times, including in the *New York Times, Publishers Weekly,* Amazon.com, *Kirkus Reviews, The Guardian,* the *Washington Post,* and *Library Journal.* He is the author of *Race and Resistance: Literature and Politics in Asian America* and the co-editor of *Transpacific Studies: Framing an Emerging Field.* His latest book is *Nothing Ever Dies: Vietnam and the Memory of War* (Harvard University Press, 2016). He is an associate professor of English and American Studies and Ethnicity at the University of Southern California.

HEIDI NORTH-BAILEY
New Zealand/Aotearoa

HORSES

The summer we moved inland, we were still covered with sand. Josie and I sat in the back of the strange car as we wound along the dusty road, staring out at the dry, flat paddocks through the real-estate man's shiny car windows.

'He must wash them every day,' I'd whispered to Josie, kicking our bare feet on the hot pavement, woozy from the sun, waiting for Dad and the real-estate man to finish in his office. Josie'd looked at me but hadn't smiled.

It was cold in here. All the windows were tightly sealed, not like Dad's car where my window was stuck halfway down because the handle was broken. I pulled my hand out of my shorts' pocket to fiddle with the electric windows and some of the sand that always lived there spilled out. It made a little trail on the smooth leather seats. Good. I hated the stupid real-estate man and what Dad would usually call his 'flashy pants' car.

All the other houses ran out and we turned down a winding gravel road; it made my stomach do these little flips inside. 'I feel funny,' I said, but quietly. I don't think Dad heard me because he was too busy listening to the real-estate man tell him about all the horses we could have.

'You like horses, don't you, girls?' he had that stupid old-person voice on, all bright and shiny and fake, like Easter egg wrapping. He tried to look at us in the rear-view mirror. I dodged his eyes and stared at the cloud of dust rising behind us. I waited for Dad to tell him we didn't ride horses. We'd never ridden horses. But he didn't.

When we finally pulled up at the gate, the house looked old and haunted. It was stuck in the middle of a lumpy paddock. It was painted a faded dark brown. The real-estate man leapt out of the car and slammed the door. He looked ridiculous in his gumboots and suit. Dad wasn't wearing a suit. I'd never seen Dad wear a suit. Not ever.

I scanned the horizon. Hills, boring trees, and some cows. 'Where's the beach?' I asked Dad. I couldn't hear the waves.

'It's only about 20 minutes' drive away.' Dad said. He had his bright voice on too.

I looked down at the ground and poked my toe hard into the cracked mud. I wanted to tell Dad we couldn't live here, it was impossible. I dug in my pockets and felt the tiny grains of sand in the creases. We were beach people. We lived by the sea. But then I saw tears welling in Josie's eyes. She stood beside me silently, her little face quiet.

Dad strode off round the back of the house with the real-estate man to look at the guttering.

'I don't like it here,' Josie whispered.

'Shut up,' I pinched her arm hard, right in the skin just under the sleeve of her T-shirt. 'Don't say anything to Dad,' I said. I felt hot and itchy inside. 'What would...' I couldn't say the word 'Mum', it got stuck in my throat, and while I was busy trying to pull it out, it hung in the empty space between us.

Josie's upper lip trembled. I put my grown-up face on and stared at her. She stared back at me with her hazel eyes upturned. I could tell she was trying really hard not to cry. Her face had got all pinched. She nodded.

Dad called us to go and look inside. Josie trailed behind me to the porch. We stepped inside and stood blinking in the sudden darkness. I let Josie take my hand. We didn't shut the front door behind us.

'This way,' Dad called. The floorboards creaked as we followed his voice down the dark hallway.

'It smells like dead people's shops,' Josie whispered to me. That's what she called second-hand shops. She was so stupid. I pinched her again.

Dad was standing in the middle of an empty room that had, once, been painted light blue. The window looked like it was glued shut. Light filtered dimly through the dusty pane.

'This is one bedroom!' Dad said. His voice filled up the room. He swung his arms around like a puppet. I looked up at the ceiling. The dirty white paint was coming off in huge flakes. Like snow. Josie kicked something and it rattled along the wooden floorboards.

'We can paint it!' Dad said brightly. He swung his arms around again, like a windmill. 'Just imagine. Any color you like! Won't that be nice?' He sounded like he might explode.

I glued my mouth shut with invisible glue like I'd learnt to in the past few months. I got a little thin line of imaginary glue and put it between my lips.

Then I had to not breathe while I counted 20 banana seconds and then the glue would be set and all the bad things would stay inside me and not come out.

Dad asked me what color I wanted to paint the room but I couldn't speak because of the glue. I heard Josie tell him she didn't want this room. I still couldn't speak because of the glue. Dad was telling me how he'd get a skylight put in, carpet. Wallpaper, even, if I wanted. But the glue was set now. I said nothing.

Then Dad told us to go back outside. He'd said he'd be there in a minute. We left him in the blue room.

Josie followed me, her hand tugging my sleeve, over the slightly uneven floor, the brown lino tilting away from us in the kitchen, past the semi-outhouse, out the back door. She was sniffling now, but really quietly, like she was trying not to, so I didn't pinch her. We stood on the matted dead grass under the sagging washing line. It was the only thing in the backyard for miles. I lifted Josie up so she could grab hold of the metal bar. The washing line groaned and creaked as I pushed her round.

When Dad came outside his face was red and blotchy. He wasn't swinging his arms around any more. He shut his wallet quickly when he saw us, but I saw the corner of the photograph peaking out from the faded tan leather. I knew what he'd been doing.

The real-estate man came striding round the side of the house, his blue and grey striped tie flying behind him.

'Well?' he asked.

'I'm not, we're just…' Dad seemed to have deflated like a balloon at the end of a birthday party. He looked at us and gestured with his hands. They rose and fell through the air. The real-estate man flashed his shiny white teeth. He stepped in close to Dad and sort of angled his body away from us.

'Look, mate, you won't find anything else in your price range. This is absolutely it.' He looked at Dad and I didn't like the look of pity on his face.

Dad's hand was on his wallet, running his fingers over the secret inside. I could tell he wanted to say something terrible so for the first time I ripped open my lips, despite the glue.

'I love it,' I said to the real-estate man. Loudly. It was surprisingly easy. I could see Dad staring at me out of the corner of my eye but I ignored him. I looked out over the lumpy paddocks. There was a gate hanging off its hinges with a soft tuft of sheep wool stuck to it. I turned and looked at Dad. His eyes were reddening and starting to spill a little. I gave him my new grown-up smile. 'We can have horses here.'

Heidi North-Bailey is from New Zealand/Aotearoa. She writes poems, short stories, screenplays and non-fiction. She has won awards for her writing, including the Asia New Zealand Short Story Competition in 2014 and the Irish Feile Filiochta International Poetry Competition in 2007. Her work has appeared in journals such as *Poetry New Zealand, Takahē* and *The 4th Floor Literary Journal*. Her first poetry collection, *Possibility of Flight*, was published in November 2015 by Makaro Press.

ANA MENÉNDEZ
United States/Cuba

GHOSTS

Anna Kralova stands outside the apartment door, listening. This irrational impulse makes her cringe, though she assumes no one is here to record her embarrassment. Anna does not believe in ghosts. She believes that when we die, we are gone forever. She believes everything we know of the world, we know through our senses, a sudden flaming vision through time. And yet how to explain this feeling? This sense of a foreign sadness that's been lodged in her throat since the young man's death.

She turns her key in the lock and opens the door. Not too slowly, not too quickly. As naturally as she can, she opens the door to her old apartment. The door swings into silence. What was she expecting? Creaking hinges? A cold spot on the floor? Footsteps? Anna smiles to herself. For days afterward, that odious old man downstairs continued to complain about phantom footfalls.

There is no one here. There is nothing here. Just Anna and her breathing. The apartment is vacant. But vacant in a way that Anna has never experienced. More of a grey absence. The once familiar floor, the little rooms, the yellow kitchen cabinets all speak now of a place hollowed of life. And the faint antiseptic clinging to the air is itself a kind of ghost, a reminder of what happened here.

Anna Kralova didn't know much about her tenant beyond a name, Yuliani Garcia. Later, she learned he had arrived from Cuba the previous year. She never met him. She'd put her place up for rent at the height of the financial crisis, after she lost her job at the paper. The idea was to go back home, but at the last moment, another job opened in Tampa photographing corporate events, and she'd taken it gratefully. She was glad to be out of the building, anyway. The man downstairs had given her grief since the day she moved in. Once, she had held an afternoon baby shower for a colleague and the man had called the police, who had showed up shame-faced at her door.

The decrepit *bručoun* had terrorized Yuliani as well. And when the agent called Anna in Tampa to give her the news, the first thing she thought was that the neighbor had shot Yuliani dead. But it was just a suicide, the agent assured her. One of many in this town. Anna remembers the agent said she was sorry – an English construction that Anna had never been able to accept. What was there to be sorry about? As if the bad that happened always had to be someone's fault.

Anna didn't respond and the agent kept talking. She told Anna not to worry, that she would handle everything. And then before hanging up, she added, 'It won't affect the value – the suicide – we don't have to disclose it.'

Ghosts were trickier, less disposed to discretion. And just to be safe, the agent suggested, she should light some sage. Anna assumed it was in jest. But then she was at Target and there, in the bargain bin, as if an ancient trickster were calling her by name, sat a big green sage candle.

Now, Anna takes the candle out of her purse and sets it on the counter. The first match she strikes is humid. The second one is weak, but Anna manages to light the wick before the match goes out. The candle flame sputters, threatens to expire and then flares with such ferocity that Anna takes a step back.

Anna was 17 when the Wall fell. Two years later, she was working for the Czech ministry of foreign affairs. Over the years, her parents had sold off pieces of jewelry, china, even the silverware her grandparents had hidden after the war, to pay for English lessons for their only daughter. Later, those lessons paid off for the entire family. It helped that Anna was pretty. But what got her into the foreign ministry was her flawless English, acquired clandestinely from an elderly British lady whose pedagogy involved memorizing long passages of English poetry.

In the early years after the revolution, Prague, like the rest of Eastern Europe, was awash in suitors: corporate, national, international. Anna worked 15-hour days, going from meeting to meeting as interpreter. She had taken the job instead of going to college. She couldn't have hoped for a better crash course in international business. Anna heard pitches from car companies, fast-food businesses, chocolate empires, all the time wondering at this new kind of twisted poetry. She understood the individual words, but couldn't make sense of them. 'If we can leverage this synergy, the impact on your market will be off the charts.' But slowly she came to understand. And, though she would never say this to anyone, she overcame the translation hurdles by understanding that these Americans were using language in the same way her own apparatchiks had done all her life. After that it became easy: substitute one nonsense phrase in English for its equivalent in Czech.

One evening, she sat in a conference room with her bosses and the representatives from USAID. Three men on their side, three men on hers. Anna had already met many Americans, but they never failed to impress. So healthy-looking, with their straight white teeth, their short hair. Cheeks gone pink in the lingering spring cold. And, of course, the smiles. She had yet to meet an American who didn't smile. She was still another year away from her first trip to the Midwest. But already she imagined a country full of men and women like this, shiny with wealth's good humor.

In contrast, her own people. 'Beaten down by history,' as her grandmother always said, with her usual abundance of drama. And maybe she was right. What did these brand-new Americans know of war or occupation? Did they even know what it was to be hungry?

The meeting started with the usual preliminaries. The Americans asked after her bosses' families, something they must have learned in a seminar somewhere and that always made Anna recoil, as if a guest had opened the refrigerator in her home without permission. Then they wandered down to the discussion. Her bosses understood English very well, but they still let her handle the interpreting. That way they couldn't be blamed – that much hadn't changed.

The men were there to talk about entrepreneurship and business. The conversation went back and forth. They were offering their expertise. The bosses were very grateful, so much work was still needed, our country so far behind Western-style development. The Americans could cover infrastructure costs, ensure there weren't too many stumbles on the road to privatization.

After an hour of this, Anna's boss turned to her and said, in Czech: 'Look, dearie, don't translate what I'm about to tell you. But can you speed this up a bit? We just want their money.'

Anna takes a few steps and stops, suddenly cold. Sharp knocking comes through the floor. Then a shaky voice cries up through the wooden slats, 'Knock it off!'

Christ. That nasty man. She stomps once on the floor in anger, then slips off her heels. After a moment, she tiptoes to the kitchen. She takes the camera out of its case, pops in the wide-angle. The investigation had taken a little more than a month. When it was over, Anna arranged to have the young man's possessions removed. She worked with the agent to clean the place. And, for an extra fee, the agency refurnished the apartment.

Mostly Ikea, Anna sees now. And the monotonous lines add to the sense of melancholy. The agent had taken some photos, but they made Anna wince. She begins to move through the apartment with her Nikon. The light is good. But when Anna checks the view screen, every photo she's taken of the kitchen is framed by grotesque shadows. She extinguishes the silly sage candle and starts over. The small living room, the bathroom. She leaves the bedroom for last. They'd had to rip out the rug here, and now Anna hesitates at the threshold. The new laminate is dark and shiny, unmarred. The double bed is made. Anna recognizes the bedspread from the catalogue. Also the nightstands and the dresser. Over the bed hangs the apartment's only piece of art, a map of the world. Anna has never got used to seeing North America in the center.

She takes a deep breath and steps into the room. He had slit his wrists. Just 21 years old and he had lain down one night as if to sleep, but instead he'd slit his wrists until all the blood drained from him. A friend had found him. Or a client – the police later told Anna that Yuliani had been working as a prostitute. Her immediate reaction was to protest as if it were her duty to preserve the honor of the dead, 'He was a masseur!' she'd cried. And the cops laughed, a laugh that in an instant burnt up the distance Anna Kralova had travelled.

Anna crouches for a shot of the closet. Walk-in closets, even small ones, are rare in buildings of this age. That will be a nice *selling point*, as the agent would say. Anna is closing the doors again, when she notices something – a shadow – on the top shelf. She stops. Not a shadow, she tells her wild heart. Not a shadow. Not a shadow. She shuts the closet door. Not a shadow, Anna. She opens it again. A dark box pushed back against a corner. She taps the light switch. A suitcase. Anna considers the situation. The suitcase might belong to one of the workers. Perhaps, Anna thinks, one of the workers stayed a few nights, unable to resist the temptation of a new home, new sheets, a different life.

Anna clings to this version as long as she can. But she is too long accustomed to seeing things clearly. No worker would have left a suitcase here. And still Anna does not move. She has shorn herself of her mother's superstitions. But she does not want to touch the effects of the dead man. She turns to leave. Someone else will remove the suitcase. Anna closes the closet doors. She begins to walk away. She will send someone, maybe one of the same workers. If it was his suitcase, he will be glad for the opportunity to take it home. And if it belonged to the dead man, someone will throw it away. Anna pictures the suitcase lying in the dumpster outside. And what of the boy's family? Wouldn't Anna, living far from home and all alone, wish a stranger to gather the small evidence of her life? Isn't that part of the respect we owe the dead?

Anna opens the closet again. The suitcase is a solid thing, a mute invitation. She stands on tiptoe and nudges it from side to side until a corner hangs over the edge. Anna grabs and yanks hard. But the suitcase is lighter than she expects and it flies across the room, landing with a crash on the new laminate before bursting open. Papers are still flying down when violent tapping echoes through the room. Anna's heart seizes. Then the disembodied voice from below, 'Knock it off!'

Jesus Mary and Joseph. Anna is afraid to move. Papers litter the room. Slowly, quietly, she begins to gather them. Receipts, letters, photographs. She sorts them in piles. Lodged into the corner of the suitcase, a brick of letters, tightly wound in rubber bands. Anna releases them and the letters fall open, hundreds, all written on airmail paper. She opens them one after the other. Long letters in a tiny script. Almost all of them begin with *Gracias por el dinero, mi hijo*. Anna's Spanish is not perfect, but she can read most of it, at least take away the sense. *Me alegro mucho. Que bonita suerte. Como te estraño.* All the words that a mother would write. About happiness and longing and the good luck that her son was enjoying in that abundant land. How pleased she was that he was making a life for himself, however much it hurt her to be so far away.

Anna sits with the suitcase for a long time, much longer than she had expected, absorbed in the story she unfolds page by page. She finds other letters, from friends, perhaps. Birthday cards, most of them hand-crafted. One card is made from pressed paper, a bird in flight with wings that open and close, like a fan. A pile of medical receipts. The results of an HIV test – negative. A Cuban passport, the photo in black and white of an impossibly young boy. Some two dozen photographs of young people, smiling at the shore, in the fields, on the great lawn of what seems a library or university.

How long ago it seems that Anna climbed these steps for the first time. How little she knew then. Spirits press down on her, and again and again she rejects them. Sends them packing, back to the pre-rational past. Not a haunting, but an echo. The boy's life a gesture pointing back to her own. A dream of a thousand iterations. From nowhere, now, comes a fragment of Yeats, a ghostly melody.

I would spread the cloths under your feet:
But I, being poor, have only my dreams;
I have spread my dreams under your feet;
Tread softly because you tread on my dreams.'

Maybe her father was right, maybe she should never have left. Now she is neither American nor Czech. Now she is some in-between thing, diminished.

'I was in Prague after the split,' the agent told her after they signed the rental lease with Yuliani. 'I loved it.'

'Yes,' Anna said. 'Americans love Prague.'

'Because of Kafka, probably,' said the agent.

Anna nodded. Of course, Kafka and the Charles Bridge. The extent of American knowledge of Prague. How could Anna explain that she didn't even read Kafka until she moved to the US? Thanks to her eccentric education, she knew more about Shakespeare and Auden, could recite long passages from Yeats many years before she made the acquaintance of Gregor Samsa.

So much time gone by. Anna grasps at the blurred edges of her childhood, the past no longer the certain shelter she imagined for herself. Is it like this for everyone, or only for those who leave? The loss of her childhood language, the acquisition of a new one, has altered the topography of memory. Her poor, lonely mother tongue has run out of stories to tell. And the present is a tyrant who speaks English. *I am old with wandering through hollow lands and hilly lands…*

How long since her last trip home? Three years? Five. Yes, it's been five years since she stood at the Palacky bridge, tracing the Vltava's black embroidery through the city, five years since she sat with her mother over a cup of tea and talked for hours about her old friends: who made it, who didn't, who got out, who stayed behind.

When she was a girl, her parents visited her mother's village in Slovakia every summer. Today the trip takes less than five hours. But in those days, it was almost a full day's journey in their old Škoda, from eight in the morning to five in the evening. They usually stayed for two weeks, setting back early on the morning of departure. But one year, they didn't leave the village until late afternoon. Night caught them on the road. And the last hours, they moved through the darkened countryside, the rocking and steady hum of the car lulling Anna in and out of sleep. As they approached Bratislava, a great glow came up behind the hills. It was as if the moon had fallen to earth.

Anna's father must have seen her pressing her face to the glass.

'That's Vienna,' he said.

'The lights of the city,' murmured her mother.

Vienna, city of great lights. And for the rest of Anna's childhood, that's what the unreachable West was, an other-worldly radiance set in the wilderness, a place where people refused to give in to the natural gloom.

And that memory loosens others. They come rushing back to Anna in her native tongue. *A to je ta krásná země, země česká, domov můj.* Her skinny schoolgirl years. A boy she loved. The first smell of summer. The lovely childhood lived in quiet obedience. And how the end of it – the protests, the thousands in the square – all tasted to her of love. That is what it was like to live inside great changes, to ache for a life viewed so long from a distance. That is what it had been like for Yuliani, more brother to Anna than either could have known.

She's been in Miami for 17 years. Three years before that in Chicago. Two years in Los Angeles. Half her life in a foreign country. Though it doesn't feel like a foreign country. The foreign country is here, Anna thinks. She is the foreign country. Fourteen years photographing strangers. How many people had she met? She's lost track. She can't remember all of them, though it occurs to her that each of them may remember her, lit up against the blazing tragedy that delivered her to their door.

Who will remember Yuliani Garcia? How did he get here? How long had he been dreaming of Miami? Anna knows almost nothing of his story. But she knows that he departed at dawn so his mother would not see his tears. Knows that the sadness of leaving was mixed with an electric anticipation that no one who has never left can understand. No, Anna does not believe in ghosts; we are our own ghosts, dragging our mournful pasts.

Anna repacks the suitcase, taking her time. She refolds the letters and secures them with the rubber band. She stacks the certificates, the birthday cards. She gathers the photographs into a pile, the strangers still laughing by the foreign sea, sweetly mocking Anna Kralova, a woman they don't even know exists. After she folds the last page, Anna closes the suitcase and sits with her head in her hands.

History seems like a big thing to those outside it. But it's experienced in miniature: a boat's humid hold, a creased passport, a small suitcase full of papers that you drag from city to city. *Nemoc na koni přijíždí a pěšky odchází.* So much lost between languages, forgotten in transit. So many dreams in this town. Miscommunications and galloping misfortunes. It was her grandmother's favorite phrase, uttered in every season: misfortune arrives on horseback and departs on foot. Her grandmother, who had survived three currencies and witnessed both the crushed Spring and the fall of the Wall. Now, she is buried in a city of Zara and Starbucks, a Prague she would scarcely recognize.

Anna will see about the papers. Maybe she will track down Yuliani's mother. Someone must remain to collect the photographs. Someone will find meaning in these fragments of a life.

After a long while, Anna stands, legs shaking, and rolls the suitcase across the unforgiving threshold as softly as she can.

Ana Menéndez was born in Los Angeles, the daughter of Cuban exiles. She is the author of four books of fiction: *In Cuba I Was a German Shepherd*, *Loving Che*, *The Last War* and, most recently, *Adios, Happy Homeland!* A former journalist, she has written about Cuba, Haiti, Kashmir, Afghanistan and India. Her work has appeared in a variety of publications including *Vogue*, *Bomb Magazine*, *Poets & Writers* and *Tin House* and has been included in several anthologies, including *Cubanisimo!* and *American Food Writing*. A former Fulbright Scholar in Egypt, she now lives in Surfside, Florida.

MATHEW HOWARD
Canada/Australia

SOMETHING LIKE JOY

Celia woke with the sunrise, high in the Rockies, chasing the zephyr memory of her dad. A year had passed since his death and for a year she'd hung suspended, strung by her feet between two stars in the airless expanse of space.

The Rockies were nothing like the big sky she'd grown up with. She looked up at the mountains, creeping gold in the early light, and knew again that the world was beautiful – tremendously, unknowingly beautiful – but also broken, the gentle snow-covered peaks and lilting passes disguising a violent rupture of rock.

A week earlier, Celia had thrown her clothes in a suitcase, tossing in her typewriter as an afterthought. She'd borrowed a friend's car and navigated the seas of grass and lunar foothills of Alberta, up through awesome passes and shining lakes, before finally arriving at Bridges Rehabilitation and Aged Care Facility, perched high where rocky field met summer snow.

Far from the bedlam she'd imagined, Celia found a place of peace and majesty. The building itself was nestled in the crux of two abutting mountains, balanced zen-like and perfect amongst the wildflowers and stones. A path span down to a spectacular glacial lake, its turquoise lined with park benches and reeds.

She'd come to retrace the last trail her father's comet had blazed.

Celia was a writer – hence the typewriter – and had requested a month-long stay to write a book, funded through a grant that didn't exist. Truthfully, she'd come with a single goal: to find a photograph of her dad.

They'd been separated when she was young and, without a photograph, her memory had begun to fail her. Was his hair blond or sandy grey? Did his tooth snaggle to the left, or was it the right? And, wrapped up in all that, did he love her? Was someone in his condition *able* to love? Was she?

So far, she'd mostly sat by the lake, trailing her feet in icy water and calling out to her father's ghost. She avoided the residents and staff, ate alone in her room. She'd searched for information about her father, asked after him feebly to no avail. She'd expected finding a photograph to be difficult. She'd expected the mystery and dead-ends. What came as a surprise was the quiet of the place, the smallness she felt amongst the towering mountains and great blackness of night. At lights out, she'd pull her curtains tight for fear the sky would crash down on her with the weight of her father's memory.

When she did dream, Celia dreamt of him, but his face was a blur, an amalgam of men, and she'd wake with a start and lie silent in the suffocating black of her room. If she felt brave, she'd finger a crack in the curtains and peer through at the glowing firmament of stars. If she felt strong, she'd breathe deeply and remember.

When she was little, Celia's father claimed to have discovered a planet. On the night of his greatest discovery, so she was told, the astrophysicist returned home to find the door ajar, his infant daughter asleep beside a note from his wife. He held Celia, tiny and perfect in his arms, and abandoned pursuit of the universe to raise her.

From as early as she could remember, his quest for wonder and awe, once satisfied by his life's work, he now trained entirely on her. In the obsidian black of her eyes, he found galaxy upon galaxy, a cornucopia of whirling constellations and bursting stars. He told her the planet had been named for her and that it teetered on the edge of the universe, a ghostly last post before the great expanse of nothing.

'Your planet is impossibly beautiful,' he told her, 'a red-hued orb of sulphur and shadow, traced with rings of silver and gold. We'll go there together, my sweet, just you and me.'

As the sun edged across the floor, Celia shook her head to loosen the past. She dressed and stepped out into the mountain light. She gripped the rail and carefully managed the steps, looking fixedly down to ensure her feet hit hard rock and not cloud. A winding gravel path carried her to the lake and her usual spot. Sitting silent and still, the past caught up to her.

Like her dad, Celia was a loner. While other kids played, Celia dreamed only of their planet and how to get there, conjuring its wild frontiers and as yet undiscovered civilizations. She'd curl next to her father to watch rocket launches on television, imagining them both on board, hand in hand, the world shrinking away in a cloud of fire and fumes.

She longed for his company. While her father dried space-food on windowsills or stitched together spacesuits to keep them warm, Celia worked only for his approval. After falling into bed, she'd hear him incanting late into the night, memorizing ancient languages or testing radio frequencies. He'd lock himself away for days, welding or hammering, emerging only to eat and rustle his daughter's hair before hiding away again.

Deep down, Celia always knew it was make-believe, but kept at the game because it was something they shared. It tethered them together, heart to heart, their planet a bridge across all that made her father different and strange.

Everything changed the night the Challenger disintegrated in fire and ash, their story along with it.

'Daddy, what happened?' Celia wailed, confused. 'Did they die? Did they make it to space?'

Celia remembered her father in the kitchen, leaned up against a wall. Face turned and shoulders stooped, the purpose of his life seared across the sky in a fiery ball. Celia had sensed the great nothingness of what was next. She had taken him by the arm.

'We'll still get there, Daddy,' she had whispered. 'We'll climb into a rowboat and cast off on a flat and silent sea. We'll sail until the stars are above us and beneath us, Daddy, and we'll float past the moon. We'll trail our toes in the gas clouds of Jupiter and crash on our planet's shores. We'll make ourselves a home – a castle on the tallest hill – and live just the two of us. OK, Daddy?'

He'd stared at the wall a while longer, Celia's heart in her throat. When she'd thought she couldn't bear the silence any longer, he'd laughed, dried his eyes and, being a man of science, launched into a lecture on quantum physics. Then he'd bumbled back to the basement. Young as she was, Celia knew she'd saved them. Their story had kept them alive.

Celia remembered all this by the lake. She fought to stay in the present, imagining her father alive and well; visits to her home, hugs and gifts and days spent sitting on the porch in the prairies. He'd find her home was cluttered with junk, just as his had been. She was a writer (technically), her walls propped up with towers of books, just as his had been. He'd find in her the same empty pull, the unchartered, unclosable vastness that they both shared and never spoke of. Maybe it was depression; maybe it was genius. Whatever it was, she knew she'd learned from him to feed it with sadness and longing.

Lost in thought, she hadn't seen the old woman slip into the gelid lake, lower herself into the water and cast off towards the other side. As Celia basked in shadow, the old woman climbed onto the opposite bank, bracing her tiny body against the cold mud, and tottered back towards the home. Oblivious, Celia watched the sun trail high across the sky, and then hours later, dip low beyond a mountain peak.

The next morning felt different somehow, the early-fall light pale but warm. Celia sensed a swell in the air, a subtle shift in season. She returned to her usual spot only to find it taken. A resident – an elderly woman, suspiciously wet – lay on the bench wrapped in a towel. Had she swum in the lake? *Could you swim in the lake?* The air was brisk, but laced with a hint of swirling warmth, and the possibility of it struck Celia like a dull punch. What had she been doing these past weeks?

The old woman's swimming costume bloomed in a pattern of red dahlias, her thin, grey hair creeping in ringlets from beneath a red latex cap. Her eyes were covered with red cat-eye sunglasses. She lay deathly still and Celia was suddenly seized by the impulse to shake her.

The woman's arm slipped sideways and Celia jumped in fright. She sensed death hovering on the gravel path behind her. She shook the woman firmly and fell backwards with a squeal as the old woman's eyes flew open in a rage.

'Get your hands off me!'

'I'm so sorry,' Celia stammered, 'I thought you were dead!'

'Grab an old lady like that and she soon will be,' the old woman snapped, wrapping the towel around her tight.

'I was worried –'

'You're casting a shadow, kid.'

'Sorry,' Celia replied, softer this time, shifting to let the pale sun fall on the old woman's paler skin. The old woman reached down and applied coconut oil to bone-thin limbs.

'I know you're Canadian, but you can calm down with the sorries,' she said with a wave. 'If you're going to stay, and clearly you are, at least have the decency to move out of what little sun the good Lord provideth up here.'

'Aren't you Canadian?' Celia replied.

'As Canadian as they come, my dear, but you'll never hear me apologizing for things I've no business apologizing for.'

'Did you swim in the lake?'

The old woman shot her a reproving look and flicked her sunglasses back onto her nose, lying back down to catch the fullness of the sun.

'Isn't it cold?' Celia offered.

'Up here, it's cold in the water and out of it. What's the difference?'

Celia sat on the ground by the bench, flummoxed.

'Aren't you a bit young to be hanging around here? Or are you a hiker with frostbite?' the woman asked. 'We get a lot of those. I found one on the doorstep last month and dragged him up the stairs all on my lonesome.'

'I'm visiting. My dad used to be a resident here and I'm –'

'Judah Jones,' the woman interrupted. 'You've got his nose.'

Celia's jaw dropped. 'Do you remember him? Not many people here do.'

'I've been here twenty-something years. I've seen people come and go. I try not to remember too much,' the old woman tapped her forehead, 'I'm saving room for the future. Jones was a difficult man. I'm surprised they let you stay.'

'I'm a writer. I told them I'm writing a novel.'

The old woman contemplated for a moment. 'Judah was quite the storyteller.'

'So you knew him well, then?'

The old woman ignored her. 'He was sick from the beginning; not right in the head. Everyone knew he'd had a rough go of things and left him well alone, as I'm sure he wanted. But he told some stories,' she chuckled, 'some truly knockout stories. He was an astronaut, apparently, and a rocket scientist, too. We understand crazy in here and don't think too much about it.'

'He *was* an astrophysicist, actually.'

The old woman sneezed and wiped her nose with her towel. 'Around here, we see quiet crazy and big bang crazy. The quiet ones gasp about and mumble to themselves. They fade into the wallpaper until they're invisible and that's that. The big bang ones – and your Judah was the biggest of the bangs – they rail and hiss and scratch their ways out.'

'So my father was unhappy?'

'Sometimes. Other times, he was over the moon,' the old woman chortled. 'What do you write?'

'Not much these days.'

'Too bad.'

As she walked back up to the home, Celia heard an almighty splash and turned to see the old woman's towel by the lakeside, a trail of bubbles strung out into the depths.

Celia strode back to her room determined to write, but the typewriter sat still as the lake. Until her father's death, she'd always been able to write. She put it down to her staccato childhood, a life lived amongst people but forever on the outside. Words usually flowed for her like light and water.

She'd decided to be a writer in her teens. Terrified by the slow emergence of her body, she'd dressed only in black; the first goth on the prairies. Celia had discovered boys, then girls, and then books after that. During her father's basement spells, she'd lock herself in her room and write until the sun came up.

In a moment of clarity, he had fixed her an old typewriter – still missing the letters p and v – so that his late-night hammering could have a softer echo as she tapped and typed two floors above. As she grew older, home-made rockets and tin-foil radars piled high amongst the stacks of magazines and dirty dishes. Laundry went undone, beds unmade. But she always had reams of stories and poems.

Her father would emerge from the basement from time to time and talk her through inventions, but her growing lack of interest gnawed at him and sent him spiralling further away from her and into himself. Some days he'd be there, alert and present, and she'd cherish the bright star-speck in his far-off eyes. He'd tell wandering stories and Celia would write them down, simplifying the confusion when he got himself lost. She wrote and wrote as he paced and laughed. On days like these, the tether between them was tight, strong.

Other days, she could feel the black hole spreading inside him, sensed its consuming sadness, a voracious hunger and pull. He would natter and jitter, then fall into a funk. Celia held his face and searched for light in his eyes, finding only dark. One day around her fifteenth birthday, she knew he'd been swallowed whole. He was telling a story and then stopped mid-sentence. She peered deep into his eyes, but their starless black was as empty as space itself.

He went first to hospital and then to the home in the Rocky Mountains. Celia moved from town to town, relative to relative, until she realized the black hole was in her, too. She saw a doctor who gave it a name. She did her best to ignore it. When the darkness came, she wrote her way through it.

Separated from her father, she thought of him often, but the tether between them hung loose. Her greatest fear was being devoured as he had. He'd write and she'd sometimes reply. She called him on the phone, but he stopped picking up. She got drunk once and wrote him an email, pouring torrents of love, but then realized he had no email address and it sat in her outbox, a murky pond.

She wanted to visit, but didn't. She moved and forgot to tell him. One day, Celia returned to a note. He was dead. After years apart, the tether between them had been stretched thin but never broken. While her feet were on the ground, she always knew her father was far above her somewhere, swimming dreamily through space. The line between them was limp at times, at other times sickeningly taut; she always thought she could reel him back to earth, whenever she so chose, but now he'd been cut loose, the thread between them piled around her in tatters.

She tore through her apartment in search of a photograph, but found none. The black hole within her clenched tight, and she realized her father lived now only in *other* people's photographs, photographs taken by mistake or chance, discarded in tattered shoeboxes or tucked deep in the dark spaces of forgotten books; photographs taken by people her father knew, or didn't know, and which she would never see. Having burned bright, he was nothing more than scattered matter and energy.

She imagined him standing off in the distance in one photo, axe in hand as he trod through a prairie field; in another, he'd stare over the shoulder of a young girl in brilliant blue; others would catch only the bend of his elbow or shiny tip of shoe. Sometimes the photographer would know him and there'd be bright eyes; other times he'd have fallen into frame by chance. These were the ones that interested Celia most, the ones where he was alien and unknowable, no longer her father, but a man on the street and nothing more. He wouldn't hold back his stormy sorrow for fear of upsetting her; he'd be utterly himself, eyes dark and brow furrowed. She'd see his angry orbit, spinning, gorging hungrily. In these photos, he'd be his most true self.

She wanted to gather all that remained of him – a stranger in strangers' albums – and put the story together piece by piece until she had him whole again, glowing bright and full as the universe, leaned up against her kitchen wall. A year later, high up in the Rockies, she had nothing and her typewriter sat silent and still.

Celia was waiting for the old woman first thing the next day. By the time she stumbled from the water, Celia was there to help. The old woman swiped the water from her eyes, fumbling through the sharper reeds and rocks. Celia held out her hand.

'No thanks,' the old woman gasped, shaking off the cold.

'You're here early. You might want to tell someone you're out here.'
'Is that so?'
'How long have you been swimming?'
'All my life,' the old woman's back straightened.
'In the lake?'
'This is my third try.'
'Then it might not be safe –'
'First thing, I'm an Olympian. Second, I've looked at this lake for twenty-something years and never realized what it was, a chance for me to do something I've always loved. So I've been swimming.' The old woman moved to leave, shooing Celia away: 'I don't know anything else about your father.'

'You know more than I do. Your name is Ruth, right? I asked one of the other residents.' Annoyed, Ruth gathered her towel to leave. Celia continued: 'My father and I were separated when I was a teenager. He had depression and God only knows what and he ended up here. We lost touch, he died a year ago and I haven't been the same since. I can't remember how he looked and I don't have a photograph of him. I'm here to find one.'

Ruth sat, quiet as the lake, brow furrowed. 'Why photographs?'
'Sorry?'
'Why photographs? What good are they?'
'I don't remember what he looks like.'
'But you remember his stories? He told wonderful stories.'
Celia thought for a moment.
Ruth continued: 'I lived across the hall from him and we were friends of sorts. He was addled and confused most days, but we'd share stories and wander about the place. We kept each other company.'
'You didn't ask him about his life?'
Ruth shook her head. 'And he didn't ask me about mine. You spend time here and you let go. You let go of faces and names. You let go of photographs.'

For days, Celia waited by the lake, but there was no sign of red dahlias. She paced the corridors and hallways, mountains cutting the light thinner as the days grew shorter and fall set in. She continued to ask around after her dad, visiting residents who thought they remembered a man named Judah, but were no longer sure.

She visited the room her father died in. A small bed was pushed into the corner, a television and chair neatly arranged on the other side. A simple rug gave the room warmth, heavy curtains splitting sunlight across a pine dresser and a dried-out plant.

She listened for her father pattering from the bed to the chair. She breathed deep and caught a scent, faint but familiar, that transported her back to the prairie. She lay on the bed just as he would have done. The bed was hard; afternoon light soft. A crack edged across the ceiling, wide enough to expose the ancient lathe above. She peered closely at the wall by the bed; thought she made out a faded scratch mark. She watched dust speckle and stray through the sunlight and held her breath; the room now as quiet as when her father had died.

Celia slowly picked through the drawers. She knew the room had a new owner now; her father had died over a year ago. Still, she was struck by the lack of photographs: no weddings, no smiling grandchildren, no summer days by the ocean. Ruth was right. Strange, she thought, how tightly people held onto the present as they approached death, how entirely they cut themselves loose from the past.

That night, Celia lay alone in the dark of her room. She awoke around midnight, untied the curtains, and left them open to the mountains and stars.

Still, the horror of a blank page.

Finally, after another sleepless night, Celia saw red down by the lakeside. Ruth lay on her towel catching the last rays of sun before the fall blew in proper. She was dripping wet and Celia again wondered whether she was dead. She pulled her cardigan around her tight.

Ruth spoke low, 'If it makes you feel better, lakes this far up are never actually warm.'

'I've been searching for you. Have you been away?'

'Sometimes an old woman doesn't want to be found.' Ruth raised her arms and legs together off the ground, spinning them in tiny wheeling motions. She began to warble, tipping her legs and arms to the right and left, then dropping them to the bench with a sigh. 'I used to be a synchronized swimmer, you know. I went to the Melbourne Olympics. I had a thing with a Russian water-polo player.'

Celia nodded. She'd heard taller stories. Ruth coughed deeply, ribs rattling.

The old woman propped herself up on her elbow. 'You seem down today,' she said.

'I don't think I'll find what I'm looking for.'

'The photograph.'

'The photograph. Or redemption. Anything really.'

'You didn't say goodbye, dear. That's all. It happens to most of us.'

'Maybe.'

'I'm sure you don't believe me, but I did go to the Olympics and I did love that Russian. I watched him bobbing in the water, all muscle and strength, and I fell in love. We had a secret affair. It was hard back then; he was a Stalinist, after all. We had to hide from his team-mates, from his coaches and the police. It was an affair of secret looks and stolen moments.

'We made love the night before his final game. I went to see him play, Russia versus Hungary, and the pool erupted in a brawl. It was Cold War on the water. The pool filled red with blood. The last I saw of my Russian, he was pulling himself from the water, blood gushing from his eye. He looked up at me in the bleachers and waved. Then he was gone.'

'I'm so sorry,' Celia offered, not sure what to say.

'I could find a photograph of him if I wanted to. I'm sure I could find *him* if I wanted to.'

'You absolutely could.'

'But I don't need to. I have the story, locked away in head and heart, and that's enough for me.'

'You were an adult. I was just a child when I last saw my dad. My memories are unclear, unformed.'

'Dear, all memories are unclear. I for one like them that way. Every time I try to remember my Russian, every time I go back and try to fill the dots, I'm *there* again, I *live* it again.'

'I can't trust my memories.'

'So fill the gaps with stories.'

'I can't do that. What's the point of that anyway?'

'A writer who doesn't tell stories,' Ruth raised an eyebrow. She flicked her sunglasses back down onto her nose and lay flat in the sun, arms crossed behind her head. When Celia didn't leave, the old woman pretended to snore.

The cold was moving in now. Mountain winds gusted and shook the old building. As her time at the home drew to a close, Celia avoided Ruth, locking herself in with yellowing archives in an increasingly desperate search. She scoured boxes and files for any trace of her dad. She invited herself into residents' rooms to search photo albums and dusty shelves. All for nought.

Her last night in the mountains, Celia pulled the curtains tight, and dreamt of whirling constellations and bursting stars, of all-devouring black holes and a rowboat cast out in a still and silent sea. When awake, she stared at a darkness filled with words she couldn't grasp.

Sometime before the dawn, overcome with terror, she realized the darkness was pouring out of her. She tried to plug the gaping hole in her chest, using her hands, the blankets and pillow. Blackness seeped from her heart, along the fine trails of her veins, bursting through her skin to consume everything.

She sat bolt upright and ran to the window, searching the morning mist for a red cap and bathers. She threw on a sweater and hurried down to the lake, slipping and grazing her knee on the loose gravel path as she went.

The fog and cold reached deep and clenched within her, growing thicker as the lake approached. Not seeing where she was going, Celia lost her footing and tipped headlong into the icy water. Cold liquid black coursed through her, filling all of her that was empty and porous, dragging her down amongst the mossy stones and reeds. Every part of her recoiled and seized. Her clothes grew heavy as her head grew light. Instead of grasping for light, Celia let herself go.

She lay still and quiet as the lake. From the sandy bottom, she looked up as her father paced and laughed across the sky. He slowly began to pull at the tether between them and for the first time in a year, it grew taut and strong. Celia felt safe. She felt light. She felt something like joy.

On the edge of consciousness, Celia glimpsed red by her on the lakebed and pulled herself sideways to take hold of Ruth's tiny bones. She lifted the old woman up, through what seemed an ocean of water, and pulled her to shore. She hit the old woman squarely in the chest, over and over, until the red dahlias jerked and wheezed.

The two women lay together in the cold mud. Through the fog, far up beyond the moon and stars, she saw her dad, smiling, the soft glimmer of her planet over his shoulder.

In the days that followed, Celia wrote: wrote of her father, her childhood, her family, her life. She wrote about everything and nothing at all. She wrote for herself. She wrote for Ruth.

When she was well enough to leave, she weaved down the gravel path to say goodbye. Celia and Ruth sat side by side, still and quiet as the lake itself.

'Can I tell you a story?' Celia asked the old woman.

'Make it a good one.'

'It's not a story, really, more of a description.'

The old woman put on her sunglasses.

'I remember a photograph, old and faded. In it, my father strides towards the camera in light grey tones, shirt open, bag slung over his shoulder and cigarette low on his lips. I'm not sure where he's coming from, or where he's going. I don't know how old he is, or who took the photo. I don't know anything about it at all, in fact, but I see something of myself in the shadows on his face, the direct stare to camera, his dazzling eyes, full as space itself.'

'That's how I remember him, too.'

Celia put her arm around the older woman and they sat a long while, the sun dipping low.

'My swimming days are over,' was all that Ruth said, 'for now.'

Celia was filled with stories, stories that brought him to life and spread about her in a blaze of color and movement. The great distance between them, finely wrought by disease and now death, was rendered nothing more than a crack.

Celia felt her father's line tug and pull. Just beyond Pluto, perched right where this galaxy melted into the next, her father sailed towards a planet of soft-red hues. She heard the thud of her father's boat as it beached on solid ground, a snap as the tether between them broke and tumbled to earth. Celia smiled. Their planet was immeasurably beautiful, dappled in soft light, ringed with bands of silver and gold.

Mathew Howard is a Canadian-Australian writer and theatre maker, who also works in politics. He was a finalist in the CBC's Canada Writes short story competition in 2013 and now lives in Sydney, Australia with his partner and two children.

OKWIRI ODUOR
Kenya

THAT BALMY SEPTEMBER DAY

The anthills crumbled that balmy September day. The garter snakes withered and the beetles toppled over and flailed about. The ground was hot and moist, throbbing, and the earthworms and millipedes and squirrels shuddered. The wind rattled the brittle leaves of the wattle trees and slammed window shutters against plaster walls. And the Thing swirled about, inky, sometimes coalescing into a freckle or a pucker, into a smudge or a smear, into a transistor radio that kept squealing, 'Haya Makanjo!'

The Thing liked purring kittens and withered potatoes and grey hairs that fell askew over a stranger's forehead. It liked mismatched socks and rickety tables and sticky coffee rings. It liked rats with bent whiskers, and water trembling inside glass tumblers, and footsteps that made wooden stairs creak. It liked dirty fingernails and cracked verandas and maggots that oozed from the corners of people's eyes.

The Thing was light as a fly, and it hovered everywhere – on the walls and in the soup bowls, inside billowing frocks and underneath banana leaves. The Thing was a thing like all things. It was a jellyfish and a wristwatch and a sunhat. It was a bottle cap and a goose-neck lamp and a set of polarizing lenses. It was a blister festering on a person's knee, and a squiggly doll sprawled inside a playpen, and yellow ghee in a bowl of pishori rice.

The houses were not houses that balmy September day. They were sticks of firewood tied together with string. The peasants sat out in the courtyard and traded shreds of fish and dollops of githeri. They traded stories of accidents they once saw, stories of containers falling off the backs of trailers and crashing five-year-old girls.

They talked and talked, but even the tom cats and the geese and the goats in the ditches knew that this talk was not talk but a type of waiting. The peasants waited for the wind to cool the tea in their mugs. They waited for the night sky to fade and for the milk bottles to clang in the carts and for the tin roof to shrivel in the afternoon sun.

They waited for the yellow air to sing and for the laundry to dance on the wash lines and for teeth to rattle in their mouths as they chewed on groundnuts. They waited for telegrams to break their hearts. They waited for the seven o'clock news to start so that they could shake their heads and say, 'Just see the type of mud this day has brought'.

They waited for sisters to scoop Tiger Bomb in their fingers and spread it over the echoing pain in their lower backs, and for brothers to tape the windows so that the evening frost would not nibble at their toes. They waited for the fog to descend, and for bedroom floors to writhe into the backseats of buses so that lovers woke up naked in the market square.

They waited to shove their burdens inside the luggage compartments of trains and to hobble away to places where the sun turned them inside out so that they were no longer themselves but the negatives of photographs in their mothers' nightstands.

The Thing turned into another thing that balmy September day. It drifted through a grove which, due to the absence of eucalypti and casuarinas and acacias, had been spared the ruthless marauding of charcoal burners. The trees were slender as pencils, huddling close, their barks covered with lichen and teeming with yellow-banded skipper caterpillars.

A stray sow rolled in its farrowing bed in the mud, groaning from the dull ache of recent parturition, still unused to the litter that tugged at its swollen tits, and so, in its heaving and gagging and buckling, almost smothering the pitiful, squealing piglets. One of the piglets lay still in a nearby pool, floating like a teabag in the muddy water, already attracting tinsel-colored flies. A dog found it, sucked the mucus from its snout and then uncurled its sticky tail and ripped it apart.

The Thing fluttered onto the ground. It rested at the feet of a young woman. The young woman's name was Chichi. Her wide-set eyes sloped downwards. She possessed the type of beauty that spread itself patiently, like a bunched-up tapestry unravelling down a wall. One had to look at her face intently to see things sprouting in it – the crinkles in her nose when she smiled, and the dimples that crimpled her chin when she laughed, and the softness in her eyes when she thought of yellow things.

Chichi slapped at a cloud of gnats. She sat on a log, and the seam of her skirt was caught in the deep furrows of the bark. The log was from a gumtree which, after years of hawing in the wind, had finally keeled over. On its bark was a cluster of canary-colored mushrooms. Chichi rummaged in her bag, found an afro comb and began to unravel her tresses.

On the back of Chichi's comb was a shard of broken mirror. The Thing stared at it, marvelling at the way it glinted in the sun. Chichi waved the comb about. 'You like the shiny shine-shine?' she cooed at the Thing.

The Thing stared into the mirror. In it was a girl – she had wispy hair and a pinched, scowling mouth.

'Who is that?' Chichi cooed. 'Is it you, my little groundnut paste?'

The Thing turned away in horror. It tried to drift off into the frangipanis, there where the air hummed and was treacly and orange, there where the Thing could wriggle and slither and contort itself into the shapes of flamingoes and cowbells and puff udders, but the lightness of its being was gone. The Thing had lost itself, had turned into another thing now – a waif-like girl with red-brown skin and fingernails like the mangled shreds of sugarcane. The Thing – the girl – wept.

The girl sought her own reflection that balmy September day – in the water jug and on the window latch, in the porridge bowl and on the paring knife. She wiggled the things inside her face, and though they looked odd and surly and incongruous, they did not feel that way at all. They felt as they had always felt before she had known that they were there inside her face – like nothing at all.

She wondered how one could have been a person for so long and never have known it. She wondered if there were people out there who lived their entire lives without ever finding out that they were people. She envied them, those people. She wanted to go back to being a Thing, to drift and flutter and squirm, to take the form of tangerine jam or of hiking boots or of soggy earthworms.

The girl memorized herself that balmy September day. She had eleven moles on her back. Sometimes she ate the skin of a pawpaw just so her lips would swell up. When the sky glowered, she banged pots and pans against the walls to chase the rain jinnis away. She flittered about like a humming bird, her giggles splattering over the front of her frock. She wore poplin petticoats beneath her frocks. She fashioned earrings out of thistles. Whenever she sneezed, she said, 'Jesus is Lord'.

The girl memorized her mother too. She liked that Chichi brushed her teeth with baking soda instead of toothpaste, that, when her head ached, she boiled the bitter bark of a neem tree and drank it with her eyes flickering open and shut. She liked that Chichi darned her socks with tacking stitches. She liked that, in the afternoons when all the chores were done, Chichi spread a mat out in the yard and sang all the Christmas carols she knew, the words curling in the air like passion-fruit tendrils.

She liked the squeak of Chichi's rubber shoes against the floor tiles. She liked the harsh smell of the talcum powder on the bureau, liked how it spilled on the floor each time Chichi used it. She liked Chichi's collection of hand-kerchiefs, liked that Chichi would wash them in salty water every Sunday.

She liked that Chichi's palms smelt like rusted safety pins, that she always used a toothpick to coax cuticles back into her nailbeds. She liked the dark crevice of Chichi's mouth, liked the wet words that fell out of it.

At night, after the laborers had dropped coins in the sugar bowl and kicked off their boots and corduroys and slid into Chichi and cried 'Hallelujah Amen', and after Chichi had washed the thicket between her legs and changed her muslin dress, and after the tin lamp had flickered out, the girl and her mother sat on the veranda and ate pumpkin soup in the moonlight, listening to the death news.

Later, they rinsed their plates in the washbowl and huddled together on the pallet. They whispered to each other late into the night.

'Mama?' the girl said.

'Yes, my little groundnut paste?'

'What if one day you were cleaning the sitting room, and you removed the cushions in the sofa set and found a million shillings? What would you do with it?'

'Where would it have come from?'

'The money tree.'

'There's no such thing as a money tree.'

'The tooth fairy.'

'You are speaking mud now.'

'Well, then, maybe a rich person died and left all their money for their child, and the child was walking down the road and the money was in their pocket, and then a big wind came and blew the money away and it flew through the window and entered our house. What would you do?'

'Smack that child across the face for being so careless.'

The girl sighed. 'Me, if I found a million shillings, I would buy one of those stone toilets that you sit on. You know them? The kind where, when you finish, blue water comes and takes your business away. It would be nice to have one, wouldn't it? Except that for the first few days I would catch a fright every time I flushed and the water roared.'

'How many stone toilets would you buy?'

'Six of them. They would all stand side by side, and some of them would remove green water and some yellow or orange or purple water, and you can go to the one that you want, depending on what color of water you want your business carried away in.'

The girl's mother laughed. 'And what color of water would you want your business carried away in?'

'Purple water.'

'Why now?'

'Because that type of water is made with gentian violet, and gentian violet is always a good thing to have around.'

The girl grew up that balmy September day. Her mother had already started to disappear – her clothes were big as tarpaulins on her now, and she sipped on bone soup and slept on the pallet even when the sun was high up in the sky.

The girl went alone to the river. She found an old canoe wedged in the muddy bank. She shoved it into the water and sat in it, her feet bunched up before her, her hair frizzing in the mist. The sky was bent and the clouds tumbled down in whorls, tangling in the dandelions and blackjacks and passion vines.

When the girl reached the other shore, she waded through the mud, tadpoles sticking to the spaces between her toes. Her dress was soaked, and it clung to her legs as she walked into the tall grass. She plucked blackberries from the bushes. The berries burst, and the juice trickled down her wrist. She sucked on them, and the juice was sickly sweet.

She found her special place – a sunflower field that sprawled as far as the eye could see. The flowers were tall as reeds, with faces that bowed at the noonday sun. The wind ruffled the girl's hair. She gathered it in a bun at the top of her head, twisting it round and round itself. Then she fell down to her knees and lay down in the flowers. She closed her eyes and was not afraid even when the wind howled like a rabid dog and even when the river rose and swirled across the sky.

The girl nursed her mother that balmy September day. She went to the butchery and fetched fresh bones for her soup. She washed the soiled sheets and hung them to dry on the veranda. She rubbed her mother's feet and her mother told her stories of sunflowers and tortoise cars and blood lilies, of hopscotch and pine needles and what happens to you if you stick spectacles to your face with saliva.

The girl studied her mother's angular forehead and sharp shoulders, studied the brown speckles in her mother's eyes. Chichi was a whisper, a sigh, the hum of bees in yellow cusps. Chichi, like the sweet scent of lavender in a stranger's hair. Chichi, like the steam that rose outside your corridor after a rain. Chichi, like incense swirling, becoming a white banner above your head.

'Tell me a story,' Chichi said.

'What type of story?'

'A good story.'

The girl tried to summon the good stories latched in the mound beneath her tongue, but it was difficult to do so when all she could see was her mother disappearing further and further inside herself. 'I have no stories left inside me,' she said.

'That is such mud,' her mother said. 'There are a thousand stories inside you. You just have to open your mouth and say them.'

The girl tore through the nettles and wattles that balmy September day, tore through the blackjack needles and kai apples. Her dress was no longer a dress but a piece of string for holding tresses up, and her face was no longer a face but a berry that someone had chewed and spat out.

She meant to run to the place where the sky creased like a nylon blouse, but her body prickled and stung and then crumpled to the ground. She was a locust and a ladybird and a snail nestled in the space between a person's toes. She was an onion bulb and a basil leaf and an asparagus stalk. She was a bead of sweat that trickled down the folds of a street preacher's neck.

The girl went to her special place and sat in the sunflowers and thought about her mother. She and her mother were lovers. She had learned that there were many types of everything a person could think of – pens and purses and pigeons. There were many types of lovers too.

Some lovers were for loving with your fingers tight over the stalks of star grass. Some lovers were for loving with deep puffs from a cigarette. Some lovers were for loving through the genteel words of greeting cards.

And some lovers, like Chichi, were for waiting for you in the place where you went to meet yourself. They were your lover because the gnawing in the deep dark places inside you eased when they sat down next to you.

These types of lovers could be cats or trees or raindrops. They could be glass jars or withering wicker chairs or peeling staircases. They could be your sister or your cobbler or your milliner. They were your lover because they loved you, and their love was banal and quiet and understated and potent. Their love was yellow like all the good things you had ever known.

The girl turned into a woman that balmy September day. Her mother was dead by then – she lay in the ground out back, there where the yard was not a yard but a tangled ball of thorn trees and wild flowers and stiff yellow grass. The girl sat alone in the kitchen, cradling a mug of bone soup.

Her silences were clammy, and they spilled over the marmalade jars and the bread trays and the soup pots, covering the floors and crawling up the walls. They seeped through the spaces beneath her toenails and through the scars on her thighs and through the slash of her navel. They seeped through her mouth when she parted her lips, and through her nostrils when she breathed, and through her eyes when she blinked.

When she grew cold, she sat on the doorstep with her back pressed to the door frame, and the sun shone into her eyes and blinded her like desire and also like hope, and it was the sort of sun which turned the insides of a person's eyelids into the color of old cream, and now she plucked handfuls of lemongrass to brew in her tea, and she lit her stove and watched bubbles wobble at the bottom of the pot, and the smell of kerosene made her think of days when she clambered into her mother's skirts during thunderstorms.

Then the sun burned her eyes and she turned into a woman, and now she spread her mother's dresses in her lap and smoothed out the creases. She tugged at the drapes and let the sunlight spill in. She fumbled and knocked over ceramic candleholders and brass bookends. She stared at the dead gnats that floated in leftover soup on the kitchen table. She lit a cigarette, took a deep puff of it and flicked ash into a pot of hydrangea.

Then she opened the back door and went out into the yard that was not a yard, and she lay on the ground next to her mother, and she sang In-Dublin's-fair-city-where-girls-are-so-pretty, and her singing was not singing but a type of waiting.

The woman went away that balmy September day. There was nothing left for her in the town, so she washed her face and changed her dress and walked and walked until the soles of her feet cracked, and she found a place where people spoke in soft voices, where people fondled nectarines and glass marbles in their pockets.

The woman sat on a stranger's wicker chair. She drank bone soup and watched the termites that crawled through the floorboards and jam jars and the broken chimney. The stranger was tall as a minaret, had eyes the color of dried figs, and, when they touched your neck or shoulder or wrist, you wanted to say, '*Niwie radhi*,' for no reason.

The stranger had a drab suspicious mouth. It had things sprouting inside it. The stranger showed them to her – rice husks and cassava flakes and regiments of safari ants.

'Now you show me yours,' the stranger said.

'My mouth is not the type of mouth which has things sprouting inside,' the woman said.

The stranger said, 'Everyone's mouth is the type of mouth which has things sprouting inside.'

The woman opened her mouth. She found things inside it – the helm of a dhow and red cardigans and off-white canvas shoes.

'What do I do with these things?' she said.

'You suck on them,' the stranger said.

They sat on a high wall with their legs dangling beneath them, and they sucked on all the strange, beautiful things they found growing inside their mouths. They watched a donkey pulling a cabbage-laden cart. They watched a woman hang her blouses on the wires of an electricity pole. They watched milk canisters topple on the neighbor's veranda. They watched a cow swish its tail, swatting at gadflies. They watched a child dig through the rubbish, pulling plastic bottles out and tossing them into his burlap bag.

The woman and the stranger pounded dried henna leaves to a fine powder, mixed it with water, and drew meandering shapes on their arms and legs. They set traps for guinea fowls, carried the birds over their shoulders, and plucked them on the muddy riverbank.

Then the stranger brought out a tonic which was made of sugar water and plums, and fed spoonfuls of it to her, and now she was the type of woman who could spin round and round on one foot without falling, the type of woman who knew how many papyrus reeds grew at the edge of the river.

The woman wandered about that balmy September day. She yearned to find earth that her feet did not already know, and doors that mumbled things to the wind, and pools of water where dragonflies circled and dipped, and nectar to dribble out of the backs of flowers and into her throat, and samosas which, when you pressed them to the roof of your mouth, tasted like henna and rosewater. She yearned to touch the words that dead lovers once wrote to each other, and to uncap vials and sniff them and dab hints of lavender onto the tenderness behind her earlobe.

She sang songs that were stringy, songs that cut the insides of her cheeks and that brought tears to her eyes, songs that cleaved onto her teeth and gums and the walls of her lips.

Sometimes she wove raffia baskets for carrying bell peppers and coriander. Sometimes she pounded yams in cracked mortars. Sometimes she thatched leaking roofs. Sometimes she waded through rice plantations, gumboots sloshing, sickle hanging at her side.

Later, she washed her face and changed her dress and walked and walked until the soles of her feet cracked. She was a transient. All the places she went were fragments of her imagination. Every crack on the ground was there because the soles of her feet liked the sensation of unevenness, and every alleyway was there because the shadows that lurked in them were the same shadows that lurked inside her.

She roamed the earth until her back stooped and her fingers gnarled and her bones creaked. Then she closed her eyes and the ground was putty beneath her feet, and she was drifting, light as a cotton ball that someone had plucked from their cardigan. The walls were silk scarves that flapped in the breeze, and the air was red and yellow and green, swirling, and she was swirling too, murmuring to the bulbuls that brushed their wings against her face, murmuring to the lizards that bobbed their heads up and down at her, and the lightness of her being returned, and she was no longer herself but a Thing that could wriggle and slither and contort itself into the shapes of flamingoes and cowbells and puff udders.

Okwiri Oduor was born in Nairobi, Kenya. Her short story *My Father's Head* won the 2014 Caine Prize for African Writing as well as Short Story Day Africa's *Feast, Famine and Potluck* story contest. She was a 2014 MacDowell Colony Fellow. She is currently at work on her debut novel and pursuing an MFA in Creative Writing at the Iowa Writers' Workshop.

DESIREE BAILEY
Trinidad & Tobago/United States

MATCHSTICK

She is still following me, the girl in the mirror, the one who moves through rooms with the lightness of ghosts, with legs thinner than a bloodless mosquito, arms long and dangling, breasts flat and shapeless as stained linen. I let my hands travel the quiet slope of my hips, and she mocks me. Her eyes tell me that I'm trapped, held prisoner in the glass.

All around me are clothes. Acid-washed jeans, stretched-cotton t-shirts, dresses with the faded prints of flowers dashed across the bed and dresser, littering the floor like shorn petals. I try on every bit of fabric I can find in my room but nothing covers me in the way that I need. I need to be swimming in the cloth, for the threads to be a shield, for no one to know the true hollows of my body.

'Mya, don't make me drag you out of that room. You shoulda been gone ten minutes ago!' Tantie Lucy slams her palms against the door. Her voice breaks the spell cast by the mirror and I tear my naked body away from the girl's sight.

I don't want Tantie to find me in the mess that I made, for her to think I am ungrateful. Wasteful and ruinous. That I only know how to shred the clean and quiet that she's built in this house, far from the razor edge of the city. I shove my legs into the jeans and force a thick oversized sweatshirt over my head though the October morning still carries the heat of the summer. Sure I'll sweat, but the sweat is better than exposing my frame.

When my mother's heart seized up in her chest it was Tantie who dragged me from her still warm body, which had collapsed in the kitchen of our ground-floor apartment. Tantie came before the ambulance. The ambulance arrived 20 minutes too late. Red and blue lights dripped down the walls, staining our photographs and my student of the month certificates. It was Tantie who locked her arms around my torso when a man and a woman appeared with the stretcher that would save no one. She stopped me from lunging at them, from grabbing them up in my fists, from kicking and biting and scratching. How dare they come now? To carry who? To save who? Tantie knew what I only came to know long after my mother flew up in the air in a black smoke. A fire could raze entire blocks to ash. A plague could cloak the buildings and gnaw down our skins. And no one would listen to our cries beating down the sky. And even if they did, they'd take their sweet time to come to our aid, moving slowly until the hour of our need had ticked away.

She rises from the pool, her white cotton dress wet and clinging, pressed against her tanned, jiggling flesh.

Slow motion. A gleaming jewel to be stroked by the men crowding the rim of the pool. The camera tenderly captures the up-and-down movement of her hips. Captures the bass and the horns riding under the rapper's blaring verse. Captures the other women too or, rather, captures hard nipples piercing the triangles of bikini tops and tiny waists and wide hips and thick thighs, some dimpled or with muscular carvings, and large, round ass cheeks spilling on the floor or in the hands or lap of some man, grinning, salivating, shifting in his chair.

I watch not because I'm transfixed by the song's rhythm. It's a good enough song, but I am not yet locked in and strapped to the metronome. I don't watch because I want to feel a small flame in the dark space between my thighs. I watch because I'm envious and I want to be what I see there on the screen. I want to crawl into those voluptuous bodies and take up residence there. To parade myself around, up and down Jamaica Avenue, holding the gaze of everyone in my radius. I imagine that I am no longer invisible, that people no longer avert their eyes from my skinny frame. No matter who I'm with or what I wear, I can make any kind of joke, argue any kind of point and I will be heard. I will be received.

Tantie says I am beautiful in the delicate way of my mother, dark and slender, akin to the stalk of a lily. I want to believe her. Better yet, I want to remember. My memory is a tide pulling backwards against the shore. The tide pulls further into the horizon, moving towards a thing I will never know, leaving shards of shell and glass naked in the sand. The photographs I have are all from the neck up. They sever the length of her. Not even the photographs can remember for me. Somewhere I heard that those caught in the ink of a photograph begin to fade when their last breath leaves, but in the photographs of her, the colors are so rich they could stain my chewed fingernails. Her eyes bore through until I can't bear to meet them with mine. I know her face, the incline of her cheeks, but the movement of her limbs and the shape of her body escape me. Locked somewhere beneath the receding tide.

I touch my stomach to the wooden floor, sprawled flat, neighboring the dust and dark held under my bed. Under my bed is where the thing that will change me lives. I thrust my arm into the dark until I feel the hard plastic of a bottle. I grab it by the throat and take a swig, not bothering to measure the amount in the lines marked on the cap. The thick, bitter syrup spreads itself across my tongue and I hold my nostrils as it courses down my throat. Soon it will settle in my stomach and gnaw at me from the inside, awakening a terrible hunger that makes me want to eat more than I want to breathe.

One day I was combing through the internet, looking for anyone who felt the way I did. With my neglected homework scattered around me, I watched hours of testimonials and confessions of girls and women embarking on what they called their weight gain journey. They sought the eye of the camera and the comments of their audience for support. They varied on the scale but most were desperate to add about 60 to 80 pounds to their frames. They were healthy and naturally slim, but were sick of being the slender ones among their families and friends, susceptible to crude jokes about needing to be stuffed with hamburgers. Sick of not being seen as sexy but simply cute or sweet. They slung their bodies across the screen, rotating to show off their progress, spouting their new-found wisdom on how to put on the pounds.

'Eat lots of meals.' 'Remember, do crunches to keep your gut down.' 'Drink a ton of water. Every day.' 'Eat, eat, eat.'

Fried plantains, cheeseburgers and whatever else I can lay my hands on. They fall without sound down a bottomless well.

'Myaaaaaaa,' Tantie calls as I reach for the doorknob to leave my room. She sits at the little dining table, sipping black coffee from her favorite mug, already dressed in her dark blue security guard uniform which is starched and ironed so that the folds of her pants resemble knives.

'What you doing in there that it take this long to get ready? You leave later and later every morning.' The sunlight shooting off her badge cuts me in the eye.

I try to tell her that I was finishing up some homework but she holds up her rough hand. 'Just start walking.'

I make my way out the house, past all the other houses, their yards dotted with flowers bracing for the oncoming blast of autumn air. I hop on the Q85 bus, pressed against the other morning commuters until we get off on Archer Avenue. We walk as fast as ants, arms and legs pushing on in unison as if responding to a higher choreography, pushing past any straggling soul who dares shatter the intricate flow.

Down into the subway on the crowded E train, I stand and hold on to the rail above my head. My eyelids are heavy and I force them open. With no seat, this is no place to fall asleep. Better to fall backwards into a pit of scorpions. Another hour until I get off. Of the train bellowing above the old tracks.

My school brags about its diversity, how it has students of all shades and nationalities, learning and growing together, united inside these grey walls. Still, there's hardly anyone who looks like me. And white is what we strive to be. When I'm here, my voice moves from my belly and into my nose and throat, rounding out the 'r's of words and curling up the ends of sentences.

I hate to stand up in front of a class or to walk my body through the hallway where the other students can catch a glimpse of my frame. Even the white girls say that I am so skinny. They offer the words like a prize, a glistening emerald, or an entrance card into the gated world of their beauty. A card saying you are not like the other black girls. Unlike them, you are delicate and small. You are something like us, or what we think ourselves to be.

I slip quietly into Mr Harrison's English class. I know he sees me but he avoids looking in my direction. This used to be my favorite class but these days it's like I'm hearing him through a body of water. His voice drifts farther and farther away. And it's not just Mr Harrison. I barely hear the voices of my other teachers. Something is keeping me from their words. All day I am cloaked in drowsiness, falling in and out of sleep. No one bothers to wake me and I only stir when the periods end and the chairs scrape the floor as everyone gets up to go to their next class. I fight the feeling but the drowsiness will not leave me. Somewhere in my fog I remember the girls online who are trying to gain weight like me. They say that the syrup works wonders. They say that it gives them confidence, that it helped them to regain their appetite when they were depressed. That it helped them arrive at the silhouette that they've always wanted. I move deeper into the fog and I hear a lone voice mention side effects. *Everybody's different so it probably won't happen to everybody. But this thing made me want to sleep all the time. My girlfriend threw it out when I almost crashed the car.*

My head clears when I leave school and take the train back to Jamaica station. I stroll down the Avenue, past the jewelry stores and DVD stalls, the clothing shops with soca music spilling out onto the sidewalk. Men make eye contact with me and immediately look down towards the rest of me, then look away as if to say, 'Nothing to see there.' I keep on walking and swaying my hips the way this avenue taught me. When you are on The Ave you cannot walk plainly and squarely, with the mere purpose of moving one foot after the other, simply to arrive at your destination. You have to sway and swing. You have to ring out with your own music, as if bells were fastened to your hips. Young, old, skinny, thick or fat. The walk has sound. But the way I see it, the girls with the butts and breasts and hips sound out the loudest.

I want to possess the power of that music, to hold it in the heat between my thighs till it drips and stains the pavement. My limbs are strong. I can walk forever, past the botánica with its dust-covered Mary reaching out with empty hands. Past the bargain stores where my mother used to buy cheap ceramic ornaments in the shape of little black girls with opened books and fat pigtailed hair. I can walk as long and strong as any of these girls on the Avenue. But my bones do not bend like theirs. My bones do not curve like the songs of sirens. They do not call out to men who stand on the sidewalk or curb before the knock-off basketball caps hanging off racks like fruits on a tree. My body does not inspire a whistle or a bold request for my number. The Avenue is filled with noise, always. But it is silent where I walk.

Tantie says I am beautiful in the delicate way of my mother. The same way of walking, the same slender frame. In Tantie's eyes I am all that is left of her sister. There are days when she looks at me as if she's looking in on something else that's hidden inside me. If I am my mother, then whose body is this? Who I am fighting to change? Who am I meeting in the mirror? Who's looking back, peering at me with blank eyes? Maybe the memory is right here, sitting in my arms and legs. If I force this body into another shape, will she leave me again?

I turn on the TV to shake the questions. I watch the videos, the curvy women moving luxuriously across the screen. There it is. The me I want to be. I push past the face of my mother and reach under the bed. In the dark there is a spiralling wind, twirling me, carrying me.

Desiree Bailey was born in Trinidad and Tobago and grew up in Queens, NY. She has a BA from Georgetown and an MFA in Fiction from Brown University. She has received fellowships from Princeton in Africa, the Norman Mailer Center and Callaloo Creative Writing Workshop. She is a recipient of the 2013 Poets and Writers' Amy Award. Her work has been published in *Callaloo, Best American Poetry, Transition* and other publications. She is currently the fiction editor at *Kinfolks Quarterly*.

VAMBA SHERIF
Liberia/The Netherlands

HOMECOMING

I had been away for 20 years. I had spent most of that time in Belgium, a period during which my country Liberia was embroiled in civil war. What was bringing me home was the death of my mother and the contradictory accounts regarding the circumstances of her death. I had arrived in Monrovia from Brussels two days before, apprehensive about the journey because of the stories of people like me who had undertaken such trips and had died of poisons mixed into their food. After the civil war, poison had replaced bullets, I had been told, and the enemy was omnipresent.

I lodged at my elder brother Edmond's, in Gardnersville, a suburb of the city, where homes stood on marshlands, and where, when it rained, the water rose and burst what remained of the sewerage. My brother had taken several dozen family members into his care, mostly youngsters whose parents had not survived the war. He was a replica of my father, at least of that single memory of my father that I had held onto for more than 30 years. The memory was of a closely shaved man with a permanent frown around his brows, a man with a polished forehead that promised infinite youth. He was a businessman, and had owned a store located on the busiest street in Wologizi, the town of my birth. I remember him sitting in an arm-chair, drumming with his fingers while I, a four-year-old, played on the floor of his bedroom in our house. He had passed on a year later, leaving behind a void that I would struggle to fill, and now he was staring at me from the face of my brother. Edmond must now have been around the same age as our father when I was born, the same height, the same temperament, his occasional outbursts of anger laced with an affecting humor for which my father was famous.

The evening before my departure to Wologizi, I sat with my brother in the living room of his home, where one of the children in his care had prepared our food. It consisted of parboiled rice served with cassava leaves and smoked fish prepared with palm oil. While we ate he told me about the war. Like our father, Edmond once had a thriving store with goods purchased from Dubai and China, right at the heart of Monrovia, on Ashmun Street, but it had been destroyed in the war. Now he had partnered with one of our cousins and had opened up a small store, where he sold office wares on Camp Johnson Road.

He had lived most of his life in Monrovia, and the stories that reached me in Wologizi during my childhood were of a fiercely ambitious man: he had opened up his first store while in secondary school, had expanded into a larger store and was about to open up a chain of stores, thereby doing what our family had been doing for ages, trading, when the war broke out. He had been married once, he told me, but his wife had left him during the war.

'At one point, she ran about Monrovia with a gun in hand with the purpose of killing me,' he told me. 'I don't know what I did to deserve such a fate. It was not an easy time then, but we survived.'

As I listened to him, I had the feeling that he needed me, needed an audience to hear his story, as if in doing so he would relieve himself of the burden it had become. The longing to tell stories about the war, which I found in my brother that night, would manifest itself in many other people. Liberians longed to tell stories of war, even the most horrific ones. 'Never ask people about the absent ones,' Edmond said, 'for you might be shocked to learn that a childhood friend, a dear aunt or an uncle had been killed, or worse, had joined the rebels in killing their own people. Just keep quiet and wait until you are told about the missing or the dead.'

It worried me that I would have to wait to be told about the war, but he meant to protect me from those horrific accounts. What he did not know was that his advice would not shield me from being broken by the accounts of my mother's death.

Later, after we had had our meal, he asked me about Belgium. 'Vali, we heard that you build cars in that country, and that your company has come to appreciate your talent so much that they've done everything to keep you from leaving them, even to visit us. Is that true? If so, then you've made us all proud.'

It was not true. I was a mere factory worker in an industrial city in Belgium, and all I did was assemble truck parts for days on end, year in, year out. But I couldn't tell him that. He wouldn't have believed me. My story, which began with me as a factory worker who worked in shifts, six or seven days a week, had elevated me to the level of a designer of trucks.

I told my brother about my early years as a refugee, about my life in a refugee camp which housed people with similar stories of war and persecution. At the camp I had as a teacher an old professor from Bosnia, and as friends a family from Ethiopia, a Ghanaian who taught me to ride a bicycle, and a Nigerian who was so smart that he succeeded in saving money in a place where all thought that was impossible. As a refugee, my life was monotonous: I would have the same breakfast every morning, bread served with cheese or jam – then stamp my card daily to prove I was present, while waiting for a decision that was certain to change my life: the decision whether I could stay or must leave the country. To fill in the hours, I managed to befriend the man who went to the city every day to rent several films for the entertainment of the refugees. Because of my love of film, I was the one who chose what we could see. In the world of the films, with their realities detached from the one at the camp, I felt at home. I would marvel at the freedom enjoyed by the volunteer workers who cooked and kept order at the camp, returning to their homes at the end of each day.

The constant news of the civil war in Liberia, which filled the papers and crowded the headlines, made me desperate to attempt to escape the cage of camp life. I learned to speak and write Flemish, and, by the time I was granted asylum, I was ready to work in the truck factory and to send most of my earnings home to those family members who had fled the war to Sierra Leone and Guinea.

'I worked seven days a week for years, trying to help the family,' I told my brother.

He nodded. 'Yes, you did,' he said. The war had broken him. He had had a stroke that had almost paralyzed him. Like the fighter that he was, he had done everything to be able to walk again, refusing to use a walking stick even during those moments when he needed it most. 'Once I become attached to it, I will never get rid of it,' he said. 'I am still fighting the effect of the stroke. One of which is that I tend to forget things.'

In dark corners of the living room, on the floor and on mats, my nephews and nieces sat, listening to us. Some were born during the war, and those who were born just before the war now had children of their own. Children had become parents who could not support their offspring, and all were dependent on my brother.

All around us, the night was restless: church songs, drums and rattles rent the air. Monrovia had turned into a noisy marketplace of God-seekers. 'The war has made people turn to the only thing that gives them some modicum of solace, and that is religion,' Edmond said. The heat was unbearable. My shirt clung to my body from sweat. And despite the care my brother had taken, spraying the bedroom and draping a huge net over the mattress that I shared with him, the mosquitoes managed to find their way to me. I hardly slept a wink. My lack of sleep, I realized, had less to do with the mosquitoes than with the death of my mother. When I attempted to inquire about the circumstances of her death, Edmond said: 'It happened a long time ago. Let it be and try to be at peace with her death.'

But I couldn't.

The driver came to pick me up at dawn. As protection against unforeseen circumstances, I decided to take some of my cousins with me as guards. We loaded the jeep with bags of rice and other foodstuffs for the family in Wologizi. By the time the city awoke, we were far beyond its borders. The driver was good. I marvelled at how he skillfully avoided the potholes that littered the roads and, when I commented on this, he said without hesitation, 'I was a driver for a rebel faction during the war'. He was sturdy like a wrestler, bowlegged and with bloodshot eyes, and he wore a cap and winter boots in a heat that had denied me sleep. The revelation numbed me; I was sitting beside a man who had actually participated in the war, who had probably killed.

The war in which he had participated began in 1989 when a rebel group, led by Charles Taylor, aimed to oust the then president Samuel Doe, who had come to power in a bloody coup in 1980. But the Liberian conflict began much earlier, during the founding of the country, when freed black slaves from America returned to Africa in 1822 to found a new republic based on liberty. These founders were at odds with indigenous groups who thrived along the coast of Liberia and in the interior. The inability to create a balanced society without discrimination ultimately led to the coup in 1980 and then to the civil war in 1989.

My driver pulled over at a roadside restaurant in a town that was swathed in dust, where the asphalt petered out into dusty roads. We had been driving for hours.

'Just imagine, Chief,' the driver told me, as we stuffed ourselves on rice served with a sauce of brown beans and smoked fish cooked with palm oil – the famous Liberian dish, *tobogee*. I was uncomfortable with the 'chief' title, for he was employing it either to mock me or to emphasize our difference, putting me on an unwanted pedestal. 'I would be speeding at 200 kilometers per hour in a jeep without a windshield, my head just below the steering wheel, for fear a sniper might snatch it off. At the back of the jeep would be a fighter with a machinegun, letting loose his fury on everything that crossed our path. The mission would be to drive right into the heart of enemy territory, and fire a few rounds of bazookas before returning to the base.' As I listened to him, it struck me that he must have been in his teens when he made those sorties. 'We won the war, Chief,' he told me.

But at what cost, I wondered, thinking of my mother. She had died when the north was cordoned off from the rest of Liberia by the rebel group to which my driver belonged, as they fought other groups for control over that territory. I was told that she had taken ill and died for lack of medicine, but a week later someone claimed to have seen her in a refugee camp in Guinea. I even had a telephone call from a cousin in Guinea saying that my mother wanted to speak with me. But the information proved baseless. My mother had indeed passed on and I was left with questions as to how she had actually died. In subsequent years, I had attempted to visit her grave but had been hampered by reports of war, by lack of adequate funds or by the terrible condition of the roads which made it impossible to travel during rainy seasons.

Once we took to the road again, dust settled with solemnity in the car, impeding breath and sometimes blinding us. Flanking the road toward the north were forests, dense, perpetual and mysterious, the greenest of the green, crowning mountains and spreading like a canopy over the earth. Towns and villages emerged before us, some abandoned, others sparsely inhabited, but always with beautiful flame trees, which my eyes would caress, as if I were seeing them for the first time. This overwhelming beauty was a stark contrast to the country's recent history. Along the road, people traded coal, vegetables or bushmeat, or waited to be given a lift.

We arrived at Wologizi just before dusk. Its suburbs were cluttered with houses so dilapidated that I could not imagine human beings inhabiting them. One of the buildings I recognized at the heart of the city was a two-story building that once belonged to a Lebanese nicknamed 'Old Baldhead'. The people of Wologizi were ingenious at giving nicknames. The best local footballer was called 'The Broom' because he swept up everything in his path with his bare feet – player, ball and all. And the child who once torched a box in which his friend was hiding in an attempt to lure him out was named 'Foday, The Torturer', which stuck so well that when I met him 20 years later, now old and wise and with a career in the agricultural sector, he was still called 'The Torturer', but always behind his back. We had a corpulent man as teacher who, because of his size, the town named after a mountain. This teacher was versed in Shakespeare and would quote lines from *Othello* and *Hamlet* as if he were from a bygone era. But his jokes were often so spicy with sexual innuendos that women fled on seeing him. Rumor had it that he slept with most of them.

The Lebanese's building was bullet-ridden, bare of paint and dark with mold, like most homes around it. The main thoroughfare, where girls fried fish and *calas* (doughnuts) at night to sell to lovers, appeared much narrower than I recalled, and the shops that once flanked it, including the gas station where checkers players often gathered to insult each other were gone.

On that road in my early teens, when I was not swimming in the nearby river, or joining friends to play out in the moonlight, I would be singing songs from Indian films, or playing the heroes or the villains of those films – so much so that those who could not afford the entrance fee would give me some coins so that I could play out the films to them, including the songs. I was so adept at this that, whenever I played the villain Amjad Khan in an Amitabh Bachchan film, my audience would scatter in fright before me. I dreamed of becoming an actor, the African Bachchan, and of going to India and taking Bollywood by storm.

My heart skipped a beat as we turned the corner and drove into a road towards home. On my right was a school building that belonged to one of my uncles, a business man who started out fetching firewood and selling it, later becoming one of the richest men in Wologizi. We drove past the school and slowly edged our way toward the compound which had once sizzled with life. I remembered that during my childhood, on any given day, there would be more than 200 people in our compound, and the drama that played out within the shaded rooms and corners had shaped my outlook on life. I stepped out of the jeep and walked toward the compound. The family was standing in a small group, consisting mostly of women and children, the remnants of what had once been the largest family in Wologizi. As the women hugged me, I could smell firewood on them, the dust of pounded rice, and the food they were preparing. I held them tight, reluctant to let go, those women of my brothers and uncles who had been killed or had died during the war.

Afterwards, I paused to take in the compound. Some of the houses, including my mother's, were gone; so were the mango and the avocado trees I had often climbed to pick their fruits. But my father's house was still standing. I entered it now in search of the room I used to share with my siblings; the room in which, when I found myself alone, I would rehearse my role in films, striving to perfect the art of impersonations, the art of speaking Hindi or Bengali or Mandarin. I would be so swept away by those roles that, whenever I emerged from them, the world looked quite unreal to me. One day, I convinced my mother to accompany me to a film in which Amitabh Bachchan, who played its hero, was killed. My mother left the cinema in tears. 'They murdered that handsome man,' she said. 'Why did they murder that good man?' That was the end of her movie adventure. But every day after school I would assist the owner of the cinema, a man with a jaundiced face who had a lilt to his steps, by running errands for him or doing chores around his house in exchange for seeing a film. The movies were invariably Indian or Chinese, some of which I saw a dozen times. The passion for film never left me. But then the war broke out in Liberia, and I had to redream my life.

On coming out of the room, I met my brother Sekou waiting for me in what was once our father's room, the largest room in the house, and was now occupied by several women. It had lost some of its former grandeur: the chair in which my father often sat, drumming his fingers on its wooden arms, was gone, as was his smell. Every trace of him had been obliterated. The wall seemed new, the fresh painting had erased the old. There are many ways of erasing the past without much effort on one's part. The attempt to keep the house standing had replaced the importance of holding onto its history: my father's presence.

'Tell me what happened to our mother,' I told my brother.

He hesitated. 'What do you mean?' he asked.

'I want to know how she died,' I said.

'It was at the height of war. She was in Koniyan and fell ill. She died for lack of medicine,' he said, avoiding my gaze.

Of all my brothers, Sekou was the one closest to me in looks and temperament. He understood my deepest fears, even with the distance that separated us, and when we communicated he would often surprise me with his insights. 'You always say that you will return home,' he once told me. 'But what is home? You've been away for so long that I don't think this is your home any more.'

Now he turned to me. 'What do you want me to tell you?' he asked. I did not answer.

My mother was the daughter of a scholar to whom miracles were attributed. It was said that no one had taught him, and he was famous for lecturing the whole night without consulting a book. Everything he owned, he shared with his brothers: he was generous to a fault. The man, after whom I was named, had risen to such a stature that the presidents of Liberia and Sierra Leone sought his advice and prayers. He always preached peace and insisted that a religion that divided brothers and sisters and made one feel superior to the other was no religion at all but a divisive doctrine. It won him many admirers but made him controversial. When he passed on in Gbarnga, a place where there was no mosque and where he was but a guest, the people of the city who did not adhere to his faith but who regarded him nevertheless as one of their own insisted that he be buried by them. The President of Liberia had to intervene, especially when the Muslims insisted that he belonged to them. The President ruled that the people of Gbarnga had the right to bury my grandfather because he died on their ground. But most important still, they loved him as much as the Muslims loved him. And so that's where his grave remains.

I remembered journeying to the shrine with my mother. I must have been six or seven years old. When we arrived we were received by dozens of people who lined the road. 'Here they come, make way,' people were saying. 'Make way, these are his descendants.' My mother and I were led to the shrine, which was covered with white sand and surrounded by slender trees. I remembered my mother kneeling on the sand and taking a handful of it, which she distributed amongst the people over and over again, until all those present had received sand from her. And then she prayed. Every day for more than two weeks, she repeated this ritual. We left the shrine with more than two dozen carriers whose sacks were filled with gifts the pilgrims had bestowed on us. My mother would always refer to that visit as one of the most memorable moments of her life.

I longed to visit her grave, but because she was buried in a nearby town, Koniyan, the townspeople asked me to wait until they were prepared to receive me. In the house allocated to me, I placed a few cousins in one room, a number of them in the other; all tested in the war, all prepared to protect me. 'Chief, I will sleep in the jeep in front of the house,' the driver said. 'No one will dare face me.' My fear was unfounded, but I did not sleep that night out of excitement. I was thinking about my mother most of the time.

The next day, dozens crowded the road in Koniyan, singing a solemn song tinged with joy. I waited for the crowd, which moved at a snail's pace down the hill and up to where I had been asked to wait. The women fell over me with hugs, their hands moving clumsily across my sweaty face. A man edged his way through the throng of women and held my hands and would not let go until we reached the grave, which was located at the heart of the town. I thought I knew the man, and it turned out that he was another cousin – the son of an uncle who lived in Sierra Leone. As we arrived at the gravesite, the crowd left us behind.

The grass around the grave had been trimmed and a hedge of bamboo enclosed it. Standing there, I remembered my mother's shimmering dark skin; I recalled the sight of her, tall and dark, as she emerged from her house in colorful wrappers and with proud headgear to lead her apprentices to the local market where she reigned supreme. The Lomas, a people who had co-existed with us for centuries, had nicknamed her, 'The Beautiful Mandingo'. Now she was no more.

One of the town elders asked me to say a few words. The words took shape in my mind but choked in my throat. The crowd burst into tears. A town elder stood up. 'Your mother's beauty was the envy of even the jinn's,' he said. 'Yes, her beauty was extraordinary. But even more than that, she was, as a human being, a replica of your grandfather. She was generous to a fault. Everything she ever earned she gave away. Let those who remember her contradict me.' And I believed him.

Later, after the elders had said some prayers, the crowd led me to the town hall. It was there that I learned the true story of my mother's fate. 'A rebel commander caught your mother and pinned her to the ground,' the town chief of Koniyan told me. 'Believe me, Vali, for I was there when it happened. He fired a whole round at her but not a single bullet touched her. Yours is a unique family. It was not a bullet that killed your mother, but illness.'

I chose not to believe him. In this anecdote, rendered so beautifully that even the most hardened skeptic would be inclined to believe it, lay the stark truth. My mother was killed by a rebel. In a tradition where truth took on many forms, I had been spared the pain of the hard truth by another, less painful truth.

In subsequent days, I learned to live with that truth. When not with the elders, whose stories almost always ended with a spark of wisdom, I would be in Wologizi, whiling away my time with childhood friends. Or I would be at the Kaihah River, where I had learned to swim. That part of the river which had once bustled with life was now shrouded in bushes. The first time I went to see it I had to cut my way to it with a machete. I remembered a tall tree from the top of which the best swimmers from the city would plunge into the river. I remembered lying in the sand with a book in hand after a swim, the world peaceful around me, the story and the world merging into one, the story becoming my story. Places like the banks of that river had formed me, so that even now, after I've been away for more than two decades, my memories keep bringing me back to it, to the scent of the trees, to the touch of the sand, to the voices of girls rising with laughter as we chased them along the sandy banks, to the smell of the earth, to the overcrowded home, to the place where I first saw daylight.

Childhood friends, whose faces I recognized but not their names, poured daily into the compound to share the past with me. Their war experiences varied: some had been forced to fight, others had stood up to the rebels. And most of them had fled the war to Guinea or Sierra Leone, or had sought refuge in the forest surrounding Wologizi until the war was over. 'When we returned to Wologizi, we met a place that had turned into the bush,' one of them told me. 'Yes, we hunted deer and opossums right where we are now sitting.'

The war made some wealthy, while others who had once been rich lost everything. The effect was so profound that, whenever I walked the streets of Wologizi, I could see that places where once the homes of the wealthy had stood were now empty, while those who had taken up the places of the wealthy were mostly strangers to me. Some of my friends, whom many had once thought of as amounting to nothing in life, now belonged to the wealthy group. The war had come and gone, reversing fortunes and leaving frustrations and unsettled scores in its wake.

The longer I stayed in Wologizi, commuting every day to Koniyan, the more I longed to return to Belgium, to the ritual of waking up in the early hours to leave for work and stand along an assembly line, feeling the hard metal, arranging parts, and then, finally, seeing the finished product, a huge truck, painted and polished, driving out of the colossal building for a test ride.

Finally, I left Wologizi early one morning, my brother Sekou and some of the cousins accompanying me.

We had been driving for hours when we saw a man standing alongside the road, waving at our car, asking for a lift. I asked the driver to stop, for we still had space for one person. When we drew up to the man, my brother said, as if he'd seen a ghost, 'Drive on, drive on quickly.'

His reaction baffled me. 'What was the matter?'

Sekou was by then sweating, and he swept his face with his hand. 'He was the man who held our mother at gunpoint in Koniyan and tried to kill her. Yes, he was the one who shot at our mother! I can never forget that face. I was there! He's the one.'

The driver sucked his teeth. 'Chief, let me handle this,' he said. Before I could say anything, he had turned the car around and was speeding toward the man.

'Wait, wait, don't do anything yet,' I said. I could not believe that I had found my mother's murderer! But the driver jumped from the car and was upon the man. He held him by the collars and dragged him to my brother.

'Do you remember this man?' the driver said, spitting in his face. 'Do you remember him?'

The man burst into tears. 'I've never seen this man before, Chief,' he said, looking at me standing a distance away, too stunned to react. 'Why are you treating me like this?'

Sekou then recounted the incident with a tremor in his voice. 'You shot our mother. Remember, the bullets were deflected, but you intended to kill her. Yes, you intended to kill her!'

'Kill an innocent woman?' protested the man. 'I was never involved in the war.'

The driver slapped him, but the man remained adamant. He was a skinny man in a worn-out shirt and trousers, his shoes patched all over – a destitute in fact.

My brother shook his head. 'I could not forget your face even after a hundred years. You were the one who wanted to kill our mother. We were fleeing to Sierra Leone and we were in Koniyan. You took our property, including my watch, the jewelry, and some other goods. You were the one who stripped me of my clothes and left me standing naked. I cannot forget your face. You were the one who shot at our mother.'

Why was my brother still insisting that our mother had survived a gunshot? I approached the man. He was trembling now, and with every step I took towards him, he withdrew into himself. At the point when I was so close to him that I could smell his fear, the man fell to his knees and held my feet. 'Don't kill me, Chief. I was never part of the war. Never killed a human being, let alone a woman.'

Then I heard my brother say, his voice sounding distant, out of this world: 'Killing him will not bring back our mother. Let him be. The war is over.'

And I turned to him. A sudden wind seemed to have risen, and a cold swept across my body. 'So you are telling me that he did kill our mother?'

My brother shook his head. 'I am telling you that our mother has passed on. Whatever you do cannot bring her back.'

The driver sucked his teeth. 'Even if we don't kill him, Chief, at least let us break his arms and legs,' he said. 'He deserves it.' But I had become paralyzed by inaction. A deep, chilly silence seemed to have descended on me, a strange cold beneath the sweat and the heat around me. It was as if I had landed in a dream in which the action was beyond my control. The man was sobbing now, his hold on my feet stronger. It was my brother who led me to the car. When I turned around, I saw that the man had not left his kneeling position.

'I swear he was the one,' Sekou said as he recounted the incident to our elder brother Edmond that night. The latter shook his head and kept silent. By then the driver had gone home, and once again the city had been plunged into a ceaseless round of church songs and drums that would go on all night long. The cold that had taken hold of me settled deep.

Vamba Sherif was born in Liberia and spent parts of his youth in Kuwait where he completed his secondary schooling. He fled the First Gulf War and settled initially in Syria and then in The Netherlands where he read Law. He has published several novels and short stories, including *The Land of the Fathers, The Kingdom of Sebah, The Witness, Bound to Secrecy* and *The Black Napoleon.* His work has been translated into many languages. Besides his love for music and films, which he reviews, he collects rare books on Africa, especially on Liberia.

ALICE MELIKE ÜLGEZER
Turkey/Australia

SECRET PIGEONS

It was Monday morning in the village and the national anthem blared out of the megaphones as it did every Monday morning. The megaphones, usually reserved for the *Ezzan*, had been strung amateurishly to various lampposts throughout the village and now the stirring patriotic lyrics that boomed forth were being buffeted down the narrow streets by a zealous wind. It was as if scores of men and women were striding, arm in arm, up and down the narrow streets, declaring their filial love. But the wind, combined with the clamor, had the unsettling effect that wind often does; wives sought to fight not just with their mother-in-laws but their husbands, children, sisters and even shopkeepers with whom they had perhaps shared an intimate disclosure the previous day. If they were able, husbands snuck out on the thin end of a fabricated excuse and headed for the touristic viewing points where they hoped to snag a young European in hot pants, preferably resembling those on the internet. Cats got scuttled across kitchens by stray boots, tea kettles were left on blazing stoves till they heated up white, smoked and cracked, and children threw stones at dogs and passing cars or tourists and when they spat, it landed smartly on their own cheeks in a fervent whip of wind.

Mustafa strode up the steep cobbled street, his hands plugged deeply in the pockets of his new Italian black leather jacket. He had bought it after sealing a particularly good deal and dusted the sleeve now. He had promised Ayşe a blender but when he saw the jacket at the market he couldn't resist. Anyway she could wait. If he felt any remorse he had buried it along with many other things.

He was on his way to Ferid the barber and, due to the ice and sleet, had parked his car a little way up the hill. The wind blew assorted bits of household debris along the sides of the road, plastic bags, torn crusts of bread, vegetable scraps. And as he pulled his beanie down the bridge of his nose, he cut a somewhat foreboding figure under the bleak and tussled sky. He noticed some of the Syrian refugee children playing up ahead. There were squatting by the side of the road tossing rocks and sticks, scrambling and leaping. They wore no shoes despite the cold and as he approached they paused in their hurlings and expectorations and regarded him curiously.

'What kind of parent lets their child go about like that?' he muttered to himself as he approached. He thought of the child he would never have and as if his thoughts had conspired with the wind a handful of blighted dust dashed him rudely across the face. He stopped in his tracks and for a blinking moment could barely see. He ground at his eyes with the stubs of his fingers as the elements whirled. Squeezed them shut and open. He heard a squall of giggles, the blustering voices of the patriots blowing furiously around. His eye stung and he felt the grains of dust at the back of his throat as his tongue fumbled over the words of the national anthem. Blinded like this, for just a moment, he was painfully aware of his fallibility. So, in an attempt to regain composure, he squinted at his digital watch. A quarter to ten. He rubbed his eyes, told himself that all was as it should be and, buoyed up by the stirring lyrics, he continued steadfastly on his way.

But as he drew nearer, one of the children came forward and peered blithely up at him while the others hung back and snickered or giggled. The child could have only been four at the most. Someone had cut his hair, perhaps himself or one of the others, and it hung across his face at a jagged, lopsided angle. Mustafa didn't know whose child he was, only that he stayed at the house of his next-door neighbor, Hamza. He was a sweet boy, if not a little slow due perhaps to trauma or brain injury, or both, and had the unnerving habit of approaching when least expected and holding out his grubby hand, as if in introduction, and then scurrying alongside one for as long as his curiosity stuck.

As he approached, Mustafa noticed an old plank of wood slung diagonal across his back that was tied with a piece of string. Looking about, he saw that the other children had similar bits of discarded wood tied over their shoulders. They began shouting and laughing as another hoisted his piece of wood and, pointing it directly at him, began to shoot it like a machine gun and shout *Allahu Akbar* before tearing off down the cobbled street.

The first child approached Mustafa now, his wooden gun slung across his chest. He smiled up at him with a simple yet disquieting smile.

'*Selam Abi,*' he panted in the only Turkish he knew and held his right hand out. It was filthy and smeared. Mustafa scowled and, digging his fists deeper into his pockets, muttered, 'Son of a prostitute.'

Urged on by this response, which of course he couldn't understand, the child picked up his pace and trotted beside him thrusting his right hand closer towards him, his gun bouncing gaily on his back.

'Me Husam!' he grinned stupidly as he jabbed a finger at his own chest.

Mustafa hurried along feeling strangely unsettled and despite himself began to curse in Turkish. 'You come to my country and beg because your pimp of a father can't feed you and here you are trying to pick my pockets,' he snarled out the side of his mouth.

Undeterred, the child reached smiling for his hand and as suddenly as a hard gust of wind threatened to unpeel the awning of a nearby shed so did Mustafa's hand whack away the child's. And at once he burst into tears, babbling in a language that neither the man nor even the other children could understand. His face turned red as he bawled and snot dribbled down his lips, and, still holding out his hand, he continued to scramble beside the man. Mustafa looked down at his desperate and innocent face. But something hardened inside him and he quickened his pace. And as he approached a nearby lamppost, a blast of the national anthem damn near backhanded him across the cheek and the child snivelled and cried, '*Mamma! Mamma!*' after his retreating figure and all the little children laughed.

Upon reaching his car Mustafa slammed the door, locked himself in and sat breathing a moment as he let the engine warm up. He bent to adjust the rear-view mirror. Then, with a particular expression reserved only for regarding himself or studying the books at his business, he gazed derisively down the length of his nose, never once meeting his own eyes. He smoothed and patted his hair, noticed the somewhat pink and blotched color of his cheeks but was relieved to see his jaw still cut a mean line.

Mustafa had always been fastidious. His dress and appearance were immaculate, as was the way he conducted his affairs. It was something he prided himself on. Even in his schoolwork as a boy and the way he'd looked after his first motorbike and first car. He remembered how his mother had told him he could be an engineer if he wanted, what with his intelligence and attention to detail. Or even a pilot. And, when his time came to marry, his family had no problems in finding any number of potential brides for him. It was just his luck (or fate), he reflected bitterly, that he had got a barren one. It had never occurred to him that the lack might lie with him. But even that hadn't stopped him taking the greatest of care with his appearance. In fact, quite the contrary, as he had something to prove.

He was a regular, for example, at Ferid's. He enjoyed his barber visits. The waiting beforehand in an easy chair, flicking through the newspapers, chatting with the local guys about business, watching the young apprentice sweep up the hair clippings. He frequented the place as much for his vanity as for his sense of belonging. Indeed the two were intimately entwined. He liked to joke about the life-size plastic dog that sat at the doorway, to give it a pat on the head and say, 'Some guard dog you've got here, Ferid. I could turn this joint over in no time if I wanted to.' And Ferid would shrug, 'Ah but business is good. So you're in luck.'

The local guys would laugh and praise his potential skills and sharp features, all agreeing he would be just the man for such a job. If ever there were one.

Mustafa hadn't ended up an engineer or a pilot as his mother had hoped but the manager of a local quarry. That was just as good, as far as he was concerned. And he liked to tell people all about it. Especially at the barber's where he had a captive audience, though he mistook their captivity for interest. It was a pumice quarry. And when the young guys looked at him blankly he would say, 'No, it's not just for those stones that your grandmother buys for her rotten feet from the market. What do you brush your teeth with? Toothpaste? Yeah, well it goes into that and into stones for building materials too. Now that's where most of the business is – a growing industry,' he would tell them, unaware of their almost total lack of interest. Education was important, he believed, and that was part of his mission at the barber's. Educating the local folk, most of whom didn't seem to know their aces from their spades, that and keeping up with the local gossip; who had ripped off whom, which foreigners had hit town lately and stayed longer than usual.

And in terms of him being meticulous, the way he conducted his affairs was no exception. He kept two mobile phones. For business, he told Ayşe. One for the quarry and a personal one, the number of which, he liked to assure her, he gave to very few people, family only. If you didn't have family then what did you have, right? It was all about keeping it sweet on the home front and so he had two. Phones that is.

But when he had started seeing Zeyneb this had caused him to re-evaluate his telephonic circumstances. He certainly couldn't give her his family number. That she wasn't. And, besides, Ayşe used to like answering his phone – when he was in the bathroom, say. It could be his mother or sister, for example. And he certainly couldn't give Zeyneb the quarry number. That wouldn't do. So it was that he purchased a third telephone. His underground line he called it. For his underground business, he'd tell himself in moments of sleazy sentimentalism. Then he would know for sure that it was she who was calling, what for and why. This certainty gave him a sense of calm and control in a situation that otherwise could have easily got out of hand in a small village like this.

But the glove box of his car sometimes got a little hectic. And then it struck him one morning on the way to the quarry. Different ringtones. The desk-phone for his work line, the crying baby, oh the irony of it, he thought bitterly, for the family line and the bullfrog for Zeyneb. This was a private joke of theirs. It was winter and, he didn't know why, but every winter he seemed to be more flatulent than in any other season. Maybe it was the heavy meals his wife cooked for him: beans and lamb, lentil soups. She never soaked them beforehand. He always told her to. But did she listen? Of course not. If she had done so, his flatulence wouldn't be twice as bad in winter as it was in summer. Anyway Zeyneb had picked up on it. Especially since it seemed to his body the appropriate response after a good session. Like digestion, he reflected now as he sat in his favorite easy chair at the barbershop, surreptitiously admiring his own reflection. So, in order to appear more charming than he in fact was, he used to joke every time he let one rip by stamping on the floor or clapping his hands and exclaiming, 'ah ha, another frog is dead' or 'the whole family is *morte*, totally *mort*, mamma, baba, baby frog.' Zeyneb never failed to giggle coquettishly at his slapstick French, swipe him on the haunches and give him a passionate kiss. So it was that Zeyneb's line rang like a bullfrog on heat.

Arriving at the barbershop this time, he hung his new black leather jacket on the clothes peg on the wall and sat down.

'So what's news, Mustafa Abi?' Ferid the barber said as he slapped the finishing touch of citrus cologne on a wincing young man's cheeks.

'You know, this and that. Work's going good.'

'I heard. You're a shark, Mustafa. Of that we can be sure. Hey boys?'

And the men sitting around waiting for a haircut all laughed.

'No, I'm not a shark,' he feigned humility. 'I'm just a good businessman. A *meticulous* businessman. If you aren't, what's the point? You tell me, Ferid Abi,' and he threw him a withering look in the mirror.

Ferid shrugged at his reflection, refusing to take the bait.

Gratified, Mustafa nodded and looked distastefully at the magazine pile that had sat on the glass-top table for as long as he could remember, at the same faded photo portraits that had been hanging in frames on the walls for years – Brad Pitt, Keanu Reeves, Sean Connery.

'You really should get some new pictures, Ferid,' he said now as he reached for a toothpick and began to turn it about in his mouth.

Ferid glanced at Mustafa's reflection in the mirror, at his expensive shoes and that new jacket. Overeducated, insolent and with too much money for his own good, he thought. But aloud he simply said, 'So how's that family of yours doing, Mustafa?'

Mustafa blanched. 'Just fine. They're doing well, thanks be to God.'

'Oh, so you've got one on the way?'

'You know very well I haven't!' he spluttered as he pulled the toothpick from his mouth.

'Oh, it's just that you said *they*,' Ferid feigned innocence. 'I thought there might be a nice surprise coming, that's all.'

'Aren't I allowed to have a mother, a sister, a father?' His face grew red and, as he leapt up from his favorite chair, he glared at the other men waiting as if to challenge them.

'Hey, easy, brother,' bargained Ferid, wondering if he didn't feel just a little bit pleased.

'I'm not your brother, you two-timing snake.' Mustafa's hands had begun to shake. He reached for the first black jacket he saw and, storming out of the barbershop, he left the door open behind him and nearly knocked over the life-size plastic dog.

If Ferid was shocked he didn't show it. He couldn't. It wasn't good for business to be partisan. Instead he said rather flatly, 'Touchy today,' and shook his head feeling what could have been a prick of remorse.

'I'd like to see little Ayşe after I had a go at her,' a young man sniggered when Mustafa was out of earshot. 'I'd give her twins.'

'Hey,' Ferid glowered at him. 'He can't help it. It could be you that it happens to.'

'I highly doubt that sir,' the young man retorted. 'You know Betül? Well, she had to go away to Istanbul for a while to see her aunt after I'd finished with her.'

The men in the barbershop guffawed.

'It's not like he can't afford to keep another wife,' added another.

'Yeah. Take that grocer what's-his-name, for example, he's got three. The dirty ox!'

'Exactly! And Mustafa's got enough money from, what is it that he does?' And here the young man appealed to his companions.

'Guns?'

'Grass?'

'Girls?'

'Oh c'mon, that's enough!' and Ferid clipped the last one smartly over the side of the head. 'Where's your honor!'

This silenced the shop somewhat and Ferid watched as Mustafa jumped into his car and swerved off down the main street.

All of a sudden, a strange noise broke the relative quiet. The men looked bewilderedly at each other and waited.

'I could've sworn I heard a frog,' said one as he sprinkled his palms with cologne.

'A what?' said another.

'A *frog*,' and the first man widened his eyes and slapped his lemony palms together.

'Don't be crazy,' snapped Ferid. 'You must've had some good stuff last night!'

But there it went again. The unmistakeable sound of a furiously croaking bullfrog. The men started peering under the chairs and the magazine table. One got down on his knees and pressing his head to the ground squinted beneath the counter.

'But no frogs live around here,' an older man said pensively.

'Oh no?' and the first man, cologne fresh, shook the leather jacket on the clothes peg. 'Well, they've migrated, mate. The water's too sweet for them to resist.' And he pulled the phone from the pocket and held it out for everyone to see.

'Whose is this?'

But before anybody could answer the frog sounded again and, turning it over, the young man looked at the screen.

'Anyone expecting a call from Zeyneb, gentlemen?'

'The *what's* too sweet for them to resist?!' one snickered.

'I heard he was hung like a donkey,' another announced.

And the men whooped and laughed.

'That sneaky fox. Pretending like he's all cut up about his little wife, when really he's doing her on the side–'

'Of the local swamp,' another put in.

'Answer it! Answer it!'

'Give that thing to me,' retorted Ferid, all of a sudden the sober proprietor. 'Poor Mustafa. What the hell would you do? Huh? Give it here!' And he snatched it from the young man. And just as he had done so, Mustafa burst back into the shop, threw the leather jacket he had mistaken for his own on the tiled floor, grabbed the phone and his own jacket and yelled at them, 'I'd sell your mothers but I'd be broke as a joke!'

There was a shocked silence as he slammed the glass door shut behind him, the blue *nazar* beads and bells jangling madly after him, the bullfrog croaking all the while. Outside he leapt into his car with the ignition still running and, skidding once in some old snow, sped off down the main street.

'Late for Zeyneb,' sneered a young man.

'You keep that to yourself, you little pimp,' Ferid glared at him. 'All of you keep it to yourselves.' He turned to address the whole shop. 'What happens in here, stays in here, you know the rule. Now come on and help me tidy this place up.'

And so it was that the town learned of Mustafa's infidelity.

'Damn Italian leather,' he cursed as he sped down the back road through the fallow fields towards the pumice quarry. His eyes stung with the wind or the dust and he swiped at them roughly, the road disappearing momentarily before him. 'Damn technology and damn women.' He glanced at himself in the rear-view mirror, his four-day growth and shaggy hair, 'and damn barbers,' and he stepped on the accelerator and sped dangerously fast down the unsealed road.

Minus ten and the air was sparkling like powdered glass as tiny specs of ice caught in the swirls of light and drifted to the ground. Ayşe watched as her neighbor Hamza walked across the flat of his roof. The national anthem blared out of the megaphones as it did every Monday morning. If Hamza had known the song he wouldn't have much cared. National anthems had got him nowhere in his country. Yet here at least was a better place than nowhere. Despite the wind raging, dark and light he stood steady on the flat concrete roof of the house, his hair an immaculate, brilliantine black, and whistled up to his pigeons as they tossed against the rubble of the sky.

It was morning also where Hamza came from, but an altogether different kind of morning. Pigeons no longer flew above the flat-topped city, children no longer played in the streets and even the dogs and cats had vanished. Neither the citadel, the market place nor the bathhouse stood intact. In fact the city was barely recognizable. Its inhabitants had all but fled and those who couldn't had been brutally savaged along with their city. Now the likes of an imported and barbarically ignorant brand of born-again butchers went about pillaging and raping, in the name of… Hamza shook his head. In the name of what? He spat at his feet. His apartment had been bombed, his business gutted, his car destroyed. He remembered one morning he and his neighbors had rushed to bury the children who'd been shot dead in the night, point blank or from the debris of barrel bombs. That was when he'd known he had to leave.

Despite the safety that he'd found, he was plagued by guilt. It tore at him from his insides, every moment of every day. His people were suffering and it seemed no one did anything about it. Except to replenish their weapon imports and perhaps pitch a few tents on the borders when the winter got too bad to bear.

He gripped a length of plastic piping in one hand and cracked it now like a whip. It smacked hard on the flat roof and the pigeons suddenly changed direction. They ducked and swerved and dipped and span. He thought of the day's work to come, the endless lugging of stones and dust. And, thrusting his body violently upward, he yelled out to his birds. His voice tearing across the roofs and through the sky, 'Areeeeaaaaaah! Arr! Arr! Arr!' The birds dashed and cartwheeled and he stood squinting up at them, shielding his eyes from the steely pale light.

In the garden next door Ayşe leant against the walnut tree and admired this young man, her new neighbor. She knew he had come from across the border but so far he'd proven himself to be a decent addition to the village. He was employed by a local man and was known to be a hard worker, honest and courteous. She wasn't sure if he had a wife or if any of the children were his. Perhaps his wife had died or been killed. That was something she would never ask.

Unbeknownst to him, Hamza was coveted by the local village women. Shrouded in the mystery that his foreign tongue provided, he was regarded with a certain fascination. Sharing tea at each other's houses, they would speculate on the size of his manhood and the special talents as a lover that he must surely have, being foreign and all. And soon it was as good as fact that he sported something the size of a small horse. Ayşe never participated in these speculative conversations that much. She would absorb herself in the task of preparing more tea and sweets for her neighbors. Yet she felt herself drawn inward with a certain tenderness she found it difficult to describe even to herself. None of the women bothered to trace the origins of their collective consensus nor to disprove its verity. That was not the point. Rather they would giggle and lament, biting their tongues at the bitter pang that was their fate of being born into this village where for the most part, they agreed, the men were sloping, slack-jawed, idle individuals rumored to do all sorts of unmentionable things. Hamza, on the other hand, may as well have been a runaway angel, escaped from a distant harem.

Something began to unwind in Ayşe as she watched fascinated from her courtyard. She thrilled silently at this man's bird language and told herself that he was just like the ancient King Suleiman. She imagined her way into the details of his form that she couldn't make out from such a distance. The crease of his eyes against the sun, the arch of his back or the line of his hands, the heat of his throat or the dark of his irises. She saw that in his hands he held a white bird. Its wings beat fast, nervous and white. She couldn't be sure that he knew she was watching but liked all the same to believe that he did. She was sure somehow that this was for her. All of it. These birds. This bright pale air. And him. He lifted his arms up now and held the bird as its wings beat furiously. Above, the pigeons suddenly changed direction and Ayşe caught a lump in her throat as she thrilled to their flight. His voice tore through the thin light and the bird flapped in his hands. And, turning, she was sure they both saw the cat creeping up the stone wall that divided them. He had greeted her before with his right hand sworn solemnly across his heart and a nod. She had nodded back but hadn't had the courage to place her own hand on her heart though, God knows, she had wanted to.

Ayşe felt a breath of wind against her face now and thought of Mount Ergeus, a hundred or so kilometers away. It would be covered in snow, she knew. The grain of the walnut bark was rough beneath her hand as she gazed at her neighbor when, all of a sudden, a voice came low behind her, acrid in a puff of smoke, 'I'm gonna finish that man off. Look at him standing there on the roof like that.'

'You're back early,' she said, startled. 'I thought you went to Ferid's?'

'All full up,' he scoffed and then cuffed her arm. 'What do you say, girl? Huh?'

But she said nothing and after a moment Mustafa added, as if for good measure, 'And his pimps of kids too.'

Ayşe started and turned to go as Mustafa made a grab for her behind. 'Who does he think he is, coming here like a Pasha?' he exclaimed as she wriggled out of his grasp. 'Only poor and stupid people with nothing to lose run away from their homes and countries like weaklings. If those maniacs came here, wife, I'd stay and shoot them myself. I swear to God.'

Ayşe smarted at his acerbic remark and pushed the bare branches of the walnut tree aside as she tried again to leave.

Mustafa towered over her, 'Huh?'

'Of course you would, my dear, of course you would,' she tremored and it was then that she saw her neighbor smile from his place on the roof as he turned to face the winter sun.

'Hey, isn't that Hamza's kid?' Mustafa stood in the back garden pissing in a clear wide arc.

Ayşe sat at the kitchen table chewing her bottom lip and, pretending she hadn't heard, continued to feed boiled eggs to the cat under the table.

'I said, isn't that Hamza's kid?' he shouted louder this time from where he stood with his back to her, his hands at his fly.

'What?' Ayşe tidied the crushed eggshells on her saucer.

'Come here!' he turned, zipping up his trousers. 'Come and look.'

Ayşe wiped her hands on her lap and, pushing the chair back, got up and walked out to where her husband stood in the light morning snow. Halfway up the small hill opposite their house some kids were playing.

'What is it?' she stood beside him.

'Look, I said,' Mustafa snapped.

Under the trees putrid smoke rose from a small fire that had been lit in a blackened tin bucket, burning with rubbish. Barefoot kids, as young as three, were running about in the snow and the mud. Each one had a wooden stick, its ends tied with string, slung across their back. Their noses were caked with dried mucus, their clothes, either too small or too big, had been hoicked on every which way and they tumbled and scrambled, shouting, kicking and yelling. And then she saw it.

Little Husam had been tied with rope around his neck and was hanging from the branches of one of the trees. His pants were muddied and soiled and he writhed and kicked out wildly as he swung and slammed into the tree trunk every so often. Beneath him a knot of kids were shouting and calling out *Allahu Akbar* as they took it in turns to thrash at him with a piece of long plastic piping. Ayşe gasped as her throat tightened with shock. Husam was sobbing as he struggled to loosen the rope around his neck and where his pink pajamas had come loose she could see the swollen red stripes that were rising quickly across his bottom.

'Didn't I tell you these people were amoral sons of prostitutes?' Mustafa blazed. 'Huh? Didn't I? And they think we're going to put their kids through school and fill up their bellies with bread and their pockets with small change?' He scowled as he craned his neck to get a better look.

Stunned, Ayşe hardly noticed the early-morning chill. 'Go and do something, Mustafa,' she placed a hand on his arm. 'You've got to tell them that this isn't right. Not here. Not anywhere.'

Mustafa sniggered. 'No use. They think they're in Iran or something. It's probably what Hamza does to his wife, that is, if he's got one. That's probably where they learnt it.'

Her hand flickered on his arm as she breathed sharply and looked away.

'I'm serious. How do you think they treat their women, huh?'

And before she had time to think she blurted out, 'They treat their women better than the men here do. I swear to God.' She had grown red in the face and stood breathless.

'You swear to God, do you?' He stood closer suddenly, his face glowering down at her.

'I am at peace with my God,' she trembled.

Mustafa scoffed and then lowered his voice carefully. 'And how is it that you know how they treat their women?'

Ayşe felt her body run cold as he waited for her answer, the kids still screaming and yelling beneath the trees.

'I can just tell,' she shook.

He looked at her blackly as the cat emerged from the kitchen and sprawled on the step, licking at its paws.

'You can just tell, can you? Well, you know what? I can *just tell* some things too. Like no matter how charming those foreign men may seem, they are worse than any village idiot round here you can imagine.'

Ayşe looked wretchedly round the garden. 'Breakfast is getting cold,' she faltered. 'Perhaps the cat's eaten all of it. Look,' and she quavered towards where it was sitting with its back paw pointed skyward.

'Damn the cat,' muttered Mustafa as he shoved past her toward the street door.

Ayşe scrambled after him feeling the bottom rush up towards her as the distance between them gaped ever wider.

'This isn't Iran,' he bellowed as he jerked the door open, the bell clanging hysterically on its wire. The kids scattered and ran to the crumbled step outside their house, laughing and trembling. 'You want to play like that, you go somewhere else!' And he stormed towards the tree where Husam was dangling, clutching at the rope around his neck, crying, his bare feet red and muddied, barely touching the ground.

Ayşe stood on the threshold wringing her hands.

'Children,' she pleaded. 'You mustn't play like this.' They giggled and stared at her from where they had clustered on Hamza's doorstep, pulling faces.

'Mustafa?' her voice trailed hopelessly. But if he heard her he didn't show it as he whipped a knife from his jacket pocket and, flicking it open, started hacking at the rope above Husam's neck that was chafed near raw.

'Sons of prostitutes,' he cursed as he worked at the rope while Husam snivelled and sniffed and the children gaped.

And just then Ayşe saw him, standing on the doorstep, the kids pulling at his sleeves and pants as they stood around sucking their fingers and picking their noses. She followed the line of his neck and jaw, the deep ox blood of his lips and something inside her fluttered and winged. She cleared her throat and he looked over. Their eyes said nothing for a moment and then, as if a rock were thrown into water, he rippled with warmth and it was all she could do to stay standing and not lose herself in the oblivion of his eyes.

The snow had begun to fall gently and Ayşe listened to it patter outside as they lay together in the afternoon. He drew his fingers up her naked side. Alone like this, she studied his face so close before her for the first time. He looked younger than she had expected. And perhaps he was. His skin glistened with the finest sheen of sweat and oil. It glowed in the pale light that came through the torn sheet across the window through which she could see the naked branches of the walnut tree in her own back garden. There were creases across the bridge of his nose where it met his forehead. And his eyes, though closer together than she had previously thought, were of the most perfect almond shape. His eyelashes were long and his nipples, of the darkest ox blood, were alert against the smooth grain of his skin. He smiled.

The fine down of hairs that covered her body stood on end and she shivered with his touch as he spoke in that language she couldn't understand.

He cupped his head in his hand and let the other drift slowly over her body. Ayşe was damp with pleasure and felt herself radiating like a small shocked sun. He laughed at the soft velvet of her earlobes and in her center she spun giddy. Too shy to look any further, she squeezed her eyes shut and the gentle fragrance of them together set her adrift in the most immaculate stillness. She lay breathing, blind and fascinated as he continued to speak quietly into her.

Husam and the other children of the house were away at a neighbor's, she understood. The young men were working on the new hotel site up the road and the old woman was out. All the same, as her intoxication ebbed, she realized what a perilous encounter it was. Behind her closed lids and the increasing rate of her heart, she tried desperately to reason with herself. Mustafa must never find out. There was no way he could. If anyone had seen her leaving the house she would say that she had merely been delivering a parcel of clothes for the children. She felt her skin rise in goose bumps with a drift of air beneath the door and wondered about the time. But, just as she was about to move, she felt the heat of his body as he leant in closer. He placed his mouth on hers and she was cast adrift again. Strangely, she felt safe and allowed herself to be held by this man whom she barely knew but had watched, together with his birds, for months now. The air drew close between them where they lay. The scent of their bodies and the subtle smoke of the wood heater drifted and clothed them and the pigeons shuffled and cooed in the eaves.

Alice Melike Ülgezer is an Australian poet and author of Turkish background. Her work is influenced by her mixed cultural heritage and most recently by the time she spent living in a small village in Central Anatolia, Turkey. Her first novel *The Memory of Salt* was published by Giramondo in 2012.

DANIEL ALARCON
Peru/United States

ABSENCE

On his second day in New York, Wari walked around midtown looking half-heartedly for the airline office. He'd decided to forget everything. It was an early September day; the pleasant remains of summer made the city warm and inviting. He meandered in and out of sidewalk traffic, marveled at the hulking mass of the buildings and confirmed, in his mind, that the city was the capital of the world. On the train, he'd seen break dancing and heard Andean flutes. He'd watched a Chinese man play a duet with Beethoven on a strange electronic harmonica. In Times Square, a Dominican man danced frenetic merengue with a life-sized doll. The crowds milled about, smiling, tossing money carelessly at the dancer, laughing when his hands slipped lustily over the curve of the doll's ass.

Wari didn't arrive at the airline office that day; he didn't smile at any nameless woman across the counter, or reluctantly pay the $100 fine to have his ticket changed. Instead he wandered, passed the time in intense meditation upon the exotic, upon the city, its odors and gleaming surfaces, and found himself in front of a group of workers digging a hole in the sidewalk at the base of a skyscraper. He sat down to have lunch and watch them. With metal-clawed machines they bored expertly though concrete. Wari had made a sandwich uptown that morning and he ate distractedly now. The people passed in steady streams, bunching at corners and swarming across intersections the instant a light changed. From a truck, the men brought a thin sapling and lowered it into their newly dug hole. They filled it with dirt. Trees to fill holes, Wari thought, amused, but they weren't done. The workers smoked cigarettes and talked loudly among themselves and then one of them brought a wheelbarrow piled high with verdant grass cut into small squares. Sod. They laid the patches of leafy carpet out around the tree. Just like that. In the time it took Wari to eat, a hole was emptied and filled, a tree planted and adorned with fresh green grass. A wound created in the earth; a wound covered, healed, beautified. It was nothing. The city moved along, unimpressed, beneath a bright, late summer sky.

He walked a little more, and stopped in front of a group of Japanese artists drawing portraits for tourists. They advertised their skill with careful renderings of famous people but Wari could only recognize a few. There was Bill Clinton and Woody Allen and the rest were generically handsome in a way that reminded Wari of a hundred actors and actresses. It was the kind of work he could do easily. The artists' hands moved deftly across the parchment, shading here and there in swift strokes. Crowds slowed to watch and the portraitists seemed genuinely oblivious, glancing up at their clients every now and then to make certain they weren't making any mistakes. When the work was done, the customer always smiled and seemed surprised at finding his own likeness on the page. Wari smiled too, found it folkloric, like everything he had seen so far in the city – worth remembering, somehow special in a way he couldn't yet name.

Wari had been invited to New York for an exhibition; serendipity, an entire chain of events born of a single conversation in a bar with an American tourist named Eric, a red-haired PhD student in Anthropology and committed do-gooder. He had acceptable Spanish and was friend of a friend of Wari's who was still at the university. Eric and Wari had talked about Guayasamín and indigenous iconography, about Cubism and the Paracas textile tradition of the Peruvian coast. They'd shared liter bottles of beer and laughed as their communication improved with each drink, ad-hoc Spanglish and pencil drawings on napkins. Eventually Eric made an appointment to see Wari's studio. He'd taken two paintings back to New York and set up an exhibition through his department. Everything culminated in an enthusiastic email and an invitation on cream-colored bond paper. Wari had mulled it over for a few weeks, then spent most of his savings on a round-trip ticket. It was the only kind they sold. Once in New York and settled in, Wari buried the return ticket in the bottom of his bag, as if it were something radioactive. He didn't know what else to do with it. That first night, when the apartment had stilled, Wari dug into the suitcase and examined it. It had an unnatural density for a simple piece of paper. He dreamed that it glowed.

Wari found Leah, his host's girlfriend, making pasta. It was still light out, and Eric wasn't home yet. Wari wanted to explain exactly what he had seen and why it had impressed him, but he didn't have the words. She didn't speak Spanish, but made up for it by smiling a lot and bringing him things.

A cup of tea, a slice of toast. He accepted everything because he wasn't sure how to refuse. His English embarrassed him. While the water boiled, Leah stood at the edge of the living room.

'Good day?' she said. 'Did you have a good day?'

Wari nodded.

'Good,' she said. She brought him the remote to the television, then turned into the small kitchen. Wari sat on the sofa and flipped through the channels, not wanting to be rude. He could hear Leah humming a song to herself. Her jeans were slung low on her hips. Wari made himself watch the television. Game shows, news programs, talk shows; trying to understand gave him a headache, and so he settled on a baseball game, which he watched with the volume down. The game was languid and hard to follow and, before long, Wari was asleep.

When he awoke, there was a plate of food in front of him. Leah was at the sink, washing her dish. Eric was home. 'Buenas noches!' he called out grandly. 'Good game?' He pointed at the television. Two players chatted on the mound, their faces cupped in their gloves.

'Yes,' said Wari. He rubbed the sleep from his eyes.

Eric laughed. 'The Yanks gonna get it back this year,' he said. 'They're the white team.'

'I'm sorry,' was all Wari could offer.

They spoke for a while in Spanish about the details of the exhibition, which was opening in two days. Wari's canvases stood against the wall, still wrapped in brown paper and marked fragile. They would hang them tomorrow.

'Did you want to work while you were here?' Eric asked. 'I mean, paint? At my department, they said they could offer you a studio for a few weeks.'

That had everything to do with the radioactive ticket interred in the bottom of his suitcase. Wari felt a tingling in his hands. He'd brought no brushes or paints or pencils or anything. He had no money for art supplies. He guessed it would be years before he would again. What would it be like *not* to paint?

'No, thank you,' Wari said in English. He curled his fingers into a fist.

'Taking a vacation, huh? That's good. Good for you, man. Enjoy the city.'

Wari asked about phone cards, and Eric said you could get them anywhere and cheap. Any bodega, corner store, pharmacy, newsstand. 'We're connected,' he said, and laughed. 'Sell them right next to the Lotto tickets. You haven't called home?'

Wari shook his head. Did they miss him yet?

'You should.' Eric settled into the couch. Leah had disappeared into the bedroom.

His host spoke to the flickering television while Wari ate.

The American embassy sits hunched against a barren mountain in a well-to-do suburb of Lima. An immense bunker with the tiled exterior of a fancy bathroom, its perimeter gate is so far from the actual building that it would take a serious throw to hit even its lowest floor with a rock. A line gathers out front each morning before dawn, looping around the block, a hopeful procession of Peruvians with their sights on Miami or Los Angeles or New Jersey or anywhere. Since the previous September, after the attacks, the embassy had forced the line even farther out, beyond blue barricades, to the very edge of the wide sidewalk. Then there'd been a car bomb in March to welcome the visiting American president. Ten Peruvians had died, including a 13-year-old boy, unlucky enough to be skateboarding near the embassy at exactly the wrong moment. His skull had been pierced by shrapnel. Now the avenue was closed to all but official traffic. The line was still there, every morning except Sundays, in the middle of the empty street.

Before his trip, Wari presented his letter and his fees and his paperwork. Statements of property, financials, university records, a list of exhibitions and gallery openings, certificates of birth and legal documents regarding a premature marriage and redemptive divorce. The entirety of his 27 years, on paper. The centerpiece of course, was Eric's invitation on letterhead from his university. Eric had let him know that this wasn't any old university. Wari gathered that he should say the name of the institution with reverence and all would know its reputation. Eric had assured him it would open doors.

Instead the woman said: 'We don't give 90-day visas any more.'

Through the plastic window, Wari tried pointing at the invitation, at its gold letters and elegant watermark, but she wasn't interested. 'Come back in two weeks,' she said.

He did. In his passport, Wari found a one-month tourist visa.

At the airport in Miami, Wari presented his paperwork once more, his passport and, separately, the invitation in its gilded envelope. To his surprise, the agent sent him straight away to an interview room, without even glancing at the documents. Wari waited in the blank room, recalling how a friend had joked: 'Remember to shave or they'll think you're Arab.' Wari's friend had celebrated the remark by shattering a glass against the cement floor of the bar.

Everyone had applauded. Wari could feel the sweat gathering in the pores on his face. He wondered how bad he looked, how tired and disheveled. How dangerous. The stale, recycled air from the plane compartment was heavy in his lungs. He could feel his skin darkening beneath the fluorescent lights.

An agent came in, shooting questions in English. Wari did his best. 'An artist, eh?' the agent said, examining the paperwork.

Wari folded his fingers around an imaginary brush and painted circles in the air.

The agent waved Wari's gesture away. He looked through the papers, his eyes settling finally on the bank statement. He frowned.

'You're going to New York?' he asked. 'For a month?'

'In Lima, they give to me one month,' Wari said carefully.

The agent shook his head. 'You don't have the money for that kind of stay.' He looked at the invitation and then pointed to the paltry figure at the bottom of the bank statement. He showed it to Wari, who muffled a nervous laugh. 'Two weeks. And don't get any ideas,' the agent said. 'That's generous. Get your ticket changed when you get to New York.'

He stamped Wari's burgundy passport with a new visa and sent him on his way.

At baggage claim, Wari found his paintings in a stack next to an empty carousel. He made his way through customs, answering more questions before being let through. He waited patiently while they searched his suitcase, rifling through his clothes. His paintings were inspected with great care, and here the golden letter finally served a purpose. Customs let him through. Wari felt dizzy, the shuffling noise of the airport suddenly narcotic, sleep calling him to its protective embrace. Ninety days is a humane length of time, he thought. Enough time to come to a decision and find its cracks. To look for work and organize contingencies. To begin imagining the permanence of goodbyes. It wasn't as if Wari had nothing to lose. He had parents, a brother, good friends, a career just beginning in Lima, an ex-wife. If he left it behind? Even a month spent in meditation – ambling about a new city, working out the kinks of a foreign language – might be space enough to decide. But two weeks? Wari thought it cruel. He counted days on his fingers: 24 hours after his paintings came down, he would be illegal. Wari had imagined that the right decision would appear obvious to him, if not right away, then certainly before three months had passed. But there was no chance of clarity in 14 days. Wari walked through the Miami airport as if he'd been punched in the face. His feet dragged. He made his flight to LaGuardia just as the doors were closing, and was stopped again at the jetway, his shoes examined by a plastic-gloved woman who refused to return his weak smiles. On the plane, Wari slept with his face flush against the oval window. There was nothing to see anyway. It was an overcast day in south Florida, no horizon, no turquoise skies worthy of postcards, nothing except the grey expanse of a wing and its contrails, blooming at the end like slivers of smoke.

Leah woke him with apologies. 'I have to work,' she said softly. 'You couldn't have slept through it anyway.' She smiled. Her hair was pulled back in a ponytail. She smelled clean. Leah made jewelry, and his bedroom, which was actually the living room, was also her workshop.

'Is okay,' Wari said, sitting up on the couch, taking care to hide his morning erection.

Leah grinned as Wari fumbled awkwardly with the sheet. 'I've seen plenty of that, trust me,' she said. 'I wake up with Eric every morning.'

Wari felt his face turn red. 'Is lucky,' he said.

She laughed.

'Where is? Eric?' he asked, cringing at his pronunciation.

'Studying. Work. He teaches undergrads. *Young students,*' she said, translating young, in gestures, as small.

Wari pictured Eric, with his wide pale face and red hair, teaching miniature people, tiny humans who looked up to him for knowledge. He liked that Leah had tried. He understood much more than he could say, but how could she know that?

He watched her for a while, filing metal and twisting bands of silver into circles. He liked the precision of her work, and she didn't seem to mind him. Leah burnished a piece, filed and sanded, bent metal with tools that seemed too brusque for her delicate hands. She held a hammer with authority, she was a woman with purpose. It was a powerful display.

'I'm finishing up,' she said finally, 'and then you can come with me. I know a Peruvian you can talk to.'

He showered and ate a bowl of cold cereal before they left for downtown. The Peruvian she knew was named Fredy. She didn't know where he was from exactly, though she was sure he'd told her. Fredy worked a street fair on Canal. Leah had won him over with a smile a few years before, and now he let her sell her jewelry on consignment. Every couple of weeks, she went down with new stuff, listened as Fredy catalogued what had sold and what hadn't, and his opinionated take on why. He lived in New Jersey now, Leah said, and had married a Chinese woman. 'They speak to each other in broken English. Isn't that amazing?'

Wari agreed.

'It must say something about the nature of love, don't you think?' Leah asked. 'They have to trust each other so completely. That window of each other that they know in English is so small compared to everything they are in their own language.'

Wari wondered. The train rattled on its way downtown. But it's always like that, he wanted to say, you can never know anyone completely. Instead he was silent.

'Do you understand me when I speak?' Leah asked. 'If I speak slowly?'

'Of course,' Wari said, and he did, but felt helpless to say much more. He noted the descending numbered streets at every stop, and followed their subterranean progress on the map. A sticker covered the southern end of the island. They got off before they reached that veiled area. On Canal, only a few blocks was enough to remind Wari of Lima: that density, that noise, that circus. The air was swollen with foreign tongues. He felt comfortable in a way, but didn't mind at all when Leah took his arm, and led him swiftly through the crowds of people. He bumped shoulders with the city, like walking against a driving rain.

Fredy turned out to be Ecuadorian, and Leah couldn't hide her embarrassment. She turned a rose color that reminded Wari of the dying light at dusk. Wari and Fredy both reassured her it was nothing.

'We're brother countries,' Fredy said.

'We share border and history,' said Wari.

The Ecuadorian was all obsequious smiles, spoke of the peace treaty that was signed only a few years before. Wari played along, shook Fredy's hand vigorously until Leah seemed at ease with her mistake. Then she and Fredy talked business, haggling in a teasing way that seemed more like flirting, and of course Leah won. When this was finished, she excused herself and drifted away to the other stands, leaving Wari and Fredy alone.

When she was out of earshot, Fredy turned to Wari. 'Don't ask me for work, *compadre*,' he said, frowning. 'It's hard enough for me.'

Wari was taken aback. 'Who asked you for work? I've got work, *cholo*.'

'Sure you do.'

Wari ignored him, inspected the table laid out with small olive forks bent into ridiculous earrings. At the other end, there were black-and-white photos of Andean peaks, silvery and snowcapped, and others of ruined fortresses of stone and colonial churches. The scenes were devoid of people: landscapes or buildings or scattered rocks carved by Incas, unified by their uninhabited emptiness. 'There's no people,' Wari said.

'They emigrated,' sneered Fredy.

'This shit sells?'

'Good enough.'

'That's my girl, you know,' Wari said all of a sudden, and he liked the tone of the lie, the snap of it, and the way the Ecuadorian looked up, surprised.

'The gringa?'

'Yeah.'

'I bet she is,' said Fredy.

Then two customers appeared, a young woman with her boyfriend. Fredy switched to English, heavily accented, but quite acceptable, and pointed to various objects, suggesting earrings that matched the woman's skin tone. She tried on a pair, Fredy dutifully held the mirror up for her, her distracted boyfriend checking out the photos. Wari wondered where Leah had gone off to. The woman turned to him.

'What do you think?' she asked, looking back and forth between Wari and Fredy.

'Is very nice,' Wari said.

'Like a million bucks,' said Fredy.

'Where's this from?' she asked, fingering the lapis lazuli stone.

'Peru,' said Wari.

Fredy shot him a frown. 'From the Andes,' he said.

'Trev,' she called to her boyfriend. 'It's from Peru! Isn't it nice?'

She pulled out a twenty and Fredy made change. He wrapped the earrings in tissue paper, and handed her a card. The couple walked away chatting. Wari and Fredy didn't speak.

Leah reappeared and Wari made sure to touch her, thoughtlessly, as if it meant nothing at all. He could feel Fredy watching them, studying each of their movements. 'Did you tell Fredy about your opening?' she asked Wari.

He shook his head. 'So modest,' Leah said, and filled in the details and, to his delight, exaggerated its importance and weight. Wari felt like a visiting dignitary, someone famous.

Wari put his arm around Leah. She didn't stop him. Fredy said it would be difficult to make it.

'OK, but maybe?' she asked.

'Please come,' added Wari, not worrying about his pronunciation.

Leaving is no problem. It's exciting actually; in fact, it's a drug. It's the staying gone that will kill you. This is the handed-down wisdom of the immigrant. You hear it from the people that wander home, after a decade away. You hear about the euphoria that passes quickly; the new things that lose their newness and, soon after, their capacity to amuse you. Language is bewildering. You tire of exploring. Then the list of things you miss multiplies beyond all reason, nostalgia clouding everything: in memory, your country is clean and uncorrupt, the streets are safe, the people universally warm, and the food consistently delicious. The sacred details of your former life appear and reappear in strange iterations, in a hundred waking dreams. Your pockets fill with money, but your heart feels sick and empty.

Wari was prepared for all this.

In Lima, he rounded up a few friends and said his goodbyes. Tentative, equivocal goodbyes. Goodbyes over drinks, presented as jokes, gentle laughter before the *poof* and the vanishing – that Third World magic. I may be back, he told everyone, or I may not. He moved two boxes of assorted possessions into the back room of his parent's house. He took a few posters off the walls, covered the little holes with white-out. He encouraged his mother to rent out his room for extra money if he didn't come home in a month. She cried, but just a little. His brother wished him luck. Wari offered a toast to family at Sunday dinner, and promised to come home one day soon. He embraced his father, and accepted the crisp $100 bill the old man slipped into his hand. And in the last days before leaving, Wari and Eric exchanged feverish emails ironing out fine points of the exhibition: the exact size of the canvases, the translated bio, the press release. All the formalities of a real opening, but for Wari, it was so much noise and chatter. The only solid things for him were the ticket and the runway and the plane and the obligatory window seat for a last, fading view of Lima. The desert purgatory, the approaching northern lights.

I'm ready, he thought.

And if no one questioned him, it's because the logic was self-evident. What would he do there? How long could he live at home? A divorced painter, sometime teacher – what does an artist do in a place like that? In America, you can sweep floors and make money, if you're willing to work – you are willing to work, aren't you, Wari?

Yes, I am.

At anything? Outdoor work? Lifting, carting, cleaning?

Anything.

And that was it. What other questions were there? He'd be fine.

Only his mother gave voice to any concerns. 'Is it about Elie?' she asked a few days before he traveled. Wari had been expecting this question. Elie, his ex-wife, whom he loved and whom he hated. At least there were no children to grow up hating him. Wari was relieved it was over, believed she must be as well.

'No, Ma,' he said. 'It has nothing to do with her.'

So his mother smiled and smiled and smiled.

In Eric's apartment, Wari daydreamed. He dressed up the lie about Leah. He lay on the couch, composing emails about her to his friends back home, describing the shape of her body, the colors of her skin. The solution to his 14-day quandary: marry her and stay, marry her and go. Marry her and it would be all the same. He imagined falling in love in monosyllables, in nods and smiles and meaningful gestures. Telling Leah the story of his life in pictograms: his modest family home. The drab, charcoal colors of his native city. His once-happy marriage and its dissolving foundations, crumbling from the inside into a perfect parody of love. It was early afternoon and Leah readied herself for a waitressing job. The shower ran. Through the thin walls he could hear the sound of the water against her body. Her light brown hair went dark when it was wet. He closed his eyes and pictured her naked body. Then Elie's.

Wari turned on the television, let its noise fill the living room. Almost a year from the attacks and the inevitable replays had begun. He changed the channel, his mind wandered: Fredy on a train home to his Chinese wife, wondering if what Wari had boasted of was true. Elie, somewhere in Lima, not even aware he was gone. Leah, in the shower, not thinking of him. On every channel, buildings collapsed in clouds of dust and Wari watched on mute, listening hopefully to Leah's water music.

Wari rapped twice on the wooden door. This was years ago. 'Chola,' he called, to the woman who would be his wife. 'Chola, are you there?'

But Elie wasn't there. She'd left the music on loud to discourage burglars. She lived in Magdalena, a crumbling district by the sea, in a neighborhood of stereos playing loudly in empty apartments. Fourteen-year-old kids cupped joints in their palms and kept a lookout for cops. They played soccer in the streets and tossed pebbles at the moto-taxis. Wari knocked again. 'She ain't home,' someone called from the street. Wari knew she wasn't, but he wanted to see her. He wanted to kiss her and hold her and tell her his good news. He was a younger, happier version of himself.

My good news, baby: his first exhibition in a gallery in Miraflores. A real opening with wine, a catalogue and they'd promised him press, maybe even half a column interview in one of the Sunday magazines. This is what he wanted to tell her.

Wari knocked some more. He hummed along to the melody that played in her apartment. He pulled pen and paper from his bag and composed a note for her, in English. They were both studying it at an institute, Elie with much less enthusiasm. English is tacky, she'd say. She mourned the passing of Spanish, the faddish use of Gringo talk. It was everywhere: on television, in print, on the radio. In cafés, their peers spoke like this: 'Si, pero asi es la gente *nice*. No tienen ese *feeling*.' Why are you learning that language, *acomplejado*, my dear Wari, you just paint and you'll be fine. She made him laugh and that was why he loved her. On a piece of paper torn from a notebook, he wrote:

I come see you, but instead met your absence.

It's perfect, he thought. He put a W in the corner, just because – as if anyone else would come to her home and leave a note like this. He tacked it to the door and walked down to the street, music serenading the walls of empty apartments. Music that slipped out into the street. He had nothing to do but wait for her. A kid on the corner scowled at him, but Wari smiled back. It was late afternoon, the last dying light of day.

The show went up, but the reception was sparsely attended. 'It's a bad time,' said Eric, with Leah on his arm. 'The anniversary has everyone on edge.'

'On edge,' Wari asked, 'is like scared?'

'Just like that,' Leah said.

Wari didn't care. He was scared too. And not because the world could explode, or because Manhattan could sink into the sea. Real fears. His paintings were glowing beneath the bright lights. A handful of people filtered in and out, sipping champagne from plastic cups. Already there was something foreign about his paintings, as if they were the work of someone else, a man he used to know, an acquaintance from a distant episode in his life. There was nothing special about them, he decided. They exist, as I exist, and that is all.

The grandiose illusion of the exile is that they are all back home, your enemies and your friends, voyeurs all, watching you. Everything has gained importance because you are away. Back home, your routines were only that. Here, they are portentous, significant. They have the weight of discovery. Can they see me? In this city, this cathedral? In this New York gallery? Never mind that it was nearly empty, and a hundred blocks from the neighborhoods where art was sold. Not for himself, but for their benefit, Wari would manufacture the appropriate amount of excitement. Make them all happy. I'm doing it, Ma, he'd say over the static. It's a bad connection, but I know now everything will be alright.

Afterwards, Eric and Leah took Wari out for drinks with some friends. He could tell they felt bad, as if they had let him down. Eric complained about student apathy. Lack of engagement, he called it. His department was in disarray, he said, they hadn't done a very good job of advertising. Leah nodded in solemn agreement. It was all words. Nothing Wari said could convince his host that he really didn't care. *I used you,* he wanted to say. *I'm not a painter any more.* But that seemed so cruel, so ungrateful, and still untrue.

'Is no problem,' he repeated over and over. 'We have good time.'

'Yes, yes, but still… I feel *bad.*'

Americans always feel bad. They wander the globe carrying this opulent burden. They take digital photographs and buy folk art feeling a dull disappointment in themselves, and in the world. They bulldoze forests with tears in their eyes. Wari smiled. He wanted to say he understood, that none of it was Eric's fault. It's what had to happen. He took Eric's hand. 'Thank you,' Wari said, and squeezed.

The bar was warm and lively. The televisions broadcasted baseball games from a dozen cities. Eric's friends congratulated Wari, clapped him on the back. '*Muy bien!*' they shouted gregariously. They wouldn't let him spend a single dollar. They bought round after round, until the lights from the beer signs were blurred neon arabesques. Wari felt it nearly impossible to understand a single word of their shouted conversations. There was a girl, a woman who kept making eyes at him. She was slight and had a fragile goodness to her. Wari watched her whisper with Leah, and they looked his way and smiled. He smiled back.

'I liked your paintings very much,' she said later. The night was winding down. Already a few people had left. Leah and Eric had separated from the group. They kissed each other and laughed and, by the way they looked into each other's eyes, Wari could tell they were in love. It made him feel silly.

He was ignoring the woman in front of him. 'Thank you,' he said.

'They're so violent.'

'I do not intend that.'

'It's what I saw.'

'Is good you see this. Violence sometime happen.'

'I'm Ellen,' she said.

'Is nice name. My ex-wife name Elie.'

'You're Wari.'

'I am.'

'How long will you stay?'

'I have 10 more days on the visa,' Wari said.

'Oh.'

'But I do not know.'

There were more drinks and more intimate shouting over the cacophony of the bar. Ellen had a sweet smile and lips he could see himself kissing. His hand had fallen effortlessly on her knee. In the corner of the bar, Leah and Eric kissed again and again. *How long will you stay I do not know. HowlongwillyoustayIdonotknow.* Wari wanted to drop his glass on the floor, but he was afraid it wouldn't shatter. He was afraid no one would applaud, no one would understand the beauty of that sound. The days were vanishing. Then he was in the street and Ellen was teaching him how to hail a cab. You have to be aggressive, she said. Does she think we don't have cabs, he wondered, shocked, does she think we ride mules? Just as quickly, he didn't care. She meant nothing by it. He could feel the planet expanding, its details effaced. Who is this woman? What city is this? The evening was warm, and the sky, if you looked straight up, was a deep indigo. They were downtown. His head was swimming in drink. I should call my mother, he thought, and tell her I'm alive. I should call Elie and tell her I'm dead.

They stood on the street corner. Cab after yellow cab rolled past Wari's outstretched arm. He was no good at it. Wari turned to find Ellen in a daze, gazing down the avenue.

'They were there, you know. Just right there.' Ellen said. She reached for his hand.

They were quiet. She pointed with two fingers in the direction of the southern horizon, toward the near end of the island, and Wari stared at a yawning space in the sky, a wide and hollow nothing.

Daniel Alarcón is a novelist and journalist who was born in Lima, Peru, and now lives in New York, US. His first book, *War by Candlelight*, was honored by the 2006 PEN/Hemingway Foundation Award. His debut novel *Lost City Radio* was published in 2007 and his most recent novel, *At Night We Walk in Circles*, was a finalist for the 2014 PEN Faulkner Award.

MANSOURA EZ-ELDIN
Egypt

LIGHT RAIN

From now on, it was going be different if you wanted, from now on we would be two people coming on rainy nights. Maybe it would turn out better that way, or at least we would be two people on rainy nights.

Julio Cortazar, from 'Meeting with Red Circle', a story inspired by a painting of the same name by the Venezuelan artist Jacobo Borges.

She found herself in the lavish airport of a foreign city with two colleagues on a business trip. The pace was rapid and people were scurrying as if their lives depended on the speed of their step. Various languages wrangled to occupy the surrounding space. She was struck by a heavy feeling of tension while her colleagues shot nervous glances. They seemed like they were ignoring her presence deliberately. Like her, they were confused, even if they tried to imitate the assured, brisk pace of other passengers. Suddenly, they disappeared from her field of vision. This did not provoke in her the least bit of fear or surprise.

'There must be a way to get to Wiesbaden!' she murmured.

She kept muttering the name: it seemed so strange. 'Wiesbaden? Why do I have to go there?' She couldn't think of a good answer.

She called to mind what she knew about the city. She only knew that it was in Germany, and that it featured in a story she loved by Julio Cortazar. It concerned Jacobo, whom the ghost of an English woman resembling a platypus tried to warn about an inevitable fate inside an empty Balkan restaurant on a rainy night in Wiesbaden. The story ended up with them both becoming ghosts waiting on rainy nights.

Thanks to dear Cortazar, the city had been transformed in her imagination into a geographical realm inhabited by ghosts trying to rescue potential victims from the clutches of steel-nerved killers who hid in a quiet restaurant lit by candles emanating a faint glow. Just the thought that Wiesbaden was her next destination was enough to send a chill through her body, as if she were the next victim looking for Jacobo and the platypus to save her.

In a short, colorful dress and stiletto high heels, she walked on the airport's shiny floor. Her steps tried to project assurance and left behind an annoying echo. Meanwhile, she was preoccupied and confused about the shortest route to Wiesbaden.

Passing through a corridor, she emerged on a set of intersecting metallic passageways. She didn't know how she had reached this point, even though she had followed the guide signs that were supposed to lead her to the train station attached to the airport.

She was alone in that forest of passageways. The impact of her steps on the metallic floor became unbearable. Her heart began to beat faster. There was no other person in this void.

Then the train station disappeared, along with the airport and its rushing passengers. She was left alone thinking that she was confined in a void. She continued walking haphazardly until she found herself in the depths of a dimly lit old warehouse full of junk and old scrap. The sound of gunfire and the smell of burning filled the space as if the whole world were on fire outside.

She spotted a steel door corroded with rust and she pushed on it. It swung open, and she went out – only to find herself in her home city, which had turned into a giant trap tarnished by thick white smoke.

The roads were packed with police officers and riot police. Security checkpoints closed off the entrances to streets, and armored vehicles encircled every inch. Nearby, a hefty 50-year-old woman in black clothes carried a bag of fruit, vegetables and loaves of fresh bread as if life were continuing as normal. She looked sullenly at a cordon of riot police. She grumbled and then raised her voice in outrage: 'Is it a war, or was there a war?!'

The woman continued on her way, thinking that she had done her share of protesting. They ignored her while they waited behind their riot shields, cautiously expectant and armed to the teeth.

Shouts and clamor could be heard from afar. The whole city was submerged in a pungent fog. She looked away from the heavy-set woman and tried not to look the soldiers and officers in the eye.

She began to run and the world expanded as old walls collapsed. It was as if she were the heroine of a computer game. She began to advance from level to level, the risk increasing with each step up. She would cross a checkpoint only to face one that was more difficult to pass. She snuck through a side street to another street even more tucked away in search of a route to the heart of events. However, a hail of bullets forced her to take cover in the entrance of a building.

She was not now wearing her colorful, short dress or her high heels that had made an annoying sound. She was now wearing tight jeans, a brown leather jacket, sneakers, and a *keffiyeh* around her neck. The airport and the metal maze became just another part of an evasive reality.

She thought of the name of the German town and shook her head languidly while contemplating the area around her. 'I'm not in Cortazar's story but in real life,' she thought.

There were no empty streets here, no pervading silence nor rainy night, but rather an area baptized in blood and blazing under mad bombing. The whole city had become a red circle packed with people letting out chants of outrage, encircled by violent men in dark uniforms.

She was no longer alone. She was now in a large crowd, a fleck in a river, a speck of sand in a burning desert. And yet she felt intensely alone. The crowd gathered in the streets, scattered under the pressure of attacks, and then regrouped.

A memory leaped to mind of herself as a questioning child with long brown hair, climbing barefoot up a flaming hot heap of sand. She stepped on the sun-scorched sand and it burned her. She lifted one foot and then the other to relieve the burn, but it was of no use.

She had to cross a vast expanse of sand after losing her shoes. She ran away in fear from a lost dog that chased her a little and then turned back, content just to watch after she left her shoes behind her.

At the top of the hill, she sat down to relax, unable to think of anything but the pain invading her from the burning sand. At the time, she was not thinking of what she would say to her mother, or of how far away she was from home. She closed her eyes and conjured up the nearby Nile as it is when it recedes in winter. She imagined herself a fleck in the water or a grain of the hill's sand, at one with her surroundings.

She immersed herself in that moment and no longer thought of anything else. Later on, after an intensive search, her family found her unconscious with sunstroke. They were worried about her and thought that she was in a critical condition, but she kept her calm smile even while she was sleeping and unable to move.

Now, years later, she was again evading the death that lurked nearby.

She coughed and cried in spite of herself, but she did not stop chanting. A marvellous buzzing sounded in her ears, as if all the world's chants throughout history were hovering around her.

She no longer remembered anything about Jacobo, the platypus, or the rainy night in Wiesbaden. The white fog grew thicker until it engulfed the horizon. A scent of burning clung to parts of the air. Frenzied trucks ran over dozens of people, and rubber fragments pierced bodies.

She left the entrance of the building and entered a narrow passageway between two streets, almost tripping on empty gas canisters. She ignored the pain in her leg and trudged on.

She dragged her leg behind her, which was now nothing but a burden, and continued on her way. Most of the shops were closed and the buildings had securely locked their gates, protecting their residents inside, some of whom began to peek with nervous curiosity from balconies or through stealthy windows at what was happening outside. Others tried to help by throwing water bottles or anything else they deemed effective onto those below, while the rest stayed holed up inside as if the building were a tender womb protecting them from the terrors outside.

She kept walking over fragmented sidewalks. Her eyes were aching and her feet could no longer support her weight. Encountering a hostile crowd, she hugged tight to a nearby metal door and found that it was unlocked. She went inside to find herself back in the dimly lit, abandoned warehouse. She scanned the room in despair for a place to rest. Eventually, she lay down on the ground and began to hover in the dark until she closed her eyes and sank into a rainy night in a cold city.

The rattle of gunfire outside seemed to her like a movie soundtrack framing the world around her. She saw herself walking under a drizzle in a foreign city with a person she didn't know – although he looked like Jacobo as she imagined him. She was more beautiful than ever, beautiful like her idea of beauty. Various scenes from her tumultuous day passed before her eyes. She heard footsteps with a metallic clang following her but, turning around, she found only nothingness. The reflection of streetlamps appeared on the rain-sodden sidewalk, which stretched out into the distance in a shimmering bolt of light.

Mansoura Ez-Eldin is an Egyptian novelist and journalist. She published her first collection of short stories, *Flickering Light*, in 2001. This was followed by three novels, *Maryam's Maze* in 2004, *Beyond Paradise* in 2009 and *Emerald Mountain* in 2014. Her work has been translated into a number of languages, including an English translation of *Maryam's Maze* by American University in Cairo Press, which came out in 2007. In 2009, she was selected for the Beirut39, as one of the 39 best Arab authors below the age of 40. *Beyond Paradise* was shortlisted for the prestigious Arabic Booker prize in 2010 and has been translated into Italian (Piemme-Mondadori, 2011) and German (Unions Verlag, 2011). *Emerald Mountain* won the award for best Arabic novel at the 2014 Sharjah International Book Fair. Her second short-story collection, *The Path to Madness*, was published in 2013 and won the award for best Egyptian collection of short stories from the 2014 Cairo International Book Fair. 'Light Rain' is a previously unpublished story translated from the original Arabic.

AMINATTA FORNA
Scotland/Sierra Leone

BITTER KOLA

My mother told me: 'Before you are married keep both eyes open and after you are married close one eye.' But when I was young I closed my ears instead. I refused to listen to my mother. All I wanted was to get as far away from her as I could, you understand? And so I did the very opposite. I knew that in so doing I might hurt myself, but it mattered more that I hurt her.

Where to begin? I gave myself away. That's the beginning and end of the same story, the whole story, start and finish. Not to become a first wife, no. Nor even a second. I threw myself away to become some man's third wife. And would you think perhaps that man came from a ruling family, or was rich, or respected, or held an honorable position in the men's society? I would understand why you might think so.

But, no. It's true to say Osman Iscandari was none of those things.

After I married I learned a lot. I did not learn so much about men – after all, Osman Iscandari was not all men. Rather I learned about myself. I learned about us. I learned about women – how we are made into the women we become, how we shape ourselves, how we shape each other.

The day I married I rode to my husband's home on a maka carried by four makamen dressed in tunics and trousers edged with green and round felt hats with long, black tassels. They jogged barefoot. At times lifting me up over roots and stumps, at other times raising me high above their shoulders as they waded through streams. I lay back and dreamed in the silence. The makamen were graceful as mimes. I admired this about them as I swung under the shade of the canopy towards the border of our chiefdom: away from my home and towards a new life with my husband.

Behind me came the load bearers carrying the luxuries bought with my bride gift – a bride gift so great it was the talk of the town. That was how everyone knew that this man loved me, from the day he came to put kola.

For days I begged my father – out of my mother's hearing – until I persuaded him to receive Osman. On my beloved's second visit I wore the new tamule and lappa he had sent for me. I stood behind my father's chair and gazed at him, unable to believe my own good fortune.

At the crossroads that marked the border the makamen lowered me to the ground. I climbed to my feet, gathering my gown up in both hands. My husband's makamen were waiting for me. Their uniforms were a little shabby: short trousers and striped shirts like a football team. Still, I determined not to let this bother me. Instead I settled on to the bed and arranged the folds of my yellow gown in a way I thought made me look elegant. The edges of the gown were scalloped and embroidered with butterflies. My mother thought I had made a foolish decision. Still, she would never allow anyone to say she had not sent a daughter to her husband in the proper manner. Early in the morning she had roused me to begin preparations. Kaolin from the river bank had made my complexion soft and even. Oil scented with lemon grass had been massaged into my skin and left my body gleaming. The soles of my feet buffed smooth. The edges of my hands and feet painted with henna to highlight the contrast of my palms and my soles with my skin. My teeth shone white from chewing egboka leaves, so bitter they numbed my tongue and left me barely able to taste a single dish of my wedding breakfast.

And when she had finished dressing me my mother placed the brocade sash over my shoulder and stepped back, nodded and left the room.

Now I smiled to myself. I imagined the expression on my husband's face when he saw me for the first time. No longer a girl, but a woman.

I lay back, propping myself up on one elbow so that I could see where we were going. It wasn't easy to do. The maka rocked so vigorously from side to side. I thought nothing of it: we were on an underused path. As we neared the town the paths would broaden and the makamen find their stride. I tried not to think too much about how crushed my gown was becoming; I concentrated instead on the sky and the ever-changing patterns in the canopy of trees.

I was thrown out of my reverie by a sharp pain.

'Be careful!'

No reply. I tried to sit upright but my arms were pinned down by the steep sides of the hammock. The rocking and jostling persisted. I began to feel nauseous, saliva flooded my mouth. I struggled so hard I all but tipped out of the hammock. The makamen came to a halt and stood watching me as I tottered to the side of the path. There, in one great heave, I deposited my wedding breakfast into the undergrowth.

And so this was how I arrived at my husband's home: my wedding gown flecked with vomit and my breath sour. Not that I need have worried. My husband was not there; in his place a message to say he was away on business. Many days passed before he returned.

In the beginning I refused to see what was in front of my face. I saw a big house with many rooms. I did not notice that it was empty as a cave, with plain walls and no furniture. I ignored the chickens that ran freely through the house, dropping their chalky turds. I failed to notice the cockroaches hiding in the crack between the door frames and the mud walls, flattening their skeletons to fit into the tiny space. I did not see the way the hill at the back rose abruptly up out of the earth, engulfing the house in its long shadow. I let my eyes pass over the bitch that lay in the sun, with swollen teats and dried blood under her tail. And I mistook the silence of my two co-wives for acceptance.

They were all signs and there would be more, surfacing one by one, floating in front of me like flotsam from a shipwreck. Even when I was drowning I dismissed them all, first with foolishness, then with pride, and finally because I had put out my own eyes with hot pokers of shame.

From the beginning my face wore a happy expression and I forced myself to act the same way. When my husband returned I knew I had been right. I saw again how handsome he was: he had only to utter my name for me to shiver – a shiver that started behind my heart, trickled down my spine, crept up the back of my neck. Any time he called me I dropped whatever I was doing and ran to him. When he praised my cooking I was in ecstasy. Each morning I woke up and told myself how lucky I was. And for a long time I believed it. The bad feeling in my heart was overtaken by another feeling, a fluttering and leaping from somewhere below my belly, like a fish jumping on a hot pan.

Maybe this is something you don't want to hear. You pity us, not so? You think we don't have the same feelings as you – because of what was taken away, that we are dead down there. No desire. We come together with a man without pleasure. You see how hard it is for me to talk about these things: we are sworn to secrecy. And so we bear your contempt. But there are some things that should be said. So that you, at least, understand. Because you are our daughter. Listen.

For us it was something special: the gifts, the food – delicacies to eat whenever you want – friendships made that last for ever, singing and dancing, the company of women. For the rest of your life, wherever you are, when you are lost or alone, you may start to sing one of those songs and, when you hear the voice of another woman join in the refrain, you know that woman is your sister. For all of us it was the first time we had been away from our mothers. That part was hard, even for me. I missed her.

That first night: sitting in the cold stream with the other girls, chewing on bitter herbs and waiting for the moment when your name was called. The circle of holes in the earth, filling up with blood. One by one. What you remember afterwards is not the pain. That is forgotten, like the pain of giving birth. No, what I remember most was the sound of a blade cutting through my own flesh. Such an ordinary sound, like a cook cutting through the flap of a chicken wing.

My mother had said to me: 'When it is over you stand up and you walk.' I promised myself I would do that. I pushed a cloth hard between my thighs. My legs trembled. I gasped for air. The pain rose in waves, crashing into me. I concentrated only on one thing – walking away from that place. One step at a time. One foot in front of the other.

Twice we are made women. For the first time when we are initiated. And the second time when we go to our husband's room. With Osman there was tenderness, yes. And pleasure, too. I wanted to go to him. I longed for it.

Osman came and went a great deal leaving me with plenty of time to myself. I was waiting to conceive. Not so easy with a husband who is never there. Balia and Ngadie, my co-wives, had their own children. Balia's children had left home, except the youngest who was already able to help her with the cooking. Ngadie had two. A girl and a boy, who were so alike I could barely tell one from the other, they flitted about silent as shadows.

I began to dream of my own children who were waiting to be born. Of course I must have sons to take care of me when I was old, but most of all I longed for a daughter – a girl whose face I might look in to see my own secrets. I began to choose names, then worried it might bring bad luck. I picked leaves from the gbono gbono tree and stirred them into my cooking so that, with God's blessing, I might fall pregnant the next time Osman was home.

There was less to do in this place than in Rofathane. There was a well for water and only a small vegetable plot. Osman earned money working as a road inspector. The colonials were busy building roads and railways up and down the country. To the big mines and down to the coast where ships waited to carry the loads away. Osman talked a lot about his job and with pride. The new roads were built of tar and as smooth as the floors in a house. People liked to spread their laundry out upon them to dry, as well as their rice and grain. Osman told me how he confiscated their washing, threatening to burn it, and swept the grain away.

Balia and Ngadie's daily routine did not alter to include me. I had no chores. Well, I didn't mind. Wasn't I the lucky one? I'd heard the tales of junior wives who found themselves pounding rice late into the night, minding other wives' small children, working long hours in the vegetable plot. With so little to do I spent my time on petty vanities. When I grew bored of those I began to look around me, searching for ways to distract myself.

A wasp with black and yellow-striped forelegs building a nest held me captive for a long time as I watched her rolling tiny balls of mud from the edge of a puddle and flying away with them to build a nest in the branches of a tree. Another day I noticed the funnel-shaped spiders' webs that blossomed in the grass every morning, sparkling with dew and lit by the sun. On another afternoon it was the fluttering black crest and blue feathers of a plantain eater – hopping up and down next to his nest, calling for his mate to come back. 'Kooroo kooroo ko ko ko ko.'

Gradually I began to notice other things.

Early in the morning I gazed out of my window. There was Ngadie walking towards the house from the direction of the grain store. The next morning I saw her again, and the next. I wondered what she could be doing there so early. The way she walked, with a great deliberateness, placing one foot in front of the other, like a person walking on the ridge between fields of crops. She didn't notice me watching her.

The next morning I woke before the light. I hurried down and hid behind the grain store. After a short time Ngadie passed by, eyes darting from side to side to see who was watching. I slipped in behind her, followed her along the path into the forest. She stepped off the path, I stepped quickly back into the trees opposite. Once, twice she glanced over her shoulder. I waited before I switched my hiding place and had her again within my sights. I waited and watched.

Ngadie stepped up to a tall palm tree, reached up and scored the trunk three times with the blade of the knife. Sap poured from the wound. Ngadie dipped her fingers into it and raised them to her lips. She tied a gourd to the trunk beneath the flow. From higher up she took down a second gourd and from the way she braced her body, I could tell how heavy it was. This she lifted to her lips. She raised her head and for an instant seemed to stare right at me. I held my breath. The seconds passed. She lifted the gourd a second time and I relaxed. When she lowered it I saw her upper lip was crested with foam.

In the days and weeks that followed I noticed how often Ngadie slipped away. And how when she came back she lifted her feet a fraction too high and put them down carefully.

I was pregnant. I was eating a mango. The mango dripped with yellow juice and sticky goodness. I was enjoying it so much I worked my way right down to the seed and sucked the last juice from the hairy flesh that clung there. The liquid trickled down my chin. Some of the strands became caught between my teeth and I stopped to pick them out. It was then I noticed Osman watching me. Recently I had often looked up to find his eyes upon me in this way. I was sure it was because he loved me and was proud of me. I smiled at him. To show how happy I was. Osman continued to look at me. He did not return my smile. He stood up and he walked away.

For some time Osman had not called me to his room. Because I was expecting a child, I thought. I didn't worry. One night, for no particular reason, I woke from a deep sleep. I lay on my back – it was difficult to sleep any other way – and I listened to the music of the raindrops dripping from the eaves of the house, striking the leaves of trees, splashing on to the ground. My eyes were closed. The noise of the rain was immense. I laid a hand on my stomach and rubbed my belly button, imagining the baby curled up inside. I was beginning to doze again when I felt the bedclothes being dragged from my body.

'Yai!' I screamed. I was being attacked by a night devil.

It wasn't a djinna. It was Osman.

'Get up!' he told me. I hastened to do as he said.

'What is it?' I asked. 'What's happening?' I tried to imagine what emergency had brought him here in the middle of the night. Osman came up close to me. Very close. He did not touch me. He sat down on the edge of the bed and was silent. I waited. My heart beat louder than the rain on the roof. It must be something very serious indeed. Then he told me to remove my clothes. I stared at him through the darkness. I wondered if I had heard correctly.

I was told a woman should never say no to her husband. 'Osman, it's late,' I began, 'and I'm sleeping.'

My husband stood up suddenly. As dark as it was, I could see his features flex. He inhaled deeply. I saw the gleam of his teeth as he smiled. I relaxed a little. When he spoke, his tone matched mine. 'Please don't disobey me. You promised you would be a good wife to me. Isn't that what you promised?' I was standing in front of him. He reached up and caressed my cheek.

I nodded, yes, I wanted to be a good wife. I was a good wife. But I was tired. Also, Osman was behaving so strangely.

He slid both hands down my arms until he had his hands in mine, whispering: 'Come, come, little one.' Still I protested. Osman's tone changed abruptly. 'I have only so much patience for this foolishness, Asana.'

There my protests ended. Osman's manner made me hesitate. Perhaps this was something between husbands and their wives that I did not understand.

In one way nothing happened that night, by which I mean Osman did not touch me. He made me stand in front of him until the rain stopped. He stared at my body, at my breasts, my belly, down below. The clouds passed from in front of the moon to reveal his expression. I was reminded of a time when I was a child and we came across the stiffened corpse of a dead dog. The eyes were gone. The lips were shrivelled, baring gums and teeth. We stared at it, prodding it with sticks – as fascinated as we were revolted.

My body was changing, it was true. My breasts were hard and taut. My nipples protruded. So, in time, did my belly button – popped out like a bubble. Veins coursed like underground rivers beneath my skin. Often I found myself flushed and covered in a sheen of sweat. I did not mind. I loved my body and its little store of surprises. Every morning I oiled my stomach and polished it until it shone, dark and round as a seed pod.

The first few times, Osman stared at me, nothing more. Sometimes he made me turn away. A rustling sound, Osman's breath came thick and fast. As my pregnancy advanced he made me stand for longer. My feet swelled, I nearly unbalanced. I was shivering and naked. I begged him to let me sleep. There came a time when the tiredness overtook the fear and I sank to the floor.

'Get up!' Osman's voice was low. It occurred to me he did not want anyone to hear us.

'No, Osman. It's enough now.'

'What? Don't you answer me back. Who do you think you are? You are my wife.'

'Yes. Your wife who is pregnant – with your child. If you want your child to be born healthy then leave me alone and let me sleep.'

My tone of voice I knew was too strong. My mother had warned me of this. I had begun to feel contempt for Osman. I couldn't help myself, I added:

'Look at yourself, Osman. What kind of man behaves this way?'

Osman stood over me. He reached down and seized my arm, tried to haul me to my feet. I let myself go limp. My weight was almost beyond his strength. Above me I could feel his rage massing, but I didn't care any more. Who was this man? Not the one I had married. Osman continued to tug at me as I sprawled on the floor.

An image leaped unbidden into my mind. Of the two of us in the middle of the night, fighting like children. Maybe I was on the verge of hysteria. I think probably I was. I couldn't help it. I laughed. A short, high-pitched shriek. The sound of the laugh sounded funny to my ears. I laughed again. I found I couldn't stop. Osman let go of me. Good, I thought. I started up from the floor. Then he kicked me. The blow landed on my buttock and set my whole body quivering. I fell forward on to my knees. Now I was on all fours. Before I could get up, he kicked me again at the base of my spine.

At first I was too angry and my anger made me stubborn. I clamped my mouth shut and held on to my screams. Osman grasped my hair, swung my head around and slapped me. I tried to crawl away from him, naked on my hands and knees. There was nowhere to go. Instead I crawled around the room as he aimed blows at me. His panting grew hoarse as he wore himself out on me. In the end I allowed him to win.

I let the tears flow. I begged him to stop.

And I opened my eyes.

And when they were finally open I learned a lot about my husband in a short time.

Osman Iscandari. Only son of his mother, a woman with a cat's cry for a voice who wore two strings of prayer beads wrapped in her headdress, a third looped around her wrist. Always sick. Always complaining her body was too warm or too cold. When she came to visit I saw the way she watched her son's face all day, waiting for his expression to change so she could jump up and fetch him a bowl of roasted groundnuts or a sweet potato cake or offer to rub his head. When we gathered to eat in the evening she picked out all the best pieces of meat from the stew and gave them to Osman. At night she sat on the verandah with his head in her lap, braiding his hair.

My husband had three sisters who were married and lived nearby, but rarely did I see them come to visit their brother. And when the youngest one of the sisters did call, I noticed the way she spoke little, only answering: 'Yes, brother,' and did not look Osman in the eye or stay to eat.

And I saw how Balia flinched when Osman raised his arm just as she bent to place a footstool underneath his feet. And I saw the way Osman smirked when he looked at her and reached slowly across himself to scratch his armpit.

Finally I noticed the way the little bitch who came to beg for scraps disappeared every time our husband was at home.

Ngadie brushed her mouth with the back of her hand and stepped back on to the path, casually – as though she had just been wandering around in the bush, in whatever ordinary way a person might wander about in the bush. She started when I called her name. I ran to catch her up. Not so easy, I held my belly with one arm and my breasts with the other.

'Wait!' I caught her arm and swung her around to face me. She glared at me.

'Let go! What's wrong with you?' She sucked her teeth: a slow, sliding sound of scorn. I did not reply. Instead I reached out and touched her face. Ngadie reared back, but I had hold of her arm. I stretched out as if to wipe a fleck of froth from the corner of her mouth. There was nothing there, but only I knew that. She was close enough for me to smell the palm wine on her breath. Her eyes held mine, yet I could see she was scanning the edges of her vision, like a dog with a stolen chicken in its jaws.

I paused. What to do next? I hadn't thought this far. I had waylaid Ngadie without knowing what it was I wanted to ask. What had I done in marrying Osman? I searched for the words and while I did so I saw the thoughts cross Ngadie's face like clouds drifting across the sky while she made up her mind what to do.

In the event Ngadie spoke first: 'So now you know. And you want to know what else there is? Isn't it?'

I nodded. I let go of her arm.

Ngadie rubbed at the place in an exaggerated sort of way. Still, she made no move to go: 'When you first arrived I looked at you. So pleased with yourself. I wondered how long it would take.' I dipped my head. 'Every time he brings one into our house he tells Balia how he is tired of us, we have no fire. Though only God and the three of us know how we came to be that way. Osman despises us. But he doesn't understand anything, he doesn't even understand the kind of man he is.'

I learned that I was not the first. There had been others.

Listening to Ngadie was like gazing at a landscape you have grown accustomed to. Only when you look at it properly you see something you had not noticed before: a termite mound like a silent sentry, a tree slowly dying, an abandoned colony of birds' nests. Ngadie and Balia, so much older. Many years had passed since the youngest of their children had been weaned.

'One of them he complained was disobedient. Told her family to come and collect her. Another one he claimed was not a virgin and that he had paid such and such amount for her bride price. Said the family let him believe it was the case. I don't know. They were quick to settle with him. The shame.' She waved a hand. Her voice was gentler now.

I was silent. Almost as an afterthought Ngadie added that she was sure Osman had other women upline who cooked for him. Otherwise there was really no reason to stay away so long.

'What am I to do?' I asked her.

Ngadie frowned and peered at me as if seeing me properly for the first time. She shrugged, her voice was brisk once more: 'What you do is up to you.' And she turned and walked away slowly down the path towards the big, empty house. Not once did she turn or look back at me.

Oh, what a fool I had been! I had stuffed my ears with straw. I had closed my eyes, refusing to see what a bad husband I was choosing for myself. I thought about my mother. What might she say? That I had been deceived by nobody but myself. The anger between us ran cold and it sprang from a place far, far back. I could not bring myself to go to her and beg.

Even in my despair I was not ready to own my mistake, I was caught in a swirling eddy, drowning, with nothing to clutch on to except my pride. I determined I would deal with Osman in my own way.

I pondered these matters as I sat on the back step. In front of me Balia's daughter caught a chicken and prepared to slit its throat with a knife. The bird was squawking, feathers fluttering. I remembered how in the village we used to wring their necks – something that had to be learned. You had to exercise a little patience, let the bird be lulled while you got a good grip. Outside the town, in a place known only as Slaughter, I had seen a Fula slay a great bull, slicing its throat with the blade as gently as if he was caressing his sweetheart.

This house I was living in contained more than one kind of hell, and I had just thought of a way to deal with one of them.

Several weeks passed. Osman came and went. When he was at home he would enter my room as he pleased and force me to play my part in his monstrous game. I offered no resistance. As the days passed Osman gradually relaxed, believing he had mastered me.

One night he fell asleep on my bed. I crept in next to him and we stayed that way until dawn.

A few days later, in the early hours of the morning, I lay awake and watched Osman. Behind the lids I could see the bulge of his eyeball, the iris trembling as he dreamed. At the corner of his mouth a bubble of spit swelled and subsided. His chest rose as he drew in shuddering breaths. In his sleep his lips curved upwards.

'Osman,' I whispered. 'Osman.' My husband jerked slightly, his mouth twitched. He turned his shoulder away. 'Wake up, Osman. Wake up.'

I let a few beats pass. Gently I shook his shoulder, taking care not to rouse him too quickly. I rocked him, whispering his name until his eyes stilled and the lids cracked open. He uttered a groan and softly sighed.

Again: 'Osman, Osman!' His eyelids opened a fraction further.

'Asana? Eh, Asana. What is it?' he mumbled, his lips struggling with the effort of forming the words, wanting to stay in the dream. The next moment his eyelids began to flutter and close as he slipped back under.

'Osman,' I said. 'Wake up and see. See what I have for you!' I groped the floor until my fingers closed around the handle of the knife. I held it up, allowing the blade to glow in the silver light. I put my lips very close to his ear, brushing the lobe. I made my voice gentle, coaxing. Osman's eyes opened. I put the blade up under his chin: the tip made a soft indentation in the flesh. 'You see what can happen, Osman? So strong but what good do your muscles do you now?' I felt his body slowly stiffen.

I laid my cheek on the pillow, let the knife down slowly and slipped it out of sight. I lay quietly. Waiting.

It happened just as I hoped. Moments later Osman sat bolt upright. He leaped from the bed. He was naked, flailing. A little deranged, really, when I set my mind back to thinking about it. Next he bent over and peered at me closely. I let my eyes open, I gazed back at him, I reached up and stroked his cheek. 'What's the matter, husband?' I asked, as though I was greatly concerned. All the time his puzzlement grew. 'What is it, Osman? Is something the matter?' I reached up, took his hand in mine and drew him back to the bed. 'A dream, that's all. Just a dream. Go back to sleep, now.' Osman hesitated and then sat down heavily. I rolled over and pretended to sleep. After a while I felt him lie down, a long way from me, right on the other side of the bed.

From that night and for the remainder of my pregnancy Osman never touched me again. I congratulated myself heartily on my cunning. I lay back on my bed and buffed my belly with Vaseline petroleum jelly.

Osman Iscandari, I chuckled, *ng ba kerot k'bana, kere ng baye erith.*

You have a big penis, but you have no balls.

My daughter arrived, as had I, at the close of the rains. Unlike me she took her time coming into this world. I bore it. After the birth my mother praised me. Nobody would ever have known a woman was giving birth in this house. At night she took the baby to her bed to let me rest, carrying her to me when she needed to feed. Still, in the hours in between I found I missed my daughter already. I could not sleep, I could not wait to hold her again. I crept into the room and lifted her from where she slumbered in the crook of my mother's body.

Kadie was named for my grandmother, who had gone the year before. Through two rains I stayed in my mother's house while I suckled her. For hours at a time I might do nothing but gaze into my daughter's deep-water eyes, at the tiny blister on her upper lip that came from sucking; feel the way she gripped my finger with her toes when I held her feet. I examined the fine, sharp creases on the soles of those same feet and the palms of her hands. What fate, I wondered, was there awaiting her that had already been decided?

One morning unseen currents stirred the air beneath a troubled sky. A pale green glow lit the village. I sat at the front of my father's house. When I was growing up I could not imagine a world beyond this one. Change came slowly to this place. My father grew ginger now, orders from the colonials. My mother counted the money, complained about the fixed prices. She brought in extra labor to meet the demand. Above the coffee trees the hills receded in shades of grey, fading slowly into the sky. A kite spiralled down. I followed its descent through the air as gently as a leaf falling from a tree. I didn't hear my father's footfall.

'You'll be going home. As soon as your husband comes.' My father spoke in statements.

I replied: 'Perhaps, but this is my home, too.'

'*Te ting.* True. But a woman's duty is to be with her husband in his home and any day now he'll be here to take you back.' I was silent. My father waited a while before continuing. 'Of course you should make him win you again. But when he has done that you will accept him and you will go.' This is the way things were in those days. My father loved me, but for him duty came first. I could not think of running away from my marriage. I could never come home. He added gently: 'You will be missed here.'

I looked up at him, remembering how I used to ride on his shoulders, how I rode on his shoulders the day we came to this place to found the village. He spoiled me so much people called me his pet deer.

'Teh, teh,' he clapped his hands for Kadie, 'teh teh.' She weaved towards him, her hand reached for the piece of sesame cake he held out. He caught her and swung her into the air, grunting with the effort it cost him.

'Yes, father.'

Sometimes I wondered how my father knew things. Only days later Osman arrived, shaking the dust out of his clothes, struggling with a cardboard suitcase of gifts: cakes of blue soap, scented hair oil, two new head-ties and many yards of the finest-grade fabric. 'Yes, yes. Come and look! All imported,' he called for everyone to hear. Some of my father's younger children and even his wives gathered around, as though Osman was a travelling salesman and not a husband come to woo his wife back. Osman flung open the suitcase and showed off each item.

I didn't mind seeing him. He was handsome, as I remembered, even sweating under the weight of the suitcase. Despite myself I smiled as I walked down the steps of the house to greet him.

Osman Iscandari. I underestimated him. Seeing him arrive at my father's house to bring me back, the sweat rolling down from his scalp, his face shining like the moon, boasting – with that stupid grin carved into his face. When I walked up the street towards that house, that empty house lying in the shadow of the earth, I had no idea of what awaited me inside.

Fourteen, fifteen maybe. Pretty enough, I'll say that. The girl scuttled forward, bending low. She began to gather up my luggage. And my, she was strong as a bush cow. The cardboard suitcase she balanced on her head while she squatted to reach for the other bundles.

I did not speak. A cousin of Balia or Ngadie? Someone's ward? A servant, even? My senior wives had not come out to meet me. A drumming in my heart, in my ears. The light receded around the edges of my vision, as though I was staring down a bat-filled tunnel. I willed myself not to look at Osman. One step at a time, one foot in front of the other. My body was shaking. The house was empty. The girl emerged from my room, she smiled and held her hands out to Kadie. I kept a firm grip of my daughter's hand. The girl's lips trembled. At that moment I caught sight of Osman mocking me, grinning at this entertainment. Not the grin of a dullard. No, rather the smirk of a hyena.

'Ah, but let me introduce you, Asana.' The voice he used was offhand. 'This is Mabinty.' Before me the girl bowed her head and dropped into a curtsey.

And that was how I met my husband's newest wife.

Osman delighted in his triumph. He did not call me to his room. When I saw that girl – humming, wandering about, toying with some new bauble, smiling stupidly even at the chickens – I recognized myself, the way I too had been.

I contemplated my position – the third wife of a man who was of a lesser family than my own, yet who treated me with contempt. Replaced by a peasant girl brought back from one of his trips – in all likelihood given to him for the price of a sack of rice.

Osman did not care that he flaunted marriage customs. One, two, three nights he was with her. And then a fourth night. I began to wonder if I would ever lie with my husband again. I wanted more children, yes. But there was something else. I was ashamed to think of it. Despite myself I was gripped by a craving I could not quell. One morning I saw Osman sitting at the front of the house waiting for Mabinty to bring his shirt. Dressed only in his trousers, slippers half on his feet, naked to the waist. I found my eyes drawn to the spirals of hair scattered across his chest, the deep ridges of his stomach in which drops of sweat glistened, the dark trail that led down from his belly button and disappeared into the waistband of his trousers. He caught me watching him and quickly I looked away.

Liquid like melted moonlight: pale, opaque, translucent. Ngadie handed me the enamel mug, hitched up her skirts and sat down on a log. The palm wine had fermented in the heat of the day. It was strong and vinegary, faintly fizzy. I took a sip, and then another, felt the trickle of warmth reach my belly. All was quiet. We were far from the house in a small clearing surrounded by palm trees: raphia palms, oil palms, coconut palms. I had already tasted the wine from all three. When I was a child I had once tried the first sap, the juice collected early in the morning. It was sweet, clear and innocent to drink. Nothing like this. I sipped again.

Ngadie had once possessed a great beauty. The traces were there in the perfect symmetry of her lips; in the gap between her front teeth considered so desirable in a woman; in the dimple on her chin that was now no more than a smudge in the soft flesh. There was delicacy, too, in the turn of her wrist as she poured the palm wine. And regret in the trembling of her fingers.

I realized, watching her, that I did not know what her face looked like when she smiled. I had never heard her laugh. I took a kola nut, split it, and passed half to her. She hesitated, her eyes held mine for a moment. Then she accepted it and thanked me.

What had become of Osman's father? I asked. Ngadie paused, the edge of the cup rested on her lower lip.

'A great man,' she replied. 'Loved by his people.' Osman had not known his father. He had been a leader who defied the pothos when they came crowning chiefs. Osman's father was one who resisted. 'He warned his brothers not to trust the pothos. He told them no white man ever gave anything without wanting more in return. They didn't listen.' The leaders seized the gifts they were offered, signing away their lands and their power with a thumbprint. In return they were given a wooden staff with a brass handle and an upholstered chair bearing the arms of the potho queen. As for Osman's father, the pothos deposed him and gave his position to a man from a rival clan. He was forced to leave his people and went to live on the other side of the land. He died. Osman grew up in his mother's family, working on the land while the sons of the new chief grew fat. Osman resented his family's poverty terribly.

Ngadie told me there were many people who believed Osman's father had been right and those people also imagined Osman had inherited his father's spirit. They waited for him to come and lead them. Osman's mother shared this belief, but the truth was, the people waited in vain. Osman did not have the stomach to be a leader. He accepted their accolades but shunned the challenge.

Balia was the daughter of one of his father's closest advisors who had joined him in exile, betrothed to Osman when they were still children. As for Ngadie, Osman had seen her beauty and wanted her for himself. Ngadie rejected his advances but Osman bided his time. The day after her father's store of seed yams burned in a fire, Osman arrived with a proposal of marriage. Her father used the bride price to rebuild his barns.

I wondered silently how Ngadie and Balia could tolerate this empty life. Ngadie swilled the liquid in her cup and spoke as if in answer to my question: 'For me and Balia, it's over. If Osman leaves us alone – then all the better.'

In his return to form Osman made a daunting adversary. He relished my humiliation. He shamed me in public: for the way I dressed, the fashion in which I styled my hair, the expression on my face. In front of his uncles he ordered me to remove a dish of fourah cakes I had prepared, insisting they were not fit to serve to guests. The room fell silent. Osman's mother was quick to support her son.

'Useless girl. No good in the kitchen!' As for Ngadie and Balia, they averted their eyes when I passed. I pretended to myself it didn't matter. Osman made people think I was a bad wife, so what?

Kadie was asleep on the bed, curled and sucking her thumb. I sat on the floor and stared into the mirror. This was what I had become – a woman who existed only as what she saw reflected in the eyes of others. I was sorry for myself and sorry for the daughter I had brought to this place.

As the days passed I tried to avoid giving Osman a reason to belittle me. I spoke only when I was spoken to, I cooked several different dishes each night it was my turn to cook – chicken rolled in spices and roasted over an open fire, yams and hot-pepper soup, fried fish and cassava bread. The time came when if he deigned to taste even one of them I sighed with relief. All day I observed his face searching for signs that might alert me to his mood.

Do you see how I was becoming like all those other women – Osman's mother, his sisters, Balia, Ngadie? All I wanted to do was to avoid the pain of humiliation. Oh, how quickly that simple wish transformed into a desperation to please – so quickly I did not even see it happening in myself. My senses were numbed, I behaved like a sleepwalker. The days passed steadily, weeks turned into months. By that time I was treating Osman as a god.

Then came the morning when Osman told me I should come to his room that night. All that day, as I waited for the evening to come, I could not concentrate on the simplest task. Twice I burned the rice until Ngadie removed the pot from my hands and gently ushered me away from the cooking place. Kind Ngadie. The dish she cooked was one of Osman's favorites. That evening I claimed it as my own and watched as Osman ate two helpings, while I managed no more than a few mouthfuls. The next night and the next she did me the same kindness.

I lay in the bed with my arms down by my sides. The last time it had been so different. Before I was shy, yes – a new bride – and yet every movement was right. This time I reached across and touched him. 'I'm here,' I said.

How could I have known these things happened to men? I had been brought up to believe men were always in a state of desire. Our mothers told us to cover ourselves when we came back from bathing. In case a man should see us. There was even a plant that grew, that closed up when you touched it with your fingertips, sometimes all you had to do was breathe upon it and the tiny ferns came together and sealed like a pair of fans. *Bom mompneh runi ngang ang bek*, it was called. Cover yourself, there's a man coming. A woman's modesty and a man's desire were what made us different from each other. Yet I knew that I felt desire, even lying there next to the man I no longer loved.

That first night Osman rejected me I was wretched. I cannot tell you. Later, alone, I wept bitterly. Osman was ashamed, though he would not show it. The second night I slipped out of my gown and lay naked beside him; I tried to reassure him, stroking him gently. But Osman covered his own shortcomings by blaming me. I was too forward, he said. No modesty. On the third and final night, when it happened again, he pointed his finger at me and called me a witch.

The next night Osman spent with Mabinty. I sat on my bed. I did not sleep. I stared into the blackness, I tried to see my future but I could see nothing. In the morning my eyes were sore from lack of sleep, I breathed deeply and walked out to the cooking place to prepare breakfast for Kadie. At the door I stopped and stared. There was Mabinty, sitting on a stool, weeping and loudly blowing her nose on her head-tie.

I lost face and regained my life, but for many years I could not see it. Nor could I see who had helped me do it.

Osman thought it was his idea to end the marriage contract and so there was no question of reclaiming the bride gift. At first I was humiliated, thrown back to my family by my husband like a no-good fish tossed back into the water.

That was the way things were for us in those days. You, I hear you talking to your friends. You have so much, but you don't even know you are alive. We had to find the answers for ourselves, to fashion them out of the thin air and seize them from the sky.

I felt I had no choice but to remain Osman's third wife, to be treated by him in any way he pleased. I was a stupid girl who had jumped into her marriage with her eyes closed. Afterwards I could see nowhere to run. It took somebody else to open a door and push me out. And that person was Ngadie, once-beautiful Ngadie. In her own fate she could see the future that was waiting for me.

Later I learned to be grateful to her and to love her for what she had done. But in the beginning I was short-sighted, I could not see beyond my own shame to the great vista that stretched out in front of me.

After many years news came that Ngadie had died. For the first time I travelled back to the place where I had been a wife. Shadows still covered the house, nothing had changed. Balia greeted me with some warmth – to my surprise, Mabinty, too. Mabinty now with rings of flesh around her waist and her neck. I held no ill-feeling towards her. As for Osman, who rose from his chair on the verandah to meet me, brushing pumpkin-seed shells from the front of his shirt and spitting the bits out the corner of his mouth, I felt nothing. I greeted him cordially and the smile he gave me in return was surely all that remained of his blurred beauty.

Ngadie was already in the ground, fleetingly mourned – a woman insufficiently loved as a daughter, unloved as a wife.

But loved as a mother. And loved still. There were Ngadie's son and daughter. Ngadie in the male. Ngadie in the female. The him and the her, the he and the she of the woman I had known. I watched them. So alike. The only difference was the way the lines of their features had been drawn, finely traced in one, the other roughly sketched in charcoal.

On a stool at the back of the house I sat next to Ngadie's daughter, untied the corner of my lappa and took out a kola nut. I unwrapped the leaves, broke off a cotyledon – she accepted it in silence, turning the piece over and over in her hand. I glanced up at her, saw the teardrops gathering along the edge of her lower eyelid, waiting to fall.

'Hush ya,' was all I said. I laid my hand on her forearm.

I bit the kola nut and helped myself to a sip of water from the ladle at my side. The water tasted fresh and pure. It was the effect of the kola: even brackish water tasted as though it had sprung from a mountainside.

'My mother once said something about you, about how you loved kola. She said that to you even bitter kola was sweet.'

The words made no sense. One time I had split kola with Ngadie. After we had become friends. Of course it hadn't been bitter kola. There was bitter kola in the calabash containing my bride gift. Kola for the good times. Bitter kola to mark the bad.

Some days later I went home. I never returned to that place. The years slid past. I watched Kadie grow alongside the next generation of coffee trees, and I grew too. In this way slowly I found myself again. Memories of Ngadie, of her daughter's words, fell out of my mind. Not for any reason. Only because they seemed to be words spoken at a time of grief, wrongly remembered. I did not believe they held any meaning for me.

One day, I found myself passing down a street in a part of the town I had never been to before. The houses had two storeys, the streets were narrow. Two women were leaning out of the shuttered windows above me, drawing their washing in from the line that hung from one window to the next. Wisps of conversation fluttered down. The women were careless, not worrying if they were overheard.

'His tinder was wet.'

I heard the laughter that followed, coarse laughter. Shocking laughter. I walked on, the phrase wound itself after me, bringing back those awful nights – those last nights I shared with my husband when I had failed to arouse him. I remembered the state to which he had reduced me – so nervous I had burned the rice.

Ngadie had offered to cook.

Three nights in a row.

His tinder was wet.

To her even bitter kola is sweet.

You see, if I hadn't become lost, I never would have walked down that street. Nor heard a woman talk about her husband's performance in that vulgar way. That started me thinking. People believe that bitter kola has the power to wet a man's tinder. Did you know that? I thought about Ngadie, of how she had offered to cook for me on those three nights and I pondered the meaning of what she had said to her daughter.

Three nights in a row.

Maybe there was a reason things happened the way they did with Osman on those three nights.

In my seat in the poda poda I sat with my basket of shopping on my lap, crushed by other people's bodies, all the time turning the thoughts around and around in my head, the way I examine a pawpaw before I buy it in the market.

To her even bitter kola is sweet.

And I saw that it had been Ngadie's doing.

I laughed out loud: a laugh like the one I had just heard. I laughed until the tears poured down my cheeks. At first the people around me wondered what was my problem. But they saw my joy was real, I was no crazy person. My laughter even became infectious, people began to giggle and before long the whole bus was laughing without even knowing why.

And through the people's laughter I heard another sound that came from far away: the strains of a simple melody. It grew louder and louder, filling my head, pushing out all the bad feelings, the anger, the resentment that had been locked inside for so many years. I became quiet, I listened. Though I had never heard it before, there and then I recognized it. And it was beautiful. The sound of Ngadie laughing in her grave.

Aminatta Forna is a fiction writer and essayist and the award-winning author of the three novels *The Hired Man*, *The Memory of Love* and *Ancestor Stones*, and the memoir *The Devil that Danced on the Water*. Born in Scotland, she was raised in Sierra Leone and Britain and spent periods of her childhood in Iran, Thailand and Zambia. She is winner of a Windham Campbell Prize and the Commonwealth Writers Best Book Prize among others, and a finalist for the Orange Prize, IMPAC, Samuel Johnson, BBC Short Story Prize and Neustadt Prizes. She is currently a Lannan Visiting Chair of Poetics at Georgetown University in Washington, DC.

NAHID RACHLIN
Iran/United States

ON HER SIDE

Janet turned to her daughter and said, 'Emma, please, we're on vacation. Let's leave our worries behind.'

But Emma did not move from her position. She was staring out of the window at the airplane's wings cutting through fluffy white clouds. Her face was wet with tears. She had started to cry after arguing with her father. It was not so much the argument that had upset Emma, Janet sensed, but what Emma viewed as her father's lack of understanding of her point of view. When she was telling him and Janet that she and her boyfriend were having problems, her father had said, 'I don't like this whole dating system to begin with.'

He too was clearly upset judging from the way he had buried his head in *Sharg*, the Farsi-language magazine, as he sat in one of the seats in the center row next to theirs. Although it was 23 years since he had emigrated from Iran to the US, he still liked to read in Farsi.

In a moment he got up. 'I have to move around a bit.' He put the magazine into the pocket in front of his seat and walked down the aisle.

Janet took out a tissue from her purse and gave it to Emma. 'Please, honey, stop crying. Your Dad is very concerned about you because he loves you so much.'

'You and Dad are only into each other, I'm at the edge of this family,' Emma said. 'You always take his side.'

'Oh, honey, how can you say that? I'm always telling him to stop interfering with your personal life.'

Emma, as if she hadn't heard her mother, turned to the window again. Janet sank into herself, thinking of all the quarrels Emma and her father had had for the last several years and all the intervening she had to do. Emma shouting, 'Dad, we live in America!' when her father told her she was not

141

allowed to date boys, and, more absurdly, that he would find a nice Iranian man for her to marry. Or when her father had argued that she should live at home and go to a local college. Janet recalled the exact dialogue between them as if it had happened just yesterday, not a year ago. He shouting at Emma, 'You're going to stay right here,' and Emma shouting back, 'I'm not going to do that, Dad. That's not how American girls are. They go away and live on their own.' Her father saying, 'Don't make me resort to force.' Emma replying, 'You can resort to what you want, I'm going away.' Her father threatening, 'Who's going to pay for that?' And Emma threatening back, 'I will. I'll get a job.'

Janet never understood why Hooshang, who had gone against his parents' expectations when he married her, an American woman, could not tolerate his daughter's attempts at independence. When she and Hooshang first met at the University of Kansas, where he was studying geology and she art, and they started going out, he said, 'I don't like the idea of arranged marriage.' After they were both finished with their studies and they went to live in Iran for two years, he always stood up for her against his parents' and other family members' restrictions. She worked at the Tehran Contemporary Art Museum, which had both modern and ancient Persian art on display. His family frowned on her going to work but Hooshang supported her. When they came to live in Long Island, her work experience in Tehran helped her get hired by the small local museum, to develop a small Persian Art collection. Hooshang was proud of that.

Maybe his attempt to raise their daughter in the traditional way was due to the fact that he couldn't bear being cut off from his past as communications between Iran and America became more strained. Since they left Iran 20 years ago, they hadn't been able to go there even for short visits because of all the turmoil there, and the strain in the Iran-America relationship. He was making his daughter a vehicle for practising some of his family's mores. He sought out Iranian friends and specialty shops and restaurants as much as he could and basked in them as in sunshine during a cold, damp winter. And now they were going to Iran, at the first window of opportunity that opened for them: he could attend a conference aimed at promoting dialogue between the two countries and he and his family were allowed special visas. Hooshang, who taught at the university in Stony Brook, was on spring break, like Emma, and Janet took off 10 days from her job at the museum. Hooshang had no family left. His parents had died and his brother, uncles and aunts had emigrated to different countries. But he yearned for the sights and sounds of his country and wanted to introduce Emma to them.

'Didn't I persuade your father to let you go away to college?' Janet said to Emma now.

Emma shrugged sulkily. It seemed to Janet that Emma was acting even younger than her age of 18. Was all this melancholy due to her problems with her boyfriend or was it something deeper? She certainly had not been herself since she came home for her spring vacation. She acted vulnerable and easily hurt. If Hooshang raised his voice ever so slightly it upset her. She had gained weight and made drastic changes in her appearance – bleaching her hair blond and wearing tinted green contact lenses. Those colors, against her olive skin, made her look artificial.

In a moment Hooshang came back and resumed reading the magazine. Emma finally stopped crying and the three of them were practically silent for the rest of the flight.

It was early afternoon by the time they got through the customs and passport lines in the Tehran airport. Janet felt nervous, and she could see Hooshang was too, as they stood in line for their passports to be checked, and Emma's headscarf kept slipping off.

Janet breathed with relief when they were finished and were outside. The minibus for the hotel was waiting and they got in. They sat next to two Iranian women talking in an animated way. When they heard Janet and Hooshang speaking in English, one of them tapped Janet on her arm and asked her questions, in a friendly way. What were they doing in Iran? How old was their daughter? How long would they be staying? Janet answered briefly. She was still in the grip of her anxieties. The bus turned into an unpaved and bumpy street with one mosque standing at its beginning and one at its end. 'This road is better for donkeys than cars,' the woman said to Janet in a joking tone. Then the bus went on to a wider avenue filled with modern, luxurious houses, buildings, hotels. In 15 minutes they were at Hafiz Hotel, which had been recently renovated and had been recommended to them.

Janet liked the hotel with its ornate, carved, wooden entrance door, marble floors, columns in the center of the lobby, a large chandelier hanging from the ceiling, but she wondered if Emma found it to be stifling. They went to the counter and registered. Then the receptionist signaled to a porter standing in a corner and he came over. 'Take them to Suite 35.'

Emma took the smaller room and Janet and Hooshang the large one. They started to unpack so that they could eat and go to bed early, exhausted as they all were from the long flight. Emma was lingering in the bathroom. She had gone there more than 10 minutes ago and was still there. Janet went over and knocked. 'Are you ready?'

'Don't rush me, Mom.' She opened the door and then turned to the mirror, combing her hair.

Janet could see that Emma had been crying again. She went over and kissed her damp cheek. 'Please try to have a good time. There's so much you can see, so much to learn on this holiday.'

Emma nodded vaguely.

Janet came back into the living room where Hooshang was sitting on the sofa watching the news on TV. 'I don't know if the news on this state-run channel can be trusted,' he said in a near whisper, as if afraid a government agent might be standing behind the door, listening.

Janet didn't respond, afraid any conversation about Iran would quickly lead to a volatile argument between Emma and her father. Though he was willing to criticize aspects of Iranian culture, not least the censorship that went on, he didn't like it when others, particularly Emma, did that.

Emma came out of the bathroom and they left. They walked towards the nearby Martyr Ali Square. The streets were teeming with people, coming back from work or other tasks. Cars and motor scooters raced by crazily. Shops carrying a wide variety of merchandise – hand-woven local carpets, clothes, gold jewelry – were filled with people haggling with the vendors. They passed a mosque, an old palace, a park, a row of art galleries.

Janet and Emma fell behind Hooshang. 'Mom, I don't feel good about anything,' Emma said.

'Why, dear? You have so much going for you. Does this have to do with Ed?'

'No,' Emma mumbled.

'Janet, Emma,' Hooshang called to them from a few feet ahead. He was standing in front of a restaurant. As they caught up with him, he said, 'Why don't we eat here?'

Mashadi Chelo Kebabi had been there when they had lived in Tehran and Janet wanted to try it again. Emma went along.

Emma seemed uncomfortable. At her age, being forced to wear a headscarf and a *manteau*, to watch what she said in public, as her father had warned her, were clearly stifling, particularly in the distraught state she was in. Janet felt a pang of guilt that she and Hooshang had pressured her to come on this trip. Emma was right, after all, that she took Hooshang's wishes into

144

consideration much more often than she did her daughter's. Maybe it had to do with the insecurities Hooshang had begun to display ever since they had immigrated to the US. During the two years in Iran, she had been the one bewildered by all the cultural rules. In the US, her territory, their roles had shifted. He wasn't quite tuned to the nuances of American culture and, worse, there was such a negative picture of Iranians in most Americans' minds. Sensing that insecurity in him, she had, it seemed to her now, often gone along with his irrational wishes.

She remembered certain incidents. Once, when Emma returned very late from a party, her father had forbidden her to attend another party for months. Janet had just gone along with that. Another time Emma wanted to stay overnight at a friend's house for a birthday party and her father had forbidden it, believing that such parties got wild. Again Janet hadn't argued on her daughter's side. True, she had tried sometimes, but many other times she had not, and with no good justification.

She came out of her thoughts with Hooshang's voice. 'Tell me about school, your roommates,' he was saying to Emma, trying to make her open up.

'It's been a pressure cooker. At midnight we lean out of the windows and scream. We're like miserable dogs howling.'

'Oh, come on, it can't be that bad. Besides, it was...' but he stopped just in time.

'I'm going to take a walk and then go back to the hotel,' Emma said, drinking the rest of her imitation cola and getting up.

'I don't know if it's a good idea, this is a big city...' Hooshang said.

'Don't worry, I'll be very careful,' Emma said.

'Do you know how to get back to the hotel?' Janet asked.

'Yes. I won't go too far.'

'Be back in one hour, then,' said Hooshang. 'Here's the extra key to the room.' He took out the key from his pocket and gave it to Emma.

As soon as Emma left, Janet said, 'Poor girl, she's so unhappy these days.'

'Aren't all American teenagers like that, confused? They want their independence but then they have to pay a price.'

'I don't know,' Janet said.

A stocky man holding a set of cards came to their table. 'Would you like me to tell your fortune?'

Janet was tempted. In the state of mind she was in, she thought it would be soothing to give in to that idea. But then she felt ridiculous. 'No, thanks,' she said.

The man walked over to the couple at the next table. They must have agreed because the man was spreading his cards in front of them.

At another table a fortune teller was using the thick Turkish coffee they served to tell the fortune of a woman who was sitting there with a little boy.

Janet and Hooshang left and when they got to their hotel room Emma hadn't returned yet.

'It was a mistake to let her go away alone,' Hooshang said.

'She's 18 years old, a woman, not a child. She's in college.'

He sat on the sofa and turned the TV onto the news again. He rephrased his previous complaint. 'All distorted.'

Janet shrugged, her mind focused on Emma. In spite of herself, she too was a little regretful to have let her daughter stay out alone. She took out a novel from her pocketbook and, sitting on a chair across from Hooshang, began to read. He kept looking at his watch.

'I'll go and look for her,' she said.

'Where are you going to look?'

'In clothing shops that are open.'

'I'll go with you.'

'It's better if I go alone, so I can talk to her when I find her.'

As Janet walked along the wide avenue, looking inside the shops, she experienced the same panic as when Emma, at the age of five, had wandered out of their house in Setauket. Janet had gone outside looking for her on the road, and had then found her walking in the woods that stretched behind their backyard. She had to remind herself again that Emma wasn't a child and had been living on her own for a year.

The air smelled of spices mingled with the scent of unfamiliar plants and diesel fumes coming out of old cars. She looked inside many shops but there was no sign of Emma. She turned towards Mellat Park. Emma could have gone there. She entered the park and looked around. It was well lit and crowded with families strolling or sitting on the grass or benches. Children were buying cotton candy and balloons from a vendor.

She walked to a dark, secluded corner. She noticed someone sitting alone on a bench. As she got closer she could make out Emma's blue *manteau*. She walked speedily towards her, calling, 'Emma, Emma.' Her feeling of relief quickly gave place to sadness at the sight of Emma sitting there, so solitary and separate. She felt even worse when she saw in the moonlight that Emma's face was again wet with tears.

She plopped herself down beside her. 'My darling, it breaks my heart to see you so upset. What's wrong? You know how much I love you, how much you mean to me.'

'If I tell you something... no... You'll tell Dad. You tell him everything.'

'I promise I won't, please tell me,' Janet said.

'Mom, I'm pregnant, two months.'

A wave of shock made Janet go hot and then cold. 'Is it Ed's, does he know about... it?'

Emma shook her head. 'I don't want him to think I'm trying to trap him.'

'Still, you could discuss it with him,' she said, barely bringing out the words.

Emma was silent, looking downward.

I should have guessed, Janet thought – all the weight Emma has gained, the ravenous way she eats. 'When we're back home I'll take you to my gynecologist. We'll get a recommendation from him what to do.' Emma probably had not thought in any rational way about what to do with the baby. She seemed to be locked in a bubble of pain about it. She put her arms around Emma and managed to say: 'Don't be so upset. We'll deal with it together.'

In a few moments they got up and went back to the hotel. Just before entering, Emma whispered, 'You won't tell Dad, will you?'

'I promise I won't,' she said, though she wondered, with a twinge of pain and bewilderment, how she was going to keep something so important from Hooshang. And anyway, how could they hide the baby once she or he was born?

'Oh, you're back,' Hooshang said as they entered. 'I'm so glad.'

Emma just wandered to her room. All Janet said to him was, 'She was in the park.'

Janet had a hard time sleeping as she lay next to Hooshang. The situation was so complicated. How were they going to deal with it, how was she going to handle it so that it was best for Emma? She remembered how she herself, growing up, had often been angry at her mother because she automatically took her father's side when certain issues and problems came up. Her mother was a passive, meek woman, and made herself subservient to her domineering, lawyer husband. She had been a social worker but, once she fell pregnant with Janet, she took some time off from work; and then Michael was born and she stayed home and never returned. The truth was that few of her mother's women friends in Houston, where she grew up, were interested in careers; they were subservient to their husbands. But still sometimes her mother had an air of defeat, even bitterness about her. When Janet had made up her mind to marry Hooshang, her father had objected. 'He's from an alien culture and religion. It will never work out.' Her mother had just agreed with him, with no analysis of her own. So Janet and Hooshang had married in a church without any family members present, hers having objected to their marriage and his being too far away. Later, when they went to live in Iran for two years, they had to be married again by a Muslim priest for her to be accepted legally as his wife.

She was full of self-blame now. Yes, I've been absorbed in Hooshang, been ignoring Emma's needs. Perhaps even her letting herself get pregnant is a cry for help, attention.

Then her mind wandered to the days when she was pregnant with Emma. She was so happy, ecstatic, during the pregnancy and then watching the baby grow. She still had some of Emma's childhood belongings – stuffed animals, a rag doll, her pink and blue receiving blankets – stored in a closet. But she had been at a stage of life when she was ready for a child. It was different for Emma. Having the child would burden her with a big responsibility at too young an age. She was perhaps right not to want to tell Ed about it. From what she had seen of him, he wasn't the type who would want to settle down. He and Emma had dated when they were in the last year of high school and then both ended up in the same university. He wanted the relationship not to be exclusive, for them to be able to see other people. He was an attractive, vivacious boy, but not reliable. Even in high school he had once stood her up on Saturday night, and Emma had discovered he had been out with another girl.

If Emma had the baby, it would set her back in her studies and would increase all the tension at home. Perhaps the only solution was an abortion. She would have to help her make that decision. Emma was obviously having a hard time sleeping also; Janet heard her get up a few times and go to the bathroom. It was practically dawn before Janet managed to fall asleep.

In the morning when Janet woke, Emma had already left the room. Hooshang was still asleep. Through the window she could see it was a sunny day. The tall cypress trees, the domes and minarets of mosques, were bathed in yellow light. She got dressed quickly to go and look for Emma. Emma was sitting on a bench in front of a small park across from the hotel. She looked deep in thought. She would have to make an important decision, Janet thought, her heart full of compassion.

My sympathy is certainly with the confused, frightened Emma, not with Hooshang, who would only blame his daughter for what had happened. And this is a time to show her that I love her at least as much as I do her father. At that moment, with the secret breathing between them, she felt closer to Emma than to Hooshang – or to anyone else in the world for that matter.

There were problems ahead and big decisions to be made, but for the time being this sense of closeness to her daughter was exhilarating.

Nahid Rachlin was born and brought up in Iran. She studied on the Columbia University Writing Program on a Doubleday-Columbia Fellowship and then went on to Stanford University MFA program on a Stegner Fellowship. Her publications include a memoir, *Persian Girls* (Penguin); four novels: *Jumping Over Fire* (City Lights), *Foreigner* (WW Norton), *Married to a Stranger* (EP Dutton-Penguin), *The Heart's Desire* (City Lights); and a collection of short stories, *Veils* (City Lights). Her website is nahidrachlin.com

SAMUEL MUNENE
Kenya

THE DAVID THUO SHOW

The First Big Quarrel happened on the eve of my 13th birthday. That was the first time Dad and Mum argued loud enough for us to hear almost every word from their bedroom. Mum accused Dad of cheating and Dad accused Mum of sleeping with her boss.

For a short period after that we didn't talk amongst ourselves. We were silent even when watching television. Then Mum started laughing mockingly whenever watching *The Jeffersons* in Dad's presence. Initially I didn't understand why Mum had suddenly developed a liking for the comedy but then I noticed how Mr Jefferson – short, bald and clumsy – looked very similar to Dad. On Thursdays Dad made sure to come home after 7.30pm, when *The Jeffersons* had been aired but in time for *Love and Hate*, another sitcom.

Dad also started laughing when watching comedies. Previously Dad had looked bored when they aired but now he loved them more than any other program. Again I didn't comprehend the change of taste until I observed he snickered only in those parts not obviously funny, when the rest of us would be silent, waiting for the punchline. His laughter had nothing to do with jokes; it was just a way of making the rest of us in the family look unintelligent.

We got the flow. Mum raised her game, for that is what it was turning out to be. Mum's favorite program was *Love Is Made Of This*, a Mexican soap opera. In it, Lorenzo, the lead character, acted the perfect husband; hard-working, rich and showering his wife with lots of gifts. Watching the program, Mum placed her hands on her chest and moaned softly. The rest of us seemed lost. The fact that we could not connect emotionally to the program as Mum did meant that we were unable to follow the complicated plot. Mum could. But given her random gasps and moans, I doubted if she understood the storyline either.

My sister Sharon preferred to be called Shaz. But I called her Wawira, the African name she hated most. I disliked her because I guessed she disliked me too. And also because she was slow. In her form-one exam she had scored one per cent in mathematics, the lowest score in the school's history.

She loved music or pretended to. She sang along to almost every song played on TV. Other than making me feel bad because I didn't know the words, it was also irritating: she reminded me of the buzz of a mosquito trying to bite. Judging by their frowns, Mum and Dad would also have preferred it if she had remained silent, but then again that was her moment of intelligence, and the unwritten rules in our house said she was not to be interrupted.

My moment to shine came during *Who Is Smarter Now?*, a show where participants were asked general-knowledge questions and the winners given prizes. I shouted answers to almost all the questions asked. Most of the times I got the answers right. When I flopped, Mum smiled and Dad coughed a little sarcastically; Sharon would sneer, then laugh out loud. I was sure that, by getting almost all the answers correct, I made her feel thick. I was not so certain about my parents. Giving accurate answers made me seem truly bright, a fact that might have made them happy though they did not show it openly. That would have been a failure on my part: I wanted to make them feel brainless and annoy them. And so, just to be positive I was getting the desired effect, I branched out into cars, which were things adults should know about. After a Mercedes E-class advertisement, I would say something as arbitrary as: 'Multiple supersonic airbags? That's a real car,' Dad owned an old Datsun.

The only time we almost talked was during the Trust condoms advertisement. At such times, if anybody had dared to say anything then the rest would have joined in enthusiastically. But no one did. The advert showed a tall, well-built man inserting a bottle into a condom. Two girls who could not have been more than 18 looked at him, giggling, while soft music played in the background. If the ad started playing, Dad would reach for a cigarette and go out on the veranda to smoke, long enough for the commercial to end.

Mum would reach out for a copy of *True Love* magazine, which she always kept by her side. She would flip through the pages and close it as soon as she heard *Maisha iko sawa na trust* (Life is Good with Trust), the condom's slogan. Sharon would look at the television but without making it obvious: she would pretend to play with her phone but her eyes would be tilted to the screen. I didn't mind the ad, but I was not about to be the only one watching it. So I would reached for the tattered copy of *James Hadley Chase* that I always carried around and fantasize about the pistol-holding girl on the cover.

Shiko, our house help, rarely watched television. She spent most of the time in the kitchen. After cooking she would sit on a chair and knit or read the bible. The only program she liked watching was *Love Is Made Of This*. She understood very little English and perhaps that's why she smiled sheepishly throughout.

Mum worked as an administrative assistant for Ndovu Tours and Travels. She was light-skinned, with long, healthy hair. Mum left for work at seven in the morning but she woke up at five, to shower and dress. Many times I had caught men ogling at her as she walked, twisting her hips. When walking side by side with Dad they looked ridiculous, the same as *The Jeffersons*. Sharon, 15 years old and with her two boyfriends, looked every inch like Lisa, the Jeffersons' daughter.

The television broke down. It was around 7pm. Dad was not home yet but the rest of us were seated watching the news when the TV went off. For a moment we just looked at each other; then Dad walked in. It took him only a few seconds to notice something was wrong.

'What have you done to the TV?' he shouted, walking to the TV stand.

Mum clicked. 'You should know better – we left you watching it last night.'

Dad fiddled with the TV's cable but it didn't power on. He then lifted and shook it a little bit. But still nothing.

He pointed at Sharon and me.

'Between the two of you, who was the first to get home?'

'But Shiko has been here the whole day. She must have done something to it.' Sharon said, pointing at Shiko who was standing in the room in silence.

'Have you ever seen me touch the TV?' Shiko snapped, her eyes fixed on Sharon. 'And wasn't it working a few minutes ago?'

'Why couldn't it wait for *Love Is Made Of This* before malfunctioning?' Mum cried, throwing her hands up.

We all stood up, moved closer to the stand and watched as Dad tried to revive it. He looked angry. He hit the television on top, then at the back but it still didn't come to life. I thought he was going to lift it up and throw it on the floor. When it became clear the TV was not going to work, we all retreated to our bedrooms.

There was no television the following night. Dad had called the technician, who said he needed at least two weeks to repair it. Dad read the newspaper as if he was to be examined on it the following day. Mum was buried in *Live Your Dreams*, a book by Joel Osborn. She placed it so close to her eyes I wondered if she was in fact reading. Sharon was grumpy and locked herself in the bedroom. It was a Monday, the day *The Beat* aired. I was crouched on a chair pretending to read a social ethics textbook. I would have preferred to talk of my nomination as a class prefect.

Shiko served the food after Sharon had come and sat next to me. Our sitting room had two sofas. Dad lay on one and Mum on the other. We sat on the smaller individual couches.

'Look at what I bought,' Shiko said, and pointed to the part of the wall next to the TV stand. We had been eating in silence.

It was a white sticker written in red: '*Christ is the head of this house. The unseen guest at every meal. The silent listener to every conversation.*'

'It's good.' Dad said, without lifting his eyes from the food.

'I like it,' Mum said. Her head bent into her food.

'Yeah, I thought it very inspiring,' Shiko said. She sounded excited. 'The man who sold it to me had so many. What other one can I buy?'

'Get something funky,' Sharon said, her voice terse. 'This one is just too old school.'

'Hear the way your children speak,' Dad said, still looking at the food.

Mum clicked. 'Aren't they your children too?' she asked.

She then stood up and went to eat in the kitchen. Shiko followed her.

Sharon left with her food to the bedroom. I finished mine and went to sleep, leaving Dad looking at the classifieds section of the newspaper.

The following evening, after Shiko served dinner, I decided to tell everyone I had emerged top in the inter-school quiz competition.

'That is the best news I have heard in this house for so long,' Dad said, food in his mouth.

'Sharon, you should work as hard as Maina,' Mum said, looking at Dad.

'Are you saying I don't work hard? That's cruel,' Sharon snapped.

'Come on, listen to what your mother is telling you,' Dad said.

Sharon went out of the sitting room, banging the door behind her.

'That girl is spoilt,' Mum said.

After that day Sharon locked herself in her bedroom until food was served. That was the only time we had any conversation. Shiko started most of it and the rest of us joined in.

'I hear Wekesa beat his wife last night,' Shiko said one evening. Wekesa was one of our neighbors.

'What kind of men still beat their wives?' Dad said. 'It's so shameful.'

'That's shameful indeed,' Mum said. 'A lawyer beating his wife?'

'But, worst of all, he beat his wife in front of the children,' Shiko said.

'In front of the children?' Mum gasped. 'What will such children think of their father when they grow up?'

Sharon must have got her second boyfriend around that time. Her first one, who called himself G, was a classmate. He wore studs and bounced when walking. He talked like the black Americans I had seen in movies.

The second boyfriend, Tim, lived not very far from our home in Nairobi's Buruburu estate. He had been in college but now I supposed he must have finished because he had bought an old Toyota and put on oversized hide wheels. It looked as if it would tip over. The car windows were tinted and the music loud.

I saw Sharon getting out of his car one evening and that's when I first suspected she was having an affair with Tim. I confirmed with Shiko.

'I saw Sharon kiss him in that car,' Shiko told me. Her lips were twisted as if talking of something filthy. 'Can't he date girls of his own age?'

Shiko was bigger than Mum but I estimated she was 10 years younger. She had lived with us for about a year. I always wondered whether she was married or had a boyfriend.

We decided against telling Dad and Mum of Sharon's exploits.

'Let's wait. She will get pregnant and everybody will know. I can't wait to see how your mother will react,' she said. I couldn't wait either.

Three weeks were gone without television. The technician had said that the television was an old model and it would take a little longer to get the right spare parts.

Then Mum started coming home late. Shiko would serve us dinner in her absence. Dad praised her food, something he didn't do in the presence of Mum. Shiko giggled at such times. Dad would casually ask us how school was. We answered enthusiastically, though, judging by his grunts, he didn't seem too interested. After dinner, Sharon and I would immediately go to bed, leaving Dad talking to Shiko. She slept in the sitting room, on the same seat Dad always sat on.

I had heard Mum say it was the tourists' peak season and there was much work to do in the office.

'I am sure they are paying overtime in dollars,' Dad said to Mum one evening when she came as we were having dinner.

She chuckled, and then said, 'I wish!'

On Sundays I was the only one left in the house. Mum would leave at around ten. 'Imagine, they can't even give us a day off,' she said. Sharon would have left earlier, saying she was going for youth service. I was sure she was spending half the day with Tim and the rest with G.

Sundays had always been Shiko's day off. She would leave around 11am, spend the day out and come back in the evening. Previously Dad had spent Sundays indoors but now he too left the house, some minutes after Shiko.

I looked forward to Sundays. Dad wrote a column in the *Sunday News – This and That, a social commentary by Daudi Thuo*. At the bottom of the article was written: *The writer is a consultant on social issues.* Dad bought and read the newspaper before going away. I had time to read the column hoping to see my name mentioned.

Sundays were also great for me because I got to read *Emotions*, a pornographic magazine, without fear that anybody would bump into me. I bought it secretly from a street vendor.

The Second Big Quarrel happened before the television was brought back. It was on a Friday. After dinner Sharon and I had left for our rooms, leaving Dad and Shiko. I didn't hear Mum come in. But all of a sudden I heard Mum's voice:

'What is happening here? Are you sleeping with my husband?'

The next thing I heard was a scuffle and things falling.

'Don't fight.' I heard Dad say in voice that was loud enough to wake anyone.

I rushed to the sitting room. Sharon opened her door and followed close behind. We found Mum and Shiko fighting. Shiko was biting Mum's hand. Dad was trying, unsuccessfully, to separate them. They saw us and somehow stopped.

Mum was crying, 'Prostitute! Go get a man of your own!'

'You are the bigger prostitute! Who doesn't know you are sleeping with that boy?' Shiko said.

Mum lunged forward. But Dad held her. 'Which boy?' Dad shouted.

'Ask the watchman. She is dropped here by some boy driving Ndovu cars. They always hug!'

I looked at Sharon. She started crying and went back to her room.

'Is that it?' Dad said. He then pushed Mum and slapped her on the face. Mum reached for a framed photo of our family and threw it at Dad. It hit him on the head. He then went for Mum but abruptly stopped and looked at me. 'What are you doing here? Go and sleep. Stupid!' he said. I went to bed, not sure who I wanted to win.

There was no breakfast the following day. I woke up earlier than usual. Shiko was not in the kitchen or where she slept. I didn't wait to find out; I just went out of the house.

When I came back from school, the door was open. I expected to find Shiko at home. But she was not in. I was going to my room when I met Sharon. Her eyes were red, like she had been crying the whole day. She hugged me and started crying. I didn't know what to do.

She told me Mum and Dad had fought again in the morning. And Mum had left carrying her largest bag.

'She said she will never come back again.'

'Where do you think she went to?' I asked.

'She said she was going kill herself,' Sharon said.

I told her all would be fine. I went and locked myself in my room. I believed Mum was joking. She couldn't just walk out on us like that. I cooked rice. Sharon refused to eat. Dad came when we were already asleep. I left him sleeping on the couch as I went to school in the morning, still in his shoes and suit.

The whole of that week Sharon refused to go to school. Dad came home very late and drunk. I stopped cooking but bought fast food. Dad always left a hundred shillings on the kitchen table.

On the Saturday, a week after Mum had left, Dad came home at seven in the evening. He brought us chips and chicken. Sharon took her share and went to her bedroom. Dad had brought a bottle of Smirnoff. He poured some in a glass, took a sip and looked at me.

'Are you all okay?' he said. It was the first time we had spoken since Mum left.

'Yes,' I said 'But I could do with some cash.'

He gave me a thousand shillings. 'Share with your sister.' I handed Sharon 400, hoping she would stop sulking. She hadn't spoken to Dad since Mum went.

I went out briefly on Sunday and bought that week's edition of *Emotions*. Dad didn't go anywhere. And Sharon was mainly in her room.

We got used to life without Mum and Shiko. Dad left us money to buy food. I bought chips and chicken every day. Sharon complained that the food was making her fat. She had started going back to school, though when she was home she spent most of her time in the bedroom. Dad came home late every day, always drunk. He gave me a thousand shillings every week, which he asked me to share with Sharon. I always gave her 400.

We didn't talk about Mum with Dad. It was as if it had never happened. But Sharon kept asking me whether I thought Mum had committed suicide. 'Don't be silly. I am sure she will come back,' I usually told her. I was trying to sound brave but I was missing Mum and wanted her to come back now. I just wanted to see her around.

One Sunday, about a month after the Second Big Quarrel, Dad left home around 8am. I thought he had gone to drink. Sharon and I had become really close, close enough to even play Scrabble together. Around one in the afternoon we saw Dad's car park in front of our house. We heard a woman laugh. We rushed to the door. There they were, Mum and Dad giggling, removing a television from the car.

Samuel Munene is a writer based in Nairobi, Kenya. He writes fiction and creative non-fiction. He has been published in various journals, including *Kwani*. Amongst other work, he co-wrote the script of the award-winning Kenyan movie, *Nairobi Half-Life*.

VANESSA BARBARA
Brazil

NELLIE

It was not that he was violent – he had never knocked Nellie about or hit her with an iron, as many of his buddies boasted of having done, but then his wife had not given him any great reasons to lose his temper. It's just that Nellie was so annoying – she was a little dumb, too slow to understand sarcasm, and sometimes had fits of absence that resembled autism. She was also somewhat plump, short and devoid of ambition. But she loved Teo with an almost childlike affection, regaled him with treats and nursing care, and so he had concluded that, all in all, Nellie would be the lesser evil.

(There was Bruna, who had an amazing body but suffered from nerves and spent entire nights crying; Luana was smart but arrogant and bossy, with hateful friends; Cecilia was simply stupid, which did not bother him so much and could even be corrected with time – after all, she could already write her name without omitting a single letter, and so well that all the aunts could decipher it without their glasses!)

Of all the women he had known, Nellie was the calmest and most obedient, and, without much thought, needing someone to keep him company, Teo decided to give her a life of great luxury and few worries.

The oldest of three sisters, Nellie had never been the smartest or the most beautiful, so it surprised everyone when she married a renowned surgeon and moved into an upscale neighborhood. She was absolutely devoted to him and did not seem to mind having to work less – perhaps only covering from time to time for a colleague on leave, or tending a more difficult patient in the small hospital where she had worked as a nurse all her life and where she had met her husband. Also she did not care when Teo finally asked her to stop working.

She just nodded – after all, the stories of the hospital that Teo told her were enough to keep her in touch. He gave her a full life, was generous and condescending. And Nellie, a simple and industrious creature, certainly liked the routine of a housewife.

So everyone found it unfair when nasty things began to happen to the couple.

The first time, he threw the cordless phone at the wall because the cable TV plan did not include the international football channels. It was Nellie's fault, so he called back the cable TV people to say that his wife was special and suffered from senile dementia, and so of course they should not, under any circumstances, consider what she said, especially when it came to contracts.

Afterwards they ordered a pizza and everything was fine.

Although, of course, she was not worthy of great loving passion with her slow and silly gestures as if she had just hit her head on the cupboard, Teo sometimes wished she did not react so calmly to his outbursts of anger, as if the fact of possessing a sober woman irritated him a little.

Other than that, they got along. They liked to play tennis together, and Teo made sure to let her win once in a while to cheer her up. While he was at work, Nellie read biology books and studied nursing, and often would call colleagues to discuss the more difficult cases. Meanwhile, Teo climbed the career ladder and in a few months was promoted to the post of chief surgeon in the hospital. This was not such a great feat, since it was an average institution with a medical team that was no more than reasonable. But he had good contacts and began to use them.

Months later, having received an exceptional proposal to run a private clinic near the hospital, Teo switched jobs. He began to treat members of congress, judges and, in the words of Nellie, migrated officially to the A side of history. The standard of living of the couple increased further and she wondered about having children, since she spent the afternoons with nothing to do and missed working, caring for others, being busy with the needs of other people.

He said he would think about it.

The second time was when Nellie invited some friends for dinner. He protested and inadvertently ended up kicking a vase. He said it had been a hard day at work and he needed a period to rest. Nellie cancelled the invitations and stood by her husband.

The third time Teo grabbed her fists, for no particular reason – just to force her to react. Thinking about it, it was obvious that she had some mental problem. So he began requiring that Nellie always remained at home with him, although his idea was to spend hours watching reruns of the Brazilian

Championship on television (because this was how marriage was supposed to be). After this incident she became more cautious. She weighed her words better, softened the bad news and walked the house like a cornered animal. Even with Teo, who never hit Nellie nor hit her with an iron.

It is true that there was an incident some time later, when Teo came back from a surgical operation that had resulted in a death and felt he did not deserve to come home and see Nellie giggling with her friends on the phone.

That's when he pushed his wife and she hit her head on the edge of the coffee table, and really lost a lot of blood. It was while Teo was trying to justify himself that she decided to leave home. She had four stitches in her forehead and refused to keep the furniture or accept financial help from Teo.

She left home and never returned.

Of course, Nellie had to go back to work. The pay was smaller and she was allocated to the burns unit where no one liked to work. She spent a few nights sleeping in her sister's room before renting a small apartment, a grim kitchenette that had no furniture, only a sleeping bag, a microwave and an old refrigerator.

Without a car, it now took her an hour and a half to get to the hospital and she had to wake up before dawn. She had no more savings – all those had been spent on the wedding party.

From the moment she hit her head on the corner of the table, however, she felt something turning inside her: the obedient girl with slow movements gave rise to a person more alert, alive, to the point of almost being angry. By the time she had lifted herself up from the carpet, her husband still shouting that it was her fault – 'See what happens when you're stubborn?' – she had already decided to leave him.

She found herself a lawyer to handle the divorce, after obtaining a reference from the local community college, which provided legal aid for low-income citizens. This was how she met Daniel, a very quiet, tall, strong young man, who in his spare time worked as a volunteer for social organizations.

Daniel was a partner in a small law firm and believed in justice, equality and the empowerment of women. He was the opposite of her ex-husband: sweet, attentive and calm, with no delusions of grandeur.

When Nellie told him the story of her separation, asking if he could refer her to someone, Daniel was almost in tears and said he would personally take care of the case. He hugged her hard and said everything would be fine.

And it even seemed that it was going to be fine: in the weeks that followed, Nellie focused on work with great tenacity and found unexpected relief in caring for the most critical patients in a unit where no one even dared to tell jokes. The burns wing was made up of people who have suffered serious accidents with fire, with up to 80-per-cent burns on their body, including their face and hands. The patients felt pain throughout the wound-cleaning process, bathings, grafts and dressing changes. It was common to have to deal with burn psychosis, a kind of sensory confusion with irrational thought patterns that occurred after septic episodes. None of the more experienced nurses wanted to work in the sector, and even doctors fled the area.

It was generally Nellie who was left to bring a mirror when the patient regained consciousness and asked to see what they looked like. At such times, she had to deal with a process similar to that of her own grief. First came the shock, then denial, searching for the lost image, despair and finally reorganization. Some children were there because of domestic abuse or household accidents. Others were adults who had survived a fire and lost their families; yet there were those who had attempted suicide by setting fire to their homes.

The term 'social death' was used both to describe the state of the patients and the staff who worked there. After years of avoiding thinking about the existence of that world, Nellie found a kind of fulfilment among patients isolated from the society of others, who, like her, also had to face all sorts of sequels and mutilations.

In those days, Nellie went to visit the lawyer more frequently, under the pretext of assembling the divorce process and discussing the litigation opportunities provided for in the legislation. Several times she raised the issue of fees, but Daniel seemed offended and replied that there was no charge for his services. She said she felt bad about it, as if Daniel were doing her a favor that implied a return, and reiterated that she would like to pay in some way, even if in many instalments.

He insisted that she did not have to.

During these afternoons, both took the opportunity to talk about other issues, such as Daniel's voluntary work, which provided assistance to poor people and led him to meet many female victims of domestic violence. He called husbands who beat their wives monsters – his voice always rose as he talked about this, at once angry and exalted.

Nellie spoke of a quiet woman she had met in the hospital who had made a great impression on her. After suffering an assassination attempt with gasoline and fire, the 34-year-old had 40-per-cent burns. She had three fingers of her right hand amputated and spent a few days unable to see due to her swollen face. When Nellie brought her the mirror for the first time, she did not recognize herself. Her husband had set her on fire, for reasons she did not explain. When the police came to question her, she mentioned an accident with the stove.

For several weeks, the woman continued to receive the visits of her husband, who brought her flowers and trinkets. Every night after the changes of her dressings, she confessed to Nellie, quietly, that she should leave the man and learn kung-fu. Both would smile at that.

After three weeks' work, Daniel determined the value of the alimony that Teo would pay. It was not very high, but it would be enough for Nellie not to have to work double shifts. Since everything was going so slowly, Daniel himself made Nellie a personal loan so she could buy a double mattress for her apartment. He also said that the ideal would be to pay for the repair of the coffee table as soon as possible, however unfair this seemed, and then include the bill in a future contested divorce, when the judge would recognize the greater guilt of one party and reward Nellie with a larger share in the division of property. (Or at least that's what she understood.)

Everything proceeded in a calm and orderly manner until, one night, Daniel invited her to dinner and confessed he was in love. They began dating in secret, although there were ethical issues regarding the involvement of an attorney with a client, and although one of Daniel's colleagues warned him of the dangers of this type of relationship.

With his case prepared, the lawyer called Teo and set a date so they could talk privately. He said Nellie was determined to ask for a contested divorce with attribution of guilt, plus alimony and division of property. Teo became angry and, out of nowhere, asked if they were dating. Daniel evaded the question and said that the meeting was strictly professional, adding that he would be willing to serve as counsel to both parties, if the surgeon agreed.

Of course, Teo did not agree and left screaming, saying that his lawyer would be in contact. The next day, Nellie deposited the money related to the repair of the glass table.

At first, Nellie's co-workers publicly defended her, condemning the conduct of the surgeon and labelling him a coward. Some volunteered to testify in her favor when the day of reckoning came. Others brought her cookies and pies in plastic bowls. The story of the divorce came to the notice of the hospital management, who expressed solidarity with the nurse. Gradually, however, after the initial shock, routine returned to the corridors and indignation faded until the incident descended into oblivion. Many of them went back to talking with the surgeon as if nothing had happened, especially after he opened a selection process for nurses in the new clinic, with high salaries and great benefits. One of the veterans speculated out loud that Nellie must have incurred her husband's anger, and from that point no one was willing to defend her. The corridors resounded with talk of her slowness of movement and her similarity to catatonic patients in the hospital.

But she did not care about this backbiting, only about looking after the burn victims, changing their dressings and providing the tragic handheld mirrors when needed.

Daniel alone protected her fervently, and she appreciated that. One Thursday night, he asked her to be his girlfriend and she hesitated, saying later that they should only decide after the divorce. The lawyer was upset and said he didn't want to lose her, but seemed to understand. He spent the night in Nellie's tiny apartment.

On Friday morning, he came out in a suit and tie for a meeting with Teo's attorney at which both lawyers agreed that a dispute settlement process would be very costly, exhausting and humiliating. Although Nellie protested, Daniel suggested that they go for a consensual divorce without assigning blame. That would speed up the process and she would not have to go through the pain of proving she had suffered domestic violence – after all, the surgeon claimed that she had only stumbled and, besides, Nellie had not reported the incident to the police and there had been no forensic examination. It would be her word against his, and the outcome would greatly depend on the judge's understanding.

'Another problem,' said Daniel, 'is that we would have to accept a lower alimony payment, but anyway the difference would not be enough to justify the headaches associated with the other process. Later on, we could claim an increase in the value.'

It was at this point that Nellie felt a strong wave of heat running from her feet to her head, as if her blood was all rising up at once, and the pressure increased to such an extent that she had to lean against the wall. She was angry – perhaps for the first time in her life. Without hesitation, she turned to the lawyer and asked if there was another way out.

Daniel said he could pursue the contested divorce, but it would be a massive job and she eventually would come up empty-handed. Nellie took a deep breath and gave her response: she wanted to go all the way, even if it took a lifetime. She spoke in a loud, clear voice, and in case he had not heard repeated herself even more strongly. She would have said it yet again, but at this point the conversation was interrupted by a phone call from a client in trouble, and Daniel had to rush out to meet him. He would return later to continue the conversation. (Nellie must actually have some problem, thought Daniel. She is unable to think logically.)

Still taken over by anger and not knowing what to do with it, Nellie decided to try something different: she went out alone and ended up in a nightclub. She returned home only in the morning with a vague memory of having been involved with a boy, whose name escaped her memory.

In her cellphone there were 12 missed calls from Daniel that she hesitated to erase. Nellie went straight to work and, at the end of the shift, decided to meet him to talk. Calm, even relieved, she told him what had happened the night before. She also said that things were very confusing and that it would probably be a mistake to get involved with him, though she liked Daniel very much and did not regret what had passed between them.

The lawyer responded by smashing his fist against the wall. Nellie recoiled, startled, thinking he might get violent. Then he stood very still, thinking. As this lasted a good five minutes, Nellie said she thought it would be prudent for her to seek another lawyer so as not to increase friction. Sarcastic, Daniel assured her that all the lawyers in the world would want such a case, as easy and clear as it was, and of course 'they wouldn't want to charge you – maybe they'd even pay you for it'. Nellie was silent, yielding to the old slowness of movement and mental block of her married days. After all, she didn't understand sarcasm. Maybe she should have insisted, but she didn't know where to turn and gave up trying.

He confessed that, at first, just before he had got involved, he had sought to transfer the case to a specialist colleague, but he had declined. 'Depending on the judge that you get – if it is a man, for example – they could interpret your case as abandonment of the home,' he said. 'You're not in a very good situation.'

Nellie swallowed. She no longer felt anger or rebellion, only a very uncomfortable apathy. Suddenly, the dead, empty look was back in her eyes

– such a muted absence of the real world, according to her ex-husband, could only be symptomatic of autism.

For some time following this night, the lawyer made no contact with Nellie, who decided to respect his silence. Moreover, the work did not let up: every day, after leaving the hospital, she went to the house of an invalid who was recovering from heart surgery and needed a strong nurse to give him a bath, change his bandages and prescribe exercises. With this, she was earning extra money to pay the debt for the mattress.

Finally, Daniel rang announcing that he had started the contended divorce proceedings, as Nellie had asked, but said that he thought it was very unlikely to result in something. He said that she had hindered things by leaving the house without notice, and that the word of a nurse might not be taken into account. Also, that they needed to meet because she had to sign a Power of Attorney.

So they did. At the time, Nellie asked if he was okay and apologized about eight times as if she had committed a crime of lèse majesté by getting involved with someone else. She said she had thought a lot about the situation and considered their relationship a mistake, since she was still very vulnerable and distressed.

In response, Daniel asked her to try again. She said no.

The process took months and required numerous hearings with the judge. During this period, Nellie barely spoke with the lawyer, who was still resentful and, after all, started dating a co-worker. Nellie asked for details about the progress of the case but Daniel did not say much, only that the process was exhausting and that Nellie had little chance, especially because of the conservative history of the judge assigned to the case.

It was as if her body were 40-per-cent burned, she thought, and at any moment someone would arrive with a mirror.

Finally, the verdict came in: it was deemed inappropriate to assign blame for the divorce, nor was there any evidence of domestic violence. In the opinion of the judge, Nellie had been wrong to leave the house (which could be interpreted as abandonment of the home), invalidating in and of itself all other claims. The scar on her forehead could have other reasons, since there had been no witnesses.

In the end, he gave the nurse alimony of half the claimed amount. Nellie also lost out on the division of property, and the judge was keen to suggest that she should be satisfied with this.

When he left, Daniel also said it was a decent settlement. 'Next time, you should...' he began, but thought better of it and did not complete the sentence.

Nellie left the court somewhat dazed and upset, but with the vague feeling that she should try kung-fu lessons.

Vanessa Barbara was born in São Paulo in 1982 and is a journalist, translator, and writer. She is a contributing opinion writer for *The International New York Times* and a columnist for the Brazilian newspaper *O Estado de São Paulo*. She is the author of two novels, *O Verão do Chibo* and *Noites de Alface*, and the graphic novel *A Máquina de Goldberg*. 'Nellie' is a previously unpublished story translated from the original Portuguese.

RET'SEPILE MAKAMANE
Lesotho

WHY TLATLAMETSI ESCAPES TO PARADISE

I am an owl. Mind you, I started off as a god.

Tlatlametsi is the bringer of hope. In the village where we live, not so far from the open steaming mountain of magic, Tlatlametsi is a deity. He can change himself into anything he wants. It depends on the season. He can vanish and appear as a cheetah that roams the forest. The elders say not to kill wild animals when Tlatlametsi is not in the village.

When I left the village they had festivities to wish me a great journey.
Me, I know Tlatlametsi. He was born here many years ago. Tlatlametsi, he gets born into different bodies. Like this one of mine. In my sleep three moons ago I became a man. When I stepped out of those sticky blankets my father's youngest wife reported to him how urgently I needed to go to the mountain. My father, Mosenene, the chief's right-hand man, took me to Tlatlametsi's house. We found a heavy bag packed ready for a journey and Tlatlametsi flipping through pages to see how many days he would need in Paradise. Passports, he called them.

Tlatlametsi touched me on the head and shook it gently.
'You, you have to learn all kinds of wisdom. Look at those eyes! Dancing eyes of wisdom,' he said.

Tlatlametsi does not give empty words. He gives gifts. He shook into me the gift of telepathy that day. They say this is the one gift he hadn't passed on. Tlatlametsi is ageing. My father says that Tlatlametsi will stop next year. He will cease to give to us. Depending on the harvest. They know, the village knows, that another Tlatlametsi has to be born among us. Same spirit. Different body.

Tlatlametsi left for Paradise recently, to replenish the strength that he spends giving us gifts. This time there is a difference, though. I can see Tlatlametsi on his journey to Paradise. He crosses oceans. Tlatlametsi flies on an aeroplane painted the blue and white of butterflies. Tlatlametsi is the only one who can fly so bravely in this whole village. Because he has the powers of a god. Well, as I said, he is a god. The village children have taken to chasing every aeroplane in the sky. Following that frosty double-line on the blue sky, they shout, as if they are singing, 'Tlatlametsi, we know you are in that flying eagle! Drop us some sweets, Tlatlametsi! Tlatlametsi! Flying magic-man Tlatlametsi!' On and on chasing aeroplanes' tails they sing, with the hope of touching his magic.

I am a hunter.

Tlatlametsi, sometimes he makes decisions and those decisions cannot be changed. It is how it is.

This time around the people of the village said there is a bad omen. Tlatlametsi should delay his trip to Paradise. Too many things blinking in the sky at night. That was even before they knew for sure that he was going to fly through that same blinking-non-stop sky. But most especially they feared that yellow full moon that set hounds howling on the eve of his departure. He should be careful, the village elders said.

But Tlatlametsi, the only voice he listens to lately is his own. Once he has set his spirit on a mission, he goes through with it. If, for example, he is carrying a message of misfortune in the village, he just reads the letter aloud, immediately, without checking first what it contains. Some people say this is a sign of wisdom too from Tlatlametsi. He gives the news quickly so people can cry and finish and go back to their lives. So in a way he is also a healer then. He knows how to deal with people's pain. He opens his hands so that your tears can fall into his palms, if you are hurting. At times Tlatlametsi cannot stop what he sees in the future. Therefore he rushes the sufferers through it quickly.

My father, whose sharp ear has made the elders rename him the quickest snake (Mosenene), and who advises the chief against jealous forces, says that when the planets roll Tlatlametsi gets confused. Especially the last full moon of the harvest – he says that this time affects and weakens Tlatlametsi so much that he has to take his rest. Only when the planets re-align does Tlatlametsi come back to himself. And back to us. That is why the elders need Tlatlametsi to take a long sleep after the last full moon when the village finishes reaping that which they have sown.

Tlatlametsi flies to a predestined country. He has a blue sparkling ball in his house that rotates. They say – or Mosenene's all-knowing snake fangs tell me – that Tlatlametsi points on this blue ball. He says it is the world. Funny, isn't it? Because the earth we are standing on is brown soil. Anyway, Tlatlametsi points at the ball with his eyes closed, and it gives him a country to go to. And he obeys.

But now that I can see Tlatlametsi, I think he has difficulties on this journey. He needs all his six passports. In each country Tlatlametsi needs to throw away a passport. He is a new person in every new place. From Newcastle to Groningen to Bordeaux, from Bordeaux to Zurich to Leipzig. He is confusing me. Where is he going? He passes a big lake and sets out for Pisa. He spends a day sleeping in Pisa and in the cool night he walks fast and covers a lot of space to reach Gallese. Tlatlametsi wants to be close to the Vatican. I wonder why.

In Gallese Tlatlametsi finds a huge house on an expansive farm. He is worried. The veins on his temples are visible. His face is tired and wrecked. If I knew my eyes would see this much exasperation on the face of my god I would have not taken this gift of telepathy. I am feeling shame. I want to turn my eyes away from Tlatlametsi. Lately my friends come around, every day, to ask questions about the whereabouts of Tlatlametsi, ever since they learned about my abilities. Also, I have gained so many marbles as all of them refuse to beat me now. Even when I don't want to tell them about Tlatlametsi, especially when things do not look good in Paradise, they come and seek me out wherever I am.

'Come outside and play with us!'

But I have many chores today.

'What kind of chores are these that turn a person away from his friends?'

I have to help milk the cows when they arrive – the herdboy has cut his forefinger with a knife, so he can't milk.

'You can't milk either! You spill all over! *Hee hee hee!*'

Yes I can!

'It's too early, anyway – our play will finish before the cows come home. Come outside!'

I have so many things to do, I have to wash the milk pails and sweep the kraals and prepare…

'You can't see Tlatlametsi any more, can you? Your eyes have lost their way to Paradise.'

Yes, I still can.

'If you can, can you tell us this then: what are the children of Paradise doing right now?'

'No! What are they wearing is a better question.'

You want me to tell you stories about everything that is happening in Paradise?

'We can't hear you properly! Come out of the house and play with us, come tell us what Tlatlametsi has been doing. Come!'

All the children of the village, even the ones who are not my friends, join in. They keep on calling me and calling me until I come out. And their faces smile. Then we run and race towards the steaming mountain and gather in the foothills, and watch the steam come out at the top. And then we play, and I beat them at most of the games. And then we sit on the rocks and talk. And tell stories.

In the roof of a farmhouse in Gallese lives a big owl.

'What kind of an owl?'

'How big are its eyes?'

'Eyes! You are still talking about eyes! I want to ask how big its ears are.'

'What is it eating in that roof? Mice?'

You ask me too many questions, all at once! I have only one mouth to feed all these ears! Listen, because I will have to run back home and finish my chores very soon.

'No, you don't! We saw your family herdboy with uninjured fingers yesterday!'

That was yesterday! Today is today! Today brings its own weather.

'So right! So right! Sorry, our friend! May lightning strike the mouths of those that ever doubt you, the visioned one, the one with a gift of seeing-away-away! Please feed our hungry ears!'

The owl scratches and scratches in the roof. Occasionally, it towit-towoos. It snores like a drunken person, this owl. The people of the house, they name it 'Federico's owl'.

'Who is this Frederico?'

Stop jumping into my mouth! *Federico* is the son of the house, a bit older than us. He goes to school though. The owl stays on top of his room, in the roof. So you can't see it. You can only hear it.

'He goes to school? *Banna*! How I wish I will go to school next year!'

'Me too!'

Do you people want to listen or do you want me to leave?

'Okay, okay, tell us more! Don't go! No more interrupting. Shut up everyone! *Liphokophoko*! Please continue, our friend.'

He is becoming a man, this Federico, leaving the boy behind.

'Like you!'
But his spirit is wild. Too wild. It needs to be captured from its prancing wildness and trained. Ah, but the children of Paradise, they do not go to the mountain. So this is too hard for this boy Federico alone.

Federico, he starts to take his father's cigars, and he also takes methylated spirit to school...

'What are cigars?'

'Shhh! Shh! Go on, our visioned one.'

He is not a friend of his father, Federico, you see. He is frightened of his father's image...

'Does his father have a powerful root-man who makes his image extra-strong?'

No – they do not have root-men in Paradise. Men make their own images there.

'How?'

'Shh! Shh! We are listening to a story, *hleng*! Please keep your questions in your pockets for a while!'

Federico is afraid the image of his father is too big. He feels he will not be able to walk in it to become a man himself. Sometimes his father, who is called Lorenzo, takes him on long foot trips to distant villages. His father's work is to discover and unearth engineering methods of old tribes called the Samnites and the Etruscans...

'Engine what?'

'Shh, people! Go on, our friend!'

But Federico wants to discover and learn something different. His heart softens at hearing the villagers his father speaks to on these trips – their tongues spouting the rich proverbs and folktales in dialects of their old tribes. Federico's hands never itch for work. Never. Only his ears have a hunger for the sounds of the villagers. And he even thinks he can hear them when he touches the ruined bridges and water passageways of the olden days that his father studies.

And he cannot tell anyone that all he wants to do is listen to these words. But he believes that the owl knows his heart. He feels very close to it. He thinks that its snoring rhythms have patterns that only he understands. But he is still afraid, you see? And he becomes more and more afraid the afraider he feels. His heart thumps and drums so loud at times that it feels like it would blow up and come out of his ears. He inhales a white powder that makes him feel a little stronger. But when he wakes up in the morning he is back where he began, with buckets and buckets of fear weighing on his shoulders…

'He should smoke *dagga*, not powders and *snuifs* like an old woman!'

He has already! They call it hashish in Paradise.

'If he is older, he should drink pineapple brew. In fact, dried grape brew is better, they say it makes you sleep veeeery nice.'

'Hush-ish you! What do you know about drinking? Your nostrils still smell of breast milk! Our friend, please tell us more.'

He burns things, Federico. Randomly. Aimlessly. He trades his father's Russian cigars for the white powder and the *dagga* at school. He mixes these things, he injects things that look like vaccines between his thighs because he thinks his parents would see his arms if he injected them there. Then he starts to walk like he is limping. Federico laughs at everything. But the sound of his fear crowds his laugh. His laughter annoys his parents, and startles his own eyes.

'He will run mad!'

'He needs whipping, as soon as possible!'

His despair makes him weak, and jumbles his thoughts. At times he does not even remember any more what it is that frightens him so, except he finds himself speaking the old tribal dialects of his people aloud at odd moments, at times when he is trying his best not to speak at all, making his friends at school giggle and call him Federico the Deep. He starts to dislike many of his friends. He becomes so worrisome that he sometimes wishes he could stay in his room and never meet people, especially the ones closest to him. He begins to sleep for too long and his parents have to shout many times to wake him up for school.

'He is lazy! I saw it right when you said his hands do not itch for work!'

Then Federico thinks that there is another self in him. Or that a messenger of God has entered him. He feels a sudden hope. He feels that his God is within reach. Which is strange for him because he has recently abandoned the faith of his family. Then, as quick as it came, that hope suddenly returns to fear. And then pain enters and tears his heart. He knows that he has to leap, to have courage and start to become a young man, but it seems impossible for him.

'This here is your growth beginning, young man. You have nothing to fear. Strong boys like you make good men.'

Federico thinks he is hearing voices in his head. He has strange dreams without endings.

'Oh no! He is definitely knocking on the door of madness!'

Federico, one night, makes the hard decision. He thinks of using his school tie, but the image that forms in his head makes him wince. He decides against the tie. And instead takes out all his magic cocktails and zols, and the needle, and spreads them on the bed. He locks the door. Takes off his clothes. Federico writes on a piece of paper and places it next to the mixtures.

'What does the note say, can you read it? Like those big names in Paradise?'

Yes, I can read it for you.

'Then do!'

It reads: *'To be continued…'*

'That's all?'

Yes, now keep quiet! Or else I won't go on…

When Federico returns from the bathroom (his plan was to be found clean in the morning), he realizes that his piece of paper has moved from his bed to the floor. He wonders where the wind came from. He picks it up. The owl in the roof is not snoring tonight. Next to Federico's last line is written: *'By whom?'*

Federico looks at this new sentence and tries the door again and again. The door is still very much locked. He looks around his room, a strange smile forms on his face, then he chuckles, then he laughs, and laughs louder, and starts jumping up and down, shouting excitedly: 'Me and Mr Owl! Me and Mr Owl have a plan, don't we?'

He quickly tires. He lies down on the tiled floor, holding onto this note. Federico stays half-awake for a while. The owl starts to snore. Then, for the first time in a long time, Federico feels safety arrive and rock him to a deep sleep.

He wakes up in the morning, clear in the head but weak. He needs food. He takes a shower. Then he brushes his teeth in circles like the way his father used to teach him when he was very young.

He then runs downstairs. His mother and father and his baby sister Luciana stare at him from the kitchen table. They think he might burn something. There have been mornings like this where he would join them at the breakfast table and swallow everything within his reach. Slices of peppers, apples, melons, tomatoes, cheese, bread and sardines. And scoops of jam, marmalade, honey and olive oil. And grapes, and eggs, and pomegranates. All at once. And then he would grab the matchbox and burn new letters just delivered from the post office, or tablecloths. Not this morning. This morning he looks at the surprised faces of his parents and says, 'Figs ripe!' in an old Florentine tongue.

'Go get them yourself,' his mother says.

He goes out and bounces back with a basket full of figs.

'What's the inspiration this morning – St Francis of Assisi?' asks his father, Lorenzo.

With his mouth full of the juicy figs Federico says, 'Something – well *Someone* really believes in me.'

'Who? The snoring owl?' his father asks, watching Federico push a third over-ripe fig into his mouth, just allowing enough space for his tongue to come out and lick the edge of his palm that's covered in juice...

'Hmm, I want some fig now!'

'Shhhhhhhhhhh!'

Federico says: 'Yes father, the owl! Can you believe it? And contrary to the beloved Saint, I am not talking to it, it is talking to me!'

And he looks like himself again, our friend Federico. He believes that somehow he is going to make it into manhood, without his mixtures...

'Without going to the mountain? How can he become a man without going to the mountain?'

He just believes it. I don't know.

'But where is Tlatlametsi, our friend?'

Tomorrow, I will tell you more tomorrow.

'We will come and fetch you. Are you watching over Tlatlametsi's house this time?'

Maybe. Time to go now.

Me, I know Tlatlametsi. I know him better than the cleverest herdboys in this village. I look after his hidden beehives in the forest when he goes away. I also watch over Tlatlametsi's secluded hut with keen eyes, especially when it prepares itself for his return after one of his long journeys. And all the plants and the bright yellow cotulas around the house, and even the smallest weeds in the thatched roof are in flower for his return.

Tlatlametsi, this is what he is very good at. He leaves the village every year after he has helped with the harvest. He lets the seasons roll. And when it gets warm he comes back to the village.

Tlatlametsi, he is the strongest man in this village. When he was just a few years over my age, he was not yet Tlatlametsi then. He was the cleverest boy already. The village people sat around the chief's kraal. They talked and talked. After three years of talking they ignited him into a god.

We need Tlatlametsi during the ploughing season. We need him when the cattle, sheep, goats and donkeys breed. The village needs Tlatlametsi too much sometimes. But he is a god. At our weakest we need a god, don't we?

Tlatlametsi's wisdom stretches to the plants. The wild ones, too. In seasons when there is no rain, Tlatlametsi goes into the forest and gets succulent roots. Sometimes wild thorns cut his legs and he bleeds a bit. When Tlatlametsi bleeds there are bad winds in the village. Tlatlametsi climbs mountains – fog and steam blinding him, he gets us wild fruit.

I am a hunter. When I go out hunting, the kill is for a hundred mouths. They have turned me into a provider for the whole village.

Each harvest I leave the village and go to a different country. It has become easier to travel to Europe. Just stay in each country for very short periods of time before their sniffer dogs pull you out. I like the olive-oil harvest here in Gallese. Your farmers are not too mean here. They pay well. And I can take a lot of oil and money home to help my people throughout the year. Our rains have been very stingy lately.

That is how I came to live in your roof, Mr Lorenzo. Each harvest I need to escape from my village, from the memory of the first harvest when they made me a diviner. I did not want it, I wanted to remain a simple hunter. The after-harvest festivities remind me of how difficult a man's work and role can be in this world.

I'm only a runner. The way I do things keeps my fellow villagers thinking I have magic. I hunt, they think the gods are providing. I speak, people hang their heads low in respect. It can be tiring.

Each time I want to go further and further away from this reality. I am like a refugee in my own body. I live for the work. Sometimes it fills me up with joy and enthusiasm and lightness of heart. Other times dread and heaviness. At times I wish I could dissolve into a bird. It was fantastic and scary too when I was up there in that roof, hearing you people tell this owl story and the stories of soldiers who lived in the roofs in your last war. I did at times believe myself an owl. My scratching and towit towoooting was very real. I wish I could have remained an owl. But Federico had to meet his pen pal. He needed to stop doubting his own sanity for a change.

I appreciate your offer, Mr Lorenzo. I have been given a good hand for the fields. The crops talk to me, or is it the other way round? Talk to your crops. They listen. But I cannot stay. I have to head back home to my village. They are my people. Without them I am not.

Ret'sepile Makamane was born and raised in Lesotho. She studied Philosophy and Theatre at the National University of Lesotho, and then moved to Johannesburg where she studied Drama and Film at the University of the Witwatersrand. She then became Commissioning Editor for the South African Broadcasting Corporation (SABC). She went to the University of Leeds in the UK on a Graça Machel Scholarship in 2008, and subsequently moved onto the MA in Creative Writing at the University of East Anglia, where she was later awarded the Charles Pick Fellowship. She spends her time between Europe and Southern Africa.

FAN WU
China/United States

NOBODY'S TALKING ABOUT FALLING IN LOVE

The girl was tall and plump, a first-year college student. As required by her university, she and other first-year students had to complete a one-month military training program before school started, in which no other classes would be held except those on ideology and Party history.

It was the third day into training. Her grass-green army jacket – in the biggest size for female students – was tucked into a brown belt and pinched tight on her shoulders and chest. Her pants fitted at the waist but stopped an inch above her ankles. She was the first in her row, arranged from tallest to shortest. There were ten rows in total – all girls – on a campus basketball court, forming a square: Unit 8. In training, boys and girls were separated, boys in odd-numbered, girls in even-numbered units. Boys from her class were in Unit 3 and trained at an outdoor stadium. At the end of the program the students would be graded according to performance. If they failed, they'd have to retake the training next year and, later, might have trouble getting a diploma.

It was a hot summer day. The girl and her classmates sweated profusely under the scorching sun but dared not wipe their faces. She looked down and saw beads of sweat on her nose. No doubt she'd get tanned or even burned on her face and neck. A few days earlier she'd had her hair cut to the bottom of her ear lobes to meet army requirements, so it wasn't long enough to protect her neck. Also, she'd gotten up too late this morning to apply sunblock. She raised her left shoulder slightly to scratch an itchy spot on her cheek, briefly easing her shoulders and bending her knees, but repositioned immediately into attention under a soldier's gaze – on each corner of the square stood a fully uniformed soldier at attention.

Their sergeant was giving a speech. Tall and barrel-chested, he stood with his feet apart at shoulder-width, his hands behind his back, his army cap covering his forehead and shading half his face. He was said to be a model soldier and the toughest instructor.

She listened for a while. What utter nonsense the man was spouting! If college students had not provoked the government with their protests one year earlier, she wouldn't have been forced to stand here, like all the other first-years across the country, on a hot summer afternoon to listen to a barely literate soldier haranguing his unwilling victims on how to become a qualified college student. She pitied the president, a highly acclaimed mathematics scholar, for having to succumb to the government to enforce military training on students.

At 1.00pm, after singing the song 'Socialism is Good', the girls were dismissed. Some collapsed on the ground, drumming their legs with their fists. Some took off their belts and used the corner of their jackets to wipe their faces. Others charged towards the canteen, which closed at 1.30pm.

She took a palm-sized mirror from her pocket and examined herself – her cheeks were red and her lips chapped; the worst was the exposed small triangle between her collarbones, pathetically burned, painful to the touch. She'd look like a dark-skinned country girl in a week, she thought. If her parents were to visit her in the next few days, they wouldn't recognize her.

She trudged towards her dorm, her stomach aching from hunger. But it wouldn't be smart to go to the canteen now: there'd be little food left, only cold egg soup and fatty meat dishes; moreover, she'd have to fight her way to the counter. The chefs, eager to get off work, must be short-tempered and would scold the students for not standing in line. She'd be better off eating her own cookies and fruit, bought from the tiny grocery store near her dorm the day she arrived at the university. It was only a week since she'd left home in Shanghai and traveled south for 15 hours by train to Guangzhou. She could have gone to a college in Shanghai, as most of her high-school classmates did – all Shanghainese believe Shanghai is the best place in China – but she had wanted to be as far from home as possible. If her parents hadn't been so adamantly opposed, she'd have applied for a school in Harbin. She wasn't afraid of her parents but arguing with them was pointless. As a compromise, she had picked this university in Guangzhou, a city economically comparable with Shanghai.

'Hey!' A male voice behind her. She didn't stop; he wouldn't be talking to her.

'Hey, you!' the voice repeated.

She turned. The sergeant was a yard behind her, accompanied by the University president and the other soldiers. On closer examination she could see the greenish shade on his shaved cheeks and chin. His nose was high between his eyebrows and wide in the middle. His hands, loosely folded in the front, were bony around the joints. Though she'd thought he was in his early thirties, she now guessed his age at between 20 and 25.

'What's up?' She didn't salute as instructed in her first class – she wasn't a soldier to begin with and it was considered free time now.

'Attention! Salute!' A soldier shouted.

She had to obey.

'What's your name?' the sergeant asked.

'Wang Qi.'

'Comrade Wang, your belt is on the wrong side and you forgot to flatten your collar on the back.'

She fixed her collar and belt – she must have been half asleep when she was putting on her uniform. Other students nearby were staring with interest, some laughing unsympathetically.

'Extend your hands,' the sergeant ordered.

Her polished purple nails gleamed in the sun like pieces of glass. The color didn't look as bright as when she'd applied it two days ago.

'Wash off the color when you come back this afternoon. No make-up is allowed during the training. And no earrings either.'

How could he have noticed those tiny stones? They were her 16th-birthday gift from her high-school boyfriend. The two of them broke up a month ago. He didn't pass the entrance exam for college and had to take a clerical job at a local travel agency. They had a big fight since he didn't want her to leave Shanghai. Why should she listen to him? No one could stop her from doing what she wanted.

As soon as the sergeant turned, she withdrew her hands. She glared at his back until he disappeared behind a wall.

Qi walked into her dorm room and tore open a bag of instant noodles. She lifted a thermos and was about to pour hot water into her lunchbox to prepare the noodles, but it was empty. The other thermos was empty, too. Her roommates must have used all the water. There was no hot water in the dorm and they had to take turns to fetch it from the canteen. Usually two thermoses a day was enough, but all three of her roommates had chosen to eat instant noodles today – each having two bags. Sang had even filled one of her plastic water bottles so she wouldn't need to buy water during the afternoon training. She was from a small town and always tight on money.

Qi could smell beef and the mix of MSG and other artificial flavors, which stirred her stomach and made her mouth water. Had she not been stopped by the sergeant, there'd have been hot water left for her. None of her roommates said a word about the empty thermoses; they all looked innocent and indifferent, eating their noodles, chatting. They must have expected her to fetch more hot water since she was the one who needed it most. Then they'd use it without any guilt – Sang had another water bottle to fill and Ting said she could eat another bag of noodles. No, she wouldn't want to be taken advantage of. She'd rather go hungry than make another trip to the canteen – she had been the one who had fetched hot water this morning.

She picked up an apple from the fruit basket on her desk, wiped it with a tissue so vigorously that it glistened as if freshly waxed and took a big bite of it – down to the core. Then she ate two over-ripe bananas whose skins had grown black spots. Nothing lasted long in this hot summer weather.

It was not until she took off her belt and uniform and lay down on the bed that the pricking pain in her back and neck hit her. Her legs were swollen from standing the whole morning. She wanted to fall asleep but the sunlight through the uncovered window was too bright. She lay idly, looking through the window at the cloudless sky. It must have been at least 40 degrees Celsius. She touched her cheeks and the patches behind her ears, reminding herself to apply sunblock this afternoon.

It was Ting who started the subject about the sergeant.

'This guy doesn't seem to have any mercy on us.'

'I heard he got a lot of awards. Maybe being tough on us will give him a promotion. I bet it will. He treats us like dirt,' Sang said.

'We're always the last to be dismissed. The girls in Chemistry and Biology returned half an hour earlier than us.' Wei released a deep sigh.

'Don't you think he's quite handsome? His eyes are so bright, and his chest... hmm, solid as a rock. Our president looked totally like an old wimp beside him.' It was Ting who had suddenly switched the direction of the conversation. She was the oldest in the dorm and the one who liked talking about men, though she claimed to be still a virgin. She had irregular and jutting teeth, which made it difficult for her to close her mouth completely.

'Men just look cool in uniform, like us girls looking nice in miniskirts,' Wei remarked and slurped the last of the noodles in her lunch box.

'But he's so damn serious. He'd look cute if he knew how to smile. When I first saw him, I thought he'd be amazed at seeing so many girls and would go easy on us.' Sang rose from her bed. 'In his barracks, I doubt he has a chance to see any girls. Even if there are some, they must be ugly and speak and act like men.'

'I thought he'd be nice to us, too. I was standing in the first row, smiling all the time but he didn't seem to notice,' Ting said, studying herself in a mirror, plucking her eyebrows with tweezers. Her mouth contorted visibly whenever she removed a hair.

'I bet he'll relax a bit later. He's probably nervous – you know, seeing so many girls in front of him,' Wei said.

'Do you think he was dreaming about sleeping with one of us when he was making the speech?' It was Ting.

Both Wei and Sang burst into laughter.

'You dirty *dirty* girl!' Wei said.

'I dare you to go ask him that question!' Sang said.

'Girls,' Qi felt she had to say something. 'After this month he and his folks will go back to their barracks in the wilderness, far away from the city, and we'll forget them altogether. Who'd be so silly as to fall in love with him?' The conversation between her roommates seemed ridiculous to her. If anything, she wanted to humiliate the sergeant, just as he had humiliated her in public earlier.

'Nobody's talking about falling in love. Just a little flirting and fun won't hurt,' Ting retorted.

'Yeah, just a little fun,' Sang agreed.

'To get through this boring month,' said Wei.

'To create a little drama and make this ordeal worthwhile.' Ting made a quick twirl in the center of the room. 'That's called Beauty Trap, one of the oldest, yet most efficient warfare strategies according to "Art of War".'

'You really mean it? Get him to fall in love with one of us, then dump him?' Qi blurted out impatiently. Had her roommates lost their minds?

'Why not? I don't see anything wrong with it?' Sang said.

'Hmm, I'm not sure,' Wei muttered.

'Sounds like fun. If he weren't so strict with us, we wouldn't be thinking about vengeance,' Ting said. 'Sang, are you going to do it?'

'Not me. My boyfriend is in the Engineering Department. He'd break up with me if he found out.'

'Don't look at me.' Wei jumped up from her chair. 'You know I won't do it.'

'I don't mind but I'm so petite, so thin. I doubt he'd fall in love with me.' Ting was barely five feet tall.

Qi could feel the stare of her roommates. If not for this morning's humiliation, she'd never have considered their proposal. But now... she remembered the sergeant's sullen face and her fellow students' laughter. For a whole month, no earrings or nail polish or perfume for her, and she'd have to get up at 5.30am every day and suffer all the physical pain. It wasn't really the sergeant's fault – he was merely an executor, an order-taker – but who else was to blame? He could have at least treated the girls a little nicer. He definitely deserved a punishment for what he had done to her and the other girls.

'What's the incentive?' she finally said.

'You don't need to fetch hot water for one month,' Ting suggested – she must have noticed how gloomy Qi was when she didn't have hot water to fix her noodles.

'For one year,' Qi said.

'That's way too long!' Sang said.

'Then you do it yourself.'

'How about half a year?' Ting offered.

'Do it yourself.'

Finally an agreement was reached, to Qi's satisfaction.

Qi was going to ask her roommates to put the agreement in writing so they wouldn't deny it after the training ended, but she was running out of time – she had to remove her nail polish and earrings and apply sunblock. She also had to fold her blanket into a rectangle, as required by the army – for some reason this took her twice as long as her roommates. When she was done with all her chores there was barely enough time to put on her uniform. She ran down the stairs to catch up with her roommates on their way to the basketball court.

A gruelling afternoon. The cement on the basketball court was blindingly bright and the air heavy and hard to breathe. The girls stood still for one hour and spent another two hours learning a marching formation used in ceremonies. One girl threw up and had to sit in the shade to take a break. Another girl was simply exhausted, her legs shaking, and had to be sent back to the dorm. These incidents didn't seem to have bothered the sergeant. Fully uniformed, he yelled his commands. 'One two one, one two one... attention... at ease... turn left... salute...' He stopped the girls often to correct their postures.

'Raise your leg! Higher, much higher. Don't let it drop.'

'Straighten your back! Look straight! You aren't in a dance club.'

'Swing your arms chest-high. Pay attention to the angle!'

Or he found other faults with them.

'Repeat the commands... louder! Much louder! I can't hear you. '

'Keep the pace! Stay in line! No break if you can't even keep the line straight!'

It was painful for Qi to keep her legs at the right angle since her pants were tight – the creases around her thighs cut into her flesh. Across the street, on another basketball court, a different unit was taking its second break. But the girls in Unit 8 hadn't even taken their first break. She cursed in her heart – to hell with the weather, to hell with the training, to hell with the government, and mostly, to hell with the sergeant – to distract herself from the pain in her thighs.

They were finally allowed to take a 20-minute break. Some girls ran to the nearby grocery store to buy water or ice cream. In her haste to get ready earlier, she'd forgotten to bring money. There, under a tree, Sang was drinking from the water bottle she had filled during lunch. She threw her roommate a vicious glance. She could have borrowed money from a girl in her class but didn't feel like talking with anyone right now. She sat down against a tree on the sidewalk on the far side of the court, her sweat-stained clothes and pants heavy as sandbags, her rubber-toed army shoes uncomfortably tight – her feet must be swollen. *I smell like a rotten egg*, she said to herself in disgust. She spread her legs and closed her eyes. Even a five-minute nap would be heaven.

'Hey, you.' She heard the sergeant's steps.

It took her a few seconds to realize he was talking to her. She leapt to her feet and saluted. She had no energy to confront him, nor did she want to get into trouble in front of her classmates.

'What's your name?'

'Wang Qi.'

'Comrade Wang, you did well in the afternoon session.'

Should she thank him for his compliment? She couldn't bring herself to do so, so she kept silent. She could smell garlic on his breath. His teeth were yellow, probably from smoking.

'Every unit needs a student leader. I think you're the best candidate. Do you want to accept this honorable role?' He softened his tone a bit and his mouth seemed to twist into a faint smile, but his erect posture remained the same. He looked no less formidable than when he was training the girls.

His proposal surprised her. Could she say 'No'? – nobody would be so stupid. She might be asked to explain why she thought she wasn't qualified, to which she had no answer. Also, he'd said it was an honorable role. Her rejection would apparently be self-denying, even self-disparaging. Maybe it'd even be added to her *dang'an*, her personal dossier, as something negative to be held against her in the future.

He stood there, motionless, blocking the sunlight. She knew he wouldn't leave until he got an answer.

'Yes, Sergeant,' she said.

Her new role was announced immediately and in the last hour of training she stood outside the square, yelling the tempo out aloud – *one two one, one two one* – while the sergeant examined and corrected each girl's posture. At first, her voice was uncertain and hesitant, seemingly forced out of her throat, but soon she mastered the task and even began to drawl the second 'one' like the sergeant did. To her amazement, as she was steering Unit 8 in different directions, pride and power filled her heart. Watching the unit move under her commands had created a distance between her and the other girls, like sitting in the audience watching a movie. She quickly noted the other girls' jealousy and indignation – especially in her roommates. Ting and Sang had stopped smiling since her appointment was announced. Even the timid Wei threw her an unfriendly glance now and then.

The following Tuesday, when it was Qi's turn to fetch hot water, she didn't do it. Though she didn't intend to carry out her end of the bargain, she felt she had the right to enjoy the privilege of not fetching hot water. After all, since she had been appointed, Unit 8 had looked much tidier and more efficient – with her assistance, the sergeant had been able to spend more time correcting the girls' postures – and was allowed to take a 20-minute break every other hour just like other units. The day the girls started the crawling drills on a dirt playground, one third finished the distance within the required time, compared with one quarter on average for other girls' units. She was not sure whether it was because the sergeant had grown more comfortable with the girls or because the girls had begun to live up to his expectations, but he looked more relaxed and would even smile or make small jokes like 'the training will tone your legs and make you look nicer in skirts.' Sometimes, Qi would be amused by the thought that Unit 8's improvement was due to the other girls' increasing jealousy and hatred of her – they seemed to have been trying hard to impress the sergeant since she was appointed.

Ten days into the training, to her surprise, her aversion to the sergeant began to fade, though she still disliked him and avoided speaking with him whenever possible. There had been little interaction between them other than brief discussions during breaks, about the unit's performance or about the next few days' schedule. As he spoke she took notes: 14 September, 15 September, 16 September...Monday, Tuesday, Wednesday... sunny, cloudy, sunny... one person absent due to toothache... the unit ran two miles in the morning... the unit learned a new song, *Returning From the Battle*... the unit will study Chairman Mao's article *About Contradiction* tomorrow. Her elegant handwriting seemed to have impressed the sergeant, who would read her notes quietly for minutes before signing his name at the end of her daily logs. The first time he signed, he hovered his pen over the paper for a long moment as if he'd forgotten his own name. When he was done, he blushed. He closed the notebook instantly before the ink was dry. Later, when Qi opened the notebook, she couldn't help laughing at his childish signature – coarsely written, it was tilted 45 degrees to the right, like a badly damaged house.

Though she still had to stand in the blazing sunlight many hours a day and had grown tanned despite the high-SPF sunblock with a whitening effect, she was getting used to the physical workout. She had even lost weight, especially in her waist and thighs. Seeing herself in the full-size mirror at the grocery store, she was amazed at how good she looked now. The government and the army could never have thought that the training they had imposed on the students as a punishment would result in such a positive outcome on a plump girl like her.

Qi and the sergeant had their first long meeting Tuesday evening during the third week. In the past two days, the girls had learned how to install, carry and aim a semi-automatic rifle. The upcoming Friday, Unit 8, with five other units, would go to a shooting range to practise, each girl given a rifle and five bullets. The sergeant would give the 'open fire' command himself, but Qi would be needed to help with taking roll, handing out guns, counting bullets, and other administrative tasks.

They were sitting inside a bookstore near her dorm. Before the meeting Qi had taken a shower and washed her hair. It felt good to be wearing her own clothes – a short-sleeved sky-blue sports shirt and a pair of denim capris. The sergeant also wore his civilian clothes – a white shirt and khaki slacks. It was the first time that Qi had seen him without his uniform. He looked young with his short hair, like some male students in her class. Ever since he had sat down he had seemed ill at ease. As he spoke he avoided eye contact. He seemed to have a hard time deciding where to put his hands – on the table, at his sides, on his lap or behind his head. His voice was jumpy and nervous, often too fast to be comprehensible, and his country accent was stronger than ever, though he was apparently trying hard to hide it.

Poor guy! Qi thought, amused. He was like a schoolboy who doesn't know what to do in front of the girl he secretly admires. Had he ever dated anyone? What had become of his usual serious expression and stiff, formal posture? Where was his authority? Without his uniform, he looked helpless and lost, like a hermit crab without its shell for shelter. This realization brought both sympathy and satisfaction to Qi. After all, the sergeant was just as real and vulnerable as everyone else; there was no reason to be afraid of him. How absurd that she and her roommates had wanted to take revenge on him!

They sank into a brief silence after discussing the plan for the upcoming shooting exercise. It was 9.30pm, half an hour from curfew for both. As the sergeant was organizing the files on the table he asked how old she was.

'18,' she said.

'My sister is 18. The first time I saw you I was surprised by how much you two are alike. She just got married to one of my childhood friends.'

Qi's face darkened – her looking like a country-born girl was quite an insult to her – but the sergeant didn't notice her displeasure.

'Oh, that's too young,' she said, trying to be polite.

'Girls in the country aren't like you city girls.'

'Are you married?' This question somehow came to her.

'No,' he smiled shyly. 'I have a girlfriend in my hometown. She's 19.'

'How did you meet?'

'Her ba is a barber and my ba used to have his hair cut by him.'

'How often do you see her now?'

'Twice a year, when I have a vacation.'

'That's not very often. Are you going to get married soon?'

'I have another two years in the army. Afterwards, I'm going to find a job in the city, as an office clerk, or something like that, and will pick her up from my village. When I have some money I'll start a small business. If I can make good money from the business, I'll buy a condo downtown. She likes going to the malls.' As the sergeant spoke he stared at the ceiling fan, his arms folded like a primary-school student in the classroom. Qi was suddenly moved by his little ambition. Really, he was a nice guy, honest and responsible, even a little handsome. And he was so tall, taller than every other guy she knew. If she had met him at college, she might...

'Why did you join the army in the first place?'

'Free food, free clothes, and you get an allowance every month. All the young men in my village are dying to get into the army. You can't be too picky if you grow up in the country.'

'Why didn't you go to college?' It was silly to ask, but she wanted to hear the answer.

'Even if my parents sold all their pigs and chickens, they wouldn't be able to afford to send me to college,' he said, without sadness. 'And I wasn't a smart kid to start with anyway.'

'If you could have chosen between college and the army, which would you have picked?'

'College wasn't an option.'

'I mean *if* you could have chosen, if you *had* the option.'

'Hmm,' the sergeant paused. 'I've never thought about that. I like being in the army.'

Qi wanted to ask more but two uniformed soldiers walked in to buy postcards and stamps. Their appearance seemed to have put the sergeant on guard. He took a look at his watch and said he had to leave.

Qi didn't return to her dorm after the sergeant left. She bought a lighter and a pack of cigarettes and went to the lake across the street. She sat on a bench and began to smoke. Along the lake, on some other benches, couples from higher grades were embracing and kissing. She smoked half a pack and it was almost midnight when she started for her dorm.

On Friday an army truck sent Unit 8 to the shooting range on the outskirts of the city. The shooting exercise went smoothly for her unit despite minor incidents: two girls opened fire before the order was issued; one was frightened after firing her first bullet and refused to continue; yet another fired her five bullets quickly, one after the other. At the end of the day her unit's average score was the highest out of the six units. A company commander announced the results and handed the sergeant and her, as Unit 8's student leader, a copper figurine of a soldier holding a gun and a triangle-shaped silk banner.

Qi suggested to the sergeant that they go out to celebrate the victory. Of course, she didn't care about the award; on the contrary, she thought it ridiculous. The only good thing about learning how to shoot was for the bragging rights – she could tell her parents and her spoiled ex-boyfriend in Shanghai: *believe it or not, I've used a rifle and shot five bullets!*

She wasn't sure why she wanted to see the sergeant again, but after her last conversation with him she wanted to learn more about him. She had to see his real self beneath the army uniform. She had to find out what was on his mind despite his surface simplicity. She didn't believe they had nothing in common. There must be something and she needed to know what it was, like a detective investigating a mystery.

But what use was this knowledge? It wasn't as if they would become friends if she knew more about him. In less than two weeks he'd be gone anyway and she'd start her normal college life – studying, partying, dating. She'd forget him and remember the training only as a joke.

Was she a little in love with him? This thought made her laugh. If she ever wrote a novel she might make the intellectual heroine fall in love with a poorly educated sergeant just for the sake of romance. This kind of cheap novel was only good for high-school girls or women going into mid-life crisis. In reality... no, it would never happen.

At last she decided not to worry about her motivation for meeting the sergeant. She was curious about him. That was it. She was a person who did what she wanted.

They met at a café off-campus, within walking distance of the university. The sergeant wore the same clothes he had worn last time, except that this time his shirt was ironed. She wore a one-piece black dress with a wide opening exposing her neck and a big portion of her shoulders. Since she had lost quite a bit weight, the dress, bought a few months ago, now hung loosely on her at her waist and hips. But she didn't care. It wasn't a date for her, nothing close to that. She ordered espresso and chocolate mousse for herself.

'Do you need help?' she asked the sergeant, who had been looking at the menu since they were seated. He shook his head and ordered a plain coffee and no pastries.

The café was tastefully decorated with museum posters and blue and yellow recessed lights. Soft and slow-paced jazz music rose from the background. As their drinks and dessert were served, she offered to share her chocolate mousse.

'Like the music?' she asked.

'Not really. It makes me sleepy.'

'Have you ever gone clubbing in the city?'

He shook his head. 'I'm only here for the training. People dance in clubs and I don't know how to dance.'

'I can teach you.'

He smiled at her, then looked away at the neon lights.

'Do you like Guangzhou?'

'Yeah, it's nice. A lot of activities. But everything is so expensive. I won't live here unless I have a good job.'

'What'd you do if you had all the opportunities you wanted?'

'I don't know.' He tilted his head – a gesture that Qi thought cute.

'I mean… if you could do whatever you wanted to do, like become a professor, or a journalist, or a doctor, or a business tycoon, or something like that, what'd it be?'

'I don't know. I'd like to start a small business, I guess.'

'Don't you have any interests?' She could feel impatience in her own voice.

'I like watching movies.'

'What kind of movies?'

'War movies, crime movies… stuff like that. The army organizes us to see a movie once a week.'

'Don't you like reading?'

'I don't read fast.'

'I can lend you books. Some are pretty easy to read.'

'We'll see about that.' He grinned.

'What do you do in your barracks every day?'

'Training or studying the latest Party documents. We play a lot of poker in our spare time. There's not much to see or do around the barracks.' He slurped his coffee. 'Too bitter!' He stuck out his tongue. He tore open four packets of sugar and poured them into his coffee.

'Aren't you… aren't you interested in having freedom?' asked Qi.

'What do you mean?' He looked into her face. 'I have freedom.'

'I mean freedom of speech, the freedom of the Press. That kind of freedom.' She leaned across the table.

'Comrade Wang,' the sergeant said, sitting straight, a coldness in his eyes. 'The problem with college students is that they're influenced too much by the Western–'

'Don't give me that crap! Be yourself for once!'

Her loud voice drew attention from other people at the café but they quickly shifted their eyes away after realizing that the little incident wouldn't evolve into something dramatic. A couple quarrelling about domestic stuff, they must have thought. Except for one man from the farthest booth, who fixed his eyes on their table for a long while. Qi recognized him – the company commander who had issued her the shooting award. He wore plain clothes today. He said something to the other two people, also in plain clothes, in his booth. Then the three of them turned to glance at her table.

Head bowed, the sergeant was playing with his almost-empty coffee mug. He spun it on the saucer, one spin after another, his mouth shut tight.

They split the bill silently and parted outside the café without saying goodbye.

Qi knew something was wrong when a different sergeant appeared for the training the next day. Their usual sergeant had to be on a special assignment, said the new sergeant, who was easy on the girls, letting them take a break every half an hour.

After a quick lunch at the canteen she returned to her dorm to take a nap. Both of the thermos bottles were full and her roommates were nowhere to be seen. They didn't show up until halfway through the afternoon training session, all looking preoccupied and exhausted. When Qi approached them during a break, they found excuses to avoid talking with her.

At 4.30, the ideology advisor in her department, a balding, fat man, appeared on the basketball court and asked for Qi. 'There's something important I must discuss with you,' he said. When the sergeant asked if she was returning to the training later, he said he wasn't sure.

Qi was ushered into a poorly ventilated conference room in her department building, surrounded by palm trees on three sides, ancient-looking with a tile roof, painted railings and round poles, like a small palace. Through a half-covered window she saw the University's motto – carved, painted in red and secured on a wrought-iron frame – above a bed of luxuriant flowers. Think Deeply, Learn Wisely, Pursue Avidly, it said.

She had to go to the bathroom before settling at the long, dark cherry-wood table. She picked a chair facing the door so she could see people in the hallway. The advisor closed the door and also lowered the crimson window curtains. The conference room looked enormous with only the two of them.

'Do you know why you're here?' asked the advisor, a pen and an oversized notebook in his hand.

She knew but she shook her head. She had to be careful with what she said.

The advisor frowned as if having seen through her lie, his double chin twisting slightly like a small animal, then he got up and went out silently, returning with a blue plastic folder. He closed the door behind him, extracted a few pages from the folder and threw them onto the table. 'Read what your roommates said about you.'

Different handwriting, which she recognized as that of Sang, Ting and Wei. All of them said she was the one who came up with the idea of seducing the sergeant and then dumping him. Nothing was mentioned about their discussion regarding the sergeant and their negotiation of how long she wouldn't need to fetch hot water. No, they said, they weren't involved in this conspiracy. She had masterminded and carried out the plan alone, though they had tried to talk her out of it. They said she was aloof and arrogant, though admitting they didn't know her well within such a short period. If not for the special relationship between her and the sergeant, they all said, she wouldn't have been appointed the unit leader. There was no vote or discussion when the sergeant made her the leader. She didn't have the qualifications to be the leader, they said. She didn't read the assigned Party documents, she liked cursing, she had sex when she was in high school, she wore make-up, she complained about the training, calling it 'destructive and a waste of time'. One thing they said they weren't sure about was if she had slept with the sergeant. But they also said that once she didn't return to the dorm until after curfew. There was more in their confessions – small things, such as her not knowing how to fold her blanket properly, she sometimes smoked in the dorm, twice she didn't fetch hot water when it was her turn.

'I didn't seduce him. I didn't do any of the things they said about me.' She raised her head, staring at the advisor, knowing that her roommates must have reached an agreement against her before being questioned. She was innocent. She was alone. She had to fight for herself. That much she knew.

'If you don't change your attitude I'll stop right here. You can talk with the Student Ideology Bureau directly.' The advisor sank into his chair, arms crossed.

She suppressed the fire in her chest, her hands under the table clenched into fists.

'Write a Penance Letter first, then I'll discuss with the Dean how to handle your case.'

'But it's all lies.' She lowered her head and softened her voice. She had to look submissive or she'd be crushed like an ant, she warned herself. 'I didn't seduce the sergeant. I wasn't dating him. I only met him twice after the training session and all we talked about was the training.'

'Talked about the training? How diplomatic! You're very smart for your age. Let me get this straight. You were at a café with him last night. You wore revealing clothes. You two were said to be intimate. If that isn't dating, what is it?'

'We were just chatting.'

'Chatting? Why did you yell at him?'

'I… we… we disagreed on certain things.'

'What things?'

She was silent.

'Now suddenly you have nothing to say?'

'We were just chatting,' she whispered.

The advisor scribbled a few lines in his notebook, then, without looking at Qi, he asked, 'Did you sleep with him?'

'No, no, no, I didn't. Never. We only chatted.'

'Why did he make you the unit leader?'

'I don't know. Maybe because I look like his sister. He told me that.'

'How convenient! Let me remind you what your roommates said about you – you wanted to seduce the sergeant so he'd treat you nicely!'

'That wasn't my idea. They started it first. They said–'

'Stop arguing!' The advisor stood up, grasping the edge of the table. 'It's a serious matter. I'm not here to play games. It's low and disgusting to play with another's emotion, not mentioning that this person is a sergeant, a model soldier, a Party member. You've disgraced your family, your class, our department, our university, and all college students.'

She was shocked by these grand accusations. She winced as if struck by a heavy blow.

'We have to notify your parents of your conduct. They'll be asked to come to the school.'

'Please don't.' She could barely hear her own voice, feeling her smallness and her inability to defend herself.

'Anything else to say?' The advisor sat down, writing more in his notebook.

She shook her head slowly. She couldn't think. Though no penalty had been announced, she felt she had already been sentenced. From now on she was a bad girl, a seducer, a criminal, someone who didn't deserve to stay in a prestigious university or any university at all.

The advisor seemed pleased with her silence. He yawned, ready to end this interrogation. As if to make her feel better, he said casually: 'It isn't all your fault. It's strictly forbidden for a soldier to date a student during the training. The sergeant should have known better.'

She wanted to ask about the sergeant. Was he okay? Where was he? What did he say about her? But her lips were trembling so much that she couldn't speak.

The advisor said that the Dean of the department would like to talk with her as well. He replaced the cap of his pen and slammed his notebook shut. 'Remember to behave properly.' He stood up, giving her a contemptuous glance. The moment he opened the door, warm, white sunlight poured in. She could hear faint marching commands – 'One two one'… 'one two one' – coming from an unidentifiable direction. It suddenly struck her that she badly wanted to go back to Unit 8, to be in the square, to march with all the other girls. Then the door was shut and the distant sound was cut off.

She waited, crying silently. She listened to every movement in the hallway. She bit her lower lip hard so as not to make a sound and every few seconds she used the back of her hands to wipe off the seemingly endless tears. In her blurred vision she saw the past 18 years of her girlhood shattered, torn, vanishing into an unknown world. But what had she done to deserve this? Didn't she graduate from high school with honors? Didn't she once win the first prize in a city-level drawing competition when she was 14? Weren't her parents so proud of her that they decorated their bedroom's walls with her pictures from different ages? Why didn't all this matter any more now? Yes, she admitted, she had flaws. She could be mean, unreasonable, vain and selfish, like many other only-child kids; she would even admit her lack of knowledge of the 1989 college students' pro-democracy protest despite her attraction to its slogans, as well as of the following crackdown by the government – she had only learned those from TV and newspapers. But weren't her classmates, including Ting, Wei, and Sang, just like her?

Not knowing how much time had elapsed, she awoke from her reverie and heard footsteps outside. She swiftly dried her eyes and cheeks with the end of her sleeve, combed her hair behind her ears with her fingers, and sat up straight: she recalled being a college student in military uniform, a newly turned adult who has barely begun to know about responsibilities, impossibilities and failures in her life, yet one who has so much to look forward to. No, she wouldn't let her dreams be squashed so easily, she resolved. She had to stay in college, had to return to Unit 8, and start life just like all the other college students. She knew she had to compromise, had to change herself, and though she hated herself for thinking like this, she was willing to do whatever it took to survive.

Whatever it took.

The footsteps stopped, followed by a slight cough.

The time had come, she thought. She took a deep breath, attempting calmness in a way that was both sad and hopeful to her. She even managed an innocent smile.

Fan Wu was born and raised in China. After college, she had varied jobs before travelling to the US to study at Stanford University. She began to write while working as a market research analyst in Silicon Valley. Wu's two novels are *February Flowers*, published in nine languages, and *Beautiful as Yesterday*. She is a Pushcart Prize nominee, with short stories published in *Granta, The Missouri Review, Ploughshares, Asia Literary Review*, and more. In addition to writing fiction, Wu has reviewed books and blogged for leading publications. She writes in both English and Chinese, and often translates between the two. Being passionate about introducing more Chinese voices to the West, Wu was a key person in setting up the inaugural Southern International Publishing Summit in China. She lives in northern California.

OLUFEMI TERRY
Sierra Leone/St Vincent and the Grenadines

SANGMELE

Fire threatens the city. He grapples the steering wheel against a sudden wind with force enough to shunt the car into the next lane of the overpass. In that moment he's aware of the helicopter passing crosswise over him. A payload of fire retardant dangles from it by a long cable. The evening on which he arrived in the South, both flame-red helicopters had been called out from the base at Newlands; it had been, he recalls, Signal Hill afire that time.

From the car radio, he learns that a stand of eucalyptus has caught fire by accident or malice, that regional topography has metastasized the flames: the encircling mountains and sea shape a funnel which sucks Karoo squalls into the city. Come morning, some quarters might need evacuation.

He's descended from the flyover and passes directly beneath the morne which burns – Lowenkop – yet can see no more than before. No smell of tinder or scorching veldgrass.

The wind has settled to rattling the window glass. He accelerates against inertia's tug: an impulse to veer onto the road shoulder, get down and locate the fire. Inertia because pulling over will make almost certain his return to Athlone once he gets back behind the wheel. He knows the city well enough to guess which precincts are likely to be cleared first because of the danger: the creole quarter Bo Kaap, with its many hovels and Kloofnek afterward.

Downslope from where he is, in Langstraat, which is the main city thoroughfare, the beating of helicopter rotors sounds very near. Two helicopters *are* out tonight: one returns loaded from the station as the other hoves out over the suburbs. The upper stories of many houses along Langstraat offer a good line of sight, and uptilted faces in the windows of

194

restaurants track the red flit of machines. *So small*, someone in Tafel bar murmurs. Others also glimpse the lone, slow lick of fire that stands up on the steepest hillside before creeping smoke swiftly covers it again. Viewed from eating rooms in the city bowl, the baleful wink is a chance the helicopters have missed. But around Lowenkop the wind is ranting; neither pilot dares approach its slopes too closely.

The chopping recedes. For many minutes, no helicopter appears in the sky and it is not long before habitual conversations resume. In the city, even the region, there is a strain of fatalism that is stoic in the teeth of nature. Here there are brush fires, slow months of sea winds and slanting winter rain, yet these are small expiations for a life lived in so vivid a terrain.

Staggering how swiftly you outdistance the middle city, the bowl as it's known, and arrive once more at its periphery. The road, which is renamed Kloofnek, rises almost its entire length and fetches him into a *carrefour*. The left arm runs toward the cable-car station within the foothills of Tafelberg, and toward the mountain itself, numen of the city. There are footpaths but no car-worthy road leads to the summit.

He continues on, the way shearing rightward, passing through stands of montane trees on the brow of a cliff. Far beneath are threads of light, slow-going or motionless, their glittering polished sharp by contrast with the ocean, which is still, unseen as dark matter save in one place where a far-out ship mooring overnight casts a poor glow. Tafelberg is at his back now and the city's grandest houses are swept from view; very many of these are now owned by famous *Uitlanders*.

On a narrow street that tips toward the Atlantic shore, he hurries into a parking berth. Close by the wall of the nearest house are two aged protea trees and, as he rears from the driver's seat, he sees movement inside the night shadow. Another someone rising up from a seated position.

A woman has gotten off an upended drinks crate which she's carried from Langa, from God knows where in the townships, and, so he will not startle, is making a wary approach. He hesitates. A car guard. This here, partway up the Twelve Apostles, is her lean, profitless patch of road. He need not have hurried parking; several spaces are available. Curbside on the ocean road is where car guards can earn 60 rands over the course of a Friday night. But men fight with razors for those stretches of turf.

She accepts the change from his hand, coins he's dug out from the car ashtray and which amount to seven rand. No nod, no smile on that young old face.

Kampsbaai is windless. The plateau down which he's descended is an effective baffle against the winds that are chivvying flames over the ridge. The ocean road runs south through here past Atlantic towns, Llandudno and HoutBaai into Kommetjie. 'Llandudno' has a queer sound, he thinks. It is not a Neolect name as the others are.

Drinking and eating establishments front the land side of the busy ocean road, many of them named in evocation of foreign Rivieras. Here is Antibes, an open-fronted establishment. Its neighbor Janeiro is decorated in a pattern of blue, green and yellow which he has seen before in some other context. A little way down the strip is a white façade featuring a single word in tricolor paint: Amalfi, which he recognizes but cannot place. Yet another bar has a self-congratulatory name: Kaapri.

Over the road is a coved arc of beach which the tourists and locals use for bathing and surfing, but the marina is not here. Sloops and sailboats are moored several kilometers north.

He pushes his way into Ayia Napa, which he likes the sound of – likes too that it means nothing to him. The interior is airless, an atmosphere blue with smoke trapped by the low ceiling.

He's already decided what he will have but he raises his hand anyway at the bar counter to beckon for the drinks sheet. And he pores over it before signalling the bartender a second time.

His first swallow is a large one. The bar teems, its fracas is belated washing over him, as if the twilight out of doors – trees hissing in the breeze, the car guards at their posts muttering of Lubumbashi – has wrapped itself about his person, a cosset just now dissipating because of the agitation of humans.

In his cocktail is too much spirit, and a poor-quality seltzer. He seldom takes liquor but there ought not to be the taste of dustiness on his tongue.

In the austral summer, as it is now, the sun is slow in climbing down the horizon but he has missed its set. What remains are rosy smears of cirrus in the upper sky. Beneath the washed-out awning deckchairs lie as though scattered, even if nearly all are turned into the same direction. Sundowner drinks are a ritual entertainment; and now, with night come down, that pent-up attention on the fading from light into darkness has dissipated in drunkenness.

The crowd is tight. On every side are bright faces, the features of which bear a stillness that is clearer proof than any slurring of words. There is no one he troubles to look at a second time. They roam about their city in the summer nights, these *kaapsjungen*, in bands of four or six, males and females matched to one another. He does not hope to recognize anyone and yet it is certain that someone present is known to him, perhaps more than one someone; if not here, in the vicinity: at the next bar or the one down the end of the strip. The country is too small for it to be otherwise.

Small likelihood, he thinks, that any in this crowd is talking about uBaba, still less thinking of him. It would satisfy his curiosity to lay hands on the Nation Father before the man dies, a longing which he's confided to no one.

The turn of his thoughts to uBaba is not idle or accidental. News had come over the car radio that the old man has regained consciousness since being rushed to hospital in the morning because of an infection in his lung, a hospital, coincidentally, which is used by his own family.

An element of the man's myth is that he had been held among lepers for 10 of the 30 years of his imprisonment: the peril of transmission was intended by the authorities to break his will. But he befriended the afflicted and tutored them in letters until his removal from that colony to a prison for those charged like himself, with a high-sounding political crime. High insurrection. Here too he was no pariah, although warders spread word among the inmates that he was a carrier of Hansen's. uBaba we Sizwe (in the old man's own tongue in full; a title of reverence) seems to have never contracted the disease but his doctors examine his eyes and fingers even now for signs of infection.

His own interest in laying hands on uBaba is unconnected to Hansen's. It is also neither recent nor down to any sentiment so mawkish as patriotism or piety. He wishes to inspect uBaba and so discover for himself the marks, physical and otherwise, that 30 years of gaol have notched in his yellowing flesh and fine bones.

The country is weaning itself off the uBaba legend – proof of it is here in this bar, where no one frets over his health. Five years earlier it would have been otherwise. And the current leaders are too preoccupied with piling wealth, with their gilt home fixtures, to fret about uBaba's growing senility. Their preparations for his death are perhaps more feverish than those of the citizens but no different. The old man cannot be dispensed with entirely but what knits the country more and more is the imperative of wealth and no earthly flesh however beatific. Those that lack faith in the national currency, the economy, apply for emigration visas.

A heave comes down the packed bodies and disrupts his thoughts. One or another of the waiters is clearing a path to serve food or drink. The manager has told his staff – *Use your elbows if you have to, the patrons are too pissed to notice.*

A moist contact of parting lips brushes his ear, someone to the back of him. He perceives what is spoken as much as hears it: – *Excuse me.*

But there's no room to yield or to turn about. This ought to be obvious. He strains his neck to see who is there for now there is a hand clasping his collarbone. A male, but only a boy is there, an adolescent. The current fashion is to tease the hair at the forehead into a thicket with gel but this one has combed his dark red hair flat over his scalp with water. He's too young to be served a drink. He tosses his head at this stranger as if to say, pass if you want to.

The boy opens and shuts his mouth, an inaudible shout. He does not know him.

Yet the youth appears to know him, or at least his name: – *Aren't you Uys?* He lets his hand be pumped while the red-haired boy tells him something he makes out only in part: – *...behind you, at KES.* A King Edward's School pupil. He thinks he's heard the name Adam. – *Let's get out of this*, the boy makes a gesture that takes in the close quarters and the overloud music and, shyly as an infant might, he takes his wrist.

Out under the bar's awning are smells of sand, asphalt, coffee rather than cigarettes. He lets himself be led. Adam halts before an unoccupied seat and leaves go of his wrist. In an adjacent chair, a woman stares at the mobile phone in her hand. Adam says a few words to her, bending low and unsmiling, before turning again toward him. He points to the empty chair.

In his hand is a tumbler with what remains of his cocktail, and he sits alongside the woman. Her hair is very black; she bears Adam no resemblance. Her unpainted right hand is extended toward him but he misses it – he's scouting for Adam, who has slipped away (curious behavior, fetching him here and then going off again). The woman says – *You're at KES as well.*

– *I matriculated*, he tells her. Her name is Tamsin and, looking at her while not making eye contact, he takes her hand. The noise outside is more varied, also quieter.

The display of her mobile phone flares once more and her eyes and forehead are illuminated. *Why dye your hair?* That is his question for her.

She has applied tint out of a packet to change her appearance, some generic apothecary product that has been laved without care or patience into the scalp. The artifice is quite deliberate and extends to the whiteness of her face and arms. Tamsin takes care to keep out of the sun, in spite of the 14 hours of sunshine each day. The use of dye is related in some way to the ample blondness not only in this bar but through and around the city. Fair hair and sun-dark skin are the emblems of the gilded austral life, which is surely a numinous gift.

In Tamsin's lap is the mobile phone which even now she's fooling with, and an old-fashioned clutch like something his own mother carries to cocktail parties. Tamsin's hands are fine as his own. Her listlessness seems unconnected to Adam's absence (where's he gone?). At intervals of less than half a minute she fingers the tiny keys of the mobile phone to consult the screen.

Tamsin too has a question (of course he knows nothing of this), which she frames in her thoughts as an aside, a confidence – It's a bit white in here – and then discards. No doubt he has observed the same and he might be made self-conscious by the remark.

The beach is slowly being abandoned. Youths mount the pavement moving in squads, and they peer into the interior of Ayia Napa. They will inspect every drinking place along the strip never noticing perhaps that the sameness is complete. Juddering music escapes the bars and joins seamlessly to the blare from cars seeping down the ocean road.

He swallows the meltwater at the bottom of his glass. Time to leave. He'll take a turn along the beach road on foot and return to the car.

The communication arrives that Tamsin has awaited. Her mobile phone flickers, once, twice. She's on her feet and she checks the screen a second time. And now Adam reappears, empty-handed. Where's he been hiding? He also stands, as Tamsin goes to Adam and speaks into his ear. Adam's head jerks in displeasure. They are talking over one another – it is obvious that a quarrel has begun and, rather than interrupt, he stands still.

Tamsin is turning away from Adam and he snatches at her elbow. He is watching the two of them, waiting for his opening to thank Adam (for what?) and leave. Tamsin's eye finds his. He's abashed, like a peeper with his eye to the keyhole. In a determined movement, she approaches very close, her nose and his own nearly touching. – *Come with me.* She has no need to shout. And her mouth smells of nothing whatever. – *I must run a quick errand, five minutes from here just up the hill. You don't mind, do you, being dragged away?*

Tamsin is the second person this evening to touch him in an over-familiar way. Adam held his wrist possessively a few moments ago; they are both KES boys, after all.

But Tamsin takes his hand now to place herself under his protection, a gesture directed at her brother. For he's sure now of the relation between Tamsin and Adam: some quality he's noticed in Adam's face, the disjointed interplay between eyes and lips, is also apparent in her features. Adam cannot be more than 16 years old but there seems to be an edginess between the boy and his sister that raises the possibility of intimacy.

He offers up no resistance, lets Tamsin tug him out of the bar, Adam following, and on to the pavement. Adam's frustration has increased. He squares off again with his sister: – *I think it's a bad idea.*

– *He's going with me,* Tamsin says, not looking at him. Her meaning is obvious. Adam's grievance is easy to guess: you don't know this oke, not even his name. School custom, the KES deference to seniority, wins out. Adam glowers at him and shoves his fingers deep into his front pockets and does not say anything; making a show of his refusal to shake hands.

Tamsin walks away. In the set of her shoulders is a kind of knowing: one or both men will follow. But Adam has ducked back indoors, leaving him to stare after Tamsin. No question of going his own way now. He dodges a shoal of pedestrians and catches her up as she's turning into the first intersection. The tilting of the road at first is small. Ahead it is very steep and a pair of gleams can be made out in the low light: reflective vests. Two parking guards have stationed themselves fully in the road for a better view downhill.

He slows his step. Tamsin's close long skirts shorten her gait. At the next junction she raises a hand in the air as one might hail a taxi. A car with headlights dimmed slides away from the opposite curb, moving low and humped over the roadway, and noses up abreast of them. The headlights are turned on. The car guards, piqued, squint and frown into the full stare of the high beams.

The door behind the driver is ajar. – *Ekow,* Tamsin says. And she says something else once she's inside the car, which he does not understand. He hears a reply before he sees who it is talking.

– *Tams.* The accent is European, but in his origins the driver is an African, and from further north and west than Mbuji Maye or Kisangani. His lips are almost the color of his very black cheeks. A foreigner twice over in this country.

He seats himself behind the driver and cants his neck so his face is invisible in the driving mirror. The dashboard is over lit and Ekow has been running the car's heating and has just shortly cut it off: the interior is uncomfortably warm. A distally familiar jazz arrangement plays, the mournful honk of horns.

Tamsin declines to make introductions. And she has inserted the entire length of the back seat between the two of them. She giggles. – *Ekow, are you cold?* He has not seen her smile, still less laugh.

Ekow is keeping to the side roads, guiding the car with an effortless skill. – *The wind up Chapmans gets cold nights.* He hunches forward with a shoulder shrug to get a good look at the face behind him. – *This your brother, Tams?* Ekow has not missed the void on the back seat. His mouth shapes a comment and then he appears to change his mind or perhaps he's taunting Tamsin. And he passes a package over his shoulder.

She accepts the padded envelope, sets it in her lap, lifts the flap and fetches out the contents. To be helpful, nothing more, Ekow switches on the console light as Tamsin hands him money in return, her fingers curled about the wadded notes – a concealment that fools no one in the car, and which anyway is needless. She signs a little sharply for the light to be put out.

– *I think we're good.* Tamsin announces brightly and she leans out across the seat to pat his knee: – *Oh, he's my foster brother.*

Ekow is too shrewd to make a response. – *I'll let you two out by the Pick n Pay, yeah?*

They are above Kampsbaai, moving at no great speed in, he suspects, a southerly direction. But he cannot be sure: Ekow has reversed direction more than once. – *What's the rush?*

– *Actually, there is, Tams.* Without transition, the car gathers speed. – *I've got to be in Constantia in 15 minutes.*

Tamsin bows her neck and her pinkie taps first one nostril, now the other. He cannot see what she's holding until she raises her fist up close to his cheek. In the fold of her fingers is a vial of powder. The physiological effects of cocaine are known to him, but his knowledge, gained from medical texts, is abstruse. He shuts his eyes and sniffs.

Ekow is easing his car to a standstill in front of a tall, well-guarded house. Driving it is no less an element of the man's trade than the substances in envelopes. Seeing the two of them out of his car, Ekow turns the music up loud, deterring further talk, and he says a curious thing: – *You'll be alright here, I think, Tams Freudfolger. Good to meet you, Tamsin's brother.*

He finds a lot to dislike in Ekow's coercive *I think*.

Tamsin rabbits her nose at him because of the cocaine and catches his elbow. Out of Ekow's presence, she is again diffident. The silver car has made a turn, moving with that low-slung, sidling movement and vanished. The course that suggests itself is to go the opposite direction, which must lead away from Constantia and the south of the peninsula. That means following the decline of the road.

Around the next house, which is unlit and untenanted – this is a neighborhood of seasonal homes – there is the open sea, the surface rippling like swartveld.

Ekow's bearings are awry, or else he's deliberately let them out too far down the coast. On foot, it is very far. Seen close to, the Kampsbaai bars had seemed a futile echo of famous resorts in other countries. At this range the neon lights – lurid greens, blues and reds – seem nothing more than a fata morgana that wavers between smudginess and cocaine clarity. Sea spray and a distance of about two kilometers produce this distortion, which is akin to looking out of a rainswept windshield.

And south of the Kampsbaaistrand, the beach, the formation of the littoral alters: there's more stone underfoot here than sand. The coast road, which they have now joined, winds along a sheer but not high bluff. Sea mist spritzes his face and bare forearms, and among the fine water droplets are some that retain the biting cold that flows up out of the South Pole.

– *He used a name as we got out. Was that Neolect? And what did he mean about Chapman's Peak?*

Tamsin furrows her top lip over her teeth; does it, without awareness, a reflex against the irritation of the chemical in her throat. – *Yes. Freudfolger. A private joke.* He hears it in her voice: she's winded. – *One of his kicks is racing around Chapman's Peak with the windows down and headlights off. That car's his fetish.*

Fetish. He has no response to the word. Tamsin, slowing, leans her head back and looks up. Some of the Apostles are visible against the moonless night. – *My father grew up here before Kampsbaai was anything, not even a village, just scrub and fynbos. He and a few other kids made their own paths through the bush.* Is she, he wonders, wanting to reassure him with talk? She ought to save her breath? They have entered an especially desolate stretch of road. – *My grandma used to go over the ridge in her little car to the Shoprite.*

A sudden high laughter up ahead, and the witter of male voices hollering at one another in Neolect and moving fast toward them, as if conjured by her talk of children roving in the bush. He's aware of it before she is; his first thought is of the pistol, cached, useless, beneath the driver seat of his car.

The road just here is flanked by a red cliff, smooth as a stone wall. He catches Tamsin's slippery-dry palm in his own and backs the two of them against it. – *Where does he live now, your father?* A hashed attempt at reassuring Tamsin and made worse by his acting perturbed. Embarrassed, he nearly lets go of her hand.

Two *jungen* of his own age come on a little in advance of three more. None is very tall; and they move with no great hurry. Their carrying voices had seemed eager, full of that impatience of the young to be elsewhere than they are. Where are they going? No taxivans ply this sea road, nothing goes south this way but private cars.

They have not been in the Kampsbaai bars, these *seuns*. They come from the beach. His reasoning staggers him. He knows by looking at the clothes on them, because their skin is brown. They are as dark as he is. *You're going native,* he tells himself. It is well known that the local creoles, the *sangmeles* as they sometimes call themselves, have an alertness for rank and caste that has been honed by the region's chattel history.

– *Hy dink hy slim,* someone of the boys is telling his mates in a cracking voice, a remark about some recent encounter, perhaps some incident on the beach. – *Thought he was clever.* They are not *skollies* but they carry an air of Saltrivier or Mannenberg.

Just in advance of Tamsin and himself, the coast road sharply bends and, owing to this curve and the *jungen* being caught up in teasing and jeering, they have not yet been seen. And it may be the physical resemblance he bears to them, and they to him, which collapses the last intervening meters. But the distinction between him and these others is also pronounced and the dissonance forces a double consciousness on him.

He is himself and in the same moment the sixth *jung* in this gang. An infiltrator holding fast to the hand of a woman who assumes a new guise in his refracted vision. The knob of one hip juts through her thin cotton skirt. She is a lone white presence on an emptied section of road, a reality that can be viewed as almost inviting violation.

Not long ago, a matter of weeks, he'd come across, while trying to improve his fluency in Neolect, a tabloid story about an assault by several males on a pubescent child. He's minded now of the incident as one local witness recounted it to the correspondent in a highly idiomatic speech: *Begin 'n trein op haar, Meinheer. They run a train on that girl.* To be certain, he'd had to look up the translation on his mobile phone.

One fragment of his splintering awareness knows Tamsin ought to be afraid, even expects it. Yet his left hand squeezes her palm to steady her. He's wishing once more the pistol were at his waist. Tamsin's face anyway shows only curiosity.

Something of these twisting feelings conveys to her. Her attention settles on his face, a flensing look which he turns from. Images flash in his eye like a nanosecond fever dream: two prostrated, shadowed forms, a sprawl of pale wrists and long-toed feet bare, contorting. One form is supine and almost entirely obscured beneath another, larger and juddering human shape. Tamsin is part of the vision. The despoiler might be himself.

He shakes his head to be rid of the hallucination and turns so that he faces the oncomers. His right arm assumes a curious position. Tamsin is almost behind him and she sees the knuckles of his right hand tuck into the waistband in back of those oddly formal trousers. The arm shapes a birdwing, with his elbow the wingtip.

The first youth has moved up almost alongside them before his chin jerks in confusion. His eyes go very round, he starts and, in the hesitation of an instant, the next boy stumbles into his back.

In five faces a flaring wonder quickly mingles with curiosity. He loosens hold of Tamsin's hand and squeezes again: an action commanding her to keep silent. Her gaze on his cheek is disturbing as a leer but he makes a point to ignore it and to look each *jung* in the face: what he perceives there is insolence, driven out by surprise, but now returning. It is his presence that draws their interest. Still, not one of the *jungen* slows or as much as glances at the odd posture of his arm. The inertia of their surprise marches them on.

A half dozen paces past, the youths erupt in a honk of laughter, amusement in a different register than from the crowing of a few moments ago. Tamsin understands little Neolect but it is obvious one of them has muttered a joke and dispelled the tension and fear.

She pulls free of his hold. She's recognized the posture of his arm, it is from a particular genre of film. And she starts out toward the neon. Has he frightened her?

❖ ❖ ❖

He and Tamsin are almost the same height. He notices it as he waits for a pedestrian signal light to change. Over this road, which intersects the coast road, is the Pick n Pay. Tamsin is close enough that he can touch her shoulder. He has trailed her almost the entire way back. The two of them, he thinks, have had a let off. Not only Tamsin.

She seems not to have arrived at the same thought. Straight-backed she goes on, whereas he stops, simply halts mid-step and allows her to leave him behind. They are not yoked together. Let her find her own way to her brother. Footgangers overtake him to either side on the pavement, the faces illuminated from below by the AMOLED light of their mobile phones. He can see no more than her head now.

He sweats in spite of the coolness off the water. The encounter down the coast road is taking on an irreal quality; in retrospect, it is like a delusion. The fear of being attacked, of the possibility that he will be required to offer himself in place of Tamsin, has taken on a sense of absurdity. The *jungen* intend sleeping on a beach somewhere, is his guess. There is a possibility of hypothermia, even in summer.

Dragging his gait, he starts walking again.

At the next corner are ten motorcycles parked in array. This style (the molded seat and airbox cover resemble the haunches of a cowering woman) is very popular in creole neighborhoods. Another sight distracts him. Girls are in the road. They have marked their faces with points and snaking lines of luminous daub. Their clothing strikes him as inapt for children as young as nine years old, which one or two among them are. Brief string skirts and halter necks are pulled tight and hard over budding breasts.

These are children, the hour is late. His face grows hot with an irritation that catches him by surprise. But they are not unchaperoned. The leader of the performing ensemble is a man of more than 40 and he wears a kirtle pattern-dyed to mimic the skin of a civet or hyena. He is easily overlooked because he sits apart, humped over his drum. He produces from it a varying rhythm, using only the heels of his hands. In spite of the precision of his beating, he has an unfocused look.

In the outdoor air the hide sounds reedy and hollow.

The girls dance a traditional dance. They, the man also, are not creoles. Their ancestral home is a province a thousand kilometers east of this city; their forefathers slaughtered every head of cattle in their herds a century ago and nearly became extinct because of it. He has no measure with which to assess the girls' skill. And for whom do they dance? Not *footgangers* who glance away from their mobile phones only long enough to glimpse into the nearest bar. The audience for the performance is behind him, where he has stationed himself to watch. One of the Kampsbaai restaurants has erected a dinner platform next to the pavement but cordoned off from it and looking over both road and bay. On the platform are six supper tables and all are occupied. The kicking and stamping and handclapping is for these diners hunkered over plates of shucked crustaceans, seared meat, potato.

He turns his back on the girls. He cannot leave off glaring at one couple on the restaurant deck. The woman and her husband are tourists, with the pillowy appearance that connotes a midlife that is both prosperous and harried. They tear at their food, avid but with little appearance of satisfaction. In their faces is an appalling, unshifting incuriosity.

They are unused, he supposes, to such prices for lobster, have never before eaten the flesh of ostriches. The rate of currency exchange vastly favors them, and they are most gorged on how little it all costs, also on the climate – 16 ruddy hours of sunshine. Enthralled to discover that in this country the blacks are pliant, even abject. In Africa, the blacks are natives of course, whereas in their own country the problem, quite the opposite, is immigrants, an inundation of dark-haired foreigners assertively hunting for jobs, getting their big-eyed kids into the best schools. Speaking their clucking tongues unashamedly in the metro.

He cannot be sure of any feeling he imputes to these tourists yet nor does he doubt them. He seldom reads the newspapers, let alone the foreign press, but he is aware of an anxious feeling in the world about migrants, which in his own country is most acute in the shanties.

Owing to the gawks of this tourist couple, he sees the dancing anew, perceives the intricate stylization he initially missed. Each girl has her role. The dancers form two lines facing one another. The row of girls nearer him bends deeply forward in obvious imitation of four-legged beasts and, tumbling one by one to the ground, they lie still. (A rehearsal perhaps of the cattle killing.)

That slaughter of a nation's entire wealth stands as one enduring enigma in the national history for it had been done on the advice of mysterious and faceless strangers with the air of seers. Kill the herds to rid your land of white men. Mysterious messengers with the appearance of seers had urged the sacrifice as a necessary step in ridding the country of Europeans.

Mass starvation had ensued. The identity of those prophets has never been discovered.

The whiff of exploitation hangs over the dancers, and this – nothing else – attracts the couple's attention. They watch to see if anyone will acknowledge the performance with a donation, whether the drummer will share the earnings with the children.

And the children? They answer blank indifference by dancing with greater and greater energy; the drummer whips them up. The girls, also the man who might be both guardian and exploiter, have nothing to sell but their culture.

He drops some notes into the battered paper cup – so easily kicked aside by heedless feet – set down on the pavement for that purpose. Straightening, he hears Tamsin's voice close at his ear.

– *I'm not going back in. That place, I mean. Let's rather sit on the beach.* He turns to face her. She is looking not at him but over his shoulder: at the children, who are still dancing.

The need to put his hands on the gun is sharp, a sudden inexplicable itch. The sensation of being exposed has returned, and Tamsin's presence is a part of it. He answers – *I'll need to get something from my car first.*

Olufemi Terry won the 2010 Caine Prize for African Writing for his story 'Stickfighting Days', and has published fiction and non-fiction online and in print. His work has appeared in The Guardian, Chimurenga and the LA Review of Books, and has been performed on stage in Germany, Switzerland and Austria. Born in Sierra Leone, he studied Creative Writing in Cape Town and currently lives in Washington, DC.

BALLI KAUR JASWAL
Singapore/Australia

INVENTIONS OF THE FUTURE

Time was running out for Mrs Eustace; she was dying of cancer. Regular treatments had stripped away her eyebrows and whenever she stooped to adjust a student's collar, a gleaming patch of her scalp was visible.

She was most enthusiastic about teaching in the mornings, after the flag-raising ceremony. Each day, the first timetabled lesson was Science, followed by Maths, recess, then English. Mrs Eustace spoke urgently, trying to tell us everything she knew before lethargy set in.

'This school building used to have no walls. The only boundaries between classrooms and the jungle were swollen tree trunks. Small monkeys and lizards passed through during the day and sat amongst the students, resting before continuing their journeys. It was an absolute thoroughfare,' she said delightedly.

We gripped our Science workbooks, figuring that this story was related to the subject, but then Mrs Eustace wrote 'thoroughfare' on the board and selected Ong Pei Fang to look it up in the Oxford Dictionary. We began rummaging through our bags for our English vocabulary exercise books. As Pei Fang struggled to lift the heavy dictionary from its shelf, Mrs Eustace switched to an entirely different topic, explaining the differences in costs of high-rise flats and landed properties. 'It's actually not that much. But with a house, you have to consider maintenance, and cars are getting more expensive.' We replaced our English books with *Primary Four Maths* and expected her to weave this narrative into a problem sum.

Sometimes lessons were more relevant to our timetabled subjects. To illustrate a point about gravity, Mrs Eustace once explained the perils of being a tightrope walker. 'Imagine all of the focus needed to defy a force like that,' she said. Then she strayed. 'Do you know that professional tightrope walkers from all over the world use the cable car lines on Sentosa Island to practise?' she asked. 'They come from China, Russia, Uzbekistan, everywhere.' We giggled at "Uzbekistan" – it sounded clumsy, a place that had no business producing tightrope walkers. 'If you look closely, you can see their shadows at night but of course, the government doesn't leave the lights on for them. Don't worry,' she added, noticing our worried expressions. 'They're very good at keeping their balance.'

Time was limited; we knew this better than any other Primary Four class in the school. By the time we returned from recess, Mrs Eustace would be weary, her eyelids dropping and voice growing whispery. Left to our own devices, we could do anything while our teacher dozed at her desk but it was streaming year. In November, all of Singapore's 10-year-olds would take an exam to determine our academic stream, and everybody in my class was determined to avoid being ordinary. We strived to enter the Gifted stream, to be guided by teachers with Masters Degrees and British enunciation. It was the swiftest pathway to future success; our country's leaders had all been Gifted, we were told. It meant that our parents – the children of peasants and laborers – could say that their toiling and sacrifices during uncertain times had been worthwhile. We dutifully followed instructions on the board for English. There were grammar exercises to complete and compositions to be written.

There was also the option of sitting in the Little Library, an area that Mrs Eustace had cleared in the corner of the classroom which contained a small shelf of books, a sunny yellow rug and some throw pillows. Earlier that year, our parents had attended an information session where the Principal had warned them about the distractions to our studies posed by story books. 'These days, books are more for entertainment than information, especially the sorts of books that children are drawn to,' Mrs Lillian Wong had said, handing out a list with titles of books in popular series. 'They can be as distracting as television, and the values they promote are just as detrimental.' Many students' parents had returned home that night and raided our shelves, culling the books which did not teach us anything we could use in an exam.

Mrs Eustace had set up the Little Library the next day. While she napped at her desk, most girls still stayed glued to their chairs, doing the prescribed activities, while a few headed straight for the Little Library. I was in the latter group but I sat aside from the other girls, who browsed the shelves as a guise for continuing their recess chatter.

It was in the Little Library one afternoon that I came across a book called *Inventions of the Future*. It had a neon blue-and-yellow cover and glossy pages. Each chapter was given the title of a year post-2000, and the new products that would be available to us by then. In 2002, there would be an invisibility machine. In 2004, a voice-sensitive pen that you could dictate your homework to. There were various models of hover boards (2002), shoes that increased walking speed (2003) and cinemas which allowed audience members to step into the screen and become part of the film (2009). The predictions stopped at the year 2012.

Mrs Eustace started the next morning's Science lesson by announcing that she would teach us the water cycle. Halfway through drawing a diagram on the board, she paused and began to tell us about the time it snowed in Singapore. We leaned forwards, captivated. Snow? In Singapore? This was a dream. 'Yes,' she said with a hint of impatience. 'Everything was covered in it.'

An excited murmur rose through the class. We were all picturing the tropical leaves dusted white when Aurelia Goh's voice rang out. 'It has never snowed in Singapore and it never will.' The murmuring stopped abruptly.

Mrs Eustace's composure was so unflinching that I wondered if her illness had affected her hearing. Finally, she replied: 'Of course it did, Aurelia, the same night Singapore won the World Cup. Those who don't remember the snow were inside watching the game. Those who were outside got a chance to experience the snow.'

Our excitement was impossible to contain. Singapore had won the World Cup? At recess that morning, we lamented all that we had missed before our time. Aurelia was unimpressed. She stalked off to the bookshop to buy a foolscap pad and, while the rest of us lined up for *roti john* and *mee siam*, she was busy writing something down. As we filed back to class, I overheard her saying, 'Mrs Eustace had better start teaching us soon or my parents will…'

During English that afternoon, Mrs Eustace reminded us to complete our composition entitled 'An Adventure at the Zoo' and then she went to sleep. I had already finished mine the night before. While other girls wrote stories about escaped lions being captured by government officials (charged with ensuring the nation's safety from wild threats), I had written about a gang of children who broke into the zoo and spent a thrilling night living like the rest of the animals. I went to Mrs Eustace's desk to hand it in but noticed the line of drool strung from her lips to her collar. Embarrassed, I took my composition back to my desk and spent the rest of the afternoon with *Inventions of the Future*. This time I studied the illustrations, putting my faith in the confident lines of a series of time-machine blueprints.

I looked up to find Aurelia Goh standing above me, holding out a sheet of paper. 'Would you like to sign my petition?'

'About what?'

'Mrs Eustace. I'm trying to get us another teacher.'

'Why?'

'We're not learning anything and it's our streaming year. Don't you want to get into a top stream?'

All I wanted was to hurry up and get to the future. A study of the book's pictures revealed that one day, we would have everything we ever wanted. Wasn't this what the Singapore pledge meant in that line about *achieving happiness, prosperity and progress for our nation*? It would happen, and not as a consequence of streaming. Aurelia's lips became a tight pencil-drawn line. 'She's sleeping,' she hissed. 'Sign my petition and we'll get a better teacher like Mrs Ng or Miss Salim.'

'I'll think about it,' I said. This was what my mother always said to door-knocking salespeople and Christians who handed out pamphlets in the bus interchange.

Aurelia tossed another look at Mrs Eustace and then turned back to me. I followed her eyes as they scanned me from head to toe. Softly, she spoke. 'Everybody else has signed it but you. Of course.' She spun around and flounced back to her seat. Shame coursed through me, as certain and visceral as blood. I was different from the other girls. My mind wandered too much. I was always the last student to line up for recess and I had missed the school bus several times because I had been mesmerized watching the other vehicles gliding in and out of their parking spaces.

All of the future inventions in the book promised distance from reality. I couldn't wait for the invisibility machine to become available. In 2003, all spectacles would come with a night vision option. In 2010, tiny television screens would be readily available and accompanied by a sort of magnifying glass which projected the images onto any blank surface. Commuter trips to Mars would be available to passengers as early as 2012.

The next day, there was a substitute teacher named Miss Ly. She stood with her back pressed against the blackboard. We stared back earnestly, waiting for the lesson to begin. We were not used to starting the morning with silence.

'Did your teacher give you any homework?' she asked.

'Yes,' we chorused. Relief seemed to loosen Miss Ly's limbs. She stepped away from the board and walked around the room, collecting our compositions.

'Will you mark these?' Aurelia asked, beaming.

'Mrs Eustace will mark them,' Miss Ly said. 'She's just resting at home at the moment but she'll be able to read your work.' Aurelia's smile faded. At recess, a regular audience of girls had started to form around her, encouraging her tirades. She regarded them with an appreciative nod. 'If she can read our compositions, she can jolly well come to school. Enough is enough.'

Parent-Teacher conferences took place before the first round of practice exams in April. My mother glanced around the room anxiously as we waited our turn. The school hall was set up with canteen tables and benches. It looked like a banquet, with teachers on one end and waiting parents and students perched in a neat row. My mother turned to my father and whispered, 'There has to be a better way to do this. No privacy – you can hear everything that teacher is saying.' Mrs Eustace was telling Janice Ting's parents that if she improved her posture, she would have an easier time paying attention during class. 'At the moment, she slouches like a foolish girl.' Janice Ting's mum gave her a light karate chop on the spine which made her shoot up, alert. 'Like that,' Mrs. Eustace said approvingly. 'There is a world of opportunities out there for young ladies who pay attention.'

When my turn came, I was nervous. Would Mrs Eustace say that I daydreamed too much? This had been a common criticism from my Primary Two and Three teachers. When she noticed me, she smiled widely and produced my composition, "An Adventure at the Zoo." 'Thirty out of thirty,' she said to my parents.

They looked puzzled and I knew why. During the briefing at the start of the year, parents and students had been told that full marks were not attainable for English. 'Because there is no right or wrong answer, it would be inaccurate to declare a story one hundred-per-cent correct,' Mrs Wong had explained.

'This was a remarkable composition. Imaginative, wild, descriptive and full of life,' Mrs Eustace said. My mum beamed, looking around the room. Suddenly she didn't mind that the whole world could hear us. 'You, my girl, have talent.'

My dad did not look so sure. He had started reading the first few lines and he had not spotted any Winning Words. Found in a book called Increase Your Word Power, these words were an impressive departure from the limited vocabulary of his generation. He tested me on my spelling sometimes and always encouraged me to use these words in my compositions for maximum marks. *The house was dilapidated and engulfed in flames. As the fires raged, pandemonium ensued.*

'Amanda is going to be a writer,' Mrs Eustace said. Mum's look of joy began to fade.

'What kind of career does a writer have?' Mum asked.

'Any kind of career she wants. She can use words to travel the world.'

My dad looked at the composition again. I followed his gaze and spotted a spelling error in the first paragraph. He didn't notice it. 'That's very good,' he murmured. Mum nodded and smiled. I could tell that they were satisfied only because Mrs Eustace's enthusiasm was infectious. With that expression of pure joy, she could have told them that I would grow up to hijack trains and they would have been pleased.

The following Monday, Mrs Eustace wasn't in class again and she didn't come back for an entire week. When she returned, she was missing more hair and her skin was sallow. She still gestured wildly as she spoke, but now movement seemed to hurt her and she winced to punctuate her enthusiastic speeches. She spent longer periods sitting at her desk and she dozed off well before assigning any work. Luckily, we all had assessment books in our bags. My parents had saved to buy *Essential Examination Practice For Streaming Success – Three Subjects.* Not only was it an encyclopedia-sized tome with color-coded sections for Maths, Science and English, there was also a sticker on the cover declaring it an UPDATED AND REVISED EDITION. I flipped through the book with little interest and was about to retreat to the Reading Corner when the English composition prompt caught my eye:

Write about the future. What will people experience 10 years from now?

I copied the prompt on a fresh piece of paper and began writing. The future, I informed Mrs Eustace, would be full of inventions. I detailed my knowledge of these gadgets which would make life easier. There would be airplanes which took only milliseconds to cross the globe and translation software which allowed us to converse with animals. Machinery would be available to make washing and drying clothes instantaneous and silent. Green vegetables would be genetically modified to have the taste and texture of chocolate.

Mrs Eustace returned for a few quiet days during which we were free to work on our own exercises while she napped at her desk. I embarked on a second draft of my composition, focusing on neatening my handwriting and putting two-finger spaces at the start of each paragraph. At some point, another Primary Four teacher walked in. She crouched next to Mrs Eustace's desk and whispered to her, patting her on the shoulder. Then she left and returned with copies of Maths and Science worksheets that she had given her class. Grateful for some guidance, the other students lapped them up but I set them aside. There were important things to tell Mrs Eustace.

She disappeared again. This time, the absence was prolonged. Concerned parents began to notice and question whether their daughters should be transferred to other classes. Aurelia Goh's petition made the rounds again. When it floated past me one afternoon on the school bus, I noticed that the signatures went on for three pages. Students who didn't even have Mrs Eustace had signed it.

'Don't give it to Amanda,' Aurelia said loudly for my benefit. 'She's the only one who doesn't agree with us.'

The only one. In Primary One, Miss Fung had exasperatedly announced, 'Amanda is the only one who hasn't changed into her PE attire yet.' The following year, in Primary Two, we had Mrs Tay. 'You all did very well on the Maths test. Only one careless girl got the final problem sum wrong.'

I ignored Aurelia and stared out the window, watching Singapore unravel. White high-rise towers faced the street like lines of soldiers waiting to salute. A woman in a batik nightdress lumbered slowly along the pavement, carrying the schoolbag of a kindergartener who skipped ahead of her. It would normally have bothered me to be so singled out but Mrs Eustace had made my difference seem like a good thing.

At home, my parents were allowing me to read story books again. When I stared off into space and Dad became impatient with me, Mum served him a reminder: 'It's that imagination of hers.'

I waited eagerly for the return of my composition but much of our classroom work seemed to disappear down a one-way path. Young substitute teachers arrived and taught what they knew. They all enjoyed pre-emptively correcting common misconceptions, perhaps hoping to be remembered for enlightening us. 'Dolphins are not fish. They're mammals. Did you know that?' Of course we knew. Mrs Eustace's commentaries had covered a great deal of accidental knowledge.

Mrs Eustace came back after the June holidays. She arrived with a glossy and neatly styled bob. 'It's a wig,' the girl next to me whispered. 'My auntie knows her from church – she lost all her hair.' Mrs Eustace had undoubtedly lost weight as well. Her watch hung slack from her bony wrist and slid up her arm when she pulled the cord to turn on the ceiling fan.

Mrs Eustace asked for volunteers to go to her car and bring up all of the work she had marked. Several girls raised their hands. 'All of you,' she said. 'There's that much marking. You've all been very busy.' She smiled proudly at us and scanned the room. I smiled back and gave her a little wave. When her eyes met mine, they grew a bit cold. Right away I assured myself that I was imagining things. Perhaps it was the wig or the lost weight which gave Mrs Eustace an appearance of severity that I had not seen before.

Mrs Eustace named one volunteer the leader; to this girl she entrusted her car keys and told the rest of the group that the work could be found in the trunk. 'Don't drive away in my car now,' Mrs Eustace said. We all laughed. I relaxed. She wasn't angry with me, and for what anyway?

The girls left and soon returned with crates of worksheets. I craned my neck and searched for my work. It took almost the entire lesson to hand everything out. My Maths assignments piled up on my desk like junk mail. My Science worksheets arrived, organized according to the unit. I noticed that nobody else had written anything on composition paper – no compositions had been assigned after all. I became anxious that my piece had been tossed out by Miss Abdul, that flighty substitute teacher who had written on the whiteboard with permanent marker.

It must have been on the very bottom of Mrs Eustace's pile because it was the last assignment to be returned. It floated onto my desk in a casual attempt by its distributor (the always considerate Serena Au, who had never defended me but also never joined in the other girls' teasing) to pretend that she had not seen the mark on it. She had. Everybody had, or at least this was how I felt. Mrs Eustace had written UNGRADED at the top in fiery red ink. Scribbled across my first paragraph, her comments were difficult to distinguish but I squinted and managed to untangle her words from mine:

Disappointing. Devoid of imagination. You weren't asked for a list of silly inventions. You were asked about the future!

The last word was underlined several times. I didn't dare to let my gaze travel to the front of the room where Mrs Eustace was standing, giving instructions now on how to avoid being splashed by the new automatic flushing systems on some public toilets. 'The trick is to hover. If your bottom touches the seat and the sensor goes off before you're ready, then you'll get wet for nothing,' she said. The class laughed appreciatively; it was good advice.

I held my composition tautly between two hands like it was a prayer book. I did not understand. The assignment had been to write about the future and this was what I had done. I had not copied the book. My composition had fitted the requirements of the exercise. During recess, I thought Mrs Eustace might ask to speak to me but she strode past our line and disappeared around the corner while the Class Monitors barked their instructions: 'Single line, arms-length space in front of you, come on, you're wasting precious recess time.' For the first time, I was not the last to get in line. Instead of going to the canteen, I ducked into the school library and asked for a dictionary. The librarian handed me a Webster's dictionary and told me I could take a seat. I remained at her counter. I just wanted to look up the word 'devoid,' to make sure I knew exactly what it meant.

I thought of Mrs Eustace's comments for the rest of the day. When she fell asleep at her desk, I avoided the Little Library. The school library was vast and white, with desks and ceiling-high shelves on which books were systematically and sensibly catalogued. The Little Library had none of that. I re-arranged the work in my folders. Being my weakest subject, Maths should take priority. I put the Maths worksheets on top of everything else and combed through my mistakes carefully, doing my problem sum corrections in green pen. I consulted my Science textbook and amended my wrong responses to multiple-choice questions on precipitation. My English worksheets were relegated to the bottom folder. I was good at grammar and vocabulary – I *spoke* English so there was really no need to spend substantial time revising the subject.

On the way home on the bus, Aurelia Goh waved around her worksheets and unleashed a fresh tirade. 'All of this work – she just gives it back and doesn't bother to explain where we went wrong? How are we going to do our exams? Now my parents will have to book extra tuition sessions for me just so I can correct all of my mistakes.'

I listened to her and she made sense. How dare Mrs Eustace pass such flippant judgment on our work when she had barely taught us anything all year? When the bus stopped to let out a few girls who lived in a cluster of blocks near Bishan Park, Aurelia strode through the aisles and handed out her petition. This time she targeted the Primary Three students, with warnings that Mrs Eustace could be their teacher next year unless we acted now. 'Think about your future,' she said. I threw out my arm and waved her down as she passed my seat.

'I'd like to sign it too.' I said it so quietly that there was a chance she would keep walking by without having heard me. But she turned, her face open with surprise, her pen ready in her small, tight fist.

I passed my streaming exams – we all did, but passing was just the beginning. Those who excelled went into Gifted but I was not one of them. I entered a respectable stream nonetheless. I took Maths and Science more seriously and started to focus on what I wanted to achieve in the future. I placed great trust in what our leaders said: the only way to stabilize our country was to keep looking forward. My parents were relieved at my renewed efforts in practical subjects. Over the years, my storybooks yellowed on the shelves. Some became infested with silverfish and had to be thrown into the pile for the bow-legged *karang guni* man's fortnightly collection.

In 1999, plans were revealed to tear down Singapore's National Library building. An old brick building hidden behind tall trees, it was a corner of peace in a bustling downtown area. The newspapers ran articles which commented on the civic protests to this change – it was rare for Singaporeans to object so vocally to government plans. I had just graduated from university and could understand what the fuss was about because I had spent many final exam periods studying there but I didn't feel strongly enough to attend the public forum. After all, the new building would be a magnificent 10-story glass and steel structure, so vast that it would appear to have infinite room for all the books in the world. Ultimately, it was decided that the old building had no aesthetic or architectural value, and it was torn down to make room for a road tunnel that would connect motorists to the city more efficiently.

I went to the National Library's final clearance sale. I was passing through town on the way to dinner with some friends one Sunday and had some time to kill. It was the last hour of the sale and most of the remainders were outdated and damaged books. I picked up a dog-eared romance novel and a copy of Stephen King's 'Carrie' with the movie tie-in cover. In Primary Six, somebody had got hold of this book and read the goriest chapters to the class between lessons while teachers were in transit in the hallways. Our reactions had oscillated between horrified squeals and collective groans. As I made my way to the cashier, a neon blue-and-yellow cover caught my eye. It was *Inventions of the Future* in the 3 For $1 bin.

It was 2004 and none of the book's promises had materialized. At dinner,

I flipped to my favorite sections and read them aloud to my friends. 'We'd have robots doing our household chores by now,' I told them. 'We'd have holiday houses on the moon.' We laughed at the book's kitschy cover, its wildly inaccurate predictions. For the first time in many years, I thought of Mrs Eustace and felt a rush of indignation as if I were back in that classroom, receiving my composition again. I remembered the relish with which I had signed that petition and the remaining months of stern, straightforward instruction from Mrs Ng, her formidable replacement.

Had my story really been so disappointing? After all, for the streaming exam, the composition prompt had been: 'Describe your dream home.' Most students had filled the exam booklet with details of landed properties with chimneys, green lawns and a basketball hoop in the driveway like houses in American sitcoms. I had started my composition by saying that my dream home was in the future, and I had described all of the fantastic gadgets and fixtures it would hold.

The composition was selected by assessors as their top pick. I was honored at a Ministry of Education ceremony for high achievers in English and presented with a plaque. It was included in a collection of top compositions for future students as well. In the introduction to my composition, the assessor had written: *This piece shows control of language, appropriate choice of vocabulary and a varied sentence structure. The student has demonstrated strong descriptive capabilities.* They had given 'My Dream Home' a mark of 28 out of 30. 'A realistic mark,' my father had said. The collection stayed on my parents' bookshelf until its pages began to curl from the humidity and tiny mites burrowed into the microfibers, at which point it was placed in the recycling pile with yesterday's newspapers.

Balli Kaur Jaswal was named the *Sydney Morning Herald*'s 'Best Australian Novelist' in 2014 for her debut novel, *Inheritance*. She has been a writer-in-residence at the University of East Anglia and Nanyang Technological University. Recently, her manuscript *Sugarbread* was shortlisted for the inaugural Epigram Books Fiction Prize in Singapore. She currently lives in Istanbul, Turkey, with her husband, where she teaches English in an international school and continues to write fiction.

CHRIS BRAZIER
England

THE AWAKENING

The day news of the Revolution reached Salmaga was a day like any other. The sun climbed high and fast into its cloudless showcase. The children ran in and out, free to come and go as they pleased provided they were still too young to help in the fields or fetch water.

Old Gerban was out in front of the *concession*, the family compound. He was in his usual place, sitting against the wall with his sightless eyes pointed towards the concrete mound that marked the tomb of his brother, once the most important man in the family. This round, raised stone was the gathering-place for the whole extended family. People passed the time of day here, and rehearsed the old stories under a big tree where the bats hung all day, their sacks of wrinkled skin decorating every branch.

Memnatu was arriving back from the well with her third bowl of water – it took four of the heavy metal bowls to fill the storage jar in her part of the concession. She looked straight ahead, thinking neither about the weight on her head nor about the perfect erectness of her posture – these were things a woman learned early, part of her sense of herself. Instead her mind ran on, as it was wont to do, worrying at the problem of her children's health. What did the baby's cough mean? And why was her daughter not holding down her food?

As she climbed the small slope towards the concession she saw a man on a bicycle pedalling furiously towards her as if he'd come from the nearby town of Garango. When he came a little closer she could see that it was Pierre. He looked very excited – his round, honest face was glowing with the effort of his ride, and he clearly wanted to be the first to break some kind of news.

'Ho! Memnatu!' he called.

'*Natizena,*' she said in greeting as he slowed up. He held out his hand for her to clasp it briefly.

'*Natizé*. Hey, what do you think? There's been a revolution in Ouaga. The army has taken power and is saying our country belongs to the people. They say everything is going to change.'

'What do they mean?'

'I'm not sure, but that's what they're saying, anyway. I'll see you later – I have to tell everyone else.' And he was away again, swinging down past the tree into the dip and on up the other side towards his own family's concession.

Memnatu looked after him in some bewilderment – she had never seen him so excited before. He was a Catholic boy with a slow but easy smile, thought to be very dependable by the elders of the village.

As if echoing her thoughts, Gerban called her over. 'I don't know why he's so worked up – nothing will change,' he said. 'Governments come and go but life here stays the same. Things are harder than they used to be, but people in Ouagadougou won't do anything about that.'

Memnatu had to agree. She didn't know much about the politics of the capital – who in the village did? – but she had never seen it affect their own lives. She moved on with her load into the concession. Its external mud walls reached up to just above head height and the conical straw roofs of the huts poked over the top at intervals. She passed into the gap that served as a gateway, and beyond into the network of passageways that veined the largest concession in the village. At least 60 people lived here, each family in its own section. Memnatu's home was typical enough – separated from the other living quarters by a chest-high wall. There were three huts here – one for Memnatu and her four children with a little courtyard outside, mud seats built into the walls; one for her co-wife Alima and her children, with a bigger courtyard that befitted her status as the first and oldest wife; and the third for their husband, Oumaru.

Memnatu poured the water down into the jar from on top of her head, temporarily setting a shimmering curtain between herself and the bright colors of her world. Then, without pausing, since there was much to be done before the sun fell, she was away again on her fourth journey to the well.

The months passed and, as Gerban had predicted, nothing changed. The millet was harvested and stored in the mini-huts that served as granaries. There did not seem to be as much grain as the year before – but then there never seemed to be as much as the year before. And, besides, Memnatu could never be sure, since only her husband could look in the granary. Just after the harvest he gave each of his co-wives a storage jar full of millet that they would be able to use in the hard times of the year. But for the most part they depended for their own and their children's staple food on the amount Oumaru carefully measured out to them every four days.

'Don't waste any of it,' he would say. As if she or Alima would ever waste food! Perhaps in the old days when the granaries were filled to overflowing, in the times Gerban would recall with such fondness for anyone who had the time to listen, wives used to be profligate with their food – but no woman of her age had ever been secure enough from the fear of hunger to be so careless. She supposed that Oumaru's imprecation was just a tradition – it was as if he had to distrust his wives on principle, as if by urging them every day to be careful he was warding off the evil spirit in them that would cause Allah alone knew what mischief if it were allowed free rein.

The rains had dwindled to nothing by October and then it was on into the dry, cool winter when nothing can be grown except tomatoes or okra for the markets if you were prepared to make the trek for sufficient water to help them grow. It was much the same as every year – the women had all their normal work but were spared the extra labor in the fields, while many of the men left to look for work elsewhere, in the towns or even on the plantations of Côte d'Ivoire. All promised to return for the rains but every year there were some that did not.

But every now and then through that year there would come rumors from the capital. The young were particularly ready to discuss the new developments, since they told of an army officer almost as young as themselves who was different from all previous leaders, who was honest and cared about the people instead of just about himself. 'Capitaine Thomas Sankara...' His name cropped up in conversations all over the village long before anyone had seen his picture.

Gerban still refused to believe that anything would change and said he could not tell whether Sankara was a good or a bad man until he had heard him speak. So Pierre brought a little radio to the concession and they listened to the impassioned voice together, Pierre translating the French into the local Bisa language as best he could, with the anxiety of the convert. When it was over and the still sound of the wind in the bat tree returned, Gerban narrowed his blind eyes as if they were peering into the distance and pronounced his verdict: 'I believe he is good, this Sankara.'

❖ ❖ ❖

In May, just before the next rains, Memnatu's third child fell ill. The baby was still healthy, protected by his breastfeeding, but four-year-old Fatimata suddenly tumbled into a raging fever. It was rare that a year passed without a child being sick with diarrhea or vomiting, and that was worrying enough, since Memnatu herself had seen many of the village children waste away into nothingness from what seemed like a trivial beginning. But this was obviously even more serious. Her own co-wife Alima had lost two of her five children in this way and they talked worriedly about what should be done.

'I think you should take her to Lembussa,' said Alima.

Memnatu sighed but agreed. Lembussa was the wise woman who'd delivered all her babies, but she had a certain reluctance about going to her with something of this sort. There was no knowing what the formidable old woman would diagnose, and Memnatu feared that she would insist on the child's clitoris being cut out, young though she was – she knew that there was already much talk around the village about her decision not to send her eldest child Salamatu to be circumcised. But she wrapped up Fatimata and carried her across the valley to another large concession, in the heart of which she found Lembussa.

'Ahsé,' said Memnatu in respectful greeting, and sat down. The old woman was a little stooped but still strong. She already knew about the little girl, and would have been surprised and offended had she not been consulted as to the requisite treatment. It didn't take her long to find out the problem, either.

'I've seen this many times before. A great bird of evil omen must have flown in from the bush and passed exactly over Fatimata while she was sleeping. All we have to do is let the wickedness out.' Lembussa went over into her hut, and emerged from the darkness with a razor blade. She laid the child on her lap and made a small but deep cut beneath the right eye, just on the cheekbone. Fatimata screamed, as much because of the iodine which Lembussa had rather reluctantly adopted as a new-fangled sterilizing agent as because of the actual incision. Memnatu gathered her daughter up hurriedly and left, pausing only to thank the old woman and to take the strip of cotton she offered as a means of staunching the blood flow.

'So Fatimata will have a scar,' she thought as she hurried away, 'as if she were a Mossi child. Still, sometimes that can look quite pretty.' She was relieved that the cut had been all that was necessary and, though she had not been sure before whether this visit would do any good, she somehow had no doubt now that Fatimata's illness would heal with her scar. And within a week the child was playing again.

Memnatu was one of the most popular women in Salmaga and she enjoyed that. She was tall and strong, and still young for her 25 years, despite her four children. Her face was not as beautiful as that of some of the other women of the area, she knew, but it was infused with such life that those comparisons were irrelevant – she looked all the time as though she were poised on the brink of laughter, as though gaiety were her most natural state. Only her breasts, pulled and pummelled into lank submission by four hungry infants, showed signs of age, along with her hands, their knuckles slightly swollen. For all the pleasures of being known and respected in the community for miles around, life was hard. She couldn't help sometimes but look back upon her childhood in Garango as a paradise, full of rain and plenty.

Her father had had three wives, so there had always been plenty of brothers and sisters to play with, though there had never seemed to be any problem with the food supply – not that she would have been told if there had been. Her father took the education of his daughters seriously and she learned in French about the world beyond the Bisa people – about her nation of Upper Volta, which had achieved its independence from France soon after her birth. She could speak French better than she read it, but either way it was enough to get by.

By the time she was 16, Memnatu was a very marriageable prospect, and three men had already staked their claims to her. There was no question which of the three she preferred. Michel was, at 18, very young as a man to be thinking of marriage, but she had known him at school and there had always been something special between them. At first it had just been a shy kind of friendship which had lapsed once Michel had left school. But they'd met once in the market in Garango and he'd asked at what age she wanted to marry, and from then on she'd known what was inside both of them. It was with some difficulty that she acknowledged this, since it was bound to cause problems – she had been raised a Muslim, while Michel was Catholic. Worse still, three years before, her sister had explored the same stony ground – she had decided to marry a Catholic boy. She had clung to resolve and her lover despite her father's anger, despite his threats that she would never see her family again. And now she was married with a child in Ouagadougou and she had a new Catholic name – Jacqueline.

Memnatu hoped that her father would have learned from the loss of one daughter. But his reaction was just the same. After a furious scene, he forbade her ever to see Michel again and swore that if she betrayed her faith by marrying the boy she would be an outcast from the family. Then he stormed out of the concession, leaving Memnatu in the throes of an awful dilemma. She walked off on her own down the road past the goat market, where the houses thread along it before giving way to open country. Once out of sight of people, she sat down at the foot of a baobab tree – a younger, less boastful version of the huge one beside the chief's concession.

In truth there was no decision to make – Memnatu had already accepted that she could not marry Michel. Knowing that made her want to be with him even more, made her insides flutter upwards as if to turn her back onto a different road. But to marry him she would have to move away and never see all the places and the people she loved – and she had loved all of them longer than she had loved Michel. They were part of herself, like this tree was part of this rock-hard earth.

She turned over a stone beside her with a strange delicacy and watched the white scorpion beneath it swing its tail from side to side, searching for the enemy that threatened it with this blinding light. Killing scorpions is almost a reflex action, something you don't think about, so hostile are we to each other as creatures, yet Memnatu carefully set the stone back in place, restoring its dark safety. Then she set off back to town to tell Michel.

The choice between her two remaining suitors was not difficult to make. Both were Muslim, both already had wives and were much older than Michel, but Oumaru was clearly the nicer of the two. He was a quiet man of 30 who exuded a kind of gentle strength. 'He's steady,' said her mother, 'he won't let you down and he won't beat you.'

What more could she ask of a husband than that? – except the means to keep her, and on that score her father was already satisfied. Oumaru had only been back in the area for six months having worked on the plantations in Côte d'Ivoire for five years. Unlike most men, he'd taken his wife and children there with him and had saved enough to clear himself of worries about any bad harvests in the next few years. Now that his father's death had brought him home to Salmaga, it seemed that a second wife would be commensurate with his new status as head of the family. And he regarded Memnatu as quite a prize, not just because she came from a good family in Garango, but because she was lively and intelligent. Not every man wanted that in a wife, but Oumaru felt sure that she would enrich his life and bring him happy, healthy children.

So Memnatu entered upon the normal married life of a Bisa woman. Only after the day's work was over and the night had come down did she have time to sit and think about the change in her life. She did not think of Michel, nor did she consider whether this new life was good, whether it suited her. She wondered only how good a wife she was making. And she yearned for the time when she would be fully accepted as a woman and as Oumaru's wife, which would not come until she had a child. She knew that the tongues of the old women would begin to wag if she showed none of the familiar signs within three months – the disgrace of infertility was a black pocket of fear inside her. So Memnatu was glad that Oumaru would come to her hut every night in those first months. He did not have to alternate between them, as Alima had just given birth and thus was still in the two-year grace period in which it is taboo for a man to have sex with his wife – a traditional protection from the rigors of non-stop pregnancy, evolved by a society without contraception.

She did not have long to wait, and the old women's tongues were stilled before the end of the three months. Memnatu's three-yearly cycle of pregnancy and respite had begun.

The winter after the Revolution there was more news from Ouagadougou, and this time it wasn't just a rustling in a far-off forest – this time there were orders for Salmaga. A young man with sparks in his eyes came from the regional capital of Tenkodogo and called a meeting to explain what had to be done. It was the villagers' first contact with a revolutionary – there were young men in Garango who fancied themselves enough to assume that name but they convinced no one. But there were no questioners of this stranger's credentials. He was no older than Pierre but he had a passion and an authority that immediately set him apart. Rumor had it that he was to be Haute-Commissaire, the most important post in the region. To be working in that big building set apart from Tenkodogo where the whites used to rule, and so young!

When he had gone, the village could talk about nothing else for days. It wasn't so much his grand words about building a new country – that could have been lifted from almost any other speech made since Upper Volta's independence. 'Words,' Gerban always said, 'words change nothing on their own.' But this new country was to be built in a different way, on their thoughts, their needs. In every village and every urban district there was to be a Committee for the Defence of the Revolution. Their own Committee would have the power to decide what happened to the village and the power to convey to the Government what the people wanted – 'the link between Sankara and Salmaga,' as the Haute-Commissaire had said, seizing on the similarity between the two names like a born orator. And what's more, this Committee was not to be nominated by the Government or by the local chief but was instead to be elected by everyone in the village, male and female alike.

'You should be choosing,' the Haute-Commissaire had advised rather fiercely, 'not the oldest people or the people with most money or those in your family, but those who believe most passionately in the Revolution, who will work hardest for development and justice.' And this was not all. At least two members of the CDR had by law to be women, and one of those had to be either the head or the deputy head of the committee.

This caused more consternation in the village than anything else. Women had gone to the meeting on the open ground beside the copse, but more because it was a big event for the village than because they expected to be involved. Making decisions was something men did, and there were many women who were not sure this new idea was a good one – it would only cause trouble and, besides, how could you argue against a man in front of all the other men? Who would be able to do that, and what man would allow his wife to take part?

Memnatu was not of this camp – she had been impressed by the Haute Commissaire's words about changing the country, about working together to make life better, and she felt inspired to think that women had a part to play in such important work. Somehow it changed the whole way she saw the Revolution. Before it had just been a different set of people in power in Ouagadougou. But the Haute Commissaire's phrase – 'this is women's revolution, too' – set her imagining women at work all over Upper Volta, not just raising children and drawing water, but also helping to make the country less poor. How it could be made less poor was beyond her understanding for the moment but it was an inspiring vision nonetheless. Perhaps for the first time, she felt connected with the nation beyond the hills, with the people away in Ouaga and Bobo, Fada and Koupela; she felt that she was not just a Bisa woman from Garango but a Voltaic, an African.

Excited as she was by her imaginings, Memnatu had no thought of standing in the CDR elections; she assumed that two of the older women in the village would be elected. But one day, as she sat sorting out husks from grains, old Gerban started a conversation on a surprising theme. It was late afternoon and he was in his normal place with the sun full on his face, feeling the light and warmth soak into his skin the more because it could not penetrate his eyes. Since she had come to the concession those ten years ago he had grown more and more fond of Memnatu – she listened to his stories and asked his advice, and he in turn found himself listening with more attention to what she said about the people and life of the village than he was wont to offer to a woman.

'What do you think about this committee idea?' he asked. Memnatu's face glowed red and, though the old man could not see her blush, her mumbled reply was enough to communicate her confusion.

'I have been thinking long and hard about this business,' continued Gerban, as if he had heard nothing, 'and I am still not sure what my opinion of it is. I can see there being trouble with the chief because he will not have the same power as before. And perhaps that's a bad thing – our traditions are our strength. But the old ways didn't stop the white men taking taxes from our grandfathers, and they haven't stopped life becoming harder. And if Sankara and that Commissaire are to be trusted, we will perhaps be able to ask for help with our problems.'

He paused, and the sound of children playing on the other side of the communal stone, Fatimata among them, momentarily had no competition. Memnatu looked at his wrinkled face with affection – so he had felt the pull, the inspiration as well. She waited for him to go on.

'As for women being on the committee, well, I know that many of the men think it is ridiculous. And perhaps when I was younger and I had to keep up my authority over my wives I would have felt the same. But to me the most important thing is that we choose the right women, who will be strong enough to tell the men what women think. That is why I think you, Memnatu, should stand for election.'

The space after his words seemed to make them echo and emphasize their enormity. When Memnatu eventually spoke it was not to offer the protest that Gerban had perhaps expected, but instead to ask a purely practical question. 'Won't the village choose someone like Lembussa rather than me?'

'Lembussa is part of the old way, as I am. She speaks no French and she does not read like you. She has no understanding of the new ideas, and I do not think she will want anything to do with them. She may cause you trouble. There is already the question of Salamatu's circumcision which hangs between you. You are still quite decided about that?'

'I am.'

'Lembussa has not persuaded you?'

'I know that it will be more difficult for Salamatu and Fatimata to find a husband. But I know also that I cannot send my daughters to be cut.' Memnatu spoke firmly but quietly – this was not a subject it would be seemly to shout about. Gerban pondered for a moment before replying.

'I suppose you brought the seed of this idea from Garango – and probably it was sown there by people from Ouaga. The world is changing, and not just because of revolutions – men are taking fewer wives, and more of the young ones leave our village and never return. It has been difficult for you to speak your mind. But Lembussa and the older women respect you more than you know – they could simply take Salamatu aside one day and use the razor but they do not. You will find your support not in the village but in this Revolution. I am the more convinced that you should stand.'

The children's voices asserted themselves again and Memnatu turned her head to look at them. There was a dispute over a small lizard, and Fatimata was arguing with one of Alima's boys for her rights to it. Even at this distance the little scar beside her nose was visible, like a reminder of the power of the old ways. Memnatu could not say what had made her so sure that cutting girls between their legs was wrong. She remembered a girl at school who had only appeared briefly after her ceremony and had died soon after. But she remembered, too, a conversation with Jacqueline about a Mossi woman in Ouaga who was said not to have been circumcised, yet who nevertheless had a husband and some fine children. The knowledge that she could not send her daughters had grown on her gradually after Salamatu's birth, a kernel of certainty deep inside that was only waiting on her recognition of it.

She recognized another kernel of certainty inside herself now. The idea was out in the sunlight, it was spoken. And it was as if she had always known that she would help the Revolution in a special way. But there was still a fire to jump over before she could participate in the election. She stood up with her bowl of grain and reached down to touch Gerban's hand. He closed his fingers around hers and bared his toothless gums in a smile.

After the meal, while the children were still sitting in her courtyard, Memnatu passed through to her husband's section of the compound. She squatted to collect his bowl but did not rise with it immediately.

'You have heard about the new committee and the elections?' she asked.

'Yes, of course.' Oumaru looked up, a little surprised. He stood rather aloof from village gossip but he had attended the political meeting with his Muslim friends, as she surely knew.

'And you know there are to be women on the Committee?' He widened his eyes in assent, beginning to realize what was coming. 'I should like to stand for election, if you will allow it.'

He looked hard at her face, thinner than it had been all those years ago when he had paid his visits to Garango, but still young and strong. He saw enough in it to realize that this was something about which she felt deeply. He motioned to her to sit down beside the wall to his right and she did so, awaiting his answer.

'When I chose you as my wife,' Oumaru began, 'I knew that I was choosing no ordinary woman. And you have proved that with your stubbornness over Salamatu's ceremony. I did not interfere since, as far as I understand, it is custom and not religious duty which makes us circumcise our daughters. And you have been a good wife aside from that – you have worked hard and borne me strong, fine children. But this revolution business is something else again. You believe, then, that it is good for our village?'

Memnatu did not answer for a second, so unaccustomed was she to being asked what she thought by any man. But when she spoke it was in a clear, firm voice. 'I believe that it is up to us all to make it good.'

'Perhaps you are right,' he said pensively. 'For myself it is enough to live and work under Allah's law, to pray for rain and a harvest that will see us through the year without hunger. Will your Revolution then guarantee these things?' He spoke a little playfully, and Memnatu knew that he did not intend her to answer. He looked up beyond the outer wall, where the stars were beginning to prick through their curtain.

'Very well, I will allow it, provided it does not interfere with your duties as a wife and mother. Like all these things, it probably will not last. But if there must be a woman on the Committee, there is no more able woman in the village than you.'

That night, as she lay in her hut surrounded by the gentle sound of her children's breathing, she stared into the darkness trying to absorb the meaning of the day. The rhythm was broken – where would this new path lead?

Memnatu took her responsibilities on the Committee for the Defence of the Revolution seriously. She had been put in charge of 'women's issues' and throughout that first year she made it her business to talk to all the women in the village about their lives, even those whom she had only known before by sight or by reputation. There were women from over the other side of the valley, for instance, beyond the well. The more forthright among the women on this fringe of Salmaga were as well known to Memnatu as their men, but there were those who kept more to themselves, and it was important that she sat with them and came to know their children and their plaints, that they came to see her as someone they could confide in. The contact cut both ways – she hoped through her discussions to push the women forward, to make them ready for the new ideas of the Revolution as the earth is made ready for seed.

This gospel quality was central to the experience of the men and women on the CDR, known by its French initials throughout Burkina Faso – on the first anniversary of the Revolution, Upper Volta had been renamed, using words from two different languages meaning 'land of the incorruptible'. The CDR members were very young – only one of the ten was over 30. And they were as eager to learn as they were to spread the word, listening carefully as Pierre read out in French the latest dictates from the National Council of the Revolution.

They applauded the new measures and understood the reasons behind them, even if how the laws would actually apply to Salmaga was often more difficult to grasp. But if some of the revolutionary changes were obscure and still distant, there was one which everybody understood and rejoiced at – all taxes on the rural population were abolished. This did more to make the revolution popular in Salmaga than any number of words, and it helped to foster the CDR's belief in itself. But they all still felt that their role was unclear and felt frustrated that change could not come faster. 'We must,' said Pierre one day at a meeting in his concession, 'be patient.'

'It is difficult to be patient,' said Memnatu in response. If any of the men present had entertained doubts about her value to the Committee, they had long ago been dispelled. They had begun to accept the Revolution's words about the equality of women, even if they had not yet realized its implications for their everyday life. Besides, Memnatu said things that were worth hearing.

'You all know Saytum, the widow,' she continued. 'She needs food – her fields grow little and she has only her children to help. Yet all of us have ignored her situation – the village looks down on her because she is poor. The CDR should be able to help her yet we are all poor, too. When will we be able to help people like Saytum?'

There was a murmur of agreement – no one knew the answer, but it was important that there should be one some time soon.

It was 1985, a year that was to test everyone's faith. By the second week in June the millet plants should have been a foot high, flecking the landscape with green. Instead the rains had not come. At the fall of the first few drops in May, Memnatu, Oumaru and Alima had sown their fields like everyone else. But those few drops were all that had fallen and they had watched the tiny green sprouts wither back into the earth.

Now they sowed a second time, unable to believe that the sky could hold back its treasure any longer. Yet every morning saw the sun clear the eastern horizon above Benin and sail upwards into the untroubled blue. Their dabas scraped the ground with a desperate rasping sound as they made the shallowest of resting-places for the seeds. Always before there had been a clear end to their work – every drop of water from the well used, every step of the journey to the fields essential. But now, as they bent over the baked soil, their pains seemed almost robbed of meaning. The earth was bitterly hard and looked dull, as though it were ready to give up its yearly struggle to bear fruit, prepared to yield prematurely to the implacable sun and sand. The redness that screamed its raw life after the rains was locked deep inside, a whisper of hope rather than a promise.

Salmaga could speak of nothing else. All other worries and wishes were forgotten. And no one was more anxious than Oumaru. Memnatu had never seen him so agitated and she did not fully understand why until he called her and Alima to him one grain-giving morning. He handed each of them their measure of millet as usual and said: 'Be sure that you do not waste this. I have a special reason for saying this, so heed me. The money I brought back from Abidjan is gone – there is no more. If the rain does not come, this year we cannot fill our empty granary with our coins.'

Memnatu stared at him, her mouth open. He had given them no sign of this, and only now that it was gone did she realize what a comfort the knowledge of those savings had been. Alima turned noiselessly and left her husband's living-room, but Memnatu stood still a moment longer and he spoke to her almost reproachfully. 'What good is your Revolution now?' he said. 'Tell Camarade Capitaine Sankara to make it rain.'

'What good is your Allah now?' she answered quietly. He raised his hand as if to strike her for the first time ever but checked himself, his anger lost in a sudden sense of defeat. Allah knew how he had prayed. The rains had been late before, or too little, but never had they failed completely, not even in the years when famine struck the north. Why did Allah not answer all their prayers? Had he not lived a devout life according to the law?

He sank on to the wall seat beside his hut. Memnatu had never seen him like this before. She felt an impulse to hold him as she would hold her son if he hurt inside but she stood her ground – a man had his pride, after all.

'If it does not rain I will have to leave in search of work,' he said, as much to himself as to his wife. 'Perhaps this marks the end of the old world.'

The village could think of nothing else but the earth and the sky, but Memnatu had other worries. Her youngest boy, Bubakar, now nearly two years old, was ill with chronic diarrhea and refused to be parted from her. She was forced to carry him everywhere with her – to the fields, to the well and on her visits – yet even then he was too miserable and restless to allow her to consign him to her back. Normally he would be quite content to be carried there within a cloth that tied round above his mother's breasts, but now she kept having to cuddle him to her as she walked, which took more out of her and kept her hands from useful work. All her children had been weakened by diarrhea at times, but so far she had been lucky and had lost none of them to its onslaughts. The Revolution had so far delivered nothing that might help – the CDR had received papers talking of the importance of people's health but there had been no sign yet of anything practical.

There was a doctor in Tenkodogo, to be sure, but it would cost money to get there, money to consult him and money for his pills – it was not even worth thinking about. And the years had not taught Lembussa a magic that would save the village children from death by diarrhea. No, there was no alternative but to carry on and hope.

Memnatu had another reason for thinking of Lembussa. Bubakar was just a few weeks away from his second birthday, and that meant Oumaru would soon resume his visits to her hut at night. And the familiar sickness and swelling would follow inevitably within a matter of months. That was the way of things for a woman. The last time she had become pregnant, she had barely reacted to it. It had occasioned neither pleasure nor regret, had been simply a part of her life and her lot. Yet she felt very differently now, and the difference made her realize how much she had changed. In the past few weeks there had been a weight tugging from below at her buoyancy, even before the anxiety about the rains had set in. It was as if the looming certainty of conception was a threat to her from outside instead of the essential part of her world that it would once have been. Previously she had had everything to gain – another child to help along the work in the fields, greater status as a mother of many, a more solid insurance policy for her old age. But now she had something to lose.

Memnatu was as clear as she had ever been about anything that she did not want another child. But what then could she do? Was it possible to stop a baby resulting from Oumaru's night visits? She knew that Lembussa could make women bleed to stop their pregnancy, but she knew also that it was a dangerous business, and she wished for another way. Jacqueline had told her about special pills that some of the women in Ouaga took to prevent a baby coming. Why were these pills only in Ouaga? Did village women not need them, too? Why could the Revolution not help her in this?

Bubakar's illness, the nagging threat of pregnancy, the lack of rain and money – all these worries somehow combined to make Memnatu doubt the Revolution more than she had since the day the Haute Commissaire had come to offer her its inspiration and its purpose. Why were the changes so slow? Did they not see these things as important?

These questions marked a small but important change in her attitude towards the Revolution. She still believed in it – it was carrying her country forward, and her with it. But whereas she had always before seen the Revolution as a path leading towards development and justice that began at Ouagadougou, now she had some sense that she needed to influence its direction. If Sankara and the National Council did not see how important to village women was the health of their children and the means to prevent pregnancy, then perhaps she should tell them.

Her heart quailed, however, at the idea of mentioning the question of stopping babies at the next CDR meeting – how could she talk of such things to men, even if they were revolutionaries? They would know how old Bubakar was, would realize that she was talking about herself. Within hours the story would be the property of the whole village and that would be humiliating for Oumaru – it would be too much to ask him to bear. But she could at least speak from her heart about her child's health and feel the whole village behind her. She made up her mind to make her protest at the next meeting.

It was the third week in June, and still the rains had not come. The CDR meeting was a subdued affair – nothing else seemed quite as important as it had done just a month ago. But Memnatu's words about the need for help with healthcare had been well enough received. She had asked if someone from the village might receive training that would teach them what to do about their children's illnesses and Pierre had undertaken to speak to people in Garango about it.

After the meeting was over he came over to talk with her – he had a proposal to make. The Government had announced a new program of military service earlier in the year – every young person was to receive three months of training, and people from the towns had to spend an extra period doing agricultural work. Pierre had come back from his own training in Tenkodogo in the spring full of his usual enthusiasm.

'You don't only learn how to be a soldier – we were taught so many other things as well. About the need to grow more food. About the problems of Africa and the need for development. And we met so many different people, too, from all over the region.'

Memnatu had been fascinated to hear about the experience but had not related it to herself. Yet now Pierre was suggesting that she should do her three months' training in Tenkodogo from October. 'It is important that women receive this training as well as men,' he said, 'and it is important that you, as a member of this CDR, should benefit from it as soon as possible.'

'But how can I? Oumaru will never agree!'

'Oumaru will have to agree – it is the law now. You could wait until next year. But will it be any better for Oumaru next year than this? I will speak to him if you would like it.'

'No, thank you. I must think first. It would mean living there in Tenkodogo for three months, as you did?'

'Yes – but you would be with other women there. Let me know your decision as soon as you can.'

Still Salmaga watched the sky. It was Ramadan, the month of fasting for Oumaru and the other Muslims, and never had there seemed so much point to their devotions. Perhaps, after all, the proof of faith that their abstinence provided would make Allah relent. But the extra little strain of not eating during all the daylight hours caught them up all the more in their own anxiety. There was talk of a special prayer session in the fields.

Then, as if by a miracle, the world regained its equilibrium. It was the night before the feast to mark the end of Ramadan and, just after darkness fell, the heavens blessed the earth with a deluge. The violence of the rain was awesome, as if it were making recompense for its tardiness by sending all its lost water at once. Within minutes the land had disappeared beneath the waves; rivers poured into the concessions, lapping up the walls and flowing unchecked into the huts, bubbling ferociously as the huge drops plunged into the tide; children threw water gleefully over each other while babies cried, alarmed to see their world so disturbed.

Within an hour it was over and the storm had moved on to offer its wild benison to another desperate part of West Africa. As the night went on and the moon reappeared, the rivers receded and became streams and then rivulets, the lakes became pools and then puddles and the soil drank its immoderate cocktail to the dregs. When the sun rose over Salmaga in the morning, everybody was smiling – full, glorious smiles that enveloped the faces of the men and women as they shouted their greetings. '*Natizena!*' '*Natizé!*' Oumaru dressed himself carefully in a rich red robe and set off on his bike for the feast. Today he would pray with more joy and gratitude than he had ever prayed before.

Memnatu bent to her work with a will. They were planting for the third and final time in all the places where the seedlings had not taken and, relieved of the doubt about its value, this was a happy labor. The earth beneath her was beautifully soft; she peeled it away with her daba instead of attacking it. More of its topsoil had been swept away by the waters, unable to resist the onslaught without tree or plant roots to bind it together, but what remained had reclaimed its rude red health. For this year at least, there would be another harvest.

Memnatu came to the end of the seeds in her calabash and went over to the sack for more. Her back ached as she stretched – but no one would begrudge such an ache on such a day. She looked around at the bending, bobbing figures of Oumaru, Alima and her own daughter Salamatu and thought of how what was in her mind now was going to affect them. Salamatu was old enough at ten to take some responsibility for looking after her brothers and sisters. Alima was good and kind, and would not mind the extra work that her co-wife's absence would bring her – she should really mind it more, for her own sake. But what of Oumaru? He would not suffer by her absence – the rains would be over by October and the harvest in, even after this late start. But what would he think of her? Would he curse her for neglecting her duty to him and to the children? Or would he be secretly proud that his wife was the first woman in the village to go away for training? She did not know – men were so transparent at times, yet so impenetrable at others.

And how would it affect her, Memnatu? To be away from home for the first time in her life, away from the rhythms of the earth and the sky, away from the demands of the well and the children. To wear the uniform of a Burkinabé soldier. To meet so many strange and different people and learn about the world beyond these hills...

It was an enormous prospect – the very thought of it set her stomach churning and made her breath catch. But it was right that she should go, and right that she should go so soon. Perhaps she would be lucky and not fall pregnant in the two months or so between Bubakar's birthday and her leaving, and then perhaps she would learn a way of preventing babies while she was in Tenkodogo, a way that would allow her to receive Oumaru without fear. Perhaps nothing would be the same again after this, her revolutionary baptism, just as nothing would be the same again for her country, her Burkina Faso. But Memnatu trusted in the future as she trusted in the ripening of the millet under her feet now that rain had fallen. She poured some more seeds into her calabash and went on with her work.

Chris Brazier has been a co-editor at New Internationalist since 1984. For most of his career he worked on the monthly magazine but for the past decade has commissioned and edited New Internationalist's books – including editing the annual anthology of the Caine Prize for African Writing. He is the author of the *NoNonsense Guide to World History, Vietnam: The Price of Peace* and *Trigger Issues: Football*. He has also written regularly for UNICEF since 1997, contributing to many of its *State of the World's Children* reports. He first visited rural Burkina Faso in 1985 and has returned to the same village every ten years since to report on changes in the lives of individuals and the community.

EDWIDGE DANTICAT
Haiti/United States

DOSAS

Elsie was with her live-in renal failure when her ex-husband called to inform her that his girlfriend, Olivia, had been kidnapped in Port-au-Prince. Elsie had just fed Gaspard, the renal patient, when her cellphone rang. Gaspard was lying in bed, his head carefully propped on two firm pillows, his bloated face angled towards the bedroom skylight, which allowed him a slanted view of a giant coconut palm that had been leaning over the lakeside house for years.

Elsie removed the empty plate from Gaspard's nightstand and wiped a lingering string of spinach from his chin. Shuffling both hands, he signalled to her not to leave the room, while motioning for her to carry on with her phone conversation. Quickly turning her attention from Gaspard to the phone, Elsie pressed it close to her lips and asked, '*Ki lè?*'

'This morning.' Sounding hoarse and exhausted, Blaise, the ex-husband, jumbled his words. His singsong tone, which Elsie often attributed to his being a singer, was gone, replaced by a nearly inaudible whisper.

'She was leaving her mother's house,' he continued. 'Two men grabbed her, pushed her into a car and drove off.'

Elsie could imagine Blaise sitting, or standing, with the phone trapped between his neck and shoulders, while he used his hands to pick at his fingernails. It was an obsession of his, clean nails. Dirty fingers drive him crazy, she'd reasoned because, like her, he was a product of grimy urban poverty and barely missed having dirty fingers all his life.

'You didn't go to Haiti with her?' Elsie asked.

'You're right,' he answered, loudly drawing an endless breath through what Elsie knew were grinding teeth. 'I should have been there.'

Elsie's patient's eyes wandered down from the ceiling, where the blooming palm had sprinkled the glass with a handful of tiny brown seeds. He'd been pretending not to hear, but was now looking directly at Elsie. Restlessly shifting his weight from one side of the bed to the next, he paused to catch his breath. He wanted her off the phone.

Gaspard had turned 70 that day and before his lunch had requested a bottle of champagne from his daughter. The daughter, who was visiting from Haiti, had gone out to procure what was surely the most expensive bottle of champagne she could find. And suddenly she was back.

'Elsie, I need you to hang up,' she said as she laid out three crystal champagne flutes on a folding table by the bed.

'Call me back,' Elsie told Blaise.

After she hung up, Elsie moved closer to the sick man's beautiful, portly daughter and watched as she gently slid a champagne flute between her father's swollen fingers.

That afternoon, Blaise called back to tell Elsie that Olivia's mother had heard from her captors. The mother had asked to speak to Olivia but her kidnappers had refused to put her on the phone.

'They want 50,000.' Blaise spoke in such a rapid nasal voice that Elsie had to ask him to repeat the figure.

'American?'

She imagined him nodding by slowly moving his egg-shaped head as he answered 'wi'.

'Does the mother have it?' Elsie asked.

'Of course she doesn't,' Blaise said. 'These are not rich people. The sister says we should negotiate. She thinks we can get it down into the tens. I can try to borrow that.'

'Jesus, Marie, Joseph,' Elsie mumbled a brief prayer under her breath. 'I'm sorry,' she told Blaise.

'This is hell.' He sounded almost too calm now. She wasn't surprised because he was always subdued by worry. Weeks after he was kicked out of the popular konpa band he founded and had been the lead singer of, he did nothing but stay home and stare into space whenever she tried to talk to him. Then too he had been calm.

Elsie's former friend Olivia was seductive. Everyone who ever met her acknowledged it. Chestnut-colored, with a massive head of hair that she always wore in a gelled bun, Olivia was beautiful. But what Elsie had first noticed about her when they'd first met was her ambition. At 33, Olivia was one of the most popular certified nurses' aides at the agency that assigned them work. Because of her good looks, relative youth and near-perfect mastery of textbook English, Olivia often got assigned the easiest patients in the most upscale neighborhoods.

Elsie and Olivia had met at a two-week refresher course for home attendants and upon completion of the course had gravitated towards one another. Whenever possible, they'd asked to work in the same group homes, caring for bedridden elderly patients.

At night, when their wards were safely in bed, they'd stay up and gossip in hushed tones, judging and condemning their patients' children and grandchildren, whose images were framed near bottles of medicine on bedside tables, but whose voices they rarely heard on the phone and whose faces they rarely saw in person.

The next morning Elsie brought Gaspard his toothbrush and toothpaste and helped him change out of his pajamas into the too small slacks and shirt he insisted on wearing in bed during the day. Just as he had every morning for the last week or so, he reached over and ran his coarse fingers across her sharp cheekbones and whispered, 'Elsie, my flower, I think I'm at the end.'

Compared to some mornings, when Gaspard would stop to rest even while gargling, he seemed rather stable. His entire body was swollen though, blending his features in a way that made him look less and less singular all the time. Soon, Elsie feared, his face might become like a balloon that someone had drawn a few dots on. Much to Elsie's and his daughter's astonishment and dismay, he was still refusing dialysis, which was the only thing that might help.

'Where's my daughter?' he asked.

The daughter was still sleeping in her old bedroom, whose walls, like the living room's, were draped from floor to ceiling with fabric. Elsie knew little about the daughter except that she'd once been a businesswoman of some kind, but was now living in Haiti. She had also been a beauty queen at some point, judging from the pictures around the house in which she was wearing sequined gowns and bikinis with sashes across her body. She had once even been Miss Haiti-America, whatever that was. Then her mother, who had initiated her in these pageants, had suddenly died, and even though this was long after she'd stopped participating in pageants, she had started eating so much that it seemed as though she'd swallowed the person she had once been. Moving back to Haiti to start a hotel with her husband had seemed like it might save her. This much Gaspard had told her, in order to explain that his daughter's visits could not always be long ones, that she could not come to stay.

'Her life hasn't been easy,' he'd said. 'I don't want you to judge her. I don't want you to think that she's deserted me like a lot of people desert old people in this country.'

'But she's here now, Mr Gaspard,' Elsie had said. 'That's what counts.'

The daughter walked to Gaspard's room as soon as she woke up. In order to avoid tiring him, they didn't speak very much, but for the better part of the morning the daughter read to him from an old book with a musical title, *Gouverneurs de la Rosée*, Masters of the Dew.

Blaise called once more that afternoon as Elsie was preparing a palm hearts, almond and avocado salad that Gaspard had especially requested. It was something his dead wife, his daughter's mother, used to prepare for him, he said, something he now wanted to share with his grown child.

'I think they hurt her, Elsie,' Blaise said. His speech was garbled and slow, as though he'd just woken up from a deep sleep.

'Why do you think that?' Elsie asked. Her thumb accidentally slipped across the blade of the knife she was using to slice the palm hearts. She squeezed the edge of the wound with her teeth, the sweet taste of her own blood filling her mouth.

'I don't know,' he said, 'I can feel it. You know she won't give in easily. She'll probably fight.'

The night Olivia and Blaise met, Elsie had taken Olivia to see Blaise's band play at Banbouni Night Club in Little Haiti. The place was owned by Luca Banbouni, a man in his early forties with a teenager's face, a Haitian of Italian origin who'd grown up with Blaise in Port-au-Prince. Elsie was so used to going to Banbouni's that she didn't even bother dressing up. She had chosen instead to wear a buttoned-up white shirt and a pair of casual dark slacks as though she were going to an office. Hungry for a night out, Olivia had worn a too tight, floor-length, sequined purple gown that she'd purchased at a thrift shop.

'It was the most soirée thing they had,' Olivia said when Elsie met her at the entrance. 'They didn't have one, but I wanted a red dress. I wanted fire. I wanted blood.'

'You wanted a man,' Elsie said.

'Correct,' Olivia said, tilting her body forward on sloped three-inch heels to plant a kiss right on Elsie's cheek. Though they'd known each other for a while, it was the first time Olivia had kissed her on the cheek. They were out to have fun, away from their ordinary cage of sickness and death. Perhaps Olivia was simply celebrating that.

Being with Olivia that night gained Elsie a few glances from several men, including Luca Banbouni, who'd never paid her much attention before. Minding the bar as usual, Banbouni sent winks and drinks their way until it was clear that Olivia only had a passing interest in him. While Elsie didn't dance that night, Olivia accepted every invitation. Several rum punches later, Olivia even got up between sets and, on a dare from Banbouni, sang, in a surprisingly pitch-perfect voice, both the Haitian and the American national anthems. After singing both songs, Olivia got a standing ovation. The crowd whistled and hooted. Put her in the band, they hollered. Make her president of both lands!

'I got a couple of loans,' Blaise announced when he called yet again a few hours later. His voice cracked and he stuttered and Elsie wondered if he'd been crying.

'I have 45 hundred now,' he added. 'Do you think they'll accept that?'

'Are you going to send the money just like that?' Elsie asked.

'I think I'll bring it,' he said, sounding as though he hadn't quite made up his mind. 'I think I'll just get on the plane tomorrow and bring it myself.'

'What if they take you too?'

Selfishly, she wondered who would be called if he were kidnapped. Like her, he didn't have any family in Miami. The closest thing he had were Banbouni and the band mates, who'd parted company with him over money problems he'd refused to discuss with her. Maybe that's why he'd wanted Olivia. Olivia would have insisted on knowing exactly what had happened with the band and why. Olivia might have tried to fix it, so that he could keep playing at all costs. Olivia believed, just as he did, that he needed all his time for his so-called music, that working as a doorman or a parking attendant might spiritually raze him.

'How do you know this isn't some kind of plot to trick you out of your money?' Elsie asked.

'Something's wrong,' he said. 'She'd never go this long without calling me.'

'You know her best,' Elsie said.

It was something she'd said to him before, when she'd desperately tried to hide her jealousy with mock suspicion.

Soon after Olivia met Blaise, she would also reach up to kiss his cheeks the way she had Elsie's.

At first Elsie had ignored this; however, every once in a while she would bring it to their attention in a jokey way by saying something like, 'Watch out sister, that's my man.' From her experience working with the weak and the sick, she'd learned that the disease you ignore is the one that kills you, so she tried her best to have everything out in the open.

Whenever Blaise asked her to invite Olivia to hear him play, she always obliged because she also enjoyed Olivia's company outside of work. And when the gigs stopped coming and he was no longer playing on the weekends, they would go out together, the three of them, to shop for groceries or see a movie, and even attend Sunday morning mass at Notre Dame Catholic Church. They were soon like a trio of siblings, of whom Olivia was the dosa, the untwinned child.

'I'm sorry I haven't called before all this.' Blaise spoke now as though they were simply engaged in the dawdling pillow talk that Elsie had once so enjoyed during their four-year marriage. 'I didn't think you wanted to hear from me.'

'That's how it goes when you divorce, *non*?' she said, 'except on occasions like this.'

She was only half listening, waiting for him to say something else about Olivia. He was slow at parcelling out news. It had taken him months to inform Elsie that he was leaving her. Perhaps it would have been easier to accept had he simply blurted something out that first night he'd laid eyes on Olivia. Then she wouldn't have spent so much time reviewing every moment the three of them had been together, wondering whether they'd winked behind her back during mass or smirked as she lay between them in the grass during their Saturday afternoon outings to watch him play soccer at Morningside Park.

'What's the news?' she asked, suddenly wanting to shorten their talk.

'They called me directly.' She could hear him swallow hard. Her ears had grown accustomed to that kind of effortful gulp from working with Gaspard and others. '*Volè yo.*' The thieves.

'What did they sound like?' She wanted to know everything he knew so she could form a lucid image in her own mind, a shadow play identical to his.

'I think they were boys, men. I wasn't recording,' he said, sounding annoyed.

'Did you ask to speak to her?'

'They wouldn't let me,' he said.

'Did you insist? Did you tell them you wouldn't send money unless you could speak to her? Maybe they don't have her any more. You said it yourself. She would fight. Maybe she escaped.'

'Don't you think I'd ask to speak to my own woman?' he shouted.

The way he spat this out irritated her. Woman. His own woman. She hated him for it. She hated them both.

'I'm sorry,' he said. 'They didn't speak to me for very long. They just told me to start planning her funeral if I don't send at least 10,000 by tomorrow afternoon.'

Just then she heard Gaspard's daughter call out from the other room. 'Elsie, can you come here please?', her voice laden with the permanent weariness of those who love the chronically ill.

'Please call me later,' she told Blaise and hung up.

When she got to Gaspard's room, the daughter was sitting there with the same book on her lap. She had once again been reading to her father when Elsie had slipped away with the intention of stacking the dishwasher with the breakfast and lunch plates, but had ended up answering Blaise's call.

'Elsie,' the daughter said, as her father pushed his head further back into the pillows. His fists were clenched in stoic agony, his eyes closed. His face was sweaty. He seemed to have been coughing. Later Elsie would have to bring in the oxygen compressor to help with his breathing.

'Yes, Madame,' answered Elsie, hoping to soften her up.

'I'm sorry,' Gaspard's daughter said while flipping through the pages of her book even while keeping her eyes on her father. 'I'm not here all the time. I don't know how you function normally, but I'm really concerned about how much time you spend on the phone.'

Elsie didn't want to explain why she was talking on the phone but quickly decided she had to. Not only because she felt the daughter was right, that Gaspard deserved more of her attention, but also because she had no one else to turn to for advice. And so she told them why the calls had come and why they were so frequent, except she modified a few crucial details. Because she was still too embarrassed by the actual facts, she told them that Olivia was her sister and Blaise her brother-in-law.

'I'm very sorry, Elsie,' the daughter immediately softened. Gaspard opened his eyes and held out his hand towards Elsie. Elsie moved towards him and grabbed it, as she did sometimes to help stabilize him when he managed to get on his feet.

'Do you want to go home?' asked Gaspard. 'We can get the agency to send someone else.'

'I'm not in her head, Papa,' the daughter said, 'but I think working is best. I live in the country, I know. Paying off these types of ransoms can ruin a person financially.'

'I don't live in the country,' Gaspard said, still trying to catch his breath. 'But I'm sure it's better not to wait. The less time your sister spends with these *malfetè*, the better off she'll be.'

He turned his face towards his daughter for final approval as she yielded and nodded in agreement.

'If you want to save your sister,' Gaspard said, with an even more winded voice now, 'you may have to give in.'

'I have 5,000 in the bank,' Elsie told Blaise when he called again that afternoon. Somehow she felt he knew that. It was roughly the same amount she'd had saved when they'd been together. She hadn't been able to add to it since her expenses had immediately doubled after their separation and quickie divorce. This is what Blaise had been trying to tell her all along. He needed that money.

Sometimes Elsie was sure she could make out the approximate time that Olivia and Blaise began seeing each other without her. Olivia started pairing up with someone else for the group-home jobs and turned Elsie down when she asked her to join the usual outings with Elsie and Blaise.

The night Blaise left their apartment for good, Olivia sat outside Elsie's first-floor window, in the front passenger seat of Blaise's red pick-up. The old pick-up was parked under a street lamp and, for most of the time that Elsie was staring through a crack in her drawn shades, Olivia's face was flooded in a harsh bright light. At some point Olivia got out of the car then disappeared behind it as though she had crouched down in the shadows to pee, then she got back in the front passenger seat, what Elsie had called to herself the wife's seat. Only when the car, packed with most of Blaise's belongings, was pulling away did Olivia finally look at the window, where Elsie quickly pulled the shades back and sank into the darkness.

The next evening Gaspard fell out of bed while reaching over to his bedside table for a newspaper. Elsie heard the thump from her bedroom and by the time she dashed down the hall, his daughter was already there, her wide bottom spiked up in the air, her face pressed against her father's. With one arm under her father's bulbous legs and the other wrapped around his back, she dragged him off the floor and raised him onto the edge of the bed.

Elsie paused in the doorway to watch as the daughter lowered her father into bed as though he were an oversized child. Raising a comforter over his chest, she gently kissed his forehead. They were both panting as their faces came apart, she from the effort of carrying and he from having been carried.

Suddenly their panting turned into loud chuckles.

'There are many falls before the big one,' he said.

'Thank God you got that good carpet,' she said.

Then, her face growing somber again, the daughter said, 'How can I leave you, Papa?'

'You can,' he said, 'and you will. You have your life and I have what's left of mine. I want you to always do what you want. I don't want you to have any regrets.'

'You need the treatment.' She pleaded. 'Why don't you accept it?'

The daughter reached over and grabbed a glass of water from the side table. She held the back of her father's head as he took a few sips. Elsie rushed over and took the glass from her as she lowered her father's head back onto the pillow. The daughter grimaced while trying to keep her tears from slipping down her face.

'I know you're having your family problem, Elsie,' the daughter said, straining not to raise her voice, 'but why did it take you so long to get here after my father fell out of this bed? I think Papa's right. I'm calling the agency tomorrow to ask for someone else.'

Elsie wanted to plead to stay. She liked Gaspard and didn't want him to have to break in someone else. Besides, after wiring all her savings to Blaise for Olivia's ransom that afternoon, she desperately needed to work. However, if they wanted her to leave, she would. She only hoped that her dismissal wouldn't cost her other jobs.

'I'll wrap things up,' she told them, 'until you get someone else.'

One night after Elsie and Olivia had heard Blaise play with his band at an outdoor festival at Bayfront Park in downtown Miami, they were walking along with a throng of people towards a parking lot when Olivia announced that she was going to find a man to move back with her to Haiti.

'Will you love him?' Elsie had asked.

Mildly drunk from a whole afternoon of beer sipping, Olivia had mumbled, '*Non*, not really.'

'How can you live without love?' Blaise had said, waxing lyrical in a way that Elsie had never heard before, except maybe when he was on stage trying to professionally seduce the women who came to hear his band with his idea of public come-ons ('You're looking like a piña colada, baby. Can I have a sip?'). Harmless stuff that Elsie was accustomed to.

'I can live without love,' Elsie had said, 'but I can't leave without money and I can't live without my country. I'm tired of being in this country. This country makes us mean.'

Elsie guessed at that moment that Olivia was still thinking about one of their patients' sons from the day before, a middle-aged man, a banker. In their presence, as they were changing shifts, the man had turned over his senile father and had slapped his father's bottom with his palm.

'See how you like it now,' he'd said.

Calling the agency that had hired them, then the Department of Social Services over a mistreated patient yet again, Olivia had barely been able to find the words.

The night of the concert, to distract Olivia from her thoughts of abused patients and marriage, and to distract each other from thoughts of losing Olivia, the three of them had returned to Blaise and Elsie's apartment and sipped some more beer. Sometime in the early-morning hours, without anyone's request or guidance, they had all fallen into bed together, exchanging touches and kisses, whose sources they weren't interested in keeping track of. That night, they were no longer sure what to call themselves. What were they exactly? A triad. A *ménage à trois*. No. Dosas. They were all dosas. All three of them untwinned, lonely, alone together.

When they woke up the next morning, Olivia was gone.

Blaise called again early the next morning just as Elsie was preparing to get up. Gaspard and his daughter were still asleep and, aside from the hum of Gaspard's oxygen compressor, the house was completely quiet.

'I shouldn't have let her go,' Blaise whispered before Elsie could say hello.

When Blaise was still with the band, he would sometimes go days without sleep in order to rehearse around the clock. By the time his gig came around, he'd be so hyper that his voice would sound mechanical, as though all emotion had been purged out of it. He sounded that way now as Elsie tried to keep up.

'We weren't getting along any more,' he said. 'We were going to break up. That's why she just picked up and left.'

The light came on in the room where Gaspard's daughter was sleeping. Elsie heard the shuffling of feet. A shadow approached. The daughter peeked in, rubbing a clenched fist against her eyes to fully rouse herself.

'Is everything all right?' she asked Elsie.

Elsie nodded. Blaise was still talking.

'I wish I'd begged her not go,' he was saying.

The daughter pulled Elsie's door shut behind her and continued towards her father's room down the hall.

'What happened?' Elsie asked. 'You sent the money, didn't you? They released her?'

The phone line crackled and Elsie heard several bumps. Was Blaise stomping his feet? Banging his head against a wall? Pounding the phone into his forehead?

'Where is she?' Elsie tried to moderate her voice.

'We had a fight,' he said. 'Otherwise she would have never gone. We had a spat and she left.'

The daughter opened the door and once again pushed her head in.

'Elsie, my father would like to see you when you're done,' she said, before pulling the door behind her once more.

'I'm sorry, I have to go,' Elsie said. 'My boss needs me. But first tell me she's okay.'

She didn't want to hear whatever else was coming, but she could not hang up.

'Even though we paid the ransom,' he said, now rushing to get his words out before she could hang up. 'They didn't release her. She's dead.'

Elsie walked back to the bed she'd called hers for the last few months and sat down. This was the longest she'd ever been at any job. For a while she had allowed herself to forget that this bed with its foamy mattress, which was supposed to use numbers to remember the shape of your body, would not always be hers. Taking a deep breath, she moved the phone away from her face and let it rest on her lap.

'Are you there?' Blaise was shouting now. 'Can you hear me?'

'Where was she found?' Elsie raised the phone back to her face.

'She was dumped at the mother's house,' Blaise shrieked like an injured animal.

Elsie ran her fingers across her cheeks where, in the darkness that had enveloped all three of them the night they'd fallen into bed together, Blaise had kissed her for the last time. That night, it had been hard for Elsie to differentiate Olivia's hands from Blaise's on her body. But, in her drunken haze, it had all felt perfectly normal, like they'd both loved him too much to restrain themselves.

Now the tears were catching her off guard, coming much quicker than she'd expected. She lowered her head and buried her eyes in the crook of her elbow.

'You won't believe it.' Blaise said frantically, garbling the words as they came through.

'What?,' Elsie said, wishing, not for the first time since he and Olivia had stopped talking to her, that the three of them were once again drunk and in bed together.

'Her mother says that, before she left the house, Olivia wrote her name on the bottom of her feet.'

Elsie could imagine Olivia, her conked, plastered hair wild, as she pulled her feet towards her face and, with a marker that she'd probably brought all the way from Miami just for that purpose, scribbled her name there. Knowing Olivia, she'd probably seen this as the only precaution against the loss of identity that follows an unclaimed abductee's beheading.

'Her mother's going to bury her in Haiti,' he said, 'in her family's mausoleum, in their village out south.'

'Are you going?' she asked.

'Of course,' he said. 'Would you–?'

She didn't let him finish. Of course she wouldn't go. Even if she wanted to, she couldn't afford the plane ticket.

Just then his line beeped twice, startling her.

'It's Haiti,' he said. 'I have to go.'

He hung up just as abruptly as he had re-entered her life.

'Elsie, are you all right?' Gaspard was standing in the doorway. Short of breath, he leaned towards one side. His daughter was standing behind with a portable oxygen tank.

Elsie wasn't sure how long they'd both been standing there. Still, she moved towards them, tightening her robe belt around her waist. Grunting, Gaspard looked past her, his eyes wandering around the room, taking in the foamy mattress and platform bed and companion dresser.

'Elsie, my daughter seems to think that she heard you crying.' Gaspard's blood-drained lips were trembling as though he were cold. 'Is your sister all right?'

Gaspard's body swayed back towards his daughter. The daughter quickly reached for him, anchoring him with one hand while balancing the portable oxygen tank with the other. With a fearful glance at Gaspard's shadow swaying unsteadily on the ground, Elsie replied, 'Please reconsider your decision to release me, Monsieur Gaspard. I won't be getting these phone calls any more.'

She was right.

He never called her again.

A few weeks later, after a long day's work, when her heart was still aching for them both, she stopped by Banbouni's, hoping Blaise might stop there one night after returning from the funeral in Haiti.

It was a week night and the place was nearly empty, except for some area college kids who Banbouni allowed to buy drinks and cigarettes without ID. Banbouni was at the bar. She walked over and sat across from him as a waitress squeezed in between the stools to collect orders.

'How are you holding up?' he asked.

'Working hard,' she said, 'to get by.'

'Still with the old people?' he asked.

'They're not always old,' she said. 'Sometimes they're young people who have been in car accidents or have cancer.'

Eventually they got to Blaise.

'Have you heard from him?' Banbouni asked.

'Not in a while,' she said.

'I hear he's living in Haiti now,' Banbouni said, while wiping the insides of a glass with a small white towel. 'He's living there with a lot of my money and most of his old band's money and from some kidnapping scam. He and Olivia are married.'

If this were happening to someone else, she would wonder why that person didn't grab Banbouni's neck and demand more details, why that person didn't pound her breasts with her fist, tear off her clothes and thrash around on the floor. But she did none of those things. It was as if suddenly some shred of doubt, which had been plaguing her, some small suspicion she'd harbored, was finally confirmed.

The last thing she remembered was seeing Banbouni grab a bottle from a mirrored table behind him then pull a glass from under the bar. But even as she was taking her first sips of whatever the potent elixir was he'd given her, she kept thinking about the details. The details. They'd been so good at the details.

Whose idea had it been, for example, to tell her that Olivia had written her name on the bottom of her feet?

Banbouni mixed her another drink. Then another. And even as the news of Olivia being alive slowly began to sink in, she was surprised that another kind of grief was lifting, that the dual ache in her heart was slowly turning to relief. So that in the end she felt less abandoned and betrayed than she did relieved.

Edwidge Danticat is the author of several books, including *Breath, Eyes, Memory* (an Oprah Book Club selection), *Krik? Krak!* (a National Book Award finalist), *The Farming of Bones, The Dew Breaker, Create Dangerously* and *Claire of the Sea Light*. She is also the editor of *The Butterfly's Way: Voices from the Haitian Dyaspora in the United States, Best American Essays 2011, Haiti Noir* and *Haiti Noir 2*. She has written five books for young adults and children – *Anacaona, Behind the Mountains, Eight Days, The Last Mapou* and *Mama's Nightingale* – as well as a travel narrative, *After the Dance*. Her memoir, *Brother, I'm Dying*, was a 2007 finalist for the National Book Award and a 2008 winner of the National Book Critics Circle Award for autobiography. She is a 2009 MacArthur fellow. Her most recent book is *Untwine*, a young adult novel.

About
New Internationalist

New Internationalist is an award-winning, independent media co-operative. Our aim is to inform, inspire and empower people to build a fairer, more sustainable planet.

We publish a global justice magazine and a range of books, both distributed worldwide. We have a vibrant online presence and run ethical online shops for our customers and other organizations.

We are an independent publisher of books, diaries and calendars. We cover global current affairs and popular reference complemented by world food and fiction, graphic non-fiction and children's. All our titles are published in print and digital formats and are available from independent stores, book chains and online retails platforms worldwide.

newint.org/books